Gli Duoi Fratelli Rivali

The Two Rival Brothers

Gli Duoi Fratelli Rivali

The Two Rival Brothers

Giambattista Della Porta

EDITED AND TRANSLATED BY
LOUISE GEORGE CLUBB

UNIVERSITY
OF CALIFORNIA
PRESS

BERKELEY
LOS ANGELES
LONDON

Library of Congress Cataloging in Publication Data

Porta, Giambattista Della, 1535?–1615.
  Gli duoi fratelli rivali = The two rival brothers.

  (Biblioteca italiana)
  Bibliography: p.
  I. Clubb, Louise George.   II. Title.   III. Title:
The two rival brothers.
PQ4630.P6G5713   852'.4   78-64458
ISBN 0-520-03786-3

University of California Press
Berkeley and Los Angeles, California

University of California Press, Ltd.
London, England

© 1980 by
The Regents of the University of California

Printed in the United States of America
Book design by Wolfgang Lederer.

1   2   3   4   5   6   7   8   9

Contents

Introduction

WHEN ALESSANDRO FERSEN'S PRODUCTION of *La fantesca* for the Teatro Stabile di Bolzano was taken on tour in the season of 1976–77, the revival and its success gave the latest sign of a perennial Italian regard for Giambattista Della Porta's comedies. Of the extant fourteen, several have been kept alive on stage, and *Gli duoi fratelli rivali* is one of these. Near the end of the Fascist period it was among Anton Giulio Bragaglia's presentations of classic national drama at the Teatro delle Arti di Roma, where it appeared in Gerardo Guerrieri's adaptation with actresses playing the rival brothers, the young Anna Proclemer in the role of Don Ignazio. *Fratelli rivali* even found its way into Fersen's recent *Fantesca* by means of some transplanted lines. Neither Della Porta's place in Renaissance drama nor the new scholarly enthusiasm for Italian theater history, however, has yet produced a modern edition of his dramatic works: Gennaro Muzio's four volumes of 1726 constitute the unique complete edition of the comedies, eight of which were republished in the 1910–11 collection of Vincenzo Spampanato; while the three plays in verse, *Il Georgio: tragedia*, *L'Ulisse: tragedia*, and *La Penelope: tragicomedia*, existed only in rare sixteenth- or seventeenth-century editions until very recently.★

To the student of Renaissance drama as an international phenomenon, Della Porta makes a particular appeal by virtue of the number of translators he quickly attracted. In England alone, three Latin and two En-

---

★The first volume of an edition of Della Porta's theatrical works by Raffaele Sirri appeared while my volume was in press: Giambattista Della Porta, *Teatro*, a cura di Raffaele Sirri, vol. 1, *Le tragedie* (Napoli, 1978). Volume 2, containing five comedies (*Olimpia*, *La fantesca*, *La trappolaria*, *Cintia*, and *La carbonaria*), is to appear in 1980.

glish adaptations of his comedies were performed at Cambridge or on the London stage in the first two decades of the seventeenth century. King James I was so delighted by *Ignoramus*, George Ruggle's Latin version of *La trappolaria*, that he commanded a second performance, and in the eighteenth century Garrick was still playing *The Astrologer*, a late updating of *L'astrologo*. Among the reasons for Della Porta's early launching abroad, his contemporaneity may have weighed most with fashionable English audiences. Born in 1535 and at work until the end of his life in 1615, a year before Shakespeare's death, Della Porta stood for the kind of comedy most admired in his own country immediately before and during the great flowering of drama in England, a period in which Catholic Italy figured in the English imagination as the civilized world's capital of luxury, depravity, willful error, secular learning and the arts.

The comedy at which Della Porta excelled belongs to an Italian Renaissance genre little remarked by most historians of English drama, despite its affinity with some of the best achievements of the Elizabethan theater. It is a comedy that could as easily be called tragicomedy. Names aside, it testifies to the Italian search for mixed genres, which by the last part of the sixteenth century had produced many variations on the better-known but different basic types of comedy established much earlier by Ariosto, Bibbiena and Machiavelli. The late variety exemplified by *Fratelli rivali* is strong in romantic elements, with a notably idealistic side and a dosage of moral rectitude amounting sometimes to didacticism. Matters thought by Renaissance theorists to be fit for tragedy are here: characters of noble rank exposed to danger or death, and moral menaces offering occasions of heroism and pathos. This is a kind of comedy that often looks back toward the medieval theater,

readmitting abstract content, symbolism, even allegory, and seeking to represent invisible realities that had been discarded in the transition from medieval to Renaissance drama, but now employing means sophisticated enough to function within contemporary structures developed for neoclassical genres. Such comedy is a continuation and reinterpretation of the humanistic idea of *commedia grave*, with the *gravità* expanded to include more varied and serious content and more significant form. Earlier sixteenth-century principles of *contaminatio* and complication of plots remain fundamental here—indeed are invoked to the limit. The essential materials of which the comedy is made, the structural formulae and units by which the elements of the *favola* acquire stage presence, come from a repertory of movable parts, combinable units or frames developed by decades of experiment. The Italian repertory of generic structures was a pool which irrigated more than local terrain. In print, in performances at courts, academies, universities and private houses, and in the adaptations transmitted by mobile troupes of the *commedia dell'arte*, the repertory was available to any place in western Europe that could afford theater. There was no center of drama on which it did not make its impression.

Della Porta's comedies exhibit the repertory in full range. He had begun writing for the stage in youth, many years before his first play saw print in 1589, and he kept it up throughout a long and primarily scientific career. From the early *Olimpia* to the late *Tabernaria*, his comedies are neoclassical, in the competitive and hospitable Renaissance sense, constructed by contamination and complication of Roman New Comedy and narrative sources. The extant fourteen have much in common, including shuffled structural units and ubiquitous reminders that Della Porta had made a translation, now lost, of Plautus's complete works. All fourteen come-

3

dies also testify to a fruitful give-and-take with the *commedia dell'arte*. In tone they vary: some are farcical, but in half a dozen the grave and romantic elements are pronounced, and to this latter group *Fratelli rivali* belongs.

No single period of Della Porta's production can be distinguished indisputably as his serious phase, for the dates of writing and of publication may, in many cases, be widely separated. When Pompeo Barbarito listed Della Porta's unpublished works as of 1591 in the preface to *La Penelope*, he did not mention *Fratelli rivali*: we may assume that it was composed during the decade before 1601, when it was printed in Venice. Two of his other comedies, *La Cintia* and *La carbonaria*, also appeared there that year. Della Porta was probably not on hand for the event. He had lived in Venice for a time in the 1580s under the patronage of Cardinal Luigi d'Este and while it is not inconceivable that he was there again in the early months of 1601, it is certain that by spring he was at home in Naples. As Ciotti's dedication in May of that year states, Della Porta was now a famous author. Sixty-five years old, he was known throughout Europe for his works on natural magic, physiognomy, cryptography and optics, and four of his plays were in print, one of them in three editions. He had come under the suspicion of the Inquisition in the 1580s because of the endorsement some of his works appeared to give to the forbidden arts of divination, judiciary astrology and other kinds of fortune-telling or prophecy. This experience probably contributed to the wariness of the dangerous implications of the traditional comic theme of fortune that marks *L'astrologo* and also coincides with the increasing gravity of character and of situation found in such comedies as *Il moro*, *La furiosa*, *La Cintia*, *La sorella* and *Fratelli rivali*.

I have singled out the last of these for a new edition and a first English translation because it is a ripe specimen of *commedia grave* and because its relation to the En-

glish stage demands acknowledgement. Stiefel long ago established it as Rotrou's source for *Célie, ou le vice-roi de Naples*, but it has escaped the notice of historians of Jacobean drama that *Fratelli rivali* was also used by at least two of Della Porta's Cambridge adapters. Walter Hawkesworth's *Labyrinthus*,[1] a Latin version of *Cintia*, contains a reference to the braggart "Marte bellonio," and Samuel Brooke's *Adelphe*,[2] a Latinized *Sorella*, takes from *Fratelli rivali* not only the names of the Count of Tricarico and of the heroine, "Charitia," but also the better part of a whole scene, the boasting contest between Martebellonio and Leccardo (I.iv). Brooke's commandeering of this dialogue is an act of dramatic *contaminatio* worthy of Della Porta himself.

Finally, *Fratelli rivali* is an analogue to Shakespeare's *Much Ado About Nothing*. D. J. Gordon has even suggested that the Carizia-Ignazio *imbroglio* was a source of the Hero-Claudio plot, a possibility not disposed of by C. T. Prouty's rebuttal based on the mistaken notion that *Fratelli rivali* was not published until 1911.[3] The first

1. Walter Hawkesworth's Latin adaptations of Della Porta's *Cintia* and Oddi's *Erofilomachia*, reentitled *Labyrinthus* and *Leander* respectively, are preserved in three manuscripts at Cambridge University. In one of these, Trinity College MS R.3.9, it is stated that *Leander* was acted in 1598. This manuscript may be a copy made for a revival in 1602, when *Labyrinthus* also was performed. Although a number of scholars have believed the two adaptations to be contemporaneous, the earliest certain date for *Labyrinthus* is 1602, as is recognized by E. K. Chambers, *The Elizabethan Stage* (Oxford, 1923), vol. 3, p. 337, and by Alfred Harbage, *Annals of English Drama*, 975–1700 (Philadelphia, 1949), pp. 72–73.

2. *Adelphe* is in Trinity College MSS R.3.9 and R.10.4. The scene from *Fratelli rivali*, not recognized as such, is included in selections from *Adelphe* printed in Appendix F to Samuel Brooke, *Melanthe: A Latin Pastoral Play of the Early Seventeenth Century*, ed. J. S. G. Bolton (New Haven, 1928), pp. 194 ff.

3. D. J. Gordon, "*Much Ado About Nothing*: A Possible Source for the Hero-Claudio Plot," *Studies in Philology* 39 (1942): 279–90; C. T. Prouty, *The Sources of Much Ado About Nothing: A Critical Study, Together With the Text of Peter Beverley's Ariodanto and Ieneura* (New Haven, 1950), p. 14 *n*18.

edition actually appeared only a year too late to have served Shakespeare for *Much Ado*, printed in 1600. In manuscript or performance, of course, *Fratelli rivali* could have been known in England before the turn of the century. But aside from those shared traits that Gordon observes, and from some others that he misses, Della Porta's contemporary and representative dramatization of the story Shakespeare used is a godsend of an instrument for the critical method of comparative literature. In this case comparison brings to light differences that, paradoxically, go farther than the similarities can do to reveal an international community of Renaissance comedy. Some of the ways Shakespeare takes with the tale are dramatic techniques generally practiced in Italy and particularly by Della Porta, but not in *Fratelli rivali*; conversely, in order to dramatize Bandello, Della Porta uses structural units which Shakespeare foregoes in *Much Ado* but employs elsewhere. The common narrative source in the two plays provides a crux, a unique point of encounter for instituting a deductive line.

Although not to be found in modern anthologies with *La fantesca*, *La sorella* and *L'astrologo*, Della Porta's comedy of the two rival brothers has sometimes been called his best. It reminded Francesco Milano of Lope de Vega. Raffaele Sirri descries in it stirrings of social protest. Whether it is the best or merely good, however, *Fratelli rivali* is extraordinarily representative of trends in late cinquecento comedy. The prologue is a statement of critical principles, claiming classical lineage and generic correctness while simultaneously asserting modern superiority. The characters have a richly articulated but occasionally self-contradictory emotional intensity that arises less from Della Porta's concern for psychological complexity than from his mastery of structures in the repertory common to literary *commediografi* and improvising *comici*. The abundance is so

great as to make the play almost a sampler of movable parts.

At the same time, *Fratelli rivali* illustrates the hybridism of Italian theater and the movement within it that produced different sorts of *tragicommedia, tragedia di fin lieto, favola comitragica* and so on. Della Porta seems to be testing the limits of *commedia grave*, stretching without breaking the rules of unity and decorum. Place is confined to a single street scene in a well-known city, time to about one day in a distant decade, so that the action is verisimilar and almost historical, but blurred and, possibly, allusive to a more contemporary reality. Written in prose and peopled by stock comic middle-class types as well as by aristocrats, proceeding through deceits, disguises and bawdry to happy marriages, but also containing threats of death, dishonor, fratricide and governmental injustice, *Fratelli rivali* remains *commedia*, but just barely. Among Della Porta's comedies, only *Il moro* goes so far toward tragedy; *La sorella, La Cintia* and *La furiosa* lack the political elements and the emphasis on rank. The seventeenth-century criticism of Teodoro Amaideno, who liked *Fratelli rivali* but objected to bringing the viceroy of Sicily (*sic*) on stage, and to the indecorum of permitting him to embrace his nephews' future wives in public,[4] suggests the diverse hazards awaiting playwrights who experimented with genre while observing its rules.

It is by the selection and disposition of plots that this baroque version of *commedia osservata* and the individual practitioners of it may immediately be recognized. The principal source of *Fratelli rivali* is Bandello's twenty-second novella, a sombre romantic tale, which its au-

4. Selections from the diary of this well-informed patron and judge of the drama have been published by Aulo Greco, "Note inedite di Teodoro Amaideno sulla commedia del Rinascimento," *Atti e Memorie dell'Arcadia*, ser. 3, vol. 5, nos. 2–3 (1971): 209–68.

thor heads thus: "Timbreo di Cardona [che] essendo col re Piero di Ragona in Messina s'innamora di Fenicia Lionata, e i vari e fortunevoli accidenti che avvennero prima che per moglie la prendesse."[5] Della Porta's choice is typical of the period: the whole century had witnessed a fashioning into *commedia* of novella material, but while the early cinquecento had given primacy to the comic tales in the *Decameron*, the later time saw these leavened with serious stories, often also from Boccaccio, as from other *novellieri* and from the Alexandrian romances that had begun to enjoy a vogue in translation.

Bandello's tale is a leisurely account of Timbreo's love for Fenicia, daughter of the noble but impoverished Lionato. Like Ariodante in Ariosto's similar story (*Orlando Furioso* V), Timbreo is persuaded by the deceits of a rival to believe that he has seen his beloved keep a night's assignation with another man. After repudiating her and believing that she consequently has sickened and died, Timbreo learns of Fenicia's innocence from the repentant calumniator and vows never to marry except as her bereaved father may dictate in satisfaction of wounded honor. A year later Lionato requires Timbreo to keep his promise, and at the culmination of the nuptial feast it is revealed that the bride is Fenicia, recovered from her nearly fatal illness and grown unrecognizably more lovely. The rival marries Fenicia's sister, Lionato's family is enriched again by the generosity of the Spanish ruler, Pedro of Aragon, and they all live happily thereafter.

The characters in the novella are verbose, especially Fenicia, who moralizes and laments at length, the range of mood is limited to a register that runs from lugubrious passion to courtly rejoicing, and the narrative shape

5. Matteo Bandello, *Le novelle*, a cura di Gioachino Brognoligo, 2a. ed. riv. (Bari, 1928), Parte I, 22, p. 283.

is linear. For transformation into *commedia* the plot had to be disposed so as to provide opportunities for encounters and revealing conversations. It needed enlargement by countermotion, funny matter and variety of tempo, tone and character, but it also needed to be reduced to fit the temporal and spatial limits that Renaissance neoclassicists deemed a sacrosanct inheritance from antiquity.

Della Porta's method of making the novella stageworthy rests on the enlarged principle of contamination, which by his time countenanced intermingling not only plots but also genres themselves, and on complication of the elements into the most intricate possible tangle. The labyrinthine pattern should appear hopelessly frustrating until suddenly resolved by a final peripety, a *coup de théâtre* with unexpected and satisfying dramatic impact producing order out of chaos and a happy ending all round.

He collapses the train of events into a day: between Tuesday morning and dinnertime Wednesday the rival loves are revealed, the lady won, the marriage arranged, the tricks planned and perpetrated, the accusation lodged, the death reported, the deceit confessed, the judgement of the municipal authority passed, giving rise to further rivalry, and at last, still in time for dinner, a happy denouement visited on everyone. All of these actions are tightly scheduled to occur more or less plausibly on a single street in Salerno. To each of the rivals—now brothers—is assigned a clever servant, and a venal parasite is brought in to play the go-between; together with a braggart captain and a bawdy maidservant, these add low echoes to the high tones. All of them multiply occasions of symmetrical confusion. Like the pattern of construction which packs the action into twenty-four hours and turns it out of doors, the added characters are borrowed from Roman New

Comedy and its Renaissance continuators. The same is true for many verbal and gestural structures. When Leccardo exasperates his impatient love-sick master by stammering his message while finding breath to explain that he is breathless, or when Don Ignazio pretends to love the count's daughter and Don Flaminio tries to call his bluff by claiming to have arranged the match, they are doing in their way what characters of Plautus, Terence and earlier cinquecento comedy have done before them. Their way also includes the formalistic game of mocking conventional structures, as when Simbolo replies to the long preamble of Ignazio's expository monologue, "I know all that very well, for I was in your service at the time."

Movable parts from the sizeable Boccaccian portion of the generic repertory also figure in Della Porta's *contaminatio*. The bed trick, or substitution of persons at assignations in dark rooms, had been a commonplace of *commedia* since Bibbiena's Decameronian *Calandria* of 1513, and the mutually disappointing encounter of Martebellonio and Chiaretta in *Fratelli rivali* is a practiced doubling of this familiar *inganno*. It simultaneously complicates the *intreccio*, intensifies the violent emotional pitch while providing a comic breather to it, and offers a moon-in-puddle reflection of the highflown love of Don Ignazio and Carizia.

A dimension that makes *Fratelli rivali* unique among Della Porta's comedies,—for they all demonstrate the principles of prefabricated assembly from materials of fiction, whether comedy or novella, ancient or recent, —is added by a historical framework of "facts" from the chronicles of his own family and of the Kingdom of Naples. Discarding Bandello's nominal association of Timbreo with Pedro of Aragon and thirteenth-century Messina, Della Porta transfers the action to sixteenth-century Salerno, a city in which his paternal relatives

had reputedly held high civil and ecclesiastical offices. This clan he brings onstage by rebaptizing Bandello's Lionato as Eufranone Della Porta. Antonio Mazza's account of prominent Salernitans from the Middle Ages to the late seventeenth century includes many "de Porta's" and one "Eufranon de Porta Vicarius Generalis Regni": no date accompanies his appointment, which in this unsystematic list is mentioned immediately after one made in 1675 and before another in 1445.[6] While the historical existence of the Eufranone of the play remains uncertain, there seems to be no doubt that his uncommon given name was used at least once by the Salernitan branch of the author's family.

In the narrated *antefatto* which Simbolo drily recognizes as a structural convention (I.i), Don Ignazio explains that the Mendozas have come to Italy with the forces of the "Gran Capitán." Gonzalo Fernández of Cordova, known to history as the Great Captain, launched his second Italian campaign in 1501, and by a victory over the French in 1503 brought the Kingdom of Naples fully under the control of Ferdinand V of Spain, the "Catholic King" (Ferdinand III of the Regno di Napoli). The new government, with Gonzalo Fernández as Ferdinand's viceroy until 1507, put the Regno into a more direct relation with the Spanish throne than had obtained under the rule of the Italianized branch of the house of Aragon in the fourteenth and fifteenth centuries. Gonzalo Fernández's appointment of the fictional lovers' uncle, Don Rodorigo, as viceroy of the province and city of Salerno is a recent event as the play opens. Don Ignazio has seen Carizia a single time, at the games that his uncle commanded to be held in honor of the new order. As Don Ignazio is very young—his rival brother is only seventeen (V.i)—and counts six months

6. Antonio Mazza, *Historiarum epitome de rebus salernitanis* (Neapoli, 1681; rpt. Bologna, 1965), pp. 95–96.

without Carizia an eternity (II.vi), it must be concluded that perhaps only about five months have passed since he fell in love at the bullfight. The temporal setting of the comedy, therefore, appears to be sometime not long after January 1504, when the Gran Capitán settled down in Naples to restore peaceful government to the Regno.

It has long been taken for granted that the events in *Fratelli rivali* are intended to occur considerably later than this. Spampanato identified the viceroy of the play with a "Roderico di Mendozza" listed by Tobia Almagiore among "Li Regente e Proregenti della G. C. [la Signoria del Gran Conestabile] della Vicaria" in the Kingdom of Naples for 1541,[7] and he speculated that this Mendoza held office in Salerno thereafter.[8] The reports that Carizia's family had been impoverished by the confiscation of property consequent to her father's part in the rebellion of the Sanseverino Prince of Salerno (I.i, II.vi), furthermore, were taken by Spampanato to mean that there may have been a real Eufranone Della Porta, perhaps a relative of the playwright, who lost his fortune through the local conflict with the viceroy of Naples, Pedro de Toledo, which ended in 1552 with the desertion to France of Ferrante, the last Sanseverino Prince of Salerno. Because of Francesco Fiorentino's facile agreement that this, and not any earlier uprising of the inflammable Sanseverino party, was the rebellion

7. Tobia Almagiore, *Raccolta de varie notitie historiche, non meno appartenenti all'historia del Summonte, che curiose* (Napoli, 1675), p. 115, in G. A. Summonte, *Dell'historia della città, e Regno di Napoli*, 2a. ed. (Napoli, 1675), vol. 4.

8. Vincenzo Spampanato, "I Della Porta ne' *Duoi fratelli rivali*," *L'Anomalo* 14, ser. 6 (agosto–dicembre 1917), *N[umero] speciale (pubblicato in dicembre 1918) . . . dedicato alla memoria di Giambattista Della Porta napoletano, precursore degli studi antropologico-criminali odierni, in occasione del busto erettogli . . .* [9 giugno 1918], pp. 199–203. This important, though brief and careless, notice refers to two MSS I have been unable to consult, but for this unwarranted conclusion it depends primarily on jumbled readings of Mazza and Almagiore.

referred to in the play, the untenable assumption has been sanctioned for a long time. Doubtless Della Porta had boyhood memories of the magnificent Ferrante Sanseverino, who offered lavish hospitality to the Emperor Charles V in Salerno, and entertained the citizenry with sumptuous productions of comedies in his Neapolitan palace; the fall and flight of this soon-to-become-legendary figure would have left an unforgettable impression on the imagination of the adolescent playwright. But associating the characters of *Fratelli rivali* with both Ferrante Sanseverino's rebellion and Gonzalo Fernández's conquest would require that the action be set simultaneously in two periods separated from each other by almost fifty years. To have allowed Don Flaminio to arrive in Italy in 1501 and yet be less than eighteen years old sometime after 1552 would be a *contaminatio* of time foreshadowing Shakespeare's bold juxtaposition in *Cymbeline* of the second century A.D. with Italian Renaissance custom. All the evidence tells against this fancy, however; sober arithmetic leads to the conclusion that Della Porta intended Eufranone's misfortunes to date, rather, from the "Congiura dei baroni" of 1485–86 against the local Aragonese king of the Regno, Ferrante or Ferdinand I, a rebellion in which Antonello Sanseverino, Prince of Salerno, played a leading and losing part. Whatever loss of surrealistic simultaneity this conclusion entails on the comedy is compensated for by gains in logic and historical verisimilitude. If Eufranone was involved in the conspiracy of the 1480s, he would be at a more likely age to have nubile daughters in 1504 than in the 1550s or later. The viceroy's unreserved condemnation as "most unjust" of the confiscation of Eufranone's property, which he will request "His Majesty" to restore (V.iv), is implausible if supposed to be pronounced by a viceroy of Philip II on an action approved by Philip's father, Charles V. It cor-

responds, however, to the spirit in which his great-grandfather, the Catholic King, attempted to douse the embers of old hostilities by restoring lands and titles to many rebel barons, including the principality of Salerno to Antonello Sanseverino's son, Roberto, in 1505.[9]

In keeping with a Renaissance tendency to the allusive use of history, Della Porta might have seen in the aftermath of the quattrocento conspiracy an instructive parallel with the condition of Salerno in his own time and a fleeting image of desirable relations between Spain and the cities of the Regno. Even for Naples itself there was propagandistic relevance in the fifth-act sketch of ideal government by an appointed resident viceroy determined to redress wrongs, responsive to civic opinion, and acting as a conduit rather than as a barrier between the city and the supreme authority of the Spanish king in Madrid. In Della Porta's time nearby Salerno had a long history of struggling to regain an autonomy lost in the late Middle Ages. Owned successively by the Colonna, Orsini and Sanseverino families, the city fought incessantly to be placed in the Royal Demesne, free of feudal overlords and answerable directly to the Spanish crown.[10] The dismantling

9. Luis Maria de Lojendio recounts that Gonzalo Fernández was reluctant to reinstate sympathizers with the cause of Anjou and to return to them the lands he had distributed among his own followers, but he had to accede to the conditions imposed by King Ferdinand's new alliance with Louis XII of France. See Lojendio's *Gonzalo de Córdoba, El Gran Capitán*, 2a ed. (Madrid, 1952), p. 314; Guido D'Agostino, "Il governo spagnolo nell'Italia meridionale (Napoli dal 1503 al 1580)," *Storia di Napoli*, a cura di E. Pontieri et al., vol. 5, no. 1 (1972), pp. 8–10; and Tommaso Pedio, *Napoli e Spagna nella prima metà del cinquecento* (Bari, 1971), p. 30, *n*8.

10. This chapter in Salernitan history is illuminated with documents from the Spanish Archivio General de Simancas by Carlo Carucci, "L'autonomia amministrativa della città di Salerno nella seconda metà del secolo XVI," *Archivio Storico della Provincia di Salerno* 3 (giugno–settembre, 1923): 128–39; and by Giuseppe Coniglio, "L'infeudazione di Salerno ed un contratto tra Nicolò Grimaldi e Filippo II," *Rassegna Storica Salernitana* 11 (gennaio–dicembre, 1951): 37–56.

of the principality after Ferrante Sanseverino's exile in 1552 aroused new hope in the Salernitans; in 1565 they raised 25,000 *ducati* as down-payment toward the city's ransom, and received from the Spanish viceregency at Naples a promise of demesnial status. Not until 1590 was the promise kept, however, for in the wake of bankruptcy in 1572, Philip II handed over Salerno in fief for 76,000 *ducati* to one of his creditors, the Genoese banker, Nicolò Grimaldi, who accepted the title of prince and the revenues as a means of recovering part of a bad debt. He seems to have taken no direct part in the government of Salerno. Describing the bureaucratic organization of the Kingdom of Naples between 1577 and 1579, Camillo Porzio mentioned that Spain provided two governors for the principality, one at Avellino for the province and another at Salerno for the city.[11] In 1584 when Grimaldi began to mortgage some of the property thus acquired, the representatives of Salerno offered the king 60,000 *ducati*, and by subsequent transaction put an end to the buying and selling of their city.

If, as seems probable, *Fratelli rivali* was written in the 1590s, it belongs to a time when Salerno had achieved its goal of independence from local hereditary princes and was ruled only by Spain, through the appointed viceroy of Naples and his representative. The unified Salerno Della Porta depicts—under a governor whom he arbitrarily calls a viceroy, with authority covering both the province and city of the former principality but responsible to the Spanish crown—is an idealized version of the system achieved in 1590, for which there was no precedent except during the hiatus between the exclusion of Antonello Sanseverino after the "Congiura dei baroni" and the reinstatement of Roberto in 1505. By

11. Camillo Porzio, Relazione del Regno di Napoli al Marchese di Mondesciar Vicerè di Napoli tra il 1577 e il 1579, in *La congiura de' baroni di Napoli contra il Re Ferdinando Primo e gli altri scritti*, a cura di Ernesto Pontieri, 2a. ed. riv. (Napoli, 1964), pp. 317–18.

manipulating history to dramatize a moment in 1504 when a Spanish viceroy of Naples, Gonzalo Fernández, has just appointed a representative to bring good government to Salerno, Della Porta may have intended to compliment the viceregency on the current state of affairs in Salerno, and implicitly to further good government throughout the Regno. Any such message might well have been communicated by means of his plays, for they had the attention of the viceregal court. Don Juan de Zuñiga, Count of Miranda, the viceroy of Naples who signed the request to the Spanish crown on 9 April 1590, that Salerno be confirmed as a city in the Royal Demesne, is known to have witnessed at least one performance of a Della Porta comedy, an elaborate production of *L'Olimpia* sometime between 1586 and 1589.[12]

The semihistorical additions accentuate the mixed generic character of *Fratelli rivali* but, like the purely fictional elements in the *contaminatio*, are assimilated by means of conventional comic structures. Don Rodorigo's political significance as Spanish governor is brought on stage through his dramatic function as the *vecchio* who is an obstacle to the *giovani* in their loves and who ultimately pardons their misdemeanors and reconciles their differences.

Inconsistencies in the heterogeneous structure, sections improperly attached or not attached at all, are not results of any fault inherent in the idea of hybridism or in the principle of assembly by parts. Rather, they must be written down to carelessness—on the part of Della Porta or, conceivably, of a professional troupe

12. In his dedication to Della Porta's *L'Olimpia* (Napoli, 1589) Pompeo Barbarito says that the comedy was performed before the viceroy, the Count of Miranda; Francesco Fiorentino establishes the *terminus a quo* as November 1586, the beginning of Miranda's viceregency, *Studi e ritratti della Rinascenza* (Bari, 1911), p. 263.

that might have transmitted the text. They are the in-consistencies that beset swift composers ill-disposed to blot a line, of the same order as the lapses that trouble those who wish for seamless perfection in Shakespeare's constructions. Della Porta engages Mon'Angiola, for example, in the structural commonplace of eavesdropping, so that she hears Don Ignazio's attempt to throw Don Flaminio off the track of his true love and mistakenly concludes that he is unfaithful to Carizia (II.iv). This unit of action had been useful to Terence and to his Italian successors, as it had to Della Porta himself in other comedies. In *Fratelli rivali* he brings it up only to drop it: the misconception, once created, pregnant with complication, is referred to no more. It causes no trouble but is never specifically resolved. Avanzino's abortive attempt to help his master is similarly baffling: once it is established that his well-intentioned officiousness threatens to wreck Don Ignazio's plan (III.vi), neither the danger nor Avanzino himself is heard of again. Aberrations in character are also created by the negligent use of standard repertory devices. Carizia, who in every other part of the comedy is seen and talked of as an almost superhuman example of dignity, decorum and divine majesty, briefly and for no ulterior ironic effect or apparent authorial reason other than the wish to raise a laugh, turns rowdy in Leccardo's account of how she rejected his pandering for Don Flaminio (I.iii). Likewise, the topos of the attack on cosmetics, comparing the false allure of ladies, who can afford them, with the solid charms of serving-maids, who cannot, is at odds with the facts when it is put into the mouth of Chiaretta and directed against the genuinely beautiful young mistress whom she loves (III.iv).

Incongruity sometimes besets the language of the comedy too, for the contemporary eclectic temper and

the repertory of shared comic terms made linguistic variation easy and contradictions inevitable. Labelling Della Porta's language baroque cannot adequately suggest either how representative of the cumulative genre are his choices of verbal structures or how distinctively his personal signature marks them. Although Chiaretta's speech on cosmetics is inappropriate to the relationship between her and Carizia, it pleases as a familiar comic turn suitable to a *fantesca*. At the same time, compared with the standard handling of the topos, as in Piccolomini's *L'Amor costante*, it is grotesquely scientific, studded with chemical and botanical terms from Della Porta's own *Magiæ naturalis*,[13] one of the "studi più gravi" to which, in the prologue, he solemnly gives precedence over his comedies.

In the more dignified speeches the imagery is florid, with less in it of carnality than of a *conceptismo* as natural to Della Porta as it is to the stately Spanish characters of the play who have the lion's share of such language. The syntax at times strikes a Ciceronian balance, but more often it piles up, clogs itself, and creates disjunctures that, thwarting logic, intensify expression of emotion and offer the actors a jagged linguistic implement for carving a dialectical edge on what might otherwise have been a rounded tedium of parisons and similes.

To the lovers it is given to speak not only as becomes their station and region but as the genre had come to dictate for *innamorati*. Although they engage in ceremonious Hispanoid exchanges, their lexicon has a stilnovist and Petrarchan foundation. This is betrayed in

13. Jo. Bapt. Portae Neapolitani, *Magiae naturalis libri XX* (Neapoli, 1589), Bk. IX. "De Mulierum Cosmetica," passim. The Italian translation, *Della Magia naturale* (Napoli: Appresso Gio. Giacomo Carlino, 1611), place, printer and date suggesting Della Porta's personal surveillance, renders the Latin terms in the words used by Chiaretta: *sollimati* for *sublimati* (p. 399), *litargiri* for *lithargyri* (p. 399), *rasura di verzino* for *brasili rasura* (p. 411).

echoes at appropriate moments: with "Oh maledetto giorno ch'io nacqui e che la viddi e che tanto piacque a gli occhi miei! Ahi dolenti occhi . . ." (III.xi), triggering memories of Petrarch's "Benedetto sia 'l giorno" (*Rime*, LXI) and Dante's "Gli dolenti occhi" (*Vita nuova*, Canzone III), Don Ignazio is reacting with the emotion and vocabulary decreed for lovers in this situation, and for which *comici dell'arte* who specialized in *innamorati* roles prepared themselves in part by memorizing quantities of Petrarchan poetry. Sometimes the Petrarchism erupts in unexpected directions. At a moment of tribulation, Don Flaminio laments, predictably, in metaphors culled from Petrarch: tempests beset him, his bark is tossed by waves of ill-fortune, he has no hope of port save one (III.i);[14] his imaged pleas are addressed, however, not to a Laura-like lady or even to the god of love, but only to the late Renaissance version of the Plautine *davos* who manages his affairs for him. More recent poets are echoed as well, Tasso most often: Madonna Angiola's description of Carizia (II.ii) evokes Armida's "canuto senno" hidden "sotto biondi capelli" (*Gerusalemme Liberata*, IV.24), and Don Ignazio's account of losing his heart while winning a bullfight is an expansion of Aminta's admission, "mentre io fea rapina

14. The ship in a sudden storm as a metaphor for dismay at a reversal of expectations was a commonplace in the poetry and prose of Cicero's and Ovid's medieval and Renaissance heirs. Karen Alison Newman has brought it to my attention that the image had been used in the genre of comedy as early as Menander's now-recovered *Samia* (III,i); see her "Mistaken Identity and the Structure of Comedy: A Comparative Study of Classical, Italian Renaissance and Shakespearean Comedy" (dissertation, University of California, Berkeley, 1978), p. 10. But Menander was not available to Della Porta, anymore than he had been to Machiavelli, who used the metaphor of the "nave vessata" in comedy (*La mandragola* IV,i) and elsewhere. Like most of his Renaissance predecessors, moreover, Della Porta amplified the ancient basic image by drawing entirely on Petrarchan clusters of details and lexicon: *tempesta, onda, pensieri, timore, timone, stella, occhi, naufragio*, etc.

d'animali, / Fui, non so come, a me stesso rapito"
(*Aminta*, I.ii).

The lovers and their social equals are also permitted a
more familiar style with fast colloquial dialogue and
proverbs, but in this line the initiative is usually taken
by their servants and social inferiors, whose range of
language is even greater than that of their masters.
Some of Leccardo's comic effects arise from his carefully rigged ignorance; still more of them depend on a
knowledge of literary allusions and techniques that en-
ables him to build parodic apostrophes to food, a kind
of verbal flight fancied by gluttons from Roman times
through the Renaissance, becoming in Della Porta's
comedies a counter-poetry of materialism. He characteristically uses the topos of obsession with food as an
instrument of comment to deflate the affectations and
exaggerations springing from less physical fixations—
swollen ideas of honor, rhapsodic love, emotional or
moral gigantism of many sorts. The *Bravure* of Francesco Andreini's famous mask, Capitano Spavento,
first published six years after *Fratelli rivali*, contain
many *ragionamenti* in which the braggart's bombast is
punctured by his mockingly simpleminded dogsbody.
Unlike Della Porta's Martebellonio, however, Spavento makes fantastic boasts about his appetite too. The
theater was the natural habitat of statement and ne-
gation in linguistic confrontations between dramatic
types: braggart versus glutton, glutton versus lover, the
combinations were many. Della Porta, whose diction
was kindled by contrast, and whose scientific work em-
braced the theory of the sympathy and antipathy of natural forces, knew better than most dramatists how to
use theatrical stock types and encounters for expression
and representation of equivalent forces in the fictional
combinations by which the art of comedy imitated nature.

By the time such late cinquecento writers as Oddi were defending Comedy's right to poach on Tragedy's preserves, the *gravità* in *commedia grave* included very serious content indeed. Serious form had been enjoined from the early days of Ariosto and Bibbiena but received new emphasis after literary playwrights observed that they were at war with the zanies of the *commedia dell'arte* and began to denigrate as "zannate" the loosely constructed licentious improvisations that were the most popular result of the rise of professional acting companies. The success of these relatively shapeless theatrical happenings seemed to many dramatists to threaten the ideals of high comic art, and although the cannier ones among them freely borrowed the players' lively devices, they simultaneously attacked the baser and more slovenly aspects of their rivals' methods. Concern for careful five-act structure, for definition of genre, for classical theory and practice, for experiment in variation and mixture of genres, for declaration of the relation to and distance from tradition and for principles of complication and unification: these were held by cultivators of *commedia grave* to distinguish their work from what they regarded as quick and easy commercial effects. Della Porta was on the one hand more open to the influence of the *commedia dell'arte* and more in favor with the actors as a source of material than most of his contemporaries; on the other, he was perennially fascinated by classical paradigms of structure. Barbarito used the term "commedia grave" to define *L'Olimpia* in introducing Della Porta's comedies to the reading public in 1589, but the *gravità* of the genre as he practiced it is more fully seen in *Fratelli rivali*. True, the evidence of sympathy with the *commedia dell'arte* is strong here, most obviously in such extended set pieces as Martebellonio's contest with Leccardo (I.iv) and Ignazio and Carizia's love scene (II.iv). But even more prominent is

21

Della Porta's seriousness about structure, set forth at the outset in the prologue, where he paraphrases Aristotle's *Poetics* to show his own adherence to the "rules" developed for the genre, then boasts of his departures and tweaks Aristotle's nose, but ends by claiming the approval of the deities of the classical tradition.

Gravità of content, though regularly interrupted by buffoonery and verbal play, shows itself throughout *Fratelli rivali* as emotional force, the kind and amount determined by a Counter-Reformation preference for turbulence, primary passions and embroidered expressions. Della Porta's additions to his sources and his elaborations of dialogue carry the brothers in their rivalry from one extreme of feeling to another and heighten the pathos in Eufranone's dignity and violently touchy sense of honor. Ideas about the proper object of representation in comedy were becoming more capacious, more hospitable to realities not perceived by the senses, to the psychological as well as the physical. The moral content is equally weighty. Carizia belongs to the late-blooming category of exemplary comedy heroine, a baroque icon of curved and florid virtue, elaborately chaste. An earlier *innamorata* in her position would likewise have guarded her virginity, as the fable requires, but Carizia is additionally concerned for appearances and reputation. She approves of her father's histrionic stance on family honor and is herself adept at demonstrating by diplomatic address and noble actions the virtues of the ideal lady. To the other characters she is a secular saint; and her name is linked with moral and theological doctrines as a model of filial piety and womanly goodness and as a beneficiary of the blessings of divine providence. In the depiction of her family, the ideal of domestic life is upheld. The antique topos of woman's nature and honor, which traditionally could produce a variety of conclusions and which had often been

developed in comedy as a show-stopping soliloquy, digressive dialogue or representation of contrasting feminine characters, appears in *Fratelli rivali* in Counter-Reformation dress. Carizia's character is elevated by artful contrast with Chiaretta's and by the chiaroscuro produced when the shadow cast by lies intrudes between the original brightness of her name and its heightened lustre as the truth is published. Her merit is discussed in the exchange between the idealistic Don Ignazio and the temporarily cynical Simbolo (I.iii) and, most typically of the age, it is glorified by theatrical representation of its effect on spectators: Simbolo is converted from scoffer to admirer by watching Carizia go through her paces (II.iv), and the amazed viceroy describes her as the star of a providential spectacle (V.iv).

The seriousness and moral contemporaneity are insistently displayed in the movement between the opposing forces at the center of the action, with Don Ignazio and his advisers pitted against Don Flaminio and his, in an *intreccio* of deceit, mistakes, accidents and illusions, woven so as to form a reminder that fortune, the traditional generator of comic action, is merely a subsidiary mechanism of the providential Prime Mover who plans happy endings. All the characters feel the power of fortune and many lament its fickleness, but Don Flaminio, the "villain," and his crew exalt it most and understand least that it is subordinate to God's providence. Don Flaminio broods more than his brother does about the amity or enmity of "contraria fortuna" to his enterprises, which are systematically presented as being morally inferior to Don Ignazio's. Flaminio would rather have Carizia as his mistress than as his wife and would be willing to settle for her sister instead (II.ix); he not only practices the venial kind of deceit that Ignazio, too, uses for self-protection, but even wrests his conscience around to let him calumniate

23

the woman he loves. Trying to justify bad means to his ends and overrating the pagan power of fortune, Don Flaminio joins Panimbolo, his domestic exponent of Realpolitik, in endorsing precisely those evil principles that an enlightened Counter-Reformation doctrine aimed to correct. Like his master, Panimbolo has a conscience, but it is no match for his arsenal of immoral plans. The arguments that he and Don Flaminio use to talk each other into bad courses are riddled with the pragmatic relativism that had become anathema to the world-view of Catholic reform. Panimbolo's wily assertions that winning is all that counts and treachery a necessary evil that can be made to appear admirable, if called by another name and judged by the outcome (III.i), are declarations of the kind set up to be knocked down by contemporary militants like Giovanni Botero and other orthodox moralists engaged in laying the ghost of the proscribed Machiavelli.

In working out the unifying theme of fraternal rivalry Della Porta also demonstrates the evolution of elementary comic mechanisms. The *inganni*, the tricks and traps of the foxy deceiver that belong to the inheritance of the genre, are present in *Fratelli rivali* both as machinery and, *in toto*, as an object of contemplation. The comedy invites thought about deceit and self-deceit, especially the self-deceit of thinking, as both Don Flaminio and Don Ignazio do (I.ii, IV.ii), that it is difficult or rare to deceive oneself. Although Don Ignazio is less deluded than Don Flaminio by the seeming omnipotence of fortune, even he, the "good" brother, takes appearance for reality. He is too ready to trust the testimony of the senses, to draw inferences from their meagre perceptions. When he judges Carizia unfaithful because he sees her skirt in his brother's hands, Don Ignazio is rashly accepting as ocular proof what is no proof at all; in his later condition of remorseful enlight-

enment, when she reappears as if from the dead, he has learned enough to be cautious about believing his eyes. His harping on the evidence of the seen belongs to the chorus of Renaissance commentary on human blindness. The theme of a true celestial vision of reality contrasted with mankind's fallacious view of appearances rested on Platonic authority, and coincided with the Christian doctrine of divine providence that was reiterated with Counter-Reformation insistence just at a time when Italian drama was most deeply under the spell of Sophocles' *Oedipus the Tyrant*, praised in the canonical *Poetics*. The preoccupation with the ironies of sight and blindness, appearance and reality, that pervade the imagery and thematics of late cinquecento tragedy and pastoral tragicomedy are manifested in comedy as emphasis on ocular mistakes and illusions, especially when seconded by darkness. The nocturnal scene in which Don Flaminio deceives Don Ignazio with a handful of clothes (while Leccardo simultaneously deceives Martebellonio and Chiaretta) and which culminates in Don Ignazio's passionate denunciation of Night (III.xi) is a piece of legerdemain in the genre of Iago's brilliant passes with Desdemona's handkerchief, making trifles light as air seem more real than reality. The trusty plot mainspring of "tricker tricked" works toward a *reductio ad divinum*. Don Flaminio exults over his brother, "il volpone è caduto nella trappola" (IV.iv), but later finds that he has dug a deeper trap for himself, when his scheme to possess Carizia seems to have killed her. The irony inherent in the mechanism is pushed so far that there is no escape from tragedy except through the ultimate comic irony of providential action.

Don Flaminio is wrong about most things, among them his uncle's professional ethics; this error introduces another grave theme. The question of good government and the ruler's duty, which in the earlier

Renaissance had engrossed such diverse minds as Erasmus, Rabelais, More, Elyot, Castiglione and Machiavelli, was hardly forgotten in the late sixteenth century. As a topos of drama it found a natural place in tragedy, in mixed drama like Shakespeare's or Lope de Vega's, and even in Italian comedy as early as the 1540s. Annibal Caro's *Gli straccioni* is laced with propaganda for the justice of Farnese rule in Rome, and a later, more typically Tridentine, adumbration of the virtues of an orthodox paternalistic government in the duchy of Ferrara is to be seen in Oddi's *Prigione d'amore*. The ruler familiar to Shakespeare's audiences, who seals and reconciles, and who may have something to learn which his involvement in the plot or his association with involved characters will teach him, is introduced by Della Porta in the figure of Don Rodorigo, the viceroy. There is no precedent for him in Bandello's novella. Although he is no *deus ex machina*—heaven does its own work, with Polisena as its messenger—, Don Rodorigo is brought onstage for the first time in the last act, charged with the duty of handing down a judgement. He recognizes that he may be required to shed the blood of a beloved nephew, and declares himself determined to do justice above all (V.i). Earlier in the play that nephew has cited his uncle's position as a guarantee to Leccardo that he may with impunity participate in the evil trick on Don Ignazio (III.ii). Even granted that Don Flaminio at this moment does not intend and cannot foresee the apparently fatal consequences that his actions will incur, his conviction that he and his accomplices are above the law, that his rank and family connections entitle him to a special dispensation, remains another of his wrong views, marked for demolition by Counter-Reformation instruction-in-action. Leccardo replies in the name of the class that pays; justice, he says with the bitterness of the underdog, is not equal for all: like a spider web,

easily torn apart by big birds, it is a fatal trap to little flies
(III.ii). This exchange was incorporated into Fersen's
1976 production of *La fantesca*, in a manoeuvre of dramatic *contaminatio* that gave an effect of free-standing
and unanswered social protest. In the comedy they
were meant for, however, Leccardo's protest and Flaminio's facile reassurance, bear a different weight, for,
contrary to Flaminio's expectations, his uncle is by no
means disposed to tamper with justice by favoring his
kin. Even though the offense has grown into a crime
punishable by death, Don Rodorigo acknowledges that
he must sentence his nephew accordingly, unless a
bloodless alternative can be found and made acceptable
to the injured party. As it happens, the offer of marriage
with the sister of Flaminio's victim does satisfy the
plaintiff, Eufranone, who is bent on restoration of hon-
or rather than on vengeance. There is no doubt, however, that the injured party holds the upper hand. If Leccardo's and Don Flaminio's expectations betray social
ills which Della Porta and his contemporaries knew all
too well, Don Rodorigo's behavior as judge represents
the ideal reformation of them. His actions in the remaining scenes further emphasize the bond between
secular and divine authority which it was a part of
church and state policy to preach. No sooner has he
brought about a fair and happy settlement of one case
than he is charged with injustice by his other nephew.
This time only a higher power can solve the difficulty,
but Don Rodorigo has the last word, and with it he
identifies that power as divine. He casts himself as a
spectator to the events and interprets them as a plan of
providence, thus authorizing the proper doctrinal view
of the situation; and by following up the resurrected
Carizia's expressions of universal forgiveness with a
legal pardon for Leccardo and a donation of his own
money to free all the prisoners in Salerno whose ac-

cusers are willing to agree to it (V.iv), the viceroy carries private moral and religious spirit into the public and political domain, managing the while to exercise both justice and mercy. He extends the happy ending beyond the characters affected by the plot, making it embrace the entire city. Thus the example of a good ruler is served up, briefly but gravely, as a subject for comedy.

The happy ending itself, the expertly deferred "lieto fine" hoped for or marvelled at by a succession of characters, had been the theme of the Second Day in the *Decameron*—that quarry of dramatic plots—and one of the generic features by which Dante had explained the title of his *Commedia*. In the cinquecento Giraldi Cinthio considered calling his experimental hybrid drama a "tragicomedia" but settled instead on "tragedia di fin lieto." The ending traditionally determinant of genre becomes in such a *commedia grave* as *Fratelli rivali* a means of moving outward, not merely beyond the immediate plot into the semihistorical reality of Salerno, with its thousands of inhabitants whose names and lives are irrelevant to the fiction, but farther still to a reality not to be seen with the physical sense of sight but only by what are neoplatonically called the "eyes of the intellect" in the prologue. As an object of representation, the invisible reality of the mysterious ways by which divine providence guides human destinies to joyful fulfillment had been available to the medieval drama which was hospitable to magic and miracles, but it was hedged with obstacles for Renaissance playwrights, inhibited by humanistic theory and by rules of the new literary criticism tending toward a realism which was physical though generalized. Many of them wished to give theatrical life to a sphere of human experience above domestic conflicts of love, money and luck in middle-class urban scenes bound by rules of unity and verisimili-

tude, but they wished to do so without sacrificing any of the conventions of neoclassical comedy. The impulse to stretch the confines of genre would be more fully indulged in the triumphant mixture of the pastoral tragicomedy, but it was at work also in the tentative association of providential pattern with intrigue plot in the *commedia grave*. The treatment of the fortuitous complications in *Fratelli rivali* reflects a Counter-Reformation eagerness to curb belief in the judiciary arts and other sorts of fortune-telling, which by implication challenged the doctrine of free will and opposed a pagan idea of fate to the Christian concept of divine providence. Della Porta himself had been warned by the Inquisition of the dangers in this regard of his own works on physiognomy and natural magic, and his circumscription of fortune's power attests his disposition to appear orthodox even in comedy. He stacks his plot to demonstrate that fortune is allowed a certain amount of play in human life, without impeding free will, but that providence sees to conclusions. The characters who attribute the happy ending to God (Polisena, Eufranone and the viceroy) are those whose virtue or authority fit them to be spokesmen for the truth. Carizia, whose will to goodness is emphasized, is both the favored child of the directing providence and its agent by reason of that goodness, while the brothers, who worry about the outcome and express fear of peripeties that might reverse the direction of events, are conscious, like their uncle and like the ideal self-aware Catholic of the period, that all the world's a stage. They see themselves as actors in a drama and, at the same time, as "real" people in "real" action. Both of them are beneficiaries of the inevitable triumph of providence over capricious fortune, whose reversals and peripeties are merely random (although it is the climax of Don Flaminio's wrong-

headedness to be slightly muddled about the final truth [V.v.]). Providence uses such turns of fortune—the peripeties born of peripeties about which Della Porta boasts in the prologue—not for the moment only but as part of an encompassing design. The deliberate *intreccio* of the plot, with its confusions, deceits and instances of mistaken reliance on the senses, becomes an image of human life with its fallacies, while the playwright's supervision and steering of the whole to a happy ending are tacitly compared to the workings of providence. Intrigue structure, originally a skeleton or organizing device, grows into a vehicle for representing fortune's games, and ends as a metaphor for a spiritual pattern believed by Tridentine Catholics to be a reality higher than that demonstrable by ocular proof. It would not do to claim consistent seriousness of purpose for this uneven play, nor to maintain that the medium here becomes the message; nevertheless, it deserves remark that structure and significance, signifier and signified never drew so close together in Italian Renaissance drama until the *commedia grave* became as grave as this.

The inevitable comparison of *Fratelli rivali* with *Much Ado About Nothing* could be marshalled to support and expand Gordon's suggestion of a debt on Shakespeare's part. Gordon thinks that such a debt would have been contracted only through intermediate lost material influenced by Della Porta, but it is not impossible that Shakespeare might have seen a manuscript of *Fratelli rivali* or even a performance by travelling *comici*. There are details in the two plays not shared with Bandello or his translators, nor yet with any versions of Ariosto's tale of Ariodante and Ginevra. Gordon mentions the plan (not carried out) for the impersonators to call one another by the lovers' names, the deceived bridegroom's public denunciation in the presence of the wed-

ding party, the use of the Spanish title "Don," and the father's willingness to believe his daughter guilty and to wish her dead. It may furthermore be observed that only Della Porta and Shakespeare add boisterous underlings and comic peace-officers and introduce the idea of fraternal hostility.

There are subcutaneous likenesses, too, that have eluded genealogists of Shakespeare's plots. The benignly ironic motif of beguiled sight in *Fratelli rivali* is paralleled in *Much Ado* by thematic play on seeing, or "noting,"[15] begun by

> CLAUDIO. Benedick, didst thou note the daughter of Signior Leonato?
> BENEDICK. I noted her not, but I looked on her.
> (I.i);

continued by the eye-deceiving disguises of a plot which ends with a proper subordination of sensory sight, expressed in Beatrice's "eye of favor," Benedick's "eye of love," and Claudio's pledging himself to the

15. I quote from *The Complete Shakespeare*, the Pelican edition under the general editorship of Alfred Harbage (New York, 1969). The editor of *Much Ado About Nothing*, Josephine Waters Bennett, observes that "nothing" was pronounced "noting" (p. 286, note to line 54); in the Variorum edition of Shakespeare, H. H. Furness goes into considerable detail, but remains skeptical as to the intentionality or significance of the pun. The best arguments against Furness are set forth by James A. S. McPeek, "The Thief 'Deformed' and Much Ado About 'Noting'," *Boston University Studies in English* 4, no. 2 (Summer 1960): 65–84. In a recent weighing of opinions about *Much Ado*, Ray L. Heffner, Jr., recognizes with some reservations "much warrant for reading the entire play as about 'noting,' in the sense of 'observing' or 'perceiving,'" ("Hunting for Clues in *Much Ado About Nothing*," in *Teaching Shakespeare*, edited by Walter Edens et al. [Princeton, 1977], p. 182), and himself follows a widespread contemporary preference for emphasizing the tragicomic character of the action and the focus on forms of deception and self-deception. The Pelican editions of *Romeo and Juliet* and of *Henry V* quoted below are by John E. Hankins and Alfred Harbage respectively.

veiled (unseen) Hero (V.iv); and confirmed by the comedy's punning title, which, in turn, is underscored by a verbal flourish,

> BALTHASAR. Note this before my notes:
> There's not a note of mine that's worth the noting.
> PEDRO. Why, these are very crotchets that he
> speaks!
> Note notes, forsooth, and nothing!   (II.iii)

The encounter between Benedick and Hero's attendant Margaret with which Shakespeare prefaces the love scene in V.ii bears to Capitan Martebellonio and the *fantesca* Chiaretta's morning-after meeting in *Fratelli rivali* IV.iii a distant resemblance, which seems closer for the brief exchange's being without known sources and, as far as the plot goes, entirely gratuitous. In the deception of Claudio, of course, Margaret performs a function equivalent to that of Chiaretta in the deception of Don Ignazio, and her gamey challenge to Benedick, "To have no man come over me? Why, shall I always keep below stairs?" is one of her many utterances more suited to a *fantesca* than to a lady-in-waiting of the governor's daughter. There is no connection between Margaret and Benedick like that between Chiaretta and Martebellonio, nor such bitter matter in their conversation, but in Shakespeare's banter,

> BENEDICK. Thy wit is as quick as the greyhound's mouth—it catches.
> MARGARET. And your's as blunt as the fencer's foils, which hit but hurt not.
> BENEDICK. A most manly wit, Margaret: it will not hurt a woman. And so I pray thee call Beatrice. I give thee the bucklers.
> MARGARET. Give us the swords; we have bucklers of our own . . . ,

the kind and the order of images—first hounds, then swords—and the male retreat covered by a show of re-

luctance to injure a woman are reminiscent of the recriminations between Chiaretta and the braggart captain. It is not irrelevant to remember also that Benedick has been linked with Spenser's Braggadochio.[16] The connection is certainly too tenuous to explain Pedro's jest about Benedick, "in the managing of quarrels you may say he is wise, for either he avoids them with great discretion, or undertakes them with a most Christian-like fear" (II.ii), but if these words do not fit Benedick, they are suitable for Braggadochio and almost formulaic for the Italian stage braggart, a stock figure developed long before Spenser or Della Porta began to write.

Tracking such resemblances is a vital enterprise of literary historiography, but it can lead into a cul-de-sac of source study. A more adventurous comparison would examine the dramatic microstructures and frames which, for want of a better word (*generici*, *dramemes* and the like failing in precision or sobriety), Mario Baratto has quizzically suggested that I call *teatrogrammi*. When each of these plays is read as a control for the other, with greater weight given to dissimilarities than to similarities, *Much Ado* yields up theatergrams not to be found in *Fratelli rivali* but which are characteristic of Italian comedy as a genre; conversely, in *Fratelli rivali* there appear theatergrams which are absent in *Much Ado* but present in other plays of Shakespeare.[17]

16. Abbie Findlay Potts, "Spenserian 'Courtesy' and 'Temperance' in Shakespeare's *Much Ado About Nothing*," *Shakespeare Association Bulletin* 17 (1942): 129–32.

17. While it is not appropriate here to go into the widely known but insufficiently studied fact of Shakespeare's awareness of the *commedia dell'arte*, nor to expound more than I have done above on the exchanges between literary *commediografi* and improvising *comici*, it should be remembered that Dogberry was originally played by Will Kempe, who had travelled in Italy and frequented theater circles there. For recent work on the subject, see Eugene Steele, "Verbal *Lazzi* in Shakespeare's Plays," *Italica* 53, no. 2 (Summer 1976): 214–22.

Plot-design used as illustration of idea is one such the-atergram, and here the dissimilarities between *Much Ado* and *Fratelli rivali* place them in different categories of *commedia grave*. Employing the principle of complication to produce not merely *inganni* and misunderstanding but *patterns* of *inganni* and misunderstanding was a technique brought almost to perfection in late cinque-cento comedies. In some of them, as in *Fratelli rivali*, the happy ending shows that the pattern was made in heav-en. Working the denouement of a tangled plot to con-firm the superiority of providence to fortune and to human shortsightedness is an exercise in dramatic sym-bolism of a very Shakespearean kind. The "providential pattern" which Arthur Kirsch has traced exclusively in *All's Well That Ends Well* and Shakespeare's late ro-mances[18] can also be seen emerging as early as *The Comedy of Errors*. But in many Italian comedies of the period the pattern of unhappy confusion which sud-denly gives birth to happy order is an end in itself. *Much Ado About Nothing* is of this kind, a fact emphasized by the title and constantly made visible by Shakespeare's changes in his sources: he reduces the difficulties but multiplies the misapprehensions and makes more ado about them, while rendering the truth of the case so per-fectly apparent that even the stupidity of the investiga-tors cannot obscure it. He does not carry the pattern to doctrinal lengths; consequently, in this feature *Much Ado* resembles *Fratelli rivali* less than it does some of the *commedie gravi* integrated by other themes than that of providence, such as Pino's *Gli ingiusti sdegni*, in which everyone is unjustly angry, or Castelletti's labyrinthine design of love's errors, *I torti amorosi*.

Shakespeare's most admired additions, Beatrice and Benedick, constitute another kind of dramatic structure

18. Arthur C. Kirsch, *Jacobean Dramatic Perspectives* (Charlottes-ville, Va., 1972), pp. 52–74.

for which a precedent existed in the Italian theatrical repertory. For their skirmishes of wit no unmistakable source has been established, although there has been an attempt to trace their ancestry to the relationship that Castiglione depicted between Emilia Pia and Gaspare Pallavicino in *Il libro del cortegiano*.[19] Shakespeare's other comedies testify to his chronic penchant for clever, sharp-tongued lovers, and if he had needed English models he could have found them in Lyly's arch dialogues, but it seems more than coincidence that in such an Italianate play as this one Beatrice and Benedick's stances and the tone of their mocking amatory exchanges are far less like Lyly's sexless volleys than like the "contrasti amorosi" from the actress Isabella Andreini's posthumously published repertory of pieces used in improvisation, and similar dialogues from the printed comedies of late cinquecento playwrights. Not the kind of *contrasto* evoked by Carizia and Don Ignazio's love scene in *Fratelli rivali*, however. While it is true that Carizia is wittier than her Bandellian and Shakespearean counterparts, Fenicia and Hero, she cannot come near Beatrice. Carizia's duet with Don Ignazio belongs with the gentler and more stately, Beatrice and Benedick's encounters with the nimblest and most provocative of the professional players' amorous contrasts. Even from the latter, moreover, the distance remains great; if Shakespeare's captivating pair inhabit a dramatic structure of relationship created in the Italian theater, they fill and transform it almost, but not quite, beyond recognition.

The love scene of *Fratelli rivali* also provides an instance of the reverse phenomenon, that is, a structure of stage action that Shakespeare takes for his own, but not to use in *Much Ado*. Don Ignazio greets Carizia's ap-

19. Mary Augusta Scott, "*The Book of the Courtyer*: A Possible Source of Benedick and Beatrice," *PMLA* 16 (1901): 475–502.

pearance at her window above him, "Già fuggono le tenebre dell'aria, ecco l'aurora che precede la chiarezza del mio bel sole, già spuntano i raggi intorno" (II.ii). There is no corresponding scene in *Much Ado* but it has not escaped scholarly attention that his speech is like Romeo's, "But soft! what light through yonder window breaks? It is the east, and Juliet is the sun . . ." (II.ii).[20] The significance of the resemblance, however, has not been pursued. *Romeo and Juliet* preceded *Fratelli rivali* in print, though perhaps not in composition. There is only a slight possibility that Shakespeare knew Della Porta's comedy, and no reason at all to think that Della Porta knew anything about Shakespeare. The physical stages for which they wrote both permitted conversation on upper and lower levels, but Shakespeare, unlike his Italian contemporary, was not constrained by rules of decorum or of unity of place to devise ways of bringing young ladies onstage while keeping them safe at home. In short, the kinship of the love scenes in *Romeo and Juliet* and *Fratelli rivali* is not to be explained by direct imitation or by the determining influence of identical stage sets and conventions. It arises from the general, rather than from the particular, and begins with lyric poetry. The lady-as-sunlight-and-dawn is a topos with classical and Provençal antecedents and a firm place in the Petrarchan tradition. Italian dramaturgy developed it into a microstructure of another genre by combining the image with a situation—the encounter of lovers, to whom Petrarchan vocabulary was categorically assigned—and with a theatrical space—the distance and rapport between the street level and the upper-storey window or balcony. Pino's *Gli ingiusti sdegni* includes a scene (I.v) in which Licinio hails Delia as his sun when she appears at her

20. Raffaele Sirri Rubes, *L'attività teatrale di G. B. Della Porta* (Napoli, 1968), p. 112.

window and says that darkness has returned when she leaves. Ercole Bentivoglio had already introduced a negative version of the compound structural motif in *Il geloso* (1544), when Fausto looks up at Livia's house, apostrophizes it as the abode of the sun and complains that Livia does not come forth (II.i). The Neapolitan poetaster Bell'umore of Castelletti's *Le stravaganze d'amore* shows off his knowledge of poetic theory and gives as an example of Tuscan love poetry the conceit: ". . . la vostra fenestra è il mio Oriente, e'l lume de l'occhi vostri è il mio Parnaso" (III.v). In Isabella Andreini's repertory there are numerous variations on this generic encounter, such as that in the "contrasto amoroso sopra la gelosia," which begins with Eliodoro greeting Theossena, "Hor sì ch'io posso dire vedendovi, ecco l'Aurora, che sponta della dorata porta d'Oriente."[21] Della Porta had already used this theatergram in *La fantesca* (II.iii) as Shakespeare also had done, minus its amorous aspect, in *Richard II* (III.iii). The various examples that can be adduced do more than establish that the same venerable topos underlies the Della Portean and Shakespearean scenes that respectively end and pause with

> CARIZIA. A Dio.
> DON IGNAZIO. Ecco tramontata la sfera del mio bel sole, che sola può far serena il mio giorno. O fenestra, è sparito il tuo pregio.   (II.iii)

and

> JULIET. A thousand times good night.
> ROMEO. A thousand times the worse, to want thy light.   (II.ii)

21. Bernardino Pino, *Gli ingiusti sdegni, comedia* (Roma, 1553); Ercole Bentivoglio, *Il geloso, comedia* [Venice, 1544], a cura di Alberto Dradi Maraldi (Torino, 1972); Cristoforo Castelletti, *Le stravaganze d'amore, comedia* (Venezia, 1584); Isabella Andreini, *Fragmenti di alcune scritture* (Venetia, 1620), p. 134.

37

The topos had been developed in Italian comedy as a mobile structure of stage action, for insertion into plots usually deriving from narrative sources, the lyric trope fused with the theatrical exigency of the *scène à faire* between lovers, with the space provided by the set and with the relative positions assigned to them in it by theoretical and practical investigations of the genre. The compound is an empirical result, a movable part forged in the Italian theater and rendered functional and variable long before it appeared among members of the common market of Renaissance drama. The fact that Shakespeare does not use it in *Much Ado*, when his source is one with Della Porta's, but does use it in his dramatization of a translation of another Italianate narrative suggests that he was familiar not merely with one Italian drama but with a repertory of dramatic structures.

Don Rodorigo de Mendoza, viceroy of Salerno, the figure of civil authority placed in a potentially tragic position of moral choice and operating as symbol of social reconciliation and as propaganda for order, is not one of the common theatergrams of character and function. But he is not unique in late *commedia grave* and therefore invites comparison with governors in several of Shakespeare's plays. Once again the key is not to be found in a common source-plot. The equivalent figure in *Much Ado*, "Don Pedro, Prince of Arragon," shares neither the moral dilemma nor the dramatic function assigned to Don Rodorigo: for similar examples of rulers used theatrically to confirm meaning and to extend it to farther fields, political or moral, we must look to Duke Solinus of Ephesus in *The Comedy of Errors*, to Prince Escalus of Verona in *Romeo and Juliet* or, with a different eye, to the duke in *Measure for Measure* and the king in *All's Well That Ends Well*.

A more familiar figure in *commedia grave* is the "donna mirabile"; the phrase is Girolamo Bargagli's, but Della Porta could properly have applied it to the character of Carizia. A variation on the standard *innamorata*, the wondrous woman appears early in Piccolomini's *L'amor costante* (1536) as a saint of love, about whom religious vocabulary is used as a metaphor, the religion in question being the cult of love. Although she comes onstage only twice, Carizia demonstrates how in the late cinquecento the figure took on more didactic orthodox spiritual weight, and was made a saint of the kind of love linked with the sacrament of matrimony and a nearly miraculous example of the virtues extolled from contemporary pulpits. Carizia imparts a sense of the supernatural, of miracle, without departing from the letter of the rule of verisimilitude or returning to medieval *rappresentazioni sacre*. Her presence creates an abstract dimension for the sporadic or subliminal dramatizing of some "realities" important to late Renaissance Christian thought but difficult to represent in a genre nominally committed to imitation of plausible reality. She is a phenomenon of which other examples are at hand in comedies of Bargagli, of Oddi and of Shakespeare.[22] Not *Much Ado* but the so-called "twin" comedies, *All's Well* and *Measure for Measure*, provide the comparable generic figures. Both plays are mixtures of tragedy and comedy, both turn on the strength and suffering of uncomfortably extraordinary women who stand in special relation to the powers of heaven and who, in different ways, preside over or ritualistically embody actions of

22. The figure is discussed more fully in my "Woman as Wonder: A Generic Figure in Italian and Shakespearean Comedy," *Studies in the Continental Background of Renaissance English Literature: Essays Presented to John L. Lievsay*, edited by Dale B. J. Randall and George W. Williams (Durham, N. C., 1977), pp. 109–32.

reconciliation and pardon. In both some critics have detected vestigial patterns of Christian ritual and even forthright Christian allegory.

Shakespeare's recasting Bandello's novella in the genre rather than in the mold of *Fratelli rivali* and Della Porta's dramatizing of the story to suggest now *Romeo and Juliet*, now *All's Well*, and sometimes even Shakespeare's crypto-pastoral celebrations of magical or divinely providential pattern, from *A Midsummer Night's Dream* to *The Tempest*, can hardly be accounted for by a universal Renaissance debt to Plautus and Terence or by the wide diffusion of novellas suitable for staging. Were *Fratelli rivali* not valued as it is by Italian tradition, or were it not so fullblown an example of a late Renaissance genre poorly represented in modern editions and translations, it would still cry out for use in dramatic criticism as an instrument of analysis that goes deeper than what Harry Levin once deplored as the Fluellen style of comparative literature:

> I warrant you sall find, in the comparisons between Macedon and Monmouth, that the situations, look you, is poth alike. There is a river in Macedon, and there is also moreover a river at Monmouth. It is called Wye at Monmouth. But it is out of my prains what is the name of the other river; but 'tis all one; 'tis alike as my fingers is to my fingers, and there is salmons in poth. (*Henry V*, IV.vii)[23]

23. The Plutarchan parody spoken by Shakespeare's Welsh captain, a classic caveat against false parallels, as used recently, for example, by G. R. Hibbard in "Henry IV and Hamlet," *Shakespeare Survey* 30 (1977): 1, was never better applied than in Levin's 1962 Washington, D.C., lecture on pitfalls in the field of comparative literature.

TEXT AND TRANSLATION

Gli Duoi Fratelli Rivali

Comedia nuovamente data in luce,
dal Signor Gio. Bat. Della Porta
Gentiluomo Napolitano.

The Two Rival Brothers

Comedy newly brought forth,
by Signor Giovanni Battista Della Porta
Neapolitan gentleman.

AL MOLTO ILLUSTRE SIGNORE
E PATRON MIO COLENDISSIMO IL SIGNOR
ALESSANDRO GAMBALONGA.[1]

Io CONOSCO MOLTO BENE che alle rare virtù e singulari
qualità di Vostra Signoria molto illustre altro presente
che questo di questa piccola operetta si converrebbe; ma
non permettendomi l'obbligo infinito che le tengo per
le molte cortesie ricevute dall'eccesso della sua benigni-   5
tà, senza alcun merito mio, nel ritorno che feci dal mio
perregrinaggio di Roma per cotesta città,[2] il soprastar
più lungo tempo senza darle qualche segno della memoria che tengo di tanta cortesia, né avendo al presente altra occasione che questa, prego Vostra Signoria ad ac-   10
cetare il poco che le do, in segno del molto che le devo,
assicurandosi che si come l'obbligo mi stringe a tener
memoria di lei, così io non sia per mancare all'occasione
ogni volta che mi si porgerà; e se bene la presente opera è
di poche carte e di poco volume, con tutto ciò essendo di   15
auttore famoso e di valore, non ho giudicato di scon-
venirsi in tutto a Vostra Signoria, la quale è da credere
che tal'ora doppo le grate occupazioni degli suoi ono-
ratissimi essercizii, dia anco recreazione all'animo con
la lettura di qualche cosa piacevole, sì come sovente   20
lo pasce di dolci con certi musicali, dando continua-
mente ricetto nella casa sua, ed a quelli della patria ed a
forastieri, purché o per pregio di lettere o di musica o di
altra nobile virtù ne siano meritevoli. Io tralascio in
questo luogo quelle lodi che a meriti suoi di ragione si   25
converrebbeno, perché quando una sola minima parte
raccontarne volessi, adulazione più tosto verrebbe giu-
dicata la mia che veridica relazione di servitore divoto

44

TO THE MOST ILLUSTRIOUS GENTLEMAN
AND MY MOST HONORED PATRON,
SIGNOR ALESSANDRO GAMBALONGA.

I AM WELL AWARE that a gift far other than this little work would befit Your most illustrious Worship, but as the infinite obligation I have to you for the many quite undeserved courtesies received from your exceeding kindness on my return through your city from a pilgrimage to Rome will not allow me to delay longer without giving some sign that I am mindful of so much courtesy, nor having for the moment any occasion but this, I pray Your Worship to accept the little that I give you in token of the much that I owe you, and to believe that as my obligation presses me to remember you, so shall I not miss the occasion whenever it may offer itself; and although the present work is of few pages and small volume, yet for all that, being by a famous and worthy author, I have judged it not altogether inappropriate to Your Worship, who, it must be supposed, sometimes after the satisfying activity of your high endeavors, may give recreation to your spirit in reading some pleasant thing, as you likewise often nourish it with the sweetness of musical entertainments, continually offering the shelter of your house to fellow citizens and to foreigners, provided they be deserving by virtue of accomplishment in letters, in music, or in some other noble study.

I omit here those praises which belong by right to your merits, for if I wished to tell even a small part of them, it would be judged flattery rather than the true account of the devoted and affectionate servant that I

ed affezionato quale io le sono; e per tale confermando-
mele ora con lettare, come già a bocca me le dedicai,   30
umilmente le baccio la mano, e le prego da Dio il colmo
di ogni sua desiderata felicità.

Di Venezia li 28. maggio 1601.
Di Vostra Signoria Molto Illustre
Devotissimo Servitore,   35
Gio. Batt. Ciotti Sanese.[3]

am; and now confirming myself such in letters, as here-
tofore with my lips I have dedicated my service to you, I
humbly kiss your hand and pray that God grant you the
happy fulfillment of your every desire.

From Venice the 28th day of May 1601.
Your Most Illustrious Worship's
Most Devoted Servant,
Giovanni Battista Ciotti of Siena.

Il luogo[1] dove si rappresenta la favola è Salerno.

Persone[2] della Favola

1 DON IGNAZIO, giovane innamorato
2 SIMBOLO, suo camariero
3 DON FLAMINIO, giovane, suo fratello
4 PANIMBOLO, suo camariero
5 LECCARDO, parasito
6 MARTEBELLONIO, capitano

2

7 ANGIOLA, vecchia
8 CARIZIA, giovane
9 EUFRANONE, vecchio
10 POLISENA, sua moglie

3

11 CHIARETTA, fantesca
12 AVANZINO, servo

4

13 Birri

5

14 DON RODORIGO, viceré della provincia

The action takes place in Salerno.

Characters in the Play

1 DON IGNAZIO, a young gentleman in love
2 SIMBOLO, Don Ignazio's manservant
3 DON FLAMINIO, Don Ignazio's brother
4 PANIMBOLO, Don Flaminio's manservant
5 LECCARDO, a parasite
6 MARTEBELLONIO, a captain

2

7 ANGIOLA, an old lady
8 CARIZIA, a young lady
9 EUFRANONE, an old gentleman
10 POLISENA, Eufranone's wife

3

11 CHIARETTA, a maidservant
12 AVANZINO, a manservant

4

13 [Three] Constables

5

14 DON RODORIGO, viceroy of the province
[SILENT CHARACTERS:
Carizia's sister Callidora,
gentlemen of Salerno, friends and relations
of the Della Porta family,
and courtiers attending the viceroy]

Prologo della comedia
Delli doi Fratelli Rivali
Del Signor Gio. Batista Della Porta

O LÀ CHE RUMORE?[1] o là che strepito è questo? egli è
possibil pure, che fra persone di valore, e di sangue illustre ci abbia a venir mischiata sempre questa vilissima
canaglia? la qual, per mostrar a quel popolazzo, che gli
sta d'intorno, che s'intende di comedie, or rugna di qua,   5
or torce il muso di là; par che le puzzi ogni cosa. «Questa parola non è boccaccevole, questo si potea dir meglio
altrimente, questo è fuor delle regole di Aristotele,[2]
quel non ha del verisimile»; pascendosi di quella aura
vilissima popolare, né intende che si dica, ed alla fine   10
viene a credere a gli altri: ed altri, pieni d'invidia e di
veleno, per mostrar che la comedia non dia sodisfazione
a gli intendenti, e che l'hanno in fastidio, empiono di
strepito e di gridi tutto il teatro. E che genti son queste
poi? qualche legista senza legge e qualche poeta senza   15
versi.[3] Credete, ignorantoni, con queste vostre chiacchiere far parer un'opera di manco ch'ella sia, come il
mondo dal vostro bestial giudicio giudicasse gli onori
dell'opere? o goffi che sete, ché l'opre son giudicate dal-
l'applauso universal de' dotti di tutte le nazioni; perché   20
si veggono stampate per tutte le parti del mondo, e tradotte in latino, francese, spagnolo, ed altre varie lingue;
e quanto più s'odono e si leggono, tanto più piacciono e
son ristampate,[4] come è accaduto a tutte l'altre buone
sue sorelle che in publico ed in privato comparse sono.[5]   25
Vien qua, Dottor della necessità,[6] che con sei tratti di
corda[7] non confessaresti una legge, che non sapendo

Prologue of the comedy of
The Two Rival Brothers
by Signor Giovanni Battista Della Porta

Ho THERE, WHAT'S THIS NOISE? Ho, what's the uproar?
Is it possible that with persons of worth and noble blood
there must always be mixed this most base and beastly trash, which, to show the surrounding mob that it
knows something about comedies, growls here and
wrinkles its snout there, as if everything stank in its nos-
trils? "This word is not authorized by Boccaccio, this
could be expressed better in another way, this is against
Aristotle's rules, this lacks verisimilitude"; feeding on
cheap popular favor, it doesn't understand whatever is
said, and ends up accepting the opinion of the crowd.
Still others, full of envy and poison, in order to show
that the comedy does not satisfy the connoisseurs, and
that they disdain it, fill the whole theater with clamor
and shouts. And what sort of people are these after all?
A few lacklaw lawyers and verseless versifiers. Do you
think, you dolts, that with your chattering, you can
make a work seem less than it is, as if the world rated the
honors of works according to your beastly judgment?
Clods that you are, these works are judged rather by
the universal applause of learned men of all nations; for
they are seen printed in all parts of the world and translated into Latin, French, Spanish and various other lan-
guages; and the more they are heard and read, the more
they please and are reprinted, as has happened to all the
other good sisters of this comedy which have appeared
in public and private. Come here, oh threadbare, un-
learned counselor, from whom not even six tugs of the
strappado could draw a law, you who, knowing noth-

della tua, prosumi saper tutte le scienze; certo che se sapessi che cosa è comedia, ti porresti sotterra per non parlarne giamai. Ignorantissimo, considera prima la favola,[8] se sia nuova, meravigliosa, piacevole, e se ha l'altre sue parti convenevoli, ché questa è l'anima della comedia; considera la peripezia, che è spirito dell'anima, che l'avviva e le dà moto, e se gli antichi consumavano venti scene per far caderla in una, in queste sue, senza stiracchiamenti, e da sé stessa, cade in tutto il quarto atto, e se miri più adentro, vedrai nascer peripezia da peripezia, ed agnizione da agnizione: ché se non fossi così cieco de gl'occhi dell'intelletto come sei, vedresti l'ombre di Menandro, di Epicarmo, e di Plauto[9] vagar in questa scena e rallegrarsi che la comedia sia gionta a quel colmo, ed a quel segno, dove tutta l'antichità fece bersaglio. Or questo è altro che parole del Boccaccio, o regole di Aristotele, il qual se avesse saputo di filosofia[10] e di altro quanto di comedia, forse non arebbe quel grido famoso che possiede per tutto il mondo. Ma tu che sei goffo, non conosci l'arte. Or gracchiate tanto che crepiate, ché il nome vostro non esce fuor del limitar delle vostre camere; né per ciò voi scemerete la fama dell'autore, la qual nasce da altri studi più gravi di questo, e le comedie fur scherzi della sua fanciullezza.[11] Or tacete, bocche di conche, e di sepolcri de morti, ché se provocarete la sua modestia, come or amichevolmente qui vi ammonisce, farà conoscer per sempre chi voi sete. Ma questi ignorantoni per la rabbia m'han fatto tralasciare il mio officio che era qui venuto a fare con voi. Or questo serva in vece di Prologo, ché l'argomento della favola lo vedrete minutamente spiegato da questi che vengon fuora.

ing of your own subject, think yourself expert in all the others; if you knew what comedy was, you would surely rather the earth opened and swallowed you than presume to discourse on the matter. Ignoramus, consider first the plot and whether it be new, arousing wonder, pleasing and well-proportioned, for the plot is the soul of the comedy; consider the peripety, which is the soul's spirit, which gives it life and motion, and if the ancients used up twenty scenes to make the peripety occur in one, in the comedies of this author the peripety occurs naturally and unforced in the course of the whole fourth act, and if you look deeper, you will see peripety born of peripety and recognition of recognition: for if the eyes of your intellect were not blind, as they are, you would see the shades of Menander, of Epicharmus and of Plautus wandering this stage and rejoicing that comedy has reached that height and that mark at which all antiquity aimed. Now this is something more important than following the vocabulary of Boccaccio or the rules of Aristotle, who, if he knew about philosophy or anything else only as much as he did about comedy, would perhaps not be so much renowned throughout the world. But you, clod, know nothing about art. Go on, all of you, and croak till you crack, for your names are unknown outside your own chambers; nor can you thus diminish the author's fame, which arises from other works more serious than this: his comedies were the sports of his boyhood. Now be still, shut up your hollow mouths, those dead men's tombs, for if you try his patience, as surely as he now admonishes you in friendly fashion, he will once and for all show you up for what you are.

But these ignoramuses have made me in my anger neglect the office I came here to perform for you. Well, let this serve as prologue, for the argument of the plot will be minutely explained by these whom you see issuing forth.

Gli Fratelli Rivali

di Giovan Battista Porta Napolitano

ATTO I

SCENA I

Don Ignazio, giovane, e Simbolo, suo cameriero.

DON IGNAZIO. Egli è possibile, o Simbolo, ch'avendo-
ti commesso che fussi tornato e ben presto, che m'abbi
fatto tanto penar per la risposta?

SIMBOLO. A far molti servigi bisogna molto tempo,
né io poteva caminar tanto in un tratto.   5

DON IGNAZIO. In tanto tempo arei caminato tutto il
mondo.

SIMBOLO. Sì, col cervello, ma io avea a caminar con le
gambe.

DON IGNAZIO. Or questo è peggio, farmi penar di   10
nuovo in ascoltar le tue scuse. Che hai tu fatto?

SIMBOLO. Son stato al maestro delle vesti.

DON IGNAZIO. Cominci da quello che manco m'importa.

SIMBOLO. Comincierò da quello che più vi piace: sono   15
stato a Don Flaminio, vostro fratello, per saper la risposta che ave avuto dal Conte di Tricarico[1] della vostra
sposa.

DON IGNAZIO. Che sai tu che questo mi piaccia?

SIMBOLO. Ve l'ho intesa lodar molto di bellezza, pre-   20
gate Don Flaminio che tratti col Conte ve la conceda,

The Rival Brothers

of Giovan Battista Porta, Neapolitan

ACT I

SCENE I

DON IGNAZIO, a young gentleman, and SIMBOLO, his
servant.

DON IGNAZIO. How is it, Simbolo, that being charged
to return quickly, you've made me suffer so long for the
answer?

SIMBOLO. To do many errands takes much time, and I
couldn't walk that far in an instant.

DON IGNAZIO. In as much time as you took, I could
have walked around the world.

SIMBOLO. Yes, with your brain, but I had to walk with
my legs.

DON IGNAZIO. Now worse still, you make me suffer
more by listening to your excuses. What have you accomplished?

SIMBOLO. I've been to the tailor.

DON IGNAZIO. You begin with the thing that matters
least to me.

SIMBOLO. Then I'll begin with what pleases you most:
I've been to your brother, Don Flaminio, to learn what
answer he's had from the Count of Tricarico about your
bride.

DON IGNAZIO. What makes you think that this pleases
me?

SIMBOLO. I've heard you praise her beauty much, you
beg Don Flaminio to persuade the Count to give her to

passegiate tutto il giorno sotto le sue fenestre; ed il pregio[2] che guadagnaste nella festa de' tori mandaste a do-
nar a lei.

DON IGNAZIO. E ciò m'importa manco del primo.   25

SIMBOLO. Sono stato a Madonna Angiola.

DON IGNAZIO. Ben?

SIMBOLO. Non era in chiesa, ché non era ancor venuta,
ed io, per avanzar tempo per gli altri negozii, non l'as-
pettai.   30

DON IGNAZIO. Per che non lasciasti tutti gli altri per
aspettar lei?

SIMBOLO. Che sapeva io che desiavate ciò? Se potesse
indovinar il vostro cuore, sareste servito prima che me
lo comandaste; e se a voi non rincrescerà comandarmi, a   35
me non rincrescerà servirvi: vi fidate di me de danari,
argenti, e gioie, e non potete fidar parole o secreti?

DON IGNAZIO. Ho celato il desiderio del mio cuore insino alla camicia che ho in dosso: ma or son risoluto fi-
darmi di te, così per obligarti a consigliarmi ed aiutarmi   40
con più franchezza, come per isfogar teco la passione:
ma un secreto sì grande sia custodito da te sotto sincera
fede di un onorato silenzio.

SIMBOLO. Vi offro fedeltà e franchezza nell'uno e nel-
l'altro.   45

DON IGNAZIO. Io ardo della più bella fiamma che sia al
mondo; ed acciò che tu sappi a puntino ogni cosa, co-
minciarò da capo. Quando venne il gran Capitano Ferrante di Corduba[3] nel conquisto del Regno di Napoli,
venner con lui molti gentiluomini e signori spagnuoli   50
per avventurieri, tra' quali fu Don Rodorigo di Mendozza mio zio, e noi fratelli; e dopo la felice conquista di
questo Regno, noi e nostro zio fummo molto largamente rimunerati da Sua Maestà di molte migliaia di
scudi d'entrata e de' primi uffici del Regno: fra gli altri   55
fu fatto Viceré della provincia di questa città di Salerno.[4]

you, you stroll all day under her windows; and you sent her the prize you won at the bullfight.

DON IGNAZIO. And that matters less to me than your first errand.

SIMBOLO. I've been to Madonna Angiola.

DON IGNAZIO. Well?

SIMBOLO. She wasn't at church, hadn't arrived yet, and so as to have time for the other errands, I didn't wait for her.

DON IGNAZIO. Why didn't you put off the others to wait for her?

SIMBOLO. How was I to know you wanted that? If I could guess what's in your heart, you would be obeyed before you could command; I serve you gladly and shall do so for as long as you'll have me. You trust me with your money, plate and jewels, so why not trust me with words or secrets too?

DON IGNAZIO. I have hidden my heart's desire even from the shirt on my back; but now I'm resolved to confide in you, both to make you advise and help me more freely, and to vent my passion to you: but so great a secret must be kept by a true oath of strict silence.

SIMBOLO. I swear faith and frankness on both counts.

DON IGNAZIO. I am ablaze with the most beautiful flame in the world; and that you may know everything exactly, I shall begin at the beginning. When the great captain Ferrante of Cordova came here at the time of the conquest of the Kingdom of Naples, with him came many Spanish gentlemen and lords as soldiers of fortune, among them my uncle, Don Rodorigo de Mendoza, and the two of us, my brother and I; after the fortunate winning of this realm, we were generously rewarded by His Majesty with property yielding many thousands of crowns and with the highest posts in the kingdom: among other things, my uncle was appointed viceroy of the province and city of Salerno.

SIMBOLO. Tutto ciò sapeva bene, ché son stato a' vostri servigi.

DON IGNAZIO. Or ei, volendo rallegrar la città di Salerno sotto il suo governo, il carnescial passato ordinò giochi di canne, e di tori[5] in piazza per i gentiluomini, ed un sollenne ballo nella sala di palazo per le gentildonne. Venne il giorno constituito, venner e canne e tori in piazza e le gentildonne in sala: fra le altre vennero due giovanette sorelle. Ma perché dico «giovanette»; ché non dico due angiolette? elle parvero un folgore che lampeggiando offuscò la bellezza di tutte le altre. E se ben Callidora la minore fusse d'incomparabil bellezza, posta incontro al sovran paragon di bellezza, a Carizia, restava un poco più languida, perché la maggiore avea non so che di reale e di maraviglioso: parea che la natura avesse fatto l'estremo suo forzo in lei per serbarla per modello de tutte l'altre opre sue, per non errar più mai. Ella era sì bella che non sapevi se la bellezza facesse bella lei, o s'ella facesse bella la bellezza. Perché se la miravi aresti desiderato esser tutto occhi per mirarla, s'ella parlava esser tutto orecchie per ascoltarla. In somma tutti i suoi movimenti ed azioni erano condite d'una soprema dolcezza. Un sì stupendo spettacolo di bellezza rapì a sé tutti gli occhi e cuori de' riguardanti: restar le lingue mute e gli animi sospesi; e se pur se sentiva un certo tacito mormorio, era che ogni uno mirava, ed ammirava una mai più udita leggiadria. Io furtivamente mirava gli occhi di Carizia, i quali quanto erano vaghi a riguardare tanto pungevano poi, e quanto più pungevano tanto più ti sentivi tirar a forza di rimirargli; e riguardando non si volean partire, come se fussero stati legati con una fune, talché non sapeva discernere qual fuse maggiore, o la dolcezza del mirare, o la fierezza delle punture: al fin

SIMBOLO. I know all that very well, for I was in your service at the time.

DON IGNAZIO. Well, then, my uncle, wishing to make the city of Salerno rejoice under his rule, last carnival ordered games of pole-casting and bullfighting in the piazza for the gentlemen and a splendid ball in the hall of the palace for the ladies. Came the appointed day, came the poles and the bulls into the square and the ladies into the hall: among them came two charming girls, sisters. But why do I say "girls"; why not say two charming angels? They were like a flash of lightning that dimmed the beauty of all the others. And though Callidora, the younger, was incomparably beautiful, placed beside the sovereign paragon of beauty, beside Carizia, she seemed slightly more languid, for the elder had an inexpressible air of majesty and of wondrousness: it seemed that nature's utmost exertion had gone into creating her, so as to keep a model for all her other works and never err again. She was so beautiful that you couldn't tell whether beauty made her beautiful or she made beautiful beauty itself; for if you looked at her, you would have wished to be all eyes so as to see her, if she spoke, all ears so as to hear her: in short, all her movements and actions savoured of a supreme sweetness. So dazzling a spectacle of beauty ravished to itself the eyes and hearts of all observers: tongues fell silent, spirits hung suspended, and if yet a kind of hushed murmur was heard, it was that everyone gazed and was amazed at an unheard-of loveliness. Furtively I gazed at Carizia's eyes, which were as lovely to look on as they were piercing to the onlooker, and the more they wounded, the more forcibly you felt drawn to gaze on them again; and gazing, one was as loth to leave as if bound by a rope, so that it could not be discerned which was greater, the sweetness of gazing or the savagery of the wounds: at last I understood that the one was medi-

conobbi che l'uno era la medecina dell'altro. E benché io   90
prevedessi che quel fusse un principio d'una fiamma
nascente, da la quale ogni mio spirito dovea arderne
crudelissimamente, pur non potea tenermi di non mirarla; onde per non esser osservato da mio fratello, il
prendo per la mano, e lo meno nello steccato.   95

SIMBOLO. Perché dubbitavate di vostro fratello?

DON IGNAZIO. Tu sai da che siamo nati, avemo sempre
con grandissima emulazione gareggiato insieme, di lettere, di scrima, di cavalcare, e sopra tutto nell'amoreg-
giare, ché ogni un di noi ha fatto professione di tor l'in-   100
namorata all'altro. Il che s'avenisse così di costei, si
accenderebbe un odio maggiore fra noi che mai fusse
stato; sarebbe un seme di far nascer tra noi tal sdegno
che ci amazzaremmo insieme senz'alcuna pietade.

SIMBOLO. Seguite, e poi?   105

DON IGNAZIO. Appena entrammo nello steccato, come in un famoso campo di mostrar virtude e valore, che
fur stuzziccati i tori, i quali furiosi e dalle narici spiranti
focoso fiato vennero incontro noi. Onde se mai generoso petto fu stimulato da disio di gloria, fu il mio in quel   110
punto; perché sempre volgea gli occhi in quel ciel di
bellezza, parea che da quelle vive stelle de' suoi begli occhi spirassero nell'anima mia così potentissimi influssi,
così infinito valore ch'io feci fazioni tali che a tutti sem-
brarono meraviglie, ch'io non solo non andava schi-   115
vando gli affronti e i rivolgimenti de' tori, ma gli irri-
tava ancora, acciochè con maggior furia m'assalissero.
Di quelli, molti ne destesi in terra e n'uccisi; ma in quel
tempo ch'io combatteva con i tori, Amor combatteva
con me. O strana e mai più intesa battaglia: onde un   120
combattimento era nello steccato apparente, ed un altro
invisibile nel mio cuore: il toro alcuna volta mi feriva
nella pelle, e ne gocciolavano alcune stille di sangue, e'l
popolo ne avea compassione; ma ella con i giri de gli occhi suoi mi fulminava nell'anima, ma perché le ferite   125

cine for the other. And even though I foresaw there the beginning of a kindling flame in which my very spirit would burn most cruelly, still I could not keep myself from looking at her; wherefore, in order not to be observed by my brother, I took his hand and led him into the ring.

SIMBOLO. Why were you suspicious of your brother?

DON IGNAZIO. You know that ever since our birth we have rivalled each other with the fiercest emulation, in our studies, in fencing, in riding, and above all in our love affairs, for each has always set out to steal the other's mistress. Should that happen this time, with her, it would kindle up a hatred between us greater than any ever before; it would be a seed from which such wrath would spring up between us as to make us murder each other pitilessly.

SIMBOLO. Go on, and then?

DON IGNAZIO. We were no sooner in the ring, as in a celebrated field for proving ability and valor, than the bulls were goaded and charged us, furious and snorting fiery breath. Whereupon, if ever noble heart was stirred by desire for glory, mine was at that moment; because I constantly turned my eyes toward that heaven of beauty, it seemed that the living stars of her beautiful eyes breathed into my soul such powerful influences, such boundless courage that I performed feats that seemed marvels to all, for not only did I not avoid the charges and reversals of the bulls, but I even goaded them to attack me more furiously. Many of them I felled and killed; but while I was fighting the bulls, Love was fighting me. Oh, strange, unheard-of battle, in which a visible combat took place in the ring and an invisible one in my heart! The bull occasionally grazed my skin, shedding some drops of blood, at which the public pitied me; but she, turning her eyes, struck my soul with their lightning, yet because these wounds were blood-

erano senza sangue, niuno ne avea compassione. De' colpi de' tori alcuni ne andavano voti d'effetto; ma quelli degli occhi suoi tutti colpivano a segno. Pregava Amore che crescesse la rabbia a' tori, ma temperasse la forza de' guardi di Carizia. Al fin io rimasi vincitore del 130 toro, ella vincitrice di me: ed io che vinsi, perdei, e fui in un tempo vinto, e vincitore, e restai nella vittoria per amore. Del toro si vedea il cadavero disteso in terra, il mio vagava innanzi la sua bella imagine. Il popolo con lieto applauso gradiva la mia vittoria, ed io piangeva la 135 perdita di me stesso. Ahi quanto poco vinsi, ahi quanto perdei! Vinsi un toro, e perdei l'anima.

SIMBOLO. Faceste tanto gagliarda resistenza a' fieri incontri de' tori e non poteste resistere a' molli sguardi d'una vacca? Come si portò vostro fratello? 140

DON IGNAZIO. Fece anch'egli grandissime prodezze.

In somma ella fu l'occhio e la perfezione de tutta la festa. Finito il gioco, fingendomi stracco, ed altre colorite cagioni, ritrassi Don Flaminio dallo steccato, il quale avea gran voglia d'uscirne, e ci reducemo a casa; ma 145 prima avea imposto ad un paggio s'avesse informato chi fusse. Andai a letto avendo il cuore e gli occhi ripieni della bellezza della giovane e l'anima impressa della sua bella imagine, onde passai una notte assai travagliata. Intesi poi la matina che era una gentil donna onestissi- 150 ma, dotata di molte peregrine virtù, di casa Della Porta, ma povera per essernole state tolte le robbe per caggion de rubellione: ché Eufranone, il padre, avea seguite le parti del Principe de Salerno.[6]

SIMBOLO. Se state così invaghito di costei, perché trat- 155 tar matrimonio con la figlia del Conte de Tricarico, e ci avete posto Don Flaminio vostro fratello per mezano?

DON IGNAZIO. Quando piace a' medici che non calino i cattivi umori ne' luoghi offesi, ordinano certi riversivi.[7]

less, no one felt pity. Some of the bulls' attacks missed their aim, but those of her eyes all hit the target. I prayed Love to increase the bulls' fury but to temper the force of Carizia's glances. In the end I was victor over the bull, she victress over me: and I who won, lost, and was at once vanquished and victor, and remained in the spoils of love. The bull's carcass was seen lying on the ground; mine was wandering before her beautiful image. The public, with happy applause, rejoiced in my victory, and I lamented the loss of myself. Alas, how little I won! Alas, how much I lost! I vanquished a bull and I lost my soul.

SIMBOLO. You so stoutly withstood the fierce onslaughts of the bulls and you couldn't resist the soft glances of a cow? How did your brother behave?

DON IGNAZIO. He too performed the greatest wonders.

In short, she was the cynosure and the perfection of the whole celebration. The game ended, pretending to be exhausted and with other plausible excuses, I drew Don Flaminio away from the ring, he was very eager to retire, and we returned home; but first I ordered a page to find out who the young lady was. I went to bed with my heart and eyes full of her beauty and my soul imprinted with her beautiful image, wherefore I passed a greatly troubled night. Then I learned the next morning that she was a most chaste noblewoman, gifted with many rare qualities, of the house of Della Porta, but impoverished by confiscation of property because of rebellion: for her father, Eufranone, cast his lot with the Prince of Salerno.

SIMBOLO. If you're so taken with her, why propose marriage with the Count of Tricarico's daughter and engage your brother Don Flaminio as go-between?

DON IGNAZIO. When physicians wish to prevent noxious humors from coagulating in the parts afflicted,

Io per ingannar mio fratello, ché non s'imagini che ami 160
costei, lo fo trattar matrimonio con la figlia del Conte.

SIMBOLO. Ben, che avete deliberato di fare?

DON IGNAZIO. Per dar fine alle tante volte desiato e
non mai conseguito desiderio, torla per moglie.

SIMBOLO. Avetici molto ben pensato prima? 165

DON IGNAZIO. E possedendo lei non sarò un terreno
iddio?

SIMBOLO. Avertite, che chi si dispone tor moglie, camina per la strada del pentimento: pensatici bene.

DON IGNAZIO. Ci ho tanto pensato ch'l pensiero pen- 170
sando s'è stancato nell'istesso pensiero.

SIMBOLO. Che sapete se vostro fratello se ne contenta,
o vostro zio, che vi vol maritar con una figlia de' grandi
de Ispagna? Poi, povera e senza dote? Si sdegnarà con
voi, e forsi vi privarà di quella parte di eredità ch'avea 175
designato lasciarvi, perché gli errori che si fanno ne' ma-
trimoni, dove importa l'onor di tutta la famiglia, si tira-
no gli odii dietro di tutto il parentado, e principalmente
de' fratelli e de' zii.

DON IGNAZIO. Pur che abbia costei per moglie, perda 180
l'amor del fratello, del zio, la roba ed ogni cosa fin alla
vita. Che mi curo io di robba? Son altro che miserabili
beni di fortuna? L'onestà, e gli onorati costumi, son i
fregi dell'anima: ricchezze ne ho tante, che bastano per
me, e per lei. Or non potrebbe essere, che trattenendo- 185
mi, Don Flaminio mi prevenisse, e se la togliesse per
moglie, ed io poi per disperato m'avesse ad uccidere con
le mie mani? Ho così deliberato, e le cose deliberate si
denno subbito esseguire.

SIMBOLO. Ecco Don Flaminio vostro fratello. 190

they prescribe certain anti-coagulants: similarly, to deceive my brother, so that he may not imagine that I love Carizia, I have him arranging the marriage with the Count's daughter.

SIMBOLO. Well, what have you decided to do?

DON IGNAZIO. To satisfy my incessant but thwarted desire by marrying Carizia.

SIMBOLO. Have you first given it careful thought?

DON IGNAZIO. Possessing her, shall I not be a god on earth?

SIMBOLO. Remember that he who resolves to take a wife, walks the way of repentance: think it over well.

DON IGNAZIO. I have thought about it so much that in the thinking the thought has tired itself out of thought.

SIMBOLO. How do you know if your brother will accept it, or your uncle, who wants you to marry the daughter of some Spanish grandee? And the lady you choose poor and dowerless to boot! He'll be angry with you and perhaps deprive you of the portion he intended to bequeath you, for errors made in marriages, where the honor of the whole family is concerned, bring in their train the hatred of the entire clan, and especially of brothers and uncles.

DON IGNAZIO. If I may but have her as my wife, let all be lost—love of brother, of uncle, property and everything, even to life itself. What do I care for property? What is it but the worthless goods of fortune? Honor and noble deeds are the ornaments of the soul: I have riches enough for myself and for her. Might it not happen, moreover, that if I restrained myself, Don Flaminio might forestall me and marry her, and I in despair would have to kill myself with my own hands? I have made up my mind; and decisions taken should immediately be put into effect.

SIMBOLO. Here comes your brother Don Flaminio.

DON IGNAZIO. Presto, presto, scampamo via, ché non mi veggia qui ed entri in sospetto di noi.
SIMBOLO. Andiamo.

SCENA II

DON FLAMINIO, giovane, e PANIMBOLO,
suo cameriero.

DON FLAMINIO. Panimbolo, quando vedesti Leccardo, che ti disse?
PANIMBOLO. Voi altri innamorati volete sentire una risposta mille volte.
DON FLAMINIO. Pur, che ti disse? 5
PANIMBOLO. Quel che suol dir l'altre volte.
DON FLAMINIO. Non puoi redirmelo? Non vòi dar un gusto al tuo padrone?
PANIMBOLO. Cose di vento.
DON FLAMINIO. Ed udir cose di vento mi piace. 10
PANIMBOLO. Che Carizia non stava di voglia, che raggionava con la madre, che ci era il padre, che venne la zia, che sopraggionse la fantesca, che come arà l'agio, parlarà, farà, e cose simili. Ben sapete che è un furfante, e che per esser pasteggiato e pasciuto da voi di 15 buoni bocconi, pasce voi di bugie e di vane speranze.
DON FLAMINIO. Io ben conosco ch'è un bugiardo, pur sento da lui qualche rifrigerio e conforto.
PANIMBOLO. Scarso conforto ed infelice refrigerio è 'l vostro. 20
DON FLAMINIO. Ad un povero e bisognoso, come io, ogni piccola cosa è grande.
PANIMBOLO. Anzi a voi, essendo di spirito così eccelso ed ardente, ogni gran cosa vi devrebbe parer poca.

DON IGNAZIO. Quick, quick, let's be off lest he see me here and become suspicious of us.

SIMBOLO. Let's go.

SCENE II

DON FLAMINIO, a young gentleman, and PANIMBOLO, his servant.

DON FLAMINIO. Panimbolo, when you saw Leccardo, what did he say to you?

PANIMBOLO. You lovers all want to hear an answer a thousand times over.

DON FLAMINIO. Yes, but what did he say to you?

PANIMBOLO. What he said the other times.

DON FLAMINIO. Can't you tell me again? Don't you want to please your master?

PANIMBOLO. They were mere nothings.

DON FLAMINIO. Then I like to hear mere nothings.

PANIMBOLO. Well, he said that Carizia was not in the mood to listen, that she was talking with her mother, that her father was there, that her aunt came, that her maid arrived, that when he has an opportunity he will speak, he will act and so on. You know very well that he's a scoundrel, and that to go on being dined and fed by you on delicious morsels, he feeds you with lies and vain hopes.

DON FLAMINIO. Certainly I know that he's a liar, but what I hear from him gives me some solace and comfort.

PANIMBOLO. Small comfort and sorry solace is what you get.

DON FLAMINIO. To a poor and needy creature like me, every trifle is great.

PANIMBOLO. On the contrary, with so high and ardent a spirit as yours, you should hold every great thing a trifle.

67

DON FLAMINIO. Il sentir ragionar di lei, di suoi pen- 25
sieri, e di quello che si tratta in casa m'apporta non poco contento e mi ha promesso alla prima commodità
darle una mia lettera.

PANIMBOLO. O Dio, v'è stato affermato per tante
bocche di persone di credito, che non sieno persone in 30
Salerno più d'incorruttibil onestà di queste, e che in
vano spera uomo comprarsse la loro pudicizia? né voi
in tanto tempo che la servite ne avete avuto un buon
viso.

DON FLAMINIO. Tutto questo so bene. Ma che vòi che 35
faccia? non posso voler altro, perché così vuole chi può
più del mio potere.

PANIMBOLO. Chetatevi, ed abbiate pazienza.

DON FLAMINIO. La pacienza è cibo o de santi, o d'animi vili.
40

PANIMBOLO. E voi amate senza goder al presente ciò
né sperar al futuro.

DON FLAMINIO. Almeno, se non ama me, non ama
Don Ignazio, e non la possedendo io non la possiede
egli. Quella sua onestà quanto più m'affligge più m'in- 45
namora: io non posso odiar il suo odio, godo del suo
disamore. Ché s'alle pene ch'io patisco s'aggiungesse il
sospetto di Don Ignazio, sarebbono per me troppo as-
pre ed insopportabili.

PANIMBOLO. Io dubbito che Don Ignazio avendo ten- 50
tata la via ch'or voi tentate, ed essendoli riuscita vana,
ch'or ne tenti una più riuscibile.

DON FLAMINIO. Don Ignazio non vi pensa né la vidde.

PANIMBOLO. Son speranze con che ingannate voi
stesso.
55

DON FLAMINIO. Facil cosa è ingannar un altro, ma ingannar se stesso è molto difficile. Io in quel giorno,
perché non avea altro sospetto che di lui, puosi effetto
ad ogni suo gesto, e conobbi veramente che non s'ac-

DON FLAMINIO. To hear him speak of her, of her concerns and of what goes on in her house, affords me no small content, and he has promised at the first opportunity to give her a letter from me.

PANIMBOLO. Oh Lord, sir, haven't you been told by many trustworthy people that there are no ladies in Salerno more incorruptibly chaste than these sisters, and that the man who thinks to buy their chastity hopes in vain?—nor, in all the time you have served the lady, have you received one favorable look.

DON FLAMINIO. I know all this very well. But what do you expect me to do? I can't wish otherwise, for so it is willed by one whose power is greater than mine.

PANIMBOLO. Calm yourself and have patience.

DON FLAMINIO. Patience is food for saints, or for base spirits.

PANIMBOLO. You love without present enjoyment or future hope.

DON FLAMINIO. At least, if she doesn't love me, she doesn't love Don Ignazio, and if I don't possess her, neither does he. The more that chastity of hers makes me suffer, the more it makes me love her: I cannot hate her hatred, I take pleasure in her not loving. For were suspicion of Don Ignazio added to the pains that I suffer, they would be too harsh for me to bear.

PANIMBOLO. I suspect that Don Ignazio, having tried the way you're taking and having failed, now attempts a more promising course.

DON FLAMINIO. Don Ignazio neither thinks of her nor has seen her.

PANIMBOLO. These are hopes with which you deceive yourself.

DON FLAMINIO. It's easy to deceive another, but very difficult to deceive oneself. That day, because I was suspicious of him alone, I watched his every move and could tell for a certainty that he was not aware of

corse di lei; per che dove girava gli occhi, li girava io; 60
dove mirava, mirava io; non diceva parola, che non la
volesse ascoltare; ed acciò che non s'accorgesse di lei, il
tolsi dalla sala e'l condussi allo steccato; e finito il gioco, venne meco a casa, cenammo, e ce n'andammo a
letto, e raggionammo d'ogni altra cosa che vedemmo 65
quel giorno, eccetto che di quelle giovani. Ché s'egli si
fusse accorto di sì inusitata bellezza, non l'arebbe tratto
tutto 'l mondo da quello steccato, da quella sala, dalle
sue falde; e quando t'imposi che ti fussi informato chi
fusse, usai la maggior diligenza del mondo ché non se 70
ne fusse accorto. Io non sono così goffo come pensi,
no. E se Leccardo, che abita in casa sua, n'avesse inteso
altra cosa, non me l'arebbe referito?

PANIMBOLO. Il parasito Leccardo? State fresco, ché
delle 24 ore del giorno, ne sta imbriaco e ne dorme più 75
di 30. Vostro fratello tanto può star senza far l'amore
quanto il cielo senza stelle, o il mar senza tempesta.

DON FLAMINIO. Egli sta invaghito e morto della figlia
del Conte de Tricarico, ed io sono mezano del matrimonio e mi ci affatico molto per tormi da questo sus- 80
petto, e m'ha dato parola che volendo dargli 40.000 docati,[1] sposarla. Ma egli non vol darne più che 30.000.

PANIMBOLO. Come può starne invaghito e morto s'ella è brutta come una simia? né credo che la torrebbe per
100.000; ed essendo egli di feroce e magnanimo spirito, 85
poco si curarebbe di 10.000 ducati, ché se li gioca in
mez'ora. Ma dubbito che essendo gran tempo esercitato
negli artificii della simulazione, che tutto ciò non dica
per ingannarvi, e vi mostrarei per chiarissime conget-
ture, ch'egli aspiri a posseder Carizia. 90

her; for where he turned his eyes, there I turned mine; where he gazed, I gazed; not a word he said escaped me; and so that he wouldn't notice her, I drew him from the hall and led him to the ring; and when the game ended he came home with me, we dined and we retired and we talked about everything we had seen that day, except those young ladies. For if he had been aware of such unusual beauty, the whole world couldn't have dragged him away from that ring, from that hall, from her skirts; and when I ordered you to find out who she was, I took the greatest care in the world to keep it from him. I'm not as awkward as you think, indeed. And if Leccardo, who lives in her house, had heard anything to the contrary, wouldn't he have told me?

PANIMBOLO. Leccardo the parasite? You're nowhere if you count on him, for out of twenty-four hours in the day, he's drunk or asleep more than thirty. Your brother can stay out of love about as well as the heavens can do without stars or the sea without storms.

DON FLAMINIO. He is dying for love of the Count of Tricarico's daughter, and I am go-between for the match and am taking a good deal of trouble in the matter so as to rid myself of this suspicion; and he has given me his word that he will marry her if her father will give a dowry of forty thousand ducats. But the Count does not wish to give more than thirty thousand.

PANIMBOLO. How can Don Ignazio be dying for love if she's as ugly as an ape? I don't think he would take her even for a hundred thousand; and being wild and liberal of spirit, he would care little for ten thousand ducats, a sum he gambles away in half an hour. I suspect, rather, that having long practice in the arts of dissimulation, he says all of this only to deceive you, and I could show you by a clear line of conjecture that he aims to possess Carizia.

71

DON FLAMINIO. Non piaccia a Dio che ciò sia, ché se per altre cortigianuccie di nulla ci siamo azzuffati insieme, pensa tu che farebbomo per costoro; e questa ingiuria io la sopporterei più volentieri da ogni uomo che da mio fratello. 95

PANIMBOLO. Egli da quel giorno della festa è divenuto un altro. Parla talvolta, sta malinconico, mai ride, mangiando si smentica di mangiare, dove primo mangiava per doi suoi pari, la notte poco dorme, sta volentieri solo, e standovi sospira, s'affligge e si crucia tutto. 100

DON FLAMINIO. Io ho osservato in lui tutto il contrario.

PANIMBOLO. Perché si guarda da voi solo, né mai lo veggio ridere, o star allegro, se non quando è con voi. Di più, non è mai giorno che non passi mille volte per 105 questa strada dinanzi alla sua casa.

DON FLAMINIO. Io non ve l'ho incontrato giamai.

PANIMBOLO. Deve tener le spie per non esservi colto da voi, e quella arte, che voi usate con lui, egli usa con voi. Ma io vi giuro che quante volte m'è accaduto pas- 110 sarvi, sempre ve l'ho incontrato.

DON FLAMINIO. Oimè, tu passi troppo innanzi, mi poni in sospetto e m'ammazzi. Ma come potrei io di ciò chiarirmi?

PANIMBOLO. Agevolissimamente: subbito che l'in- 115 contrate, diteli che il Conte è contento dargli i 40.000 scudi pur che la sposi per questa sera; e se non troverà qualche scusa per isfuggir, o prolungar le nozze, cavatemi gli occhi.

DON FLAMINIO. Dici assai bene, ed or ora vo' gir a tro- 120 varlo e fargli l'ambasciata.

PANIMBOLO. Ascoltate, dateli la nuova con gran allegrezza, e mirate nel volto e ne gli occhi, osservate i co-

DON FLAMINIO. God forbid, for if we have come to blows before this over worthless little tarts, think what we would do over ladies such as these; this affront I could bear better from any man alive than from my brother.

PANIMBOLO. Since the day of the festival he has become another man. He speaks little, he acts melancholy, he never laughs, at table he forgets to eat, whereas he used to eat enough for two of his size, he sleeps little at night, he prefers to be alone, and, being so, he sighs and wholly afflicts and torments himself.

DON FLAMINIO. I have observed exactly the opposite behavior in him.

PANIMBOLO. Because he is on guard against you alone, nor do I ever see him laugh or be merry except when he is with you. Moreover, not a day goes by that he doesn't take this street a thousand times to pass by her house.

DON FLAMINIO. I have never met him here.

PANIMBOLO. He must keep spies to prevent his being caught here by you, and that art which you practice on him, he practices on you. But I swear that every time I've happened to pass by, I've met him here.

DON FLAMINIO. Alas, you go too far, you cast me into doubt and slay me. How can I resolve this suspicion?

PANIMBOLO. Very easily: as soon as you see him, tell him that the count is willing to give a dowry of forty thousand crowns, provided that the marriage take place this evening; and if he doesn't find some excuse for avoiding or postponing the wedding, gouge out my eyes.

DON FLAMINIO. A very good plan; I'll go find him right away and deliver this message.

PANIMBOLO. Listen to me first: give him this news very joyfully and watch his face and his eyes with care,

73

lori, ché ne cambierà mille in un ponto, or bianco, or
pallido,[2] or rosso, osservate la bocca con che finti risi. 125
Insomma ponete effetto a tutti i suoi gesti, che troverete
quanto ve dico.

DON FLAMINIO. Così vo' fare.

PANIMBOLO. Ma ecco la peste de' polli, la destruzione
de' galli d'India,[3] e la ruina de' maccheroni! 130

SCENA III

LECCARDO, parasito, PANIMBOLO, DON FLAMINIO.

LECCARDO. [*da sé*] Non son uomo da partirmi da una
casa tanto misera prima che non sia cacciato a bastonate?

PANIMBOLO. Leccardo sta irato. Ho per fermo che non
arà leccato ancora, ché niuna cosa fuor che questa basta a
farlo arrabbiare. 5

LECCARDO. [*da sé*] È forse che debba soffrir così mise-
rabil vita per i grassi bocconi che m'ingoio, una insalatuccia, una minestra de bietole, come fusse bue? Bel
pasto da por innanzi alla mia fame bizzarra!

PANIMBOLO. Ogni sua disgrazia è sovra il mangiare. 10

LECCARDO. [*da sé*] Digiunar senza voto? forse che almeno una volta la settimana si facesse qualche cenarella
per rifocillar i spiriti!

DON FLAMINIO. L'hai indovinata, non ha mangiato ancora. 15

LECCARDO. [*da sé*] Però non è meraviglia se mi sento
così leggiero: non mangio cose di sostanza.

DON FLAMINIO. Lo vo' chiamare.

PANIMBOLO. Non l'interrompete, di grazia; dice assai
bene, loda la largità del suo padrone. 20

DON FLAMINIO. Volgiti qua, Leccardo.

observe his color, for he will turn a thousand shades in an instant, first white, then deathly pale, then red, observe his mouth with its forced laughs. In short, mark his every action, for you'll find that all I say is true.

DON FLAMINIO. I'll do so.

PANIMBOLO. But here comes the chickens' plague, the turkeys' scourge, and the ruin of the macaroni!

SCENE III

LECCARDO, parasite, PANIMBOLO, DON FLAMINIO.

LECCARDO. [*apart*] Am I one to stay in such a poverty-stricken house until I'm chased out with a stick?

PANIMBOLO. Leccardo is angry. I'm sure that means the old lickchops hasn't lapped up anything yet today, for nothing else is enough to enrage him.

LECCARDO. [*apart*] It's not as if I had to endure such a miserable life, is it, for the sake of the fat tidbits I swallow: a wretched little salad, a soup of beet-greens, as if I were an ox? A fine repast to put before my savage hunger!

PANIMBOLO. All his misfortunes are connected with eating.

LECCARDO. [*apart*] Fasting for no vow? If even once a week there were a cosy little supper to rekindle my spirits!

DON FLAMINIO. You've guessed it: he hasn't eaten yet.

LECCARDO. [*apart*] So it's no wonder I feel so light; I don't eat anything substantial.

DON FLAMINIO. I'll call him.

PANIMBOLO. Oh, please don't interrupt him; he speaks well, he praises his master's liberality.

DON FLAMINIO. Over here, Leccardo.

75

LECCARDO. O signor Don Flaminio, a punto stava col pensiero a voi!

DON FLAMINIO. Parla, ché la tua bocca mi può dar morte e vita. 25

LECCARDO. Che son serpente io, che con la bocca do morte e vita? la mia bocca non dà morte se non a polli, caponi, e porchette.

PANIMBOLO. E li dài morte e sepoltura ad un tempo.

DON FLAMINIO. Lasciamo i scherzi; ragionamo di Carizia, ché non ho maggior dolcezza in questa vita. 30

LECCARDO. Ed io quando ragiono di mangiare e di bere.

DON FLAMINIO. Narrami alcuna cosa, racconsolami tutto. 35

LECCARDO. Ti sconsolerò più tosto.

DON FLAMINIO. Potrai dirmi altro che non mi ama? lo so meglio di te, l'incendio è passato tanto oltre che mi pasco del suo disamare: di' liberamente.

LECCARDO. Vedi questi segni e le lividure? 40

DON FLAMINIO. Tu stai mal concio; chi fu quel crudelaccio?

LECCARDO. La tua Carizia me l'ha fatte.

DON FLAMINIO. Mia? perché dici « mia », se non vòi dir « nemica »? Ma pur com'è passato il fatto? 45

LECCARDO. Oggi, perché stava un poco allegretta, lodava la sua bellezza; ella ridea. Io, vedendo che sopportava le lodi, prendo animo, e passo innanzi. « Tu ridi e gli assassinati dalla tua bellezza piangono e si dolgono, ché quel giorno che fu la festa de' tori, innamorasti tutto 50 il mondo! » Ella più rideva ed io passo più innanzi: « e fra gli altri ci è un certo che sta alla morte per amor tuo! »

DON FLAMINIO. Tu te ne passi troppo leggiermente, raccontamelo più minutamente.

LECCARDO. Oh Don Flaminio, sir, I was just thinking of you!

DON FLAMINIO. Speak, for your mouth can give me death or life.

LECCARDO. What, am I a serpent that I can give death or life with my mouth? My mouth gives death only to chickens, capons, and suckling pigs.

PANIMBOLO. And it gives them death and burial simultaneously.

DON FLAMINIO. Enough joking; let us speak of Carizia, for there is nothing sweeter to me in life.

LECCARDO. And nothing sweeter to me than to speak of eating and drinking.

DON FLAMINIO. Give me some news: comfort me.

LECCARDO. I am more likely to discomfort you.

DON FLAMINIO. What worse can you say than that she doesn't love me? I know that better than you do. I am so far gone in the fire of love that I nourish myself with her unloving: speak freely.

LECCARDO. Do you see these marks and bruises?

DON FLAMINIO. You are in a sorry state: who used you so cruelly?

LECCARDO. Your Carizia did it.

DON FLAMINIO. Mine? Why do you call her "mine," unless you mean "my enemy"? But just what did happen?

LECCARDO. Today, because she was a little bit merry, I praised her beauty; she laughed. Seeing that she permitted the compliments, I took courage and went farther, saying, "You laugh and the victims of your beauty weep and lament, for on the day of the bullfights everyone fell in love with you!" She laughed still more and I went still farther, "And, among others, there is one in particular who is dying for love of you!"

DON FLAMINIO. You're going too fast: tell me everything in detail.

77

LECCARDO. Appena finì le parole, che vidi sfavillar gli 55
occhi come un toro stuzzicato, e la faccia divenir rossa
come un gambaro. Tosto mi die' un sorgozzone che mi
troncò la parola in gola, e dato di mano ad un bastone
che si trovò vicino, lo lasciava cadere dove il caso il por-
tava, non mirando più alla testa che alla faccia o al collo; 60
cade' in terra, mi die' colpi allo stomaco, e calci, che se
fusse stato un ballone me aría fatto balzar per l'aria, in-
giuriando mi « roffiano, » e che lo volea dir ad Eufranone suo padre.

DON FLAMINIO. Non spaventarti per questo, ché le 65
donne al principio sempre si mostrano così ritrose; si
ammorbiderà ben sì. Ma abbi pazienza, Leccardo mio,
ché de' colpi delle sue mani non ne morrai.

LECCARDO. Le tue belle parole non m'entrano in capo
e mi levano il dolore e la fame. 70

DON FLAMINIO. Faremo che Panimbolo ti medichi e ti
guarisca.

PANIMBOLO. Io ho recette esperimentate per le tue
infirmità.

LECCARDO. Dimele per amor de Dio! 75

PANIMBOLO. Al gorguzale ci faremo una lavanda di lacrima,[1] e di vin greco molte volte il giorno.

LECCARDO. O bene! ho per fermo che tu debbi esser
figlio di qualche medico; e se non guarisce alla prima?

PANIMBOLO. Reiterar la ricetta. 80

LECCARDO. Almeno per una settimana! Che faremo
per li denti?

PANIMBOLO. Uno sciacquadenti di vernaccia di Paula,[2] o di vin d'amarene.[3]

LECCARDO. Tu ti potresti addottorare. Ma per far 85
maggior operazione bisognarebbe che i liquori fusser
vecchi.

PANIMBOLO. N'avemo tanto vecchi in casa c'hanno la
barba bianca.

LECCARDO. E per lo stomaco poi? 90

LECCARDO. The words were hardly out of my mouth when I saw her flash her eyes like a goaded bull and blush red as a crayfish. Whack, she gave me a wallop that cut short the word in my throat, and catching up a stick that came to hand, she let it fall at random, not aiming at my head more than at my face or neck. I fell to the floor; she sent blows to my stomach and such kicks that if I'd been a ball she'd have made me bounce in the air, denouncing me as a pimp and threatening to tell her father, Eufranone.

DON FLAMINIO. Don't take fright at this, for women always act reluctant this way at first; she will soften, no doubt. But be patient, friend Leccardo, for blows from her hands will not kill you.

LECCARDO. Your soothing words don't persuade or relieve my pain and hunger.

DON FLAMINIO. We'll have Panimbolo treat and heal you.

PANIMBOLO. I have sure cures for your ailments.

LECCARDO. Tell them to me, for the love of God!

PANIMBOLO. For your gullet we prescribe gargling with Lachryma Chrysti and Greek wine several times a day.

LECCARDO. Oh, excellent! I'm convinced that you must be the son of some physician. And what if I don't recover right away?

PANIMBOLO. We'll repeat the prescription.

LECCARDO. For at least a week! What shall we do for my teeth?

PANIMBOLO. A tooth-rinsing of *vernaccia di Paula* or of cherry cordial.

LECCARDO. You deserve a doctor's degree. But for greater efficacy the liquors ought to be old.

PANIMBOLO. At home we have some so old that they have white beards.

LECCARDO. And then for the stomach, what?

PANIMBOLO. Bisogna tor quattro pollastroni, e fargli buglir ben bene, e poi colar quel brodo grasso in un piatto, e porvi dentro a macerar fette de pan bianco, ed acciò che non esalino quei vapori dove sta tutta la virtù, bisogna coprir che venghino ben stufati; poi spargervi 95 sopra cannella pista, e farà un eccellente rimedio. All'ultimo, un poco di caso marzollino[4] per un sigillastomaco.

LECCARDO. Veramente da te si devriano torre le regole della medicina: andamo a medicar presto, ché m'è salito 100 addosso un appetito ferrigno, e tanta saliva mi scorre per la bocca che n'ho ingiottito più de una carrafa; la medicina m'ha reinfrescato il dolor delle piaghe, e m'ha mosso una febre alla gola che mi sento mancar l'anima.

PANIMBOLO. Con certe animelle di vitelluccie ti ripor- 105 rò l'anima in corpo.

[LECCARDO.] Se fussi morto e sepellito resuscitarei per farmi medicar da voi. Don Flaminio, avessi qualche poco di salame o di cascio parmigiano in saccoccia?

DON FLAMINIO. Orbo, questa puzza vorrei portar 110 adosso io?

LECCARDO. Ma che muschio, che ambra, che aromati preziosi odorano più di questi?

DON FLAMINIO. Leccardo mio, come io so medicar i tuoi dolori, così vorrei che medicassi i miei! 115

LECCARDO. Non dubitar, ché quando toglio una impresa, più tosto muoio che la lascio.

DON FLAMINIO. Vieni a mangiar meco questa mattina.

LECCARDO. Non posso, ho promesso ad altri.

DON FLAMINIO. Eh, vieni. 120

LECCARDO. Eh, no.

PANIMBOLO. Mira il furfante: se ne muore, e se ne vuol far pregare!

THE TWO RIVAL BROTHERS I.III

PANIMBOLO. We must take four capons and boil them all the way down, then strain the rich broth into a dish and put slices of white bread to soak in it, and to prevent evaporation of the steam containing the powerful essence, we must cover them until thoroughly permeated, then sprinkle ground cinnamon on top, and it will be an excellent remedy. Last, a bit of March cheese as a finishing touch to the meal.

LECCARDO. Truly, the laws of medicine ought to be founded on your knowledge. Let's go medicate quickly, for a gripping appetite has seized me and so much saliva is running around my mouth that I've swallowed more than a bottleful. The medicine has renewed the pain of my wounds and brought on such a fever in my throat that my spirit faints within me.

PANIMBOLO. By means of some inspired veal sweetbreads, I'll reinspirit your insides.

LECCARDO. Were I dead and buried, I would rise again just to be medicated by you. Don Flaminio, would you by any chance have a scrap of salami or Parmesan cheese in your pocket?

DON FLAMINIO. Idiot, you think I'd carry about such a stink?

LECCARDO. But what musk, what ambergris, what costly aromatics are more fragrant?

DON FLAMINIO. Leccardo my friend, I wish you could cure my ills as I can yours.

LECCARDO. Never fear, when I undertake something I do it or die.

DON FLAMINIO. Come eat with me this morning.

LECCARDO. I can't: I'm engaged elsewhere.

DON FLAMINIO. Ah, do come.

LECCARDO. Ah, no.

PANIMBOLO. Look at the scoundrel: he's dying to come but he wants to be begged!

DON FLAMINIO. Fa' ora a mio modo, ch'una volta io
farò a tuo modo.   125

LECCARDO. Son stato invitato da certi amici ad un
buon desinare, ma vo' ingannargli per amor vostro.

DON FLAMINIO. Va' a casa, ed ordina al cuoco che t'a-
parecchi tutto quello che saprai dimandare, e fa' colla-
zione; tra tanto che sia apparecchiato, serò teco, ché vo 130
per un negozio.

LECCARDO. Ed io ne farò un altro, e sarò a voi subbito.

Vedo il Capitan Martebellonio: non ho visto di lui il
maggior bugiardo; sta gonfio di vento come un ballone
ed un giorno si risolverà in aria. Ha fatto mille arti, pri- 135
ma fu sensale, poi birro, poi aiutante del boia, poi ruffiano, e pensa con le sue bravate atterrire il mondo, e
stima che tutte le gentildonne si muoiano per la sua bellezza.

Ben trovato il bellissimo e valerosissimo Capitan 140
Martebellonio!

SCENA IV

MARTEBELLONIO, Capitano, e LECCARDO.

[MARTEBELLONIO.] Buon pro ti faccia, Leccardo mio!

LECCARDO. Che pro mi vol far quello che non ho
mangiato ancora?

[MARTEBELLONIO.] So che la mattina non ti fai coglier
fuor di casa digiuno.   5

LECCARDO. E che ho mangiato altro che un capon
freddo, un pastone, una suppa alla franzese, un petto di
vitella allesso, e bevuto così alto alto diece voltarelle?

[MARTEBELLONIO.] Ecco, non ti ho detto invano il
buon pro ti faccia.   10

DON FLAMINIO. Do as I ask now, and another time I'll do things your way.

LECCARDO. I've been invited by some friends to a good meal, but I'll disappoint them for your sake.

DON FLAMINIO. [*to Panimbolo*] Go home and order the cook to prepare a lunch of the best of everything you can think of. By the time it's ready I'll be with you; meanwhile, I have a matter to attend to.

[*Panimbolo departs*]

LECCARDO. So have I, and then I'll join you instantly.

[*Don Flaminio departs*]

I spy Captain Martebellonio coming this way. I've never seen a greater liar: he's as full of wind as a balloon and someday he'll dissolve into air. He has had a thousand trades: first he was a fence, then a flatfoot, then a hangman's helper, then a pimp; and he thinks his windy threats terrify the world and supposes that every woman alive is dying for his charms.

Well met, most handsome and brave Captain Martebellonio!

SCENE IV

MARTEBELLONIO, captain, and LECCARDO

MARTEBELLONIO. Good hap to you, friend Leccardo.

LECCARDO. What good can happen from the nothing I've had to eat yet?

MARTEBELLONIO. Come now, I know that in the morning you're never caught abroad on an empty stomach.

LECCARDO. What have I eaten besides a cold capon, a pasty, some wine-sops French style, a boiled breast of veal, or drunk besides ten little draughts about so big?

MARTEBELLONIO. There, I was right to say "good hap to you."

83

LECCARDO. Quelle cose son digeste già, e fatto sangue nelle vene; ma lo stomaco mi sta voto come un tamburro. Ma voi adesso vi dovete alzar da letto, e far castelli in aria, eh?

[MARTEBELLONIO.] Ho tardato un pochetto, che ho atteso a certi dispacci.   15

LECCARDO. Per chi?

[MARTEBELLONIO.] Per Marte l'uno, e l'altro per Bellona.

LECCARDO. Chi è questo Marte? Chi è questa Bellona?   20

[MARTEBELLONIO.] Oh tu sei un bel pezzo d'asino!

LECCARDO. Di Tunisi[1] ancora.

[MARTEBELLONIO.] Non sai tu che Marte è dio del quinto cielo,[2] il dio dell'armi, e Bellona delle battaglie?

LECCARDO. Che avete a far con loro?   25

[MARTEBELLONIO.] Non sai che son suo figlio e son lor luogo tenente dell'armi e delle battaglie in terra, com'eglino tengono il possesso dell'armi nel cielo? però il mio nome è di Martebellonio.

LECCARDO. E per chi gli mandate il dispaccio?   30

[MARTEBELLONIO.] Per un mozzo di camera.

LECCARDO. Come? gli attaccate l'ale dietro per farlo volar nel cielo?

[MARTEBELLONIO.] L'attacco le lettere al collo con un sacchetto di pane che basti per quindici giorni, poi lo   35
piglio per lo piede, e me lo giro tre volte per la testa, e l'arrondello nel cielo: Marte, che sta aspettando, come il vede, il prende e ferma; si non, che ne salirebbe sin alla sfera stellata.[3]

LECCARDO. A che effetto quel sacco di pane?   40

[MARTEBELLONIO.] Ché non si muoia di fame per la via; Marte, avendo inteso gli avisi, spedisce le provisio-

84

LECCARDO. Those things have already been digested and become blood in my veins, yet my stomach is as empty as a drum. But you, you must be just out of bed and daydreaming, eh?

MARTEBELLONIO. I delayed a bit, attending to certain dispatches.

LECCARDO. For whom?

MARTEBELLONIO. One for Mars and the other for Bellona.

LECCARDO. Who is this Mars? Who's Bellona?

MARTEBELLONIO. Oh, you're a jackass!

LECCARDO. A regular Tunisian.

MARTEBELLONIO. Don't you know that Mars is the god of the fifth heaven, the god of arms, and Bellona the goddess of battles?

LECCARDO. What have you to do with them?

MARTEBELLONIO. Don't you know that I am his son and their lieutenant for arms and battles on earth, they being in command of arms in heaven? That's why my name is Martebellonio.

LECCARDO. And by whom do you send him the dispatch?

MARTEBELLONIO. By a serving boy.

LECCARDO. What? You stick wings on his back to make him fly to heaven?

MARTEBELLONIO. I attach letters to his neck with a little bag of bread, enough to last fifteen days, then I take him by the foot and I swing him around my head three times and sling him into the sky. Mars, watching for him, when he sees him coming, grabs and stops him; otherwise, he would sail all the way up to the starry sphere.

LECCARDO. What's the bag of bread for?

MARTEBELLONIO. So that he doesn't die of hunger on the way. Mars, having understood the message, sends the requested provisions and throws the boy back

ni, e lo manda giù. Come il veggio cader dal cielo come una nubbe, vengo in piazza e lo ricevo nella palma, ché si desse in terra, se ne andrebbe fin al centro del mondo. 45

LECCARDO. Che bevea? il mangiar il pane solo l'ingozzava e potea affogarsi, o si morì di sete?

[MARTEBELLONIO.] Bevé un canchero, che ti mangia![4]

LECCARDO. [*da sé*] O s'è bella questa: degna di un par vostro! 50

[MARTEBELLONIO.] Ti vo' raccontar la battaglia ch'ebbi con la Morte.[5]

LECCARDO. Non saria meglio che andassimo a bere due voltarelle per aver più forza, io di ascoltare, e voi di narrare? 55

[MARTEBELLONIO.] Il ber ti apportarebbe sonno, ed io non te le ridirei se mi donassi un regno. I miei fatti son morti nella mia lingua, ma per lor stessi sono illustri, e famosi, e si raccontano per istorie. Sappi che la Morte prima era viva, ed era suo ufficio ammazzar le genti con 60 la falce. Ritrovandomi in Mauritania, stava alle strette con Atlante, il qual per esser oppresso dal peso del mondo, era mal trattato da lei; io, che non posso soffrir vantaggi, li toglio il mondo da sopra le spalle, e me lo pongo su le mie.[6] 65

LECCARDO. [*da sé*] Sarà più bella della prima!

Ditemi, quel gran peso del mondo come lo soffrivano le vostre spalle?

[MARTEBELLONIO.] Appena mi bastava a grattar la rogna. Al fin, lo posi sovra questi tre diti, e lo sostenni 70 come un melone.

LECCARDO. Quando voi sostenevate il mondo, dove stavate, fuori o dentro del mondo?

[MARTEBELLONIO.] Dentro il mondo.

down. When I see him falling from heaven like a cloud, I come out in the piazza and catch him in the palm of my hand, for if he hit the ground, he would go right on down to the center of the earth.

LECCARDO. What did he drink? Eating bread by itself might choke him and he could have strangled. Or did he die of thirst?

MARTEBELLONIO. He drank a pox, may it take you!

LECCARDO. [aside] Oh, this is a good one, worthy of the likes of you!

MARTEBELLONIO. I want to tell you about the battle I fought with Death.

LECCARDO. Wouldn't it be better if we went and drank a couple to strengthen us, me for listening and you for telling?

MARTEBELLONIO. Drinking would make you sleepy, and I wouldn't tell you twice if you gave me a kingdom. My deeds are never on my lips, but have spread their own fame and are told of in histories.

Know then, that Death used to be alive and it was her work to kill people with a scythe. Happening to be in Mauritania, I found her at odds with Atlas, whom she tormented while he bore the weight of the world. As I can't stand to see unfair advantage taken, I transferred the world from his shoulders to mine.

LECCARDO. [aside] This is going to be better than the first one!

Tell me, the great weight of the world, how did your shoulders bear it?

MARTEBELLONIO. It was just barely heavy enough to scratch me where I itched. Finally, I put it on these three fingers and held it up like a melon.

LECCARDO. When you supported the world, where were you, out of the world or in it?

MARTEBELLONIO. In the world.

LECCARDO. E se stavate di dentro, come lo tenevate di 75
fuori?

[MARTEBELLONIO.] Volsi dir di fuori.

LECCARDO. E se stavate di fuori, eravate in un altro
mondo e non in questo?

[MARTEBELLONIO.] O sciagurato, io stava dove stava 80
Atlante quando anch'egli teneva il mondo.

LECCARDO. Ben, bene, seguite l'abbattimento.

[MARTEBELLONIO.] Mona[7] viva, sentendosi offesa
ch'avessi dato aiuto al suo nemico, mi mirava in cag-
nesco, con un aspetto assai torbido ed aspro, e con 85
ischernevoli parole mi beffeggiava; la disfido ad uc-
cidersi meco; accettò l'invito, e perché avea l'elezion
dell'armi, si volse giocar la vita al ballonetto.

LECCARDO. Perché non con la falce?

[MARTEBELLONIO.] Ché ben sapea la virtù della mia 90
Dorindana.[8] Constituimmo per lo steccato tutto il
mondo: ella n'andò in oriente, io in occidente.

LECCARDO. Voi elegeste il peggior luogo, perché il sole vi feriva ne gli occhi, e poi quello occidente porta seco
mal agurio che dovevate esser ucciso.[9]   95

[MARTEBELLONIO.] L'arte tua è della cucina, ed appena
t'intendi se la carne è ben allesa; che tema ho io del sole?
Con una cera torta lo fo nascondere coperto d'una nube.
Poi uccidente è quello che uccide; io avea da esser l'uccidente, ella l'uccisa.   100

LECCARDO. Seguitte.

[MARTEBELLONIO.] Il ballonetto era la montagna di
Mauritania; a me toccò il primo colpo: percossi quella
montagna così furiosamente che andò tanto alto che
giunse al ciel di Marte, e non la fece calar giù in terra per 105
segno del valor del suo figlio.

LECCARDO. Così privasti il mondo di quella montagna. Ma quella che ci è adesso, che montagna è?

LECCARDO. And if you were in it, how did you hold it from outside?

MARTEBELLONIO. I meant to say I was outside it.

LECCARDO. And if you were outside, were you in another world and not in this one?

MARTEBELLONIO. Oh, wretch, I was where Atlas was when he held up the world.

LECCARDO. All right, all right, continue with the battle.

MARTEBELLONIO. Lively Lady Death, offended because I had aided her enemy, glared at me with a very lowering and harsh expression, and mocked me with scornful words. I challenged her to mortal combat: she accepted the invitation, and as she had the choice of arms, decided to play ball to the death.

LECCARDO. Why not fight with her scythe?

MARTEBELLONIO. Because she well knew the power of my Dorindana. For our playing field we designated the whole world: she went to the east, I to the west.

LECCARDO. You chose the worst place, for the sun shone in your eyes; and besides, the west was a bad omen that you would be going west for good.

MARTEBELLONIO. Your business is the kitchen and about that you barely know enough to judge if the meat is done. I fear the sun? With one scowl I make him take cover behind a cloud. Besides, it is not the one standing to the west whose sun is setting: I was to be the killer, she the killed.

LECCARDO. Go on.

MARTEBELLONIO. The ball was the mountain of Mauritania. I had the first turn: I struck that mountain so fiercely that it went all the way up to the sphere of Mars, who kept it there as a sign of his son's valor.

LECCARDO. So you deprived the world of that mountain. But the one there now, what mountain is that?

[MARTEBELLONIO.] Oh, sei fastidioso! Ascolta se vòi; se non, va' e t'appicca. 110

LECCARDO. Ascolterò.

[MARTEBELLONIO.] Ella dicea aver vinto il gioco, perché era imboccato il ballonetto; la presi per la gola con duo diti e l'uccisi come una quaglia. Talché non è più viva, ed io son rimasto nel suo ufficio. Ma scostati da 115 me, ch'or che mi sento inbizzarrito, che non ti strozzi.

LECCARDO. Oimè che occhi stralucenti!

[MARTEBELLONIO.] Guardati che qualche fulmine non m'esca da gli occhi e ti brusci vivo.

LECCARDO. [da sé] Tutta l'istoria è andata bene; ma ve 120 sete smenticato che non fu ballonetto, ma ballongrande e tanto grande che non si basta ingiottire.

Ma io ti vo' narrar una battaglia ch'ebbi con la Fame.

[MARTEBELLONIO.] Che battaglie, miserello?

LECCARDO. La Fame era una persona viva, macra, sot- 125 tile, ch'appena avea l'ossa e la pelle, e soleva andar in compagnia con la Carestia, con la Peste, e con la Guerra, ché n'uccideva più ella che non le spade. Ci disfidammo insieme: lo steccato fu un lago di brodo grasso, dove notavano caponi, polli, porchette, vitelle, e buoi intieri in- 130 tieri: qui ci tuffammo a combattere con i denti. Prima ch'ella si mangiasse un vitello, io ne tracannai duo buoi, e tutte le restanti robbe; e perché ancora m'avanzava appetito, e non avea che mangiare, mi mangiai lei; così non fu più Fame al mondo, ed io sono suo luogote- 135 nente, e ho due fami in corpo, la sua e la mia. Ma prima che queste due fami [mi mangino], andiamo a mangiare; se non, che mi mangiarò te intiero intiero; Dio ti scampi dalla mia bocca!

[MARTEBELLONIO.] Tu sei un gran bugiardo! 140

LECCARDO. [da sé] Voi sete maggior di me, son un vostro minimo.

MARTEBELLONIO. How annoying you are! If you want to listen, do; if not, go hang yourself.

LECCARDO. I'll listen.

MARTEBELLONIO. She claimed to have won the game, because the ball was swallowed up; I took her by the throat with two fingers and I killed her like a quail. So she's no longer alive, and I am left in her place. But keep clear of me, now I feel my rage coming on, look out that I don't strangle you.

LECCARDO. Oh, what glaring eyes!

MARTEBELLONIO. Look out that lightning doesn't strike from my eyes and burn you alive.

LECCARDO. [aside] The whole story went well; but you forget to say it was not a batting ball but a big balloon, too big to swallow.

But now I'll tell you about a battle I had with Hunger.

MARTEBELLONIO. What battles are these, you little pipsqueak?

LECCARDO. Hunger once was a live person, lean and thin, barely skin and bones, and she used to go about with Famine and Plague and War, and she killed more people than swords could do. We challenged each other: the field of combat was a lake of rich broth, swimming with capons, chickens, suckling pigs, calves and whole beeves: into this we plunged to fight with our teeth. Before she could eat one calf, I gulped down two beeves and everything else besides; and because I was still hungry and had nothing left to eat, I ate her; so there was no more Hunger in the world, and I am left in her place, her lieutenant, with two hungers in me, hers and mine. But before these two hungers [devour me], let's go eat immediately; otherwise I'm going to eat you—whole. God save you from my jaws.

MARTEBELLONIO. You're a big liar!

LECCARDO. [aside] You're a bigger one: I'm a tiny speck by the side of you.

[MARTEBELLONIO.] Dimmi un poco, quanto tempo è che Callidora non t'ha parlato di me?

LECCARDO. Ogni ora che mi vede, e che quando pas- 145
segiate così altiero dinanzi le sue fenestre, spasima per il fatto vostro.

[MARTEBELLONIO.] Io so molto ben che la poverella si deve strugger per me, ché n'ho fatto struger dell'altre. Ma io vorrei venir presto alle strette. 150

LECCARDO. Ella desia che fusse stato; e se voi mi pascete ben questa sera, io vi recarò buone novelle, e vi do la mia fede.[10]

[MARTEBELLONIO.] Guardati, non mi toccar la mano, ché se venisse stringendo te ne farei polvere, ché strin- 155
gono più d'una tanaglia.

LECCARDO. Cancaro, bisogna star in cervello con voi!

[MARTEBELLONIO.] Quando mi porterai nuova che vada a giacer con lei, ti farò un pasto da re.

LECCARDO. [da sé] Prima sarò morto che sia pesta la 160
pasta per questo pasto!

[MARTEBELLONIO.] Io ti farei mangiar meco, ma perché oggi è martedì, in onor del dio Marte non mangio altro che una insalatuccia di punte di pugnali, quattro ballotte di archibuggio in cambio d'ulive, due balle 165
d'artigliaria in pezzi con la salsa, un piatto di gelatina di orecchie, nasi e labra di capitani e colonelli, spolverizzati sopra di limatura di ferro come caso grattuggiato.

LECCARDO. Che sete struzzo che digerite quel ferro?

[MARTEBELLONIO.] Lo digerisco, e diventa acciaio. 170

LECCARDO. Dovete tener l'appalto con i ferrari dell'acciaio che cacate?

[MARTEBELLONIO.] Andrò a consultar un duello, e tornando mangiaremo; così ad un tempo sodisfarò alla mia fama, ed alla tua fame. 175

MARTEBELLONIO. Tell me now, how long is it since Callidora has spoken of me to you?

LECCARDO. She does so every time she sees me, and when you stroll so haughtily beneath her windows, she yearns after you.

MARTEBELLONIO. I know very well that the poor little thing must be pining for me; I've made women pine before. But I'd like to come to grips with her quickly.

LECCARDO. She wishes it were already done; and if you feed me well this evening, I'll bring you some good news, here's my hand on it.

MARTEBELLONIO. Look out, don't touch my hand, for if I should grip yours I would crush it to dust; my fingers grip harder than pincers.

LECCARDO. Pox! One has to be careful with you!

MARTEBELLONIO. When you bring me word that I can lie with her, I shall give you a banquet fit for a king.

LECCARDO. [aside] I'll be long passed away before the pasta is pounded for that repast.

MARTEBELLONIO. I'd have you dine with me, but because today is Tuesday, the day of Mars, in honor of the god I eat only a small salad of dagger points, a few harquebus bullets instead of olives, a couple of shattered cannon balls with sauce, a plate of jellied ears, noses and lips of captains and colonels, dusted over with iron filings in place of grated cheese.

LECCARDO. Are you an ostrich that you can digest that iron?

MARTEBELLONIO. I digest it and it becomes steel.

LECCARDO. Shouldn't you make a deal with the ironsmiths for the steel you shit?

MARTEBELLONIO. I am going now to adjudicate a duel and when I return, we'll eat: thus I'll simultaneously satisfy us both, the famous and the famished.

[*Martebellonio departs.*]

LECCARDO. Già si è partito il pecorone; se non fusse che alcuna volta mi fa certe corpacciate stravaganti in casa sua, non potrei soffrir le sue bugie. Mangia la carne mezza cruda e sanguigna, e dice che così mangiano i giganti, e che vuol assuefarsi a mangiar carne umana, e 180 bersi il sangue de' suoi nemici; non arò contento se non li fo qualche burla.

Andrò in casa di Don Flaminio, che deve aspettarmi.

ATTO II

SCENA I

DON IGNAZIO, e SIMBOLO.

DON IGNAZIO. Dura cosa è l'aver a far con i servidori: sa ben Simbolo quanto desio di andar a trovar Mon'Angiola, e non ritorna. Ma eccolo: come hai fatto aspettarmi tanto, o Simbolo?

SIMBOLO. Come saprete quanto ho fatto in vostro ser- 5 viggio, mi lodarete della tardanza. Sappiate che incontrandomi con Don Flaminio, mi domandò con grande instanza di voi, e domandando io la caggion di tanta instanza, rispose che non voleva dirlo se non a voi solo: mi lascia, e m'incontro con Panimbolo, il quale altresì mi 10 dimandò di voi, e pregandolo mi dicesse che cosa chiedeva da voi, disse in secreto, che Don Flaminio aveva conchiuso col Conte di Tricarico il matrimonio de la figlia, e che vi vuol dar 40 mille ducati, pur che foste andato a sposarla per questa sera. 15

DON IGNAZIO. Ohimè, che pugnale è questo che mi

LECCARDO. He's gone, the blockhead! If it weren't that occasionally he stands me some big bellyfuls in his house, I couldn't bear his lies. He eats meat half raw and bloody, saying that giants do so and that he wants to accustom himself to devouring human flesh and drinking the blood of his enemies. I won't rest content until I've played some trick on him.

Now I'll go to Don Flaminio's house; he must be expecting me.

ACT II

SCENE I

DON IGNAZIO, and SIMBOLO.

DON IGNAZIO. It's a hardship to have to depend on servants: Simbolo knows very well how eager I am to call on Madonna Angiola, and yet he doesn't return. But here he is. Oh, Simbolo, why have you made me wait so long?

SIMBOLO. When you know how well I've served you, you'll praise my tardiness. What happened was that I encountered Don Flaminio, and he asked me very urgently where to find you; and when I asked the reason for such urgency, he answered that he would not say except to you. He leaves me, and I meet Panimbolo, who likewise asked for you; and when I begged him to tell me what he wanted from you, he told me secretly that Don Flaminio had come to terms with the Count of Tricarico about his daughter's marriage to you, and that the Count agrees to give forty thousand ducats as dowry, provided that you marry her this evening.

DON IGNAZIO. Alas, what dagger is thrust through my

spinge nel core? mi rompi tutti i disegni, e conturbi quanto avea proposto di fare: me hai morto!

SIMBOLO. Io, acciaché non vi trovasse prima di me, e vi cogliesse all'improviso, corro di qua, corro di là per trovarvi, né lascio luoco, dove solete pratticar, che non avesse cerco. Fra tanto considerava fra me stesso cotal nuova: cado in pensiero che sia un fingimento di vostro fratello di scoprir l'animo vostro, se stiate innamorato d'alcuna donna.

DON IGNAZIO. Buon pensiero, per vita mia!

SIMBOLO. Per chiarirmi di ciò, con non men subito che ispedito consiglio me ne vo in casa del Conte di Tricarico, e non vedo genti, né apparecchi di nozze. Piglio animo, ed entro con iscusa di cercar Don Flaminio, e me ne vo insin in cucina, e non vi veggio né cuochi, né guattari. Dimando di Don Flaminio, e mi rispondono che è più di un mese che non l'han veduto; mi fermo, e veggio il cappellano; entro in ragionamento con lui, e mi dice che il Conte questa mattina è gito a Tricarico a caccia, e mi disse che molti giorni sono che del matrimonio più non si tratta; anzi stima che Don Flaminio vuol dargli la baia.

DON IGNAZIO. O Simbolo, che sia tu benedetto mille volte, ch'avendomi con la prima nuova tolto l'anima, con questa me l'hai riposta in corpo; quando mi disobligarò di tanto obligo?

SIMBOLO. Or dunque, venendo a voi Don Flaminio a farvi la proposta, acciaché più l'ingranniate e confirmiate nel suo proposito, mostrate grandissima allegrezza, accetate l'offerta, e si dice per questa sera, e voi diteli per allora.

DON IGNAZIO. Or questo sì che non farò io, ché non mi basteria il cuor mai.

SIMBOLO. Sarà forza che lo facciate.

heart? You destroy all my plans and overthrow all that you proposed to do for me: you have slain me!

SIMBOLO. So that he wouldn't find you before I could, and take you unawares, I run here and there seeking you, I neglect none of your usual haunts. Meanwhile I pondered this news: whereupon it occurs to me that it is probably a fiction invented by your brother to discover your true mind, to find out if you are in love with any other lady.

DON IGNAZIO. A clever thought, on my life!

SIMBOLO. To satisfy myself on that score, I no sooner had this idea than I put it into effect and go to the house of the Count of Tricarico, and there I see neither people nor preparations for a wedding. I pluck up my courage and enter, with the excuse of seeking Don Flaminio, and I go all the way into the kitchen without seeing cooks or scullions. I ask after Don Flaminio, and they reply that they haven't seen him there for over a month. I stop and see the chaplain: I fall into conversation with him, and he tells me that this morning the count went to Tricarico to hunt, and that for many days there has been no discussion of the marriage, and, indeed, that the count even thinks that Don Flaminio is trifling with him.

DON IGNAZIO. O Simbolo, bless you a thousand times, for although you robbed me of my soul with your first news, you have restored it to my body with this last! How can I ever repay you?

SIMBOLO. Now, therefore, when Don Flaminio comes to deliver the proposal, in order to deceive him further and confirm him in his belief, appear very happy, accept the offer, and if he says the wedding must be tonight, agree to it.

DON IGNAZIO. Now this I will not do, not I, my heart would fail me.

SIMBOLO. You absolutely must do it.

97

DON IGNAZIO. Mi farei uccider più tosto.

SIMBOLO. E se non volete, farete che vostro fratello s'accorga che stiate innamorato di Carizia, e come uomo di torbido e precipitoso ingegno vi preverrà a torsela per moglie, o verrete a qualche cattivo termine insieme. 55

DON IGNAZIO. Dubbito di non incorrere in qualche inconveniente peggiore.

SIMBOLO. Che cosa di mal di ciò ne può avvenire?

DON IGNAZIO. Son disposto far quanto tu mi consigli. 60

SIMBOLO. Ecco Madonna Angiola che viene a casa.

SCENA II

ANGIOLA, SIMBOLO, DON IGNAZIO.

ANGIOLA. [da sé] Conosco a prova che il peso de gli anni è il maggior peso che possa portar l'uomo su la sua persona, poiché in sì breve viaggio che ho fatto son così stanca come si avesse portato qualche gran soma.

DON IGNAZIO. Va' innanzi a toglierle la via. 5

ANGIOLA. [da sé] Son inciampata con Don Ignazio, c'ho cercato fuggir con ogni industria, ché so che cerca parlarmi di Carizia mia nipote; né vorrei che prorumpesse in qualche cosa men ch'onesta.

DON IGNAZIO. Signora Angiola, ho desiato gran tempo ragionar con voi d'un negozio importantissimo. 10

ANGIOLA. Eccomi al vostro commodo: ben la priego a non trattarmi di cosa che men che onesta non sia.

DON IGNAZIO. Certo non farei tanto torto alla sua bontà, alla mia qualità, né all'importanza del negozio: né il tempo richiede questo. 15

ANGIOLA. Poi che le vostre costumate parole, degne

DON IGNAZIO. I'd rather kill myself.

SIMBOLO. If you don't, you'll make your brother aware that you're in love with Carizia, and with his quick, unscrupulous wit, he'll forestall you by marrying her, or things will come to a bad pass between you somehow.

DON IGNAZIO. I'm afraid of running into worse trouble.

SIMBOLO. What harm could come of it?

DON IGNAZIO. Very well, I'll do what you advise.

SIMBOLO. Look, here's Madonna Angiola coming home.

SCENE II

ANGIOLA, SIMBOLO, DON IGNAZIO.

ANGIOLA. [apart] I know from experience that the weight of years is the heaviest that man can bear, for this short a trip has tired me as much as if I had carried some great burden.

DON IGNAZIO. Accost her and bar the way.

ANGIOLA. [apart] I have run headlong into Don Ignazio, whom I diligently tried to flee, for I know that he seeks to speak to me of my niece Carizia, but I would not want him to burst out with something less than honorable.

DON IGNAZIO. Lady Angiola, I have long wished to discuss with you a matter of very great importance.

ANGIOLA. I am at your service: I pray you truly not to speak to me of anything less than honorable.

DON IGNAZIO. Certainly I would not so offend your goodness, my own self-respect, nor the importance of the matter; nor does the occasion so require.

ANGIOLA. Since your well-mannered words, truly

veramente di quel cavaliero che voi sete, m'hanno sgombro dal cuor ogni sospetto, eccomi pronta ad ogni vostro comando. 20

DON IGNAZIO. Sappiate, madre mia, che da quel giorno, che non so si debba chiamarlo felice o infelice per me, che vidi la bellezza e l'oneste maniere di Carizia vostra nipote, m'hanno impiagata l'anima di sorte che, se voglio guarire, è bisogno ricorrere a quel fonte donde 25 sol può derivar la mia salute.

ANGIOLA. Signor Don Ignazio, so dove va a ferir lo strale del vostro raggionamento.

DON IGNAZIO. Non ad altro che ad onesto ed onorato fine. 30

ANGIOLA. Perdonatemi se così immodestamente vi rompo le parole in bocca: sappiate che se ben Carizia mia nipote è giovane, nasconde sotto quella sua età acerba virtù matura: sotto quel capel biondo, saper canuto: sotto quel petto giovenile, consiglio antico; e se 35 ben è povera d'oro, l'onore non li fa conoscer bisogno alcuno, perché si stima ricca d'onore, e di se stessa; e nella sua onestà s'inchiude il suo tesoro, e la sua dote. Onde non sperate che'l falso splendor d'oro o di gioie le appanne gli occhi, né col mostrarvi vinto della sua bel- 40 lezza, di vincer lei, o col mostrarvi ubidiente, trionfar della sua volontà, o col mostrarvi servo, signoreggiarla: perché il vostro sperar fia vano, e la moverete più tosto ad odio che ad amarvi.

DON IGNAZIO. Signora, io n'ho più timore veder i suoi 45 lumi turbati di sdegno contra di me, da' quali depende il maggior contento ch'abbi nella vita, che perder l'istessa vita: e vi giuro per quel cielo, e per colui che ci alberga dentro, ch'amo le sue bellezze come modesto sposo, e non come lascivo amante; ché chi ama la bellezza, e non 50 l'onore, non è amante, ma inimicissimo tiranno.

worthy of such a nobleman, have dispersed all doubt from my heart, I am ready to perform your every command.

DON IGNAZIO. Know then, mother, that from the day—I cannot tell whether it should be called happy or unhappy for me—on which I beheld the beauty and modest manners of your niece Carizia, they have so wounded my soul that, wishing to be healed, I must appeal to the only source from which my health can spring.

ANGIOLA. My lord Don Ignazio, I know where the arrow of your discourse aims to strike.

DON IGNAZIO. Only at a chaste and honorable goal.

ANGIOLA. Forgive me if thus boldly I stop the words in your mouth. Know that even if my niece Carizia is young, she hides ripe virtue under her green age, hoary wisdom under that blonde hair, mature counsel under that young breast; and though she is poor in gold, her honor prevents her feeling any want, for she thinks herself rich in honor and integrity; within her chastity are enclosed her treasure and her dowry. Wherefore do not hope that the false splendor of gold or of jewels may becloud her eyes; nor that by showing yourself conquered by her beauty, you may conquer her; or that by showing yourself obedient, you may triumph over her will; or by showing yourself her servant, you may become her master; because your hope will be vain, and you will move her rather to hate than to love you.

DON IGNAZIO. My lady, I fear to see her radiant beams dimmed by disdain for me—those eyes on which depend the greatest happiness that I may have in life—more than I fear to lose life itself; and I swear to you by yonder heaven and by Him who dwells therein, that I love her beauties as a chaste bridegroom and not as a wanton lover; for he who loves beauty and not honor is not a lover but a most inimical tyrant.

101

ANGIOLA. Dubito che non mi proponiate un infame amore, sotto una onorata richiesta di nozze.

DON IGNAZIO. O Iddio, non mi conoscete nel fronte, e ne gli occhi pregni di lacrime, l'effetto della mia fede, che son ridotto all'ultimo termine della mia vita, ché se non voglio morire, son constretto toglierla per moglie? 55

ANGIOLA. Ditemi di grazia che cosa desiate da lei?

DON IGNAZIO. Se non che pregarla che m'accetti per sposo, pur se non sdegna così basso sogetto. 60

ANGIOLA. Non sapete voi meglio di me che questo ufficio convien farsi col padre, e non con lei, perché non lice ad una donzella dispor di se stessa?

DON IGNAZIO. Io non cerco altro da lei in ricompensa del singular amor che le porto che sia favorito da lei dir- 65 glielo con la bocca, e con le mie orecchie sentir le sue parole, e pascer per quel breve momento gli occhi miei avidi ed affamati, in così lungo digiuno, della sua vista; ché da quel giorno della festa non fu mai possibile di rivederla. 70

ANGIOLA. Se ben quel che mi chiedete non abbi molto dell'onesto, pur traporrò l'autorità mia per quanto val appo lei d'indurlaci, ché, raggionandosele de voi, ho conosciuto nel suo animo non so che di tacito con- sentimento; fra tanto che attendete la risposta, potrete 75 trattenervi qui intorno, ché io vo' entrar in casa.

DON IGNAZIO. Che dici, Simbolo?

SIMBOLO. Ad una dura e faticosa impresa vi sete posto.

DON IGNAZIO. Per lei tutte le fatiche e le durezze mi 80 sono care, né mai le grandi imprese si vinsero senza gran fatiche.

SIMBOLO. Perdete il tempo.

ANGIOLA. I fear you may be proposing an infamous love under cover of an honorable offer of marriage.

DON IGNAZIO. Oh God, do not my face and my eyes pregnant with tears give visible proof of my faith, that I have reached the uttermost pass of my life, that if I am not to die, I must have her for my wife?

ANGIOLA. Tell me, if you please, what do you ask of her?

DON IGNAZIO. Only that I may be allowed to pray her to accept me as her husband, if she does not despise so unworthy a subject.

ANGIOLA. Do you not know better than I that such an office should rather be undertaken to her father than to her, for a maiden is not permitted to dispose of herself?

DON IGNAZIO. I seek from her no greater return for the singular love I bear her than to be allowed to tell her of it with my own mouth, and to hear her words with my own ears, and for that brief moment to feed my avid and famished eyes with the sight of her after so long a fast; for since the day of the celebration it has been impossible to see her again.

ANGIOLA. Although what you ask of me is not over-honorable, I shall nevertheless interpose my authority, whatever it is worth, to induce her to it; for conversing of you, I have sensed in her an indefinable feeling of unspoken consent. While awaiting the answer, you may stay hereabouts, for now I am going inside.

[*Angiola goes within.*]

DON IGNAZIO. What say you, Simbolo?

SIMBOLO. You have put yourself to a hard and toil-some task.

DON IGNAZIO. For her sake all toils and hardships are dear to me, nor were great undertakings ever accomplished without great labors.

SIMBOLO. You are wasting your time.

DON IGNAZIO. E che tempo più degnamente potrà perdersi come nell'acquisto de sì degno tesoro? 85

SIMBOLO. E che acquistate poi? l'amor d'una donna che si cambia di momento in momento.

DON IGNAZIO. Sì, delle vili e populari; ma quelle di reale animo come costei, amando, amano insino alla morte. 90

SIMBOLO. Tutte le donne sono d'una medesima natura.

DON IGNAZIO. Tu poco t'intendi di nature di donne. Ma non ingiuriar lei, perché ingiurii me: taci?

SIMBOLO. Taccio. 95

DON IGNAZIO. Già fuggono le tenebre dell'aria,[1] ecco l'aurora che precede la chiarezza del mio bel sole, già spuntano i raggi intorno, veggio la bella mano che con leggiadra maniera alza la gelosia; o felici occhi miei, che siete degni di tanto bene! 100

SCENA III

CARIZIA, DON IGNAZIO, SIMBOLO.

CARIZIA. Signor Don Ignazio, poi che Angiola mia zia mi fa fede della vostra onorata richiesta, io non ho voluto mancare dalla mia parte; eccomi, che comandate?

DON IGNAZIO. Io comandare, che mi terrei il più avventurato uomo che viva, se fusse un minimo suo schiavo? Voi sete quella che solo avete l'imperio d'ogni mia voluntà, ed a voi sola sta impor le leggi, e romperle a vostro modo. 5

CARIZIA. Vi priego a spiegarmi il vostro desiderio con le più brevi parole che potete. 10

DON IGNAZIO. And can time be lost more worthily than in acquiring so worthy a treasure?

SIMBOLO. What do you acquire after all? A woman's love, something that changes from one minute to the next.

DON IGNAZIO. Yes, that is true of ordinary and common women; but those of regal spirit like her, when they love, love till death.

SIMBOLO. All women have the same nature.

DON IGNAZIO. You know very little about the nature of women. But don't defame her, for thereby you defame me: will you hold your tongue?

SIMBOLO. I'm holding it.

[*A shutter opens.*]

DON IGNAZIO. Now darkness flees from the air, here is the dawn preceding the brightness of my beautiful sun, now its rays are breaking through all around: I see her lovely hand with graceful gesture lifting the shutter. O happy my eyes, to be worthy of such a boon!

SCENE III

CARIZIA, DON IGNAZIO, SIMBOLO.

CARIZIA. [*from the window*] My lord Don Ignazio, since my aunt Angiola assures me that your request is honorable, I shall not refuse to match your courtesy; here I am, will you command me?

DON IGNAZIO. I command? I, who would consider myself the most fortunate man alive if I could be the least of your slaves? You are she who holds complete empire over my every wish, and to you alone is it given to impose laws and break them at your pleasure.

CARIZIA. I pray you to express your wish in as few words as possible.

DON IGNAZIO. Signora della vita mia (e perdonatime si
ho detto «mia», ché dal giorno che la viddi la consacrai
alla vostra rara bellezza), io non desio altro in questa vita
che essere vostro sposo, e perdonate all'ardire che pre-
sume tanto alto.   15

CARIZIA. Caro signore, io ben conosco la disagua-
glianza de' nostri stati, e la mia umile fortuna, a cui non
lice sperar sposo sì grande di valore e di richeza come
voi; però ricercate altra che sia più meritevole d'un vostro pari, e lasciate me poverella ch'umilmente nel mio   20
stato mi viva: la mia sorte mi comanda ch'abbia l'occhio
alla mia bassa condizione. So che lo dite per prendervi
gioco di me: la mia dote e la mia richezza s'inchiude
nella mia onestà, la quale inviolabilmente nella mia povertà custodisco.   25

DON IGNAZIO. Troppo suntuosa è la vostra dote, signora, la quale quanto più dimostrate sprezzarla, più l'in-
grandite: le vostre ricchezze sono inestimabil tesoro di
tante peregrine virtù, le quali resiedeno in voi come in
suo proprio albergo. Meriti ordinari si possono con le   30
parole lodare, ma i gradi infiniti si lodano meraviglian-
do, e con atti di riverenza tacendo si riveriscono. Ma voi
lo dite acciò che io n'abbia scorno, ché troppo povero
mercante a così gran fiera compaia per comprarla; e veramente, meritarei quel scorno che mi fate, se non ve-   35
nissi ricchissimo d'amore; ché non basta comprarse l'infinito valore de' vostri meriti, se non con l'infinito
amore che le porto.

CARIZIA. So che in una mia pari non cadono tanti meriti, e per non poter trovar parole condegne per rispon- 40
derli, vi risponde tacendo il core.

DON IGNAZIO. Signora, ecco un anello, nel cui dia-
mante sono scolpite due fedi;[1] tenetelo per amor e segno
del sponsalizio. Il dono è picciolo ben sì, ma si considerate l'affetto di chi lo dona, egli è ben degno di lei.   45

CARIZIA. Il dono è ben degno di lui; nondimeno. . . .

DON IGNAZIO. Sovereign of my life (and forgive me for calling it "mine," for from the day I saw you I consecrated it to your rare beauty), I desire nothing in this life but to be your husband; and forgive the ardor which aspires so high.

CARIZIA. My lord, I well know the inequality of our conditions and my humble fortune, which forbids me to look for a husband of such nobility and wealth as you are; therefore seek another more worthy of such as you, and leave me, poor creature that I am, to live humbly in my station: my lot requires me to remember my lowly place. I know that you speak as you do but to make sport of me: my only dowry and riches are in my honor, which in my poverty I inviolably guard.

DON IGNAZIO. All too sumptuous, my lady, is your dowry, which you increase the more you seem to despise it. Your riches are a priceless treasure of many rare virtues, which dwell in you as in their natural home. Ordinary merits can be praised with words, but infinite degrees are praised with wonder and are worshipped silently with acts of reverence. But you speak thus to scorn me as a merchant too poor to purchase at so great a fair; and truly I should deserve your scorn, did I not come very rich in love, for nothing is great enough to purchase the infinite worth of your merits except the infinite love I bear you.

CARIZIA. I know that so many merits cannot be in such as I, and because I cannot find words equal to yours, my heart answers you silently.

DON IGNAZIO. My lady, on the diamond of this ring are engraved two hands clasped; take it for love and as a pledge of our nuptials. The gift is small, certainly, but if you consider the affection of him who gives it, it is well worthy of you.

CARIZIA. The gift is indeed worthy of him who gives

Ma ben sapete che il rigor dell'onestà delle donzelle non permette ricever doni.

DON IGNAZIO. Signora, non fate tanto torto alla vostra nobilità, né tanto torto a me: rifiutar il primo dono di un sposo. Accetatelo, e se non merita così degno luogo delle vostre mani, poi buttatelo via.

CARIZIA. Or sù accetto, e gradisco il vostro dono, e me lo pongo in dito; e non potendo donarvi dono condegno, ché nol consente la mia povertà, vi dono me stessa, ché chi dona se stessa non ha magior cosa da donare; e questo anello, come cosa mia, ve lo ridono in caro pegno della mia fede.

DON IGNAZIO. Acceto l'anello, ed accetto l'offerta della sua persona; e se ben ne sono indegno, amor mi sforza ad accettarla. In ricompensa non so che darle se non tutto io, e se ben disseguale alla sua grandezza, accettatelo come io ho accettata la sua persona.

CARIZIA. Comandate altro?

DON IGNAZIO. Vi priego a trattenervi un altro poco, acciochè gli occhi mei abbino il desiato frutto di lor desiderio.

CARIZIA. I prieghi de' padroni son comandi a' servi, e se ben i rispetti delle donzelle non patiscano tanto, pur per un marito si deveno rompere tutti i rispetti; ecomi apparecchiata a far quanto mi comandate.

DON IGNAZIO. Cara padrona, mi basta l'animo solo; so ben che la mia richiesta sarebbe a voi di poco onore; mi contento che ve n'entriate, pregandovi che in questo breve spazio, che non siamo nostri, di far buona compagnia al mio core, che resta con voi, né si partirà da voi mai; e ricordatevi di me.

CARIZIA. Non riccordandomi di voi, mi smenticarei di me stessa.

DON IGNAZIO. Amatemi come amo voi.

it; nevertheless. . . . But you well know that the rules of maiden honor forbid accepting gifts.

DON IGNAZIO. My lady, do not wrong your own nobility nor me by refusing a bridegroom's first gift. Accept it, and if it is not worthy to grace your hands, throw it away.

CARIZIA. Well, then, I accept and am grateful for your gift and I place it on my finger; and being unable to make you an equal gift, for my poverty forbids, I give you myself, for he who gives himself has no greater thing to bestow; and this ring, as my own possession, I return to you in dear pledge of my faith.

DON IGNAZIO. I accept the ring and I accept the offer of yourself; although I am unworthy, love forces me to accept it. In return I do not know what to give you except all of me; and although it is less great, accept it as I have accepted your gift of yourself.

CARIZIA. Will you command me farther?

DON IGNAZIO. I pray you to remain a little longer, so that my eyes may have the desired fruit of their yearning.

CARIZIA. The prayers of masters are commands to their servants, and although considerations of maidenly behavior forbid, for a husband all considerations must be overruled: here I am, ready to do whatever you command.

DON IGNAZIO. Dear mistress, the generosity of your spirit alone suffices. I know that my request would be less than honorable to you; I am content that you return indoors, praying you that in this brief space of time in which we do not belong to each other, you will keep good company with my heart, which remains with you never to depart; and remember me.

CARIZIA. Not to remember you would be to forget my very self.

DON IGNAZIO. Love me as I love you.

CARIZIA. Troppo vile ed indegna è quella persona che si lascia vincere in amore, e se piacerà a Dio che siamo nostri, allora faremo contesa chi amerà più di noi, ed io da la mia parte non mi lasciarò avanzare da voi. A Dio.

DON IGNAZIO. Ecco tramontata la sfera del mio bel 85 sole, che sola può far sereno il mio giorno. O fenestra, è sparito il tuo pregio, o Dio, che cosa è nel cielo che sia più bella di lei, se splendori, sole, luna, stelle e tutte le bellezze del cielo son raccolte nel breve giro del suo bel volto? Ahi, ché se prima ardea, or tutto avampo, ché per 90 non averla tanto tempo vista, i carboni erano sopiti sotto la cenere; or per la sua vista han preso vigore, m'hanno acceso ne l'alma un tal incendio che son tutto di fuoco.

SIMBOLO. Poiché sete sazio della sua vista, partiamoci. 95

DON IGNAZIO. Che sazio? gli occhi miei, in così lungo digiuno assetati, nel convivio della sua vista se l'han bevuta di sorte che son tutto ebro d'amore. Anzi questo convito mi è paruto la mensa di Tantalo,[2] dove quanto più bevea, men sazio mi rendeva, e più ingordo ne di- 100 veniva; anzi nel più bel godere è sparita via, ed io mi sento più assetato che mai; anzi mi par ch'ancor mi sieda ne gli occhi, e ci sento il peso della sua persona.[3] O alta possanza di celeste bellezza!

SIMBOLO. Se vi dolete per troppa felicità, che farete 105 nelle disgrazie?

DON IGNAZIO. Questa felicità mi dà presagio di mal più acerbo, ché amandola non riamato, quanto amarò riamato? più m'infiammarò di quel desiderio, di cui sempre son stato acceso. Ma dimmi, che ti par di lei? 110

CARIZIA. Base and unworthy indeed is he who lets himself be outdone in love; and if it please God that we belong to one another, then shall we contend to prove which of us loves most, and I for my part shall not let you surpass me. Farewell.

[*Carizia closes the shutters and disappears.*]

DON IGNAZIO. There sets the sphere of my beautiful sun which alone makes fair my day. Oh window, your glory has vanished. Oh God, what thing in heaven can be more beautiful than she, if brightness, sun, moon, stars and all the beauties of heaven are gathered in the small round of her lovely countenance? Alas, if I burned before, now I blaze, for not having seen her for so long, the coals were smothered beneath the ashes; now from the sight of her they have gained strength and have lighted in my soul such a conflagration that I am all aflame.

SIMBOLO. Since you've had enough of seeing her, let's go.

DON IGNAZIO. Enough? My eyes, parched by so long a fast, at the banquet of her appearance have drunk so deeply that I am reeling with love. Nay, this feast seemed to me the repast of Tantalus, at which the more I drank, the less I was satisfied and the thirstier I became; nay, at the moment of greatest delight, she disappeared, and I feel more parched than ever; nay, it seems to me that she still keeps her seat in my eyes, and there I feel the weight of her being. Oh lofty power of heavenly beauty!

SIMBOLO. If you mourn for excessive happiness, what will you do in misfortune?

DON IGNAZIO. This happiness presages a fiercer torment, for if I can love her without requital, how much shall I love when I am loved in return? I shall burn still more with that desire which has always inflamed me. But tell me, what do you think of her?

SIMBOLO. Ella è non men bella di dentro che di fuori: mirate con che bel modo non ha voluto accetar il vostro dono, né rifiutarlo; e se il dono era magnifico e reale, ella è stata più magnifica e reale a non lasciarssi vincere da tanta ingordiggia. 115

DON IGNAZIO. Simbolo, sapresti indovinar in qual parte della casa ella sia?

SIMBOLO. Che posso saper io?

DON IGNAZIO. Non vedi là dove l'aria è più tranquilla e tutto gioisce? ivi è la sua persona. 120

SIMBOLO. Ah, ah, ah! Ecco Don Flaminio, state in cervello.

SCENA IV

DON FLAMINIO, DON IGNAZIO, ed ANGIOLA
[e SIMBOLO]

DON FLAMINIO. Oh, signor Don Ignazio, voi siate il ben trovato.

DON IGNAZIO. E voi il ben venuto, carissimo fratello.

ANGIOLA. [da sé] Mi manda Carizia, la mia nipote, se posso spiar alcuna cosa del matrimonio suo e che si dice 5 di lei.

DON FLAMINIO. Poni mano a darmi una buona mancia, ché onoratissimamente me l'ho guadagnata.

DON IGNAZIO. Non so che offerirvi in particolare, se sete padrone di tutta la mia robba. 10

ANGIOLA. [da sé] Certo ragionano del matrimonio de mia nepote; vo' star da parte in quel vicolo, per ascoltar che dicono.

DON FLAMINIO. Veramente la merito, perché ci ho faticato, e se ben l'un fratello è tenuto por la vita per 15 l'altro, pur in cosa di gran sodisfazione non si vieta che non si faccino alcuni compimenti fra loro.

SIMBOLO. She is no less beautiful within than without: look with what grace she contrived neither to accept nor to refuse your gift; and if the gift was magnificent and regal, she was more magnificent and regal in not allowing herself to be moved by desire to possess it.

DON IGNAZIO. Simbolo, can you guess in which part of the house her room is?

SIMBOLO. How should I know?

DON IGNAZIO. Don't you see, there where the air is most serene and all is joyful? There is she.

SIMBOLO. Ha, ha, ha! Here comes Don Flaminio, be on guard.

SCENE IV

Don Flaminio, Don Ignazio, Angiola, and Simbolo
[Panimbolo and Avanzino, silent].

DON FLAMINIO. My lord Don Ignazio, well met!

DON IGNAZIO. And welcome to you, dearest brother!

ANGIOLA. [apart] My niece Carizia sends me to see if I can spy out anything about her marriage and what is being said of her.

DON FLAMINIO. Prepare to give me a good reward, for I have most honorably earned it.

DON IGNAZIO. I don't know what to offer in particular, as you are already master of all I possess.

ANGIOLA. [apart] Surely they discuss my niece's marriage: I'll draw apart into that alley to hear what they say.

DON FLAMINIO. Truly I deserve it, for I've taken pains; and although brothers are bound in duty to lay down their lives for each other, still, for an especially pleasing service some special acknowledgments are not forbidden.

DON IGNAZIO. Mi sottoscrivo a quanto mi tassarete.

ANGIOLA. [*da sé*] Fin qui va bene il principio.

DON IGNAZIO. Dite di grazia, non mi tenete più 20
sospeso.

DON FLAMINIO. Già è conchiuso il vostro matrimonio.

ANGIOLA. [*da sé*] L'ho indovinata, che ragionan del
matrimonio di Carizia.

DON IGNAZIO. Con la figlia del Conte de Tricarico.   25

DON FLAMINIO. Già è contento darvi i 40 mille ducati
di dote, e ha fermati i capitoli, pur che l'andiate a sposar
per questa sera.

DON IGNAZIO. O mio caro fratello, o mio carissimo
Don Flaminio, ché più desiderata novella non aresti 30
potuto darmi in la mia vita!

ANGIOLA. [*da sé*] Ohimè, che cosa intendo? Dice che
ha conchiuso il matrimonio con la figlia del Conte di
Tricarico con 40 mille scudi di dote.

DON FLAMINIO. Con patto espresso ch'abbiate a spo- 35
sarla per questa sera.

DON IGNAZIO. Or tal patto, non potrò osservarlo.

DON FLAMINIO. Come?

DON IGNAZIO. Perché non basterei a contener me stesso in tanto desiderio, di non gir a sposarla or ora.   40

[SIMBOLO.] [*da sé*] Finge assai bene, e dubbito che a
questa volta l'ingannatore restarà ingannato.

ANGIOLA. [*da sé*] Or va' e fidati d'uomini, va'; o uomini traditori!

DON FLAMINIO. Egli ha voluto giungervi quella clau- 45
sula perché l'era stato riferito che eravate innamorato e
morto per altra.

DON IGNAZIO. Non mi ricordo aver mai amato così ar-
dentemente come Aldonzina[1] sua figlia, ché se ben ho
amato molto, l'amor è stato assai più finto che da vero; e 50

DON IGNAZIO. I bind myself to pay whatever you may levy.

ANGIOLA. [*apart*] So far this promises well.

DON IGNAZIO. Tell me, I pray, do not keep me any longer in suspense.

DON FLAMINIO. Your marriage is arranged.

ANGIOLA. [*apart*] I guessed it: they are speaking of Carizia's marriage.

DON IGNAZIO. With the daughter of the Count of Tricarico.

DON FLAMINIO. He has now agreed to the dowry of forty thousand ducats and has signed the contracts, with the provision that you wed her this very evening.

DON IGNAZIO. Oh my dear brother, oh my dearest Don Flaminio, in all my life you could not have given me more welcome news!

ANGIOLA. [*apart*] Alas, what do I hear? He says he has arranged a marriage with the daughter of the Count of Tricarico with a dowry of forty thousand crowns.

DON FLAMINIO. On the specific condition that you must wed her this evening.

DON IGNAZIO. Now with that condition I cannot comply.

DON FLAMINIO. Why not?

DON IGNAZIO. Because I'd be unable to restrain myself from rushing to marry her this instant.

SIMBOLO. [*aside*] He acts the part very well, and I suspect that this time the tricker will be tricked.

ANGIOLA. [*apart*] So, this is how you can trust men, go to! Oh men, what traitors!

DON FLAMINIO. He added that clause because he'd been told that you were pining for love of someone else.

DON IGNAZIO. I can't remember ever loving anyone as ardently as I do his daughter Aldonzina, and though I may have had many love affairs, my love has been far

mi son dilettato sempre dar la burla or a questa, or a
quell'altra.

ANGIOLA. [da sé] O che vi siano cavati quei cuori pieni
d'inganni, or va' ti fida, va': e chi non restarebbe ingan-
nata da loro?   55

DON IGNAZIO. Ma per torlo da questo sospetto, andiamo ora a sposarla, andiamo, caro fratello; non mi far
così strugere a poco a poco; ché dubito non rimarrà
nulla d'intiero in sin a sera.

DON FLAMINIO. L'appontamento è stato per la sera che   60
viene, e credo ha chiesto il termine per non trovarsi forsi
la casa in ordine ed andando così all'improviso, forsi li
daremo qualche disgusto, e forsi vi perderete di riputazione; però abbiate pacienza per un poco d'intervallo di
tempo.   65

[SIMBOLO.] [da sé] Non dissi ch'arebbe sfugito d'an-
darvi? abiam vinto.

DON IGNAZIO. Dubbito di non potervi ubidire.

DON FLAMINIO. Forsi non sarà in casa.

ANGIOLA. [da sé] Mira che desiderio, e che ardore!   70

DON IGNAZIO. Ma andiamo a vedere.

DON FLAMINIO. Panimbolo, va' a casa del Conte.

DON IGNAZIO. Vien qua, Avanzino, va' a casa del
Conte, e vedi se il Conte de Tricarico è in casa.

DON FLAMINIO. Essendovi, andrò ad avisarlo io pri-   75
ma, verrò a trovarvi, e vi andaremo insieme.

DON IGNAZIO. Noi dove ci trovaremo?

DON FLAMINIO. In casa.

DON IGNAZIO. Andate, or sù.

ANGIOLA. O Dio, che ho inteso, o Dio, che ho veduto,   80
ed è possibile che si trovi così poca fede negli uomini?
Or chi avesse creduto che Don Ignazio, venutomi tanto

more feigned than true; I have always amused myself by trifling, first with one girl, then with another.

ANGIOLA. [apart] Oh your deceitful hearts should be cut out! Trust them who will! But who wouldn't be deceived, so plausible as they seem?

DON IGNAZIO. But to free him from suspicion, let's go now to wed her; come, dear brother, do not let me waste away little by little, for I fear there will be nothing left of me by evening.

DON FLAMINIO. The appointed time was this evening, and I think perhaps he requested this stay because the house is not in order, and if we went there now unexpectedly, perhaps we should annoy him and perhaps lower your reputation; therefore, be patient for a very little while.

SIMBOLO. [aside] Didn't I say that he would back down and avoid going? We've won.

DON IGNAZIO. I doubt that I can restrain myself as you command.

DON FLAMINIO. He may not even be at home.

ANGIOLA. [apart] See what desire and what eagerness!

DON IGNAZIO. But let's go and see.

DON FLAMINIO. Panimbolo, go to the Count's house.

DON IGNAZIO. Here, Avanzino, go to the house of the Count of Tricarico and see if he is at home.

DON FLAMINIO. Should he be, I'll go first to inform him, then fetch you and we'll go there together.

DON IGNAZIO. Where shall we meet?

DON FLAMINIO. At home.

DON IGNAZIO. Then go, quickly.

[All depart but Angiola.]

ANGIOLA. Oh God, what have I heard, oh God, what have I seen, is it possible, then, that there is so little faith among men? Now who would have believed that after importuning me about Carizia for so long, with so

117

tempo appresso per parlarmi, e con tante affettuose parole, con tante lacrime e promesse, non fusse tutto fuoco e fiamme per Carizia? Or gite, donne, e date credito a   85
quelle simulate parole, a quelle lacrime traditrici, a quei
finti sospiri, ed a quelle fallaci promesse: movetivi a
pietà di loro, perché tal volta li veggiate piovere dal
volto tempesta di amarissime lacrime; credete a quei
giuramenti, a quei spergiurii! Come si salverà onor di   90
donna già mai se li sono tesi tanti laccioli? Andrò a casa,
e non li narrerò nulla di ciò; ch'avendola io spinta a rag-
gionar con lui, sarebbe donna, a vedersi così spregiata e
tocca su l'onor suo, di morirsi di passione.

SCENA V

DON FLAMINIO, PANIMBOLO.

DON FLAMINIO. Ecco, o Panimbolo, che, tu non avendo voluto credere a quanto io te diceva, che Don Ignazio
non s'accorse quel giorno di Carizia, e che è molto invaghito della figlia del Conte, per far a tuo modo, e per
iscoprir l'animo suo, l'avemo detto che'l matrimonio   5
del Conte era conchiuso; e vedesti con che pronto animo, e con che accesa voglia, volea sposarla allora allora
e non aspettar insino alla sera.

PANIMBOLO. Così son sicuro io che Don Ignazio sta
innamorato d'altra, come che son vivo. Ma come ch'e-   10
gli è d'ingegno vivace e pronto, imaginatosi la fraude,
rispose in cotal modo.

DON FLAMINIO. Mi doglio del tuo mal preso consiglio.
Ecco, andrà, o mandarà in casa del Conte, e come saprà
che è più d'un mese che non vi son ito, scoprirà tutta la   15
bugia, mi terrà sempre per un bugiardo e bisognando
non mi crederà la verità istessa.

many loving words, with so many tears and promises, Don Ignazio was not all fire and flames for her? Let that be a lesson to you, women: go on and believe those feigned words, those treacherous tears, those counterfeit sighs and those fraudulent promises; let yourselves be moved to pity men because sometimes you see tempests of bitter tears pouring from their faces; believe those sworn oaths, believe those perjuries! How can woman's honor ever be safe when so many snares are laid for it? I shall go home and not tell Carizia anything of this, for having been persuaded by me to speak with him and now seeing herself thus despised and her honor blemished, she is of that stamp of woman who would die of chagrin.

SCENE V

Don Flaminio, Panimbolo.

DON FLAMINIO. So there, Panimbolo, because you wouldn't believe me that Don Ignazio did not notice Carizia that day and is deeply in love with the count's daughter, we followed your plan to know his mind and told him that the marriage was arranged with the count; and you saw how readily, with what hot desire, he wanted to marry her immediately and not wait till evening.

PANIMBOLO. As sure as I'm alive, Don Ignazio is in love with someone else. But being of lively and ready wit and perceiving the trick, he answered in that way.

DON FLAMINIO. I regret your ill-taken advice. Now he'll go or send word to the Count's house, and when he learns that I haven't gone there for more than a month, he'll discover the whole deceit, think me a liar ever after, and even in real need never believe anything I say, not even truth itself.

PANIMBOLO. Bisogna con una nuova bugia salvar la vecchia bugia; andiamo a casa del Conte, e rimediamo in alcun modo. 20

DON FLAMINIO. Andiamo, e se uscirò con onor mio da questa bugia, un'altra volta non sarò così prodigo del mio onore.

SCENA VI

EUFRANONE, DON IGNAZIO.

EUFRANONE. [*da sé*] Veramente chi ha una picciola villa non fa patir di fame la sua famigliola: di qua s'hanno erbicine per l'insalate, e per le minestre, legna per lo fuoco, e vino, che se non basta per tutto, almeno a soffrir più legiermente il peso della misera povertà. O 5 me infelice se, fra l'altre robbe che mi tolse il rigor della rubellione, mi avesse tolta ancor questa; mi ho colto una insalatuccia; ché chi mangia una insalata, non va a letto senza cena.

DON IGNAZIO. Eufranone carissimo, Dio vi dia ogni 10 bene.

EUFRANONE. Questa speranza ho in lui.

DON IGNAZIO. Come state?

EUFRANONE. Non posso star bene essendo così povero come sono. 15

DON IGNAZIO. Servitivi della mia robba, ché è il maggior servigio che far mi possiate. Copritevi.[1]

EUFRANONE. È mio debito star così.

DON IGNAZIO. Usate meco troppe cerimonie.

EUFRANONE. Perché mi sete signore. 20

DON IGNAZIO. Vi priego che trattiamo alla libera.

EUFRANONE. Orsù, per obedirvi. [*da sé*] Non so che voglia costui da me; mi fa entrar in sospetto.

120

PANIMBOLO. We must save the old lie with a new one: let's go to the count's house and remedy things somehow.

DON FLAMINIO. So be it, and if I come through this deceit with my honor unscathed, I'll not be so careless of it again.

SCENE VI

EUFRANONE, DON IGNAZIO.

EUFRANONE. [apart] Truly he who has a small country estate may keep his family from hunger. From the farm come greens for salads and soups, wood for the fire and wine, which, if it does not cure all ills, at least somewhat eases the burden of wretched poverty. Oh, I would be unhappy indeed if, along with the other property confiscated in penalty for the rebellion, this farm too had been taken from me! I have gathered quite a good little salad; well, as they say, "He who eats a salad, does not go supperless to bed."

DON IGNAZIO. Eufranone, my very dear sir, may God give you every blessing.

EUFRANONE. So do I hope from Him.

DON IGNAZIO. How are you?

EUFRANONE. I cannot be well, being so poor.

DON IGNAZIO. Take my possessions as yours, for you would be doing me the greatest possible service. Cover your head, I pray.

EUFRANONE. I owe you this observance.

DON IGNAZIO. You do me too much honor.

EUFRANONE. Because you are my lord.

DON IGNAZIO. Let us be more free with each other, I beg you.

EUFRANONE. Very well then, to obey you. [aside] I don't know what this one wants from me: he makes me suspicious.

121

DON IGNAZIO. Or veniva a trovarvi.

EUFRANONE. Potevate mandar a chiamarmi, ché serei 25
venuto volando.

DON IGNAZIO. Son molti giorni che desio esservi parente, e son venuto a farmevi conoscere per tale, ché veramente sete assai onorato e da bene.

EUFRANONE. Tutto ciò per vostra grazia. 30

DON IGNAZIO. Anzi per vostro merito.

EUFRANONE. Non mi conosco di tanto preggio che sia
degno di tanta cortesia.

DON IGNAZIO. Siete degno di maggior cosa. Io vi
chieggio la vostra figliola con molta affezione. 35

EUFRANONE. Stimate forsi, signore, ch'essendo io povero gentiluomo, venda l'onore de mia figliuola? Veramente non merito tanta ingiuria da voi.

DON IGNAZIO. Non ho detto per farvi ingiuria, ché
non convien ad un mio pari, né voi la meritate: ve la 40
chiedo per legittima moglie, se conoscete che ne sia
degno.

EUFRANONE. Essendo voi così ricco e di gran legnag-
gio, non convien burlar un povero gentiluomo, e vostro servidore. 45

DON IGNAZIO. Mi nieghi Dio ogni contento se non ve
la chiedo con la bocca del core: ch'io non torrò altra
sposa in mia vita che Carizia, ed in pegno dell'amore,
ecco la fede:[2] accoppiamo gli animi come il parentado.

EUFRANONE. Signor mio caro, io so ben quanto gli 50
animi giovenili sieno volubili, e leggieri, e più pieni di
furore che di consiglio, e che subbito che gli montino i
capricci in testa, si vogliono scapricciare, e passato quel-
l'umore, restano come si di ciò mai non ne fusse stata
parola, ed in un medesimo tempo amano e disamano 55
una cosa medesima; non vorrei che si spargesse fama per
Salerno che m'avete chiesto mia figlia, ché come in Sa-

DON IGNAZIO. I have come on purpose to see you.

EUFRANONE. You could have sent for me; I would have come flying.

DON IGNAZIO. For many days I have wished to become your relation, and I am here to make myself known to you as such, for truly you are honorable and virtuous.

EUFRANONE. Such good opinion derives from your graciousness.

DON IGNAZIO. From your own merit, rather.

EUFRANONE. I do not consider myself worthy of so much courtesy.

DON IGNAZIO. You are worthy of still more. I ask for your daughter, with great affection.

EUFRANONE. Perhaps you think, my lord, that being but a poor gentleman I would sell my daughter's honor? Truly I do not deserve such insult from you.

DON IGNAZIO. I intended no insult, for that does not become me nor do you deserve it: I ask for her as my lawful wife, if you think me worthy of her.

EUFRANONE. Being so rich and of such high lineage, you should not make fun of a poor gentleman, your servant.

DON IGNAZIO. May God deny me all happiness if my mouth is not speaking for my heart: I shall never in my life marry anyone but Carizia. And as a pledge of love, here is my hand on it: let us join our hearts as we join our houses.

EUFRANONE. My dear lord, I know well how fickle and light young spirits are, more full of passion than of counsel; and that they want instant satisfaction of every capricious wish, and when the fancy has passed, it is as if no word of it had ever existed; at one and the same moment they can love and not love one and the same thing. I should not like the word to spread through Salerno that you have asked me for my daughter, for here when

lerno si parla una volta di nozze, dicono «Son fatte, son fatte»: e poi se per qualche disgrazia non si accapassero, restasse la mia figliola oltraggiata nell'onore, stimando 60 esser rifiutata per alcun suo mancamento, e mi toglieste quello che non potete più restituirmi, ed io vorrei morir mille volte prima che ciò m'accadesse. Voi altri signori ricchi stimate poco l'onor de' poveri, e noi poveri gentiluomini, non avendo mo altro che l'onore, lo stimia- 65 mo più che la vita. Però lo priego ad ammogliarsi con le sue pari, e lasciar che noi apparentiamo fra' nostri.

DON IGNAZIO. Eufranone mio carissimo, Dio sa con quanto dolore or ascolto le vostre parole, e se mi pungano sul vivo del cuore; io non merito da voi esser tacciato 70 di vizio di leggierezza, nascendo il mio amore da un risoluto ed invecchiato affetto dell'anima mia, ch'avendo fatto l'ultimo mio forzo di resistere al suo amore, dopo lunghissimo combattimento, le sue bellezze son restate vincitrici d'ogni mia voglia. 75

EUFRANONE. Vi priego a pensarvi sù sei mesi prima, e se pur dura la voglia, allor me la potrete chiedere, ed io vi do la mia fede serbarla per voi in sin a quel tempo.

DON IGNAZIO. Sei mesi star senza Carizia? più tosto potrei vivere senza la vita, e ben sapete che l'amante non 80 ha maggior nemico che l'indugio.

EUFRANONE. A questo conosco l'impeto giovenile, che quanto con maggior violenza assale, tanto più tosto s'intepidisce.

DON IGNAZIO. Ogni parola che vi esce di bocca mi è un 85 can rabbioso che mi straccia il petto. Il mio amore è immortale, e la mia fé, che or stimate leggiera, la conoscerete fermissima a gli effetti.

EUFRANONE. È contento il vostro zio, e fratello del matrimonio? 90

a marriage is but mentioned once, everyone says "'Tis done, 'tis done!", and then if by some misfortune it were not to take place, to see my daughter left with her honor defamed—people thinking that she had been rejected because of some fault—and to have you take from me what you can never restore: I would sooner die a thousand times than that such a thing should happen. You rich noblemen think little of the honor of the poor, and we poor gentlemen, with nothing left us now but honor, we prize it more than life. Therefore I beg you to seek a wife among your equals and let us ally ourselves with ours.

DON IGNAZIO. Eufranone, dearest sir, as God is my witness, I hear your words now with sorrow and they pierce my heart to the quick! I do not deserve your charge of dissolute lightness, my love being born from a resolute and matured affection of my soul; for although I resisted loving her with all my strength, after long combat her beauties emerged the conquerors of my every wish.

EUFRANONE. I beg you to think on it first for six months, and if your wish still endures, then you may ask me for her, and I pledge my faith to keep her for you until that time.

DON IGNAZIO. Six months without Carizia? I could sooner live without life itself; you know that delay is a lover's worst enemy.

EUFRANONE. Your words betray the impetuousness of youth: the more violent its assault, the sooner it grows cool.

DON IGNAZIO. Each word that issues from your mouth is a rabid dog which tears my breast. My love is immortal, and my faith, which you now consider light, you shall know by its effects to be unshakeable.

EUFRANONE. And are your uncle and your brother pleased with this match?

DON IGNAZIO. Farò che si contentino.

EUFRANONE. Fate che si contentino prima, e poi effettuaremo il matrimonio.

DON IGNAZIO. L'amor mio non può patir tanto indugio; anzi mi maraviglio che dal giorno della festa come 95
sia potuto restar vivo senza lei.

EUFRANONE. Lo dico ad effetto ché forsi non contentandosi del matrimonio, inventassero qualche modo
per disturbarlo, onde venissi a perdere quel poco di
onor che mi è rimasto. 100

DON IGNAZIO. O Dio, quanta tema e quanto sospetto!

EUFRANONE. Chi poco ha, molto stima e molto teme.
Ma voi sete informato dell'infortunio che ho patito nella
robba, che non solo non ho da poter dar dote ad un par
vostro, ma meno ad un povero mio pari? 105

DON IGNAZIO. Ho inteso che per aver voluto seguir le
parti Sanseverinesche[3] siate caduto in tanta disgrazia;
ma io ho stimato sempre d'animi bassi e vili coloro che
s'han voluto arricchire con le doti delle mogli. Io prendo la vostra destra, e non la lascierò mai se non la mi 110
prometteti.

EUFRANONE. Temo prometterlavi. Non so che nuvolo
mi sta dinanzi al core.

DON IGNAZIO. Eufranone, mio padre, vi prego a darlami con vostro consenso, ché non mi fate far qualche 115
pazzia; non mi sforzate a far quello per forza che me si
deve per debito d'amore; appena posso contenermi ne'
termini dell'onestà. Son risoluto averla per moglie ancor che fusse sicuro perder la robba, la vita, l'onore, per
non dir più. 120

EUFRANONE. Signore, perdonatemi se mi fo vincere
dalla vostra ostinata cortesia; ecco la mano in segno d'amicizia e di parentado, avertendovi di nuovo che non ho
dote da darvi.

DON IGNAZIO. I shall see to it that they be pleased.

EUFRANONE. See to that first, and then we shall make the match.

DON IGNAZIO. My love cannot bear such delay. Indeed I am amazed that I have been able to live without her since the day of the festival.

EUFRANONE. I am concerned lest, perhaps being displeased with the match, they invent some excuse for breaking it off, by which I should lose what little honor remains to me.

DON IGNAZIO. Oh God, what fear and what suspicion!

EUFRANONE. He who has little, prizes and fears for it much. But are you aware of the loss of property I have suffered, so that I cannot provide a dowry fitting for a bridegroom of your wealth, nor even for one in my own poor circumstances?

DON IGNAZIO. I have heard that because you cast your lot with the house of Sanseverino, you have fallen into this misfortune; but I have always considered it base and low-spirited in a man to marry for money. I grasp your hand and shall never release it unless you promise her to me.

EUFRANONE. I fear this promise. A sort of misgiving clouds my heart.

DON IGNAZIO. Eufranone, my father, I beseech you to give her to me with your consent, and not push me to some act of madness. Do not force me to take by violence what should be bestowed on me as the due of my love. I can hardly contain myself within the bounds of chaste honor. I am resolved to have her for my wife, even were I sure on that account to lose my property, my life, my honor, to say no more.

EUFRANONE. My lord, forgive me if I allow myself to be won over by your persistent courtesy; here is my hand in sign of friendship and alliance, again with the warning that I can give no dowry.

DON IGNAZIO. Ed ancor che me la voleste dare, non la 125
vorrei. Conosco non meritar tanta dote quanta ne porta
seco. Vo' che si facci festa bandita, si conviti tutta la nobiltà di Salerno, adornisi la sala di razzi, faccisi un solenne banchetto, adornisi la sposa di gioie, perle, e di
drappi d'oro, e non si lasci a dietro cosa per dimostrar 130
l'interno contento dell'animo mio.

EUFRANONE. V'ho detto quanto sia mal agiato di far
questo.

DON IGNAZIO. A tutto provederò ben io; mandarò il
mio cameriero ché proveda quanto fia di mestiero.   135

EUFRANONE. Quando verrete a sposarla?

DON IGNAZIO. Vorrei venir prima che partirmi da voi.
Ma perché l'ora è tarda, verrò domani all'alba; ponete il
tutto in ponto per quell'ora.

EUFRANONE. Si farà quanto comandate.   140

DON IGNAZIO. Io non vo' trattener più voi, né me
stesso: andrò a mandarvi quanto ho promesso.

EUFRANONE. Andate in buon'ora.

O Dio, che ventura è questa! Desidero communicar
una mia tanta allegrezza con alcuno. Ma veggio Polise- 145
na, la mia moglie, che vien a tempo per ricever da me
così insperato contento.

SCENA VII

POLISENA, moglie, ed EUFRANONE.

POLISENA. [da sé] Veggio il mio marito su l'uscio, più
del solito allegro.

Gentil compagno mio, che ci è di nuovo?

EUFRANONE. Buone novelle.

POLISENA. Ma non per noi.   5

DON IGNAZIO. And even if you could, I would not take it: I know I am undeserving of such a dowry as she intrinsically possesses. I wish a feast to be proclaimed, all the nobility of Salerno invited, the hall decked with tapestries, a solemn banquet prepared, the bride adorned with gems, pearls and cloth of gold, and nothing omitted that may give outward show of my inner joy.

EUFRANONE. I have told you how ill I can afford to do such things.

DON IGNAZIO. Nay, I shall provide it all; I shall send my servant to see to everything.

EUFRANONE. When will you come to wed her?

DON IGNAZIO. I wish I could come this instant, before taking leave of you. But as the hour is late, I shall come tomorrow at dawn; have all in readiness at that hour.

EUFRANONE. Whatever you command shall be done.

DON IGNAZIO. I must not delay you nor myself any longer: I shall go and send you all I have promised.

EUFRANONE. Go in happiness.

[*Don Ignazio departs.*]

Oh God, what good fortune is this! I long to share my delight with someone. Good! I see Polisena, my wife, who comes opportunely to receive from me this most unhoped-for joy.

SCENE VII

POLISENA, wife, and EUFRANONE.

POLISENA. [*apart*] I see my husband in the doorway, more cheerful than usual.

Sweet companion, what news?

EUFRANONE. Good news.

POLISENA. But not for us.

EUFRANONE. Per che no?

POLISENA. Per che siamo così avezzi alle sciagure che, volendoci favorir la fortuna, non trovarebbe la via.

EUFRANONE. Abbiam maritata Carizia.

POLISENA. Eh? e con chi? con quel Dottor della neces- 10
sità,[1] nostro vicino?

EUFRANONE. Con un meglior del Dottore.

POLISENA. Con quel Capitan Martebellonio bugiardo vantatore?

EUFRANONE. Con un gentiluomo. 15

POLISENA. Quel gentiluomo poverello che ce la chiese l'altro giorno? e che val nobilità senza denari? Avete l'esempio in noi.

EUFRANONE. Non l'indovinaresti mai.

POLISENA. Dimmelo, marito mio, di grazia, non mi 20
far così struggere di desiderio.

EUFRANONE. Non vo' farti più penare: con Don Ignazio di Mendozza.

POLISENA. Quel nipote del Viceré della provincia che combaté quel giorno con i tori? 25

EUFRANONE. Con quel' istesso.

POLISENA. Egli è possibile, marito mio, che tu vogli così beffarmi, e rallegrarmi con false allegrezze? il caldo del piacere, che già mi scorrea per tutte le vene, mi s'è raffreddato e gelato. 30

EUFRANONE. Giuro per la tua vita, così a me cara come la mia, che lo dico da senno.

POLISENA. E chi ha trattato tal matrimonio?

EUFRANONE. Egli istesso; né ha voluto partirsi da me se non gli la prometteva. 35

POLISENA. Quando egli la vidde mai?

EUFRANONE. Quel giorno che fu la festa in palazzo.

POLISENA. O somma bontà di Dio, quanto sei grande; e quanto sono secreti i termini per i quali camini, quando ti piace favorir i tuoi devoti! Tu sai, marito mio, che 40

EUFRANONE. Why not?

POLISENA. Because we're so much accustomed to misfortunes that, should fortune wish to favor us, she'd lose her way.

EUFRANONE. We've made a match for Carizia.

POLISENA. Eh, and with whom? With that threadbare doctor, our neighbor?

EUFRANONE. With someone better than the doctor.

POLISENA. With that Captain Martebellonio, the liar and boaster?

EUFRANONE. With a gentleman.

POLISENA. That poverty-stricken gentleman who asked us for her the other day? And what good is nobility without money? You have an example in us.

EUFRANONE. You'd never guess.

POLISENA. Tell me, husband, please; don't let curiosity devour me.

EUFRANONE. I'll not prolong your suffering. With Don Ignazio de Mendoza.

POLISENA. The nephew of the viceroy of the province, who fought the bulls that day?

EUFRANONE. The very one.

POLISENA. Is it possible, husband, that you wish thus to tease and cheer me with false joys? The warm pleasure which but a moment ago was running through all my veins is now cooled and frozen.

EUFRANONE. I swear by your life, as dear to me as my own, that I speak in earnest.

POLISENA. And who arranged such a marriage?

EUFRANONE. He himself; nor would he depart without my promise of her.

POLISENA. When did he ever see her?

EUFRANONE. The day of the festival at the palace.

POLISENA. Oh supreme goodness of God, how great you are, and how secret are the ways you walk, when it pleases you to favor your worshipers! You know, hus-

Carizia appena sale[2] fuor di casa il Natale e la Pasqua, così per l'incommodità delle vesti, come che è di sua natura malinconica, e se quei giorni che si preparava la festa, le venne un disio che mai riposava la notte e'l giorno, pregandomi che vi la conducesse; e ributtandola io che non avea vesti ed abbegliamenti da comparir tra tante gentildonne sue pari, disse che le volea torre in presto dalle sue conoscenti, da chi una cosa e da chi un'altra; ce lo promisi, tenendo per fermo che a lei fusse impossibile tanta manifattura; s'affaticò tanto con le sue amiche che accommodò sé e Callidora. Or io, non potendo resistere a tanti prieghi, chiesi licenza a voi, e ve la condussi; or chi arebbe potuto pensare che indi avea a nascere la sua ventura? 45 50

EUFRANONE. Chi può penetrar gli occulti secreti di Dio? 55

POLISENA. O Iddio, che mai vien meno a chi pone in te solo le sue speranze, ella si è sempre raccomandata a te, e tu li hai esaudite le sue preghiere, rimunerata la sua bontà e l'ubidienza estraordinaria che porta al suo padre e sua madre. 60

EUFRANONE. Ho tanto giubilo al core che mi trae di me stesso.

POLISENA. Se ben i padri s'attristano al nascer delle femine con dir che seco portano cattivo agurio di certa povertà, e di poco onore, pur son state molte che hanno inalzato il suo parentado, come speriamo di costei. 65

EUFRANONE. Ella è una gran donna, e non m'accieca la benda del soverchio amore; mai si vide tanta saviezza e bontà in una fanciulla. 70

POLISENA. Vorrei dir molto delle sue buone qualità che voi non sapete, ma le lacrime di tenerezza non me le lasciano esprimere.

EUFRANONE. Va' e poni lei e la casa in ordine.

band, how Carizia hardly stirs from the house even at Christmas and Easter, as much because of poverty of wardrobe as because of her melancholy nature, and how in the days of preparation for the festival, she conceived such a desire to attend it that she rested neither night nor day, begging me to take her there; and I refusing because she had no clothes nor ornaments good enough to appear among ladies of her rank, she said she wanted to borrow them from her acquaintances, one thing from one, one from another. I promised, thinking it impossible for her to carry out such a scheme; she exerted herself so much among her friends that she outfitted herself and Callidora. Unable then to resist such entreaties, I asked your permission and took her to the festival. Now who would have thought that thence her good fortune was to be born?

EUFRANONE. Who can penetrate the hidden secrets of God?

POLISENA. Oh God, Thou who never failest him who puts his hopes only in Thee, she has always relied on Thee, and Thou hast heard and answered her prayers, rewarded her goodness and the extraordinary obedience she pays her father and her mother.

EUFRANONE. I have such joy in my heart that I am beside myself.

POLISENA. Although fathers lament the birth of daughters, saying that they bear a bad omen of certain poverty and small honor, yet there have been many who have exalted their families, as we hope of her.

EUFRANONE. She is a great lady; and I am not blindfolded by excessive love. Greater wisdom and goodness in a maiden were never seen.

POLISENA. I should like to tell you much you do not know about her good qualities, but tears of tenderness hinder my expression.

EUFRANONE. Go, prepare her and the house.

133

POLISENA. E con che la ponemo in ordine? 75

EUFRANONE. Ecco genti cariche di robbe; ho per fermo che le mandi Don Ignazio; conosco il suo cameriero.

SCENA VIII

SIMBOLO, EUFRANONE, POLISENA.

SIMBOLO. Signor Eufranone, il mio signor Don Ignazio vi manda questi drappi di seta e d'oro per le vesti di Carizia, e della sorella, e vostra moglie; ecco i maestri che faticheranno tutta la notte ché sieno finite per domani all'alba; ecco i razzi per la sala e camere; in questa 5 scatola son collane, maniglie, oro, perle, gioie, ed altri abbegliamenti necessarii. Questo sacchetto di scudi per lo banchetto, ed altri bisogni, che spendiate largamente in fargli onore, ch'egli supplirà al tutto; che in sì poco tempo, non ha potuto far più, e che andrà sopplendo di 10 passo in passo.

EUFRANONE. Tutto stimo sia più tosto soverchio che manchevole, e so che ci onora non secondo il nostro picciolo merito, ma secondo le sue gran qualitadi.

SIMBOLO. Dice che se bene son immeritevoli di tanta 15 sposa, col tempo farà conoscere la sua amorevolezza, e se comandate altro.

EUFRANONE. Che ci ha onorato più del dovere, e bisognando, gli lo faremo intendere.

SIMBOLO. A Dio, signori. 20

EUFRANONE. Ecco, o moglie, che non ho mentito punto di quanto t'ho detto.

POLISENA. A Dio solo si dia la gloria, ché noi non siamo meritevoli di tanti favori per li nostri peccati.

134

POLISENA. And with what can we prepare it?

EUFRANONE. Here come people laden with goods. I am sure they are sent by Don Ignazio; I know his servant.

SCENE VIII

SIMBOLO, EUFRANONE, POLISENA.

SIMBOLO. My lord Eufranone, my lord Don Ignazio sends you these stuffs of silk and gold for the garments of Carizia and her sister and your wife; here are the craftsmen who will labor all night to finish them by dawn; here are the hangings for the hall and the chambers; in this box are necklaces, bracelets, gold, pearls, jewels and other seemly adornments. This little sack of crowns is for the banquet and other needs so that you may spend freely to do him honor, for he will furnish all; but on such short notice he has been unable to do more and will go on supplying as needs arise.

EUFRANONE. I judge all this excessive rather than lacking, and I know that he honors us not according to our small deserts but according to his own great goodness.

SIMBOLO. He says that although these things are unworthy of such a bride, with time he shall demonstrate the fullness of his love, and he desires to know if you have any other commands.

EUFRANONE. Tell him that he has honored us more than he should, and in case of further need, we shall inform him.

SIMBOLO. Farewell, noble sir and lady.

EUFRANONE. You see here, oh wife, that I have not lied a jot in what I told you.

POLISENA. To God alone must the glory be given, for we in our sinfulness do not deserve so many favors.

135

EUFRANONE. Moglie, va' e fa' quanto t'ho detto, ché io 25
andrò a convitar per domani tutti i parenti, e la nobiltà
di Salerno.

SCENA IX

DON FLAMINIO, PANIMBOLO, LECCARDO.

DON FLAMINIO. Io vo' far prima ogni sforzo se posso
indurla ad amarmi, e quando non mi riuscirà, non man-
carà ricercarla per moglie; lo vo' lassar per l'ultimo, ché
son risoluto non viver senz'ella, o sua sorella.

PANIMBOLO. Voi trattando per via del parasito, e con 5
lettere, e per modi così disconvenevoli, in cambio d'a-
marvi, vibrarà contro voi fiamme di sdegno, perché
stimarà esser oltraggiata da voi ne' fatti dell'onore.

DON FLAMINIO. Non vedi Leccardo come sta allegro?

PANIMBOLO. Averà bevuto soverchio, e sta ubbriaco. 10

LECCARDO. [da sé] O Dio, dove andrò per trovar Don
Flaminio?

DON FLAMINIO. Cerca me.

LECCARDO. [da sé] Corri, volta, trotta, galoppa, e
dàgli così felice novella. 15

DON FLAMINIO. Se ben lo veggio allegro, mi sento un
discontento nel core: e se ben ho voglia d'intenderlo, li
vo innanzi contro mia voglia.

LECCARDO. O signor Don Flaminio, buona nuova; la
mia lingua non t'apporta più male novelle! 20

DON FLAMINIO. E la mia ti apporterà grande utile.

LECCARDO. Non sapete il successo?

DON FLAMINIO. Non io.

LECCARDO. Come nol sai, se 'l sa tutto Salerno?

EUFRANONE. Wife, go and perform what I have ordered, for I am going now to invite for tomorrow all our relatives and the nobility of Salerno.

SCENE IX

DON FLAMINIO, PANIMBOLO, LECCARDO.

DON FLAMINIO. First I want to make every effort to induce her to take me as her lover, and failing that, I can ask for her in marriage. I'll leave that as a last resort, since I am determined not to live without her, or her sister.

PANIMBOLO. Your approach to her through the parasite and with letters and such improper means, will have her shooting flames of anger instead of loving you, for she'll feel that you've affronted her honor.

DON FLAMINIO. Do you see how joyful Leccardo looks?

PANIMBOLO. He has probably drunk too much and got soused.

LECCARDO. [apart] Oh Lord, where shall I go to find Don Flaminio?

DON FLAMINIO. He's looking for me.

LECCARDO. [apart] Race, curvet, trot, gallop to give him such happy news.

DON FLAMINIO. Although I see him joyful, I feel a discontent in my heart: and although I want to hear him, I go unwillingly to meet him.

LECCARDO. Oh, my lord Don Flaminio, good news! My tongue brings you bad news no more!

DON FLAMINIO. And mine shall bring great benefit to you.

LECCARDO. Do you know what has happened?

DON FLAMINIO. Not I.

LECCARDO. How is that, when all Salerno knows it?

DON FLAMINIO. Nol so, ti dico.   25

LECCARDO. O nieghi, o fingi per burlarmi.

DON FLAMINIO. In cosa ch'importa non si deve bur-
lare.

LECCARDO. Io penso che tu vogli burlar me.

DON FLAMINIO. La burla insino adesso l'ho ricevuta in   30
piacere, ma or mi dà noia.

LECCARDO. Lasciarò le burle, e dirò da dovero.

DON FLAMINIO. Or di', in nome di Dio, e non mi tener
più in bilancia: parla.

LECCARDO. Ho tanto corso che non posso parlare; non   35
ho fiato.

DON FLAMINIO. Prendi fiato; se non, che farai perdere
il fiato a me.

LECCARDO. Per la soverchia stanchezza mi sento mo-
rire.   40

DON FLAMINIO. Dammi la nuova prima, e mori quando ti piace.

LECCARDO. Quanto ho più voglia di dire, manco
posso.

DON FLAMINIO. Dimmelo in una parola.   45

LECCARDO. Non si può; perché è cosa troppo lunga,
né si può esprimere in una parola; e la stanchezza m'ha
tolto il vigor del parlare.

DON FLAMINIO. Mentre hai detto questo, aresti detto
la metà.   50

LECCARDO. La vostra Ca . . . Cari . . . Carizia . . .[1]

DON FLAMINIO. La mia Carizia . . . , oh buon principio; spediscela, di grazia.

LECCARDO. . . . sarà vo . . . vostra.

DON FLAMINIO. Leccardo mio, parla presto, non mi   55
far così morire; come sarà mia?

LECCARDO. Manda a tor diece caraffe di vino per inu-
midir il palato e la gola, che stanno così secchi che non
ne può uscir la parola.

DON FLAMINIO. Arai quanto vorrai, e 20 e 30. Ma parla   60
presto.

DON FLAMINIO. I don't know it, I tell you.

LECCARDO. You deny it or pretend to, as a joke on me.

DON FLAMINIO. An important thing is no joking matter.

LECCARDO. Well, I think you're joking with me.

DON FLAMINIO. I've taken this joke with pleasure so far, but now it bores me.

LECCARDO. I'll leave off joking and tell you truly.

DON FLAMINIO. Then tell, in God's name, and don't keep me any longer in suspense: speak.

LECCARDO. I've run so hard that I can't speak: I've lost my breath.

DON FLAMINIO. Then find it again; otherwise you'll make me lose mine for good.

LECCARDO. I'm so worn out I think I'm dying.

DON FLAMINIO. Give me your news first and then die when you please.

LECCARDO. The more I want to speak, the less I can.

DON FLAMINIO. Tell me in a word.

LECCARDO. That can't be, because it's too long and can't be said in a word, and fatigue has robbed me of strength to speak.

DON FLAMINIO. In the time it took to say this much, you could have told me half of it.

LECCARDO. Your Ca . . . Cari . . . Carizia . . .

DON FLAMINIO. My Carizia. . . . A good beginning! Hurry up, for pity's sake.

LECCARDO. . . . will be you . . . yours.

DON FLAMINIO. Leccardo, friend, speak quickly, don't kill me like this. How will she be mine?

LECCARDO. Send for ten carafes of wine to moisten my palate and throat, which are so dry that the words can't come out.

DON FLAMINIO. You shall have as many as you like, twenty, thirty. But speak quickly.

LECCARDO. La vostra Carizia è maritata.

DON FLAMINIO. Maritata? Tu sia il mal venuto con questa nuova; e questa è l'allegrezza che mi portavi?

LECCARDO. Io non penso che possa esser migliore. 65

DON FLAMINIO. E dove la fondi?

LECCARDO. Non mi avete voi detto che non la desiate per moglie? Come il marito scassa la porta la prima volta, ella resta aperta per sempre; e ben sapete che le donne la custodiscono insino a quel ponto, poi ci ponno passar 70 quanti vogliono, ché non si conosce, né vi si fa danno: ecco, la goderete, ed io non sarò il mal venuto.

DON FLAMINIO. Veder la mia Carizia in poter d'altri per un sol ponto, ancor che fusse per certo possederla per sempre, non mi comportarebbe l'animo di soffrirlo; 75 e con chi è maritata?

LECCARDO. Bisogna che cominci da capo.

DON FLAMINIO. O da capo, o da piedi, pur che la spedischi tosto.

LECCARDO. Entrando in casa viddi che si facea un 80 grande apparecchio d'un banchetto, e tutto ciò con real magnificenza. Io adocchiai certe testoline di capretto, le rubai e me le mangiai in un tratto; or mi gridano in corpo «be, be», ascoltate; e le vorrei castigare.

DON FLAMINIO. Tu castighi or me, ché i tuoi tratteni- 85 menti mi son lanciate nel cuore.

LECCARDO. Ivi eran mandre di vitelle, some di capponi impastati, monti di cacio parmigiano, il vino: uh, a diluvio!

DON FLAMINIO. Vorrei saper con chi è maritata. 90

LECCARDO. Bisogna vi si dica il tutto per ordine; lascio i pastoni, i pasticci, i galli d'India, . . .

DON FLAMINIO. . . . piccioni e simili, basta, sù.

LECCARDO. Non vi erano piccioni altrimenti.

LECCARDO. Your Carizia is promised in marriage.

DON FLAMINIO. Promised in marriage? Curse you for this news! And this is the joy you were bringing me?

LECCARDO. I don't think it could be better.

DON FLAMINIO. And what do you base that on?

LECCARDO. Haven't you told me that you don't want her for your wife? When a husband has broken down the door the first time, it remains open forever; well you know that women guard it up to that point, then they let pass as many as will, for nobody knows and it does no harm. So there, you'll enjoy her and I'll not be cursed.

DON FLAMINIO. To see my Carizia in the power of another for a single moment, even were I sure to possess her forever—my spirit could not bear it. And whom is she to marry?

LECCARDO. I must begin from the beginning.

DON FLAMINIO. Begin where you will, as long as you hurry it up.

LECCARDO. When I entered the house I saw that a great banquet was in preparation, and all with royal magnificence. I cast an eye on some little goats' heads, stole and gobbled them up in a wink; now they are bleating in my belly "be, be," you hear? And I'd like to purge me of them.

DON FLAMINIO. As it is, you're punishing me, for your longwinded fooleries are spear thrusts to my heart.

LECCARDO. There were herds of veal, loads of capons in pastry, mountains of parmesan cheese, the wine— oh, in a flood!

DON FLAMINIO. I wish to know whom she is to marry.

LECCARDO. I must tell you everything in order. I pass over the pasties, the pies, the turkeys, . . .

DON FLAMINIO. . . . pigeons and the like—enough of that, go on.

LECCARDO. No, there were absolutely no pigeons.

141

DON FLAMINIO. O che vi fussero, o che non vi fussero, 95
poco importa.

LECCARDO. Dico che non vi erano, e dicean che son
caldi per natura, e che arebbono fatto male al fegato.

DON FLAMINIO. Vorrei che ragionassi del fatto mio.

LECCARDO. E del fatto vostro si ragiona; a voi tocca, 100
ché si vi fusser stati piccioni, non arei mangiato teste di
capretti.

DON FLAMINIO. O Dio, che sorte di crucifiggere è
questo; lassa le baie; di' quel ch'importa.

LECCARDO. Non è cosa che più importi ad un banchet- 105
to che non vi manchi cosa alcuna, anzi abbondantissimo
di robbe, ben apparecchiate, e condite, e poste a tempo e
con ordine a tavola.

DON FLAMINIO. Tu ti trattieni in questo, ed io sudo
sudor di morte. 110

LECCARDO. Eccovi il mantello, fatevi vento, rinfre-
scatevi.

DON FLAMINIO. Sarà ancor finito tanto apparecchio?

LECCARDO. Non è finito ancora.

DON FLAMINIO. Almen s'è detto assai; torniamo a noi. 115

LECCARDO. Quando io viddi i cuochi occupati in partire e distribuire le robbe, fingendo aiutarli mi trametto,
e ne trabalzo le teste di capretti, . . .

DON FLAMINIO. Or sù te le mangiasti, l'hai detto
prima. 120

LECCARDO. Come dunque volea mangiarmele crude?
bisognava che fussero prima cotte; se volete indovinar,
indovinate a voi stesso quanto desiate saper da me.

DON FLAMINIO. Il malanno che Dio dia a te, ed alle tue
chiacchiare! 125

DON FLAMINIO. Whether there were or not is of little importance.

LECCARDO. I tell you there were none, and it's usually said that they are too hot by nature and would be bad for the liver.

DON FLAMINIO. I wish you would speak of my business.

LECCARDO. It is your business I speak of: it concerns you, for if there had been pigeons, I wouldn't have eaten kids' heads.

DON FLAMINIO. God almighty, what a crucifixion this is! Stop clowning; come to the matter.

LECCARDO. Nothing matters more at a banquet than for there to be no lack of anything but, rather, an abundance of good things well-prepared and well-seasoned and served up at the right time and in the right order.

DON FLAMINIO. You amuse yourself with this and I sweat the sweat of death.

LECCARDO. Here is your cloak: fan yourself with it, cool yourself off.

DON FLAMINIO. Is all this preparation of the banquet finished yet?

LECCARDO. Not yet.

DON FLAMINIO. Well, enough has been said about it; let us return to our matter.

LECCARDO. When I saw the cooks busy portioning and distributing the food, pretending to aid them I slipped in and whisked away the kids' heads, . . .

DON FLAMINIO. All right, you ate them up, you said so before.

LECCARDO. What, you think perhaps I wanted to eat them raw? First they had to be cooked. If you want to be a guesser, then guess by yourself what you want to know from me.

DON FLAMINIO. God's pox on you and your chattering!

143

LECCARDO. Se non lasciate parlar a me prima, come volete che parli io?

DON FLAMINIO. Parla in tua mal ora, e finiscila presto!

LECCARDO. Se non mi lasciate parlare non finirò mai.

DON FLAMINIO. Sto per accommodarmi la cappa 130 sotto, e sedermi in terra, per ascoltare con maggior agio.

LECCARDO. Tacete mentre parlo.

DON FLAMINIO. Comincia presto, che fai? Sto attaccato alla corda, no' senti' mai in mia vita la maggior 135 pena.

LECCARDO. Voi state mal contento, e se non vi vedo allegro, non posso parlare.

DON FLAMINIO. Che cagion ho io di star allegro?

LECCARDO. Donque taccio, poi che non ascoltate con 140 allegrezza.

DON FLAMINIO. Se non con allegrezza, al meno con pacienza; di' sù.

LECCARDO. Io mi accorgo che bugliva una gran caldaia d'acqua per ispiumar i pollami e spelar gli animali; 145 fingendo stuzzicar il fuoco, vi butto dentro le testoline, . . .

DON FLAMINIO. Or lasciamo dentro la caldaia il ragionamento di ciò; cotte che furo te le mangiasti, buon pro ti faccia, finimola presto. 150

LECCARDO. Venne un altro cuoco, e s'accorge ch'ave buttato le testoline dentro la caldaia, . . .

DON FLAMINIO. Ohimè, ci è gionta un'altra persona, e se il parlar di uno era così lungo, or che vi è gionta un'altra persona, sarà altro tanto. 155

LECCARDO. Oh, oh, che m'era smenticato il meglio; prima che venisse quel cuoco . . .

DON FLAMINIO. Quando pensava che fusse alla metà dell'istoria, ci avevi lasciato il principio, ed or al principio bisogna dar un altro principio. 160

LECCARDO. Se non volete ascoltar, io taccio.

LECCARDO. If you don't let me talk to begin with, how do you expect me to say anything?

DON FLAMINIO. Speak or be damned, and quickly!

LECCARDO. If you don't let me speak, I'll never finish.

DON FLAMINIO. I'm going to spread my cape under me and sit down on the ground, so as to listen with greater ease.

LECCARDO. Hush while I speak.

DON FLAMINIO. Begin quickly, what are you waiting for? I'm on the rack, I never felt worse pain in my life.

LECCARDO. You're displeased, and if I don't see you happy I can't speak.

DON FLAMINIO. What reason have I to be happy?

LECCARDO. If you won't listen happily, then I won't say a word.

DON FLAMINIO. If not happily, at least patiently: go on, speak.

LECCARDO. I noticed a large cauldron of water boiling for taking the feathers off the fowls and the hair off the beasts; pretending to stir up the fire, I threw the kids' heads into it, . . .

DON FLAMINIO. Now let's leave the account of all that in the cauldron. When they were cooked you ate them, good health to you; let us finish it quickly.

LECCARDO. Along came another cook and noticed that I had thrown the heads into the cauldron, . . .

DON FLAMINIO. Oh Lord, another character enters the tale; and if the talk about the one was this long, with the addition of another there will be that much more again.

LECCARDO. Oh oh, I forgot the best part! Before that cook came along . . .

DON FLAMINIO. When I thought you were in the middle of the story, it seems you had left out the beginning, and now at the beginning you have to go and put another beginning.

LECCARDO. If you don't want to listen, I'll keep quiet.

DON FLAMINIO. Eh, parla col diavolo!

LECCARDO. Non parlo col diavolo io.

DON FLAMINIO. E tu parla con Dio.

LECCARDO. Or questo sì, *Innomine Domini*. 165

DON FLAMINIO. *Amen.*

LECCARDO. Voi dite «*amen*» come fosse al fine, e non sete ancora al principio.

DON FLAMINIO. Spediscimi per amor di Dio!

LECCARDO. Sei bello e spedito. Carizia è maritata con 170 un parente del Viceré della provincia.

DON FLAMINIO. Se tu dici da senno, m'uccidi, se da burla, dove ci va la vita mi ferisci troppo acerbamente. Sai tu il nome del marito?

LECCARDO. Sì, bene; ma non me ne ricordo, perché 175 era troppo intricato.

DON FLAMINIO. Ricordati bene.

LECCARDO. Spitazi . . . Pignatazio; il nome s'assomigliava al spedo, o pignato, e però me ne ricordo.

DON FLAMINIO. Fosse Don Ignazio? 180

LECCARDO. Sì sì, Don Ignazio, Spedazio.

DON FLAMINIO. M'hai ucciso, m'hai morto, le tue parole mi sono spiedi e spade che m'hanno mortalmente trafitto il cuore. Or sì che m'hai portato la morte nella lingua. 185

LECCARDO. Dubito averla portata a me stesso, ché per la mala novella, non serò più medicato come oggi.

DON FLAMINIO. Da questo principio posso indovinar la mia sciagura; più dolente uomo di me non vive sopra la terra! 190

LECCARDO. Al fin il mal bisogna sapersi, ché si possa rimediar a tempo, e dicevano che le nozze si facevano domani all'alba.

DON FLAMINIO. Tanto men spazio di tempo è dato alla mia vita. Una tempesta di pungenti pensieri m'ha ferito 195 il core, una nuovola di malinconia m'ha circondato l'a-

DON FLAMINIO. Oh, for the devil's sake, speak!

LECCARDO. I don't speak for the devil, not I.

DON FLAMINIO. Well, then in God's name, speak.

LECCARDO. Now that I will, yes, *in nomine Domini.*

DON FLAMINIO. *Amen.*

LECCARDO. You say "*amen*" as if it were the end, and you aren't even at the beginning yet.

DON FLAMINIO. Dispatch me from this misery, for the love of God!

LECCARDO. It's done, you're dispatched. Carizia is to marry a relative of the viceroy of the province.

DON FLAMINIO. If you mean what you say, you kill me; if you jest, you deal me a mortal wound. Do you know the name of her husband-to-be?

LECCARDO. Yes, quite well; but I don't remember it, because it was too complicated.

DON FLAMINIO. Try hard to remember.

LECCARDO. Spitazio, Potazio: the name was like a spit or a pot, and that's how it sticks in my mind.

DON FLAMINIO. Might it be Don Ignazio?

LECCARDO. Yes, yes, Don Ignazio, Spitazio.

DON FLAMINIO. You've killed me, slain me, your words are spits and swords which have fatally pierced my heart. Now truly you have dealt me death with your tongue.

LECCARDO. I fear I've dealt it to myself, for in return for the bad news I'll get no more of that medication I had today.

DON FLAMINIO. From this beginning I can guess my ill fortune; no more woeful man than I lives on earth!

LECCARDO. But after all, evil must be known if it is to be remedied in time, and they say that the wedding will take place tomorrow at dawn.

DON FLAMINIO. Just so little time is left me to live. A tempest of stinging cares has wounded my heart, a cloud of melancholy has surrounded my soul, already

147

nima, già la gelosia ha preso possesso del mio core. Non posso fingermi più ragioni contro me stesso per trasviarla. Ahi, che da quel giorno maledetto che la viddi, ho portato sempre questo sospetto attraversato nell'alma; e come il condennato a morte, ogni romor che sente, ogni uscio che s'apre, gli par il boia che venghi, e gli adatti il capestro al collo, così ogni parola, ogni motivo di mio fratello, mi parea che mi la togliesse! Ahi, che mai l'ho desiata come adesso; ché mai si conosce il bene se non quando si perde! Io non basto né posso vivere; se non m'ucciderà il dolore, m'ucciderò con le mie mani. 200 205

PANIMBOLO. Padrone, voi sete ben avezzo a i casi de l'una, e l'altra fortuna; reggetevi con maturo consiglio, bisogna dar fine all'ostinazione, e nelle cose impossibili far buon cuore ed abbandonar l'impresa, e prender una risoluzione tanto onorata quanto necessaria. 210

DON FLAMINIO. Panimbolo, se sei così di vile animo, non avilir e spaventar l'animo mio; se pensi rimovermi da sì bella impresa, ammazzami prima. Io non vo' andar incontro alla fortuna, né restar così vinto alla prima battaglia, né lasciar cosa intentata fin alla morte. 215

PANIMBOLO. Orsù, facciasi tutto il possibile, ch'avendo a morire, quando s'è fatto quanto umanamente può farsi, si muor più contento. Andiamo in palazzo, informiamoci del fatto. Leccardo, trattienti da qua intorno, ch'avendo bisogno di te, non abbiamo a cercarti. Va', e vieni. 220

LECCARDO. Andrò, e verrò. 225

jealousy has taken possession of my heart. I can no longer invent arguments to turn it aside. Alas, from that cursed day when I saw her, I have borne this suspicion athwart my soul; and as to one condemned each noise he hears, each door that opens, seems to be the hangman come to adjust the noose to his neck, so to me every word, every motion of my brother seemed a sign that he would take her from me! Alas, I have never desired her as I do now; for "one knows not the good except it be lost!" I cannot, may not live; if sorrow does not kill me, my own hands shall.

PANIMBOLO. Master, you are used to the chances of both kinds of fortune. Bear up philosophically, you must end this obstinacy, and when things are impossible, take heart, abandon the enterprise, and assume a fortitude as honorable as it is necessary.

DON FLAMINIO. Panimbolo, if your spirit is thus base, don't abuse and affright mine; if you think to turn me from so fine an enterprise, kill me first. I don't intend to welcome ill fortune, nor to let the first battle defeat me, nor to leave anything unattempted, even to death.

PANIMBOLO. On then, let's do the utmost, for, having to die, one dies happier if everything humanly possible has been tried. Let's go to the palace and learn the facts of the case. Leccardo, stay nearby, so that if we should need you we won't have to search for you. Go and come.

LECCARDO. I'll go and I'll come.

ATTO III

SCENA I

DON FLAMINIO, PANIMBOLO.

DON FLAMINIO. Battuto da così crudel tempesta di contraria fortuna, la qual mi spinge addoso onde sopra onde, l'anima mia stordita dalla paura ondeggia in una gran tempesta, e sta turbata di sorte che non credo viva al mondo oggi uomo che sia aggirato da varii pensieri 5 come io: temo di molte cose e fra tanto timore non so in che risolvermi; una sola forza nascosa mi toglie ogni espedito consiglio; temo il genio del mio fratello, che sempre suol dominarmi; e se bene son abbandonato dalla fortuna, non abbandonarmi ancor tu; fa' che se 10 non posso vincere, almen non resti vinto da lui. Tu sei il mio timone, e la mia stella; gli occhi miei non mirano se non in te solo; non patir che facci naufragio.

PANIMBOLO. Questa tempesta che minaccia naufragio, questa istessa vi condurrà in porto. 15

DON FLAMINIO. Non posso soffrir che mio fratello abbi saputo far meglio di me.

PANIMBOLO. S'egli ha saputo fare, voi saperete disfare.

DON FLAMINIO. Io molte volte dalli tuoi astuti inganni 20 d'invecchiata prudenzia ho conseguito molti disegni, de' quali t'ho grande obligo.

PANIMBOLO. Io non ho mai fatto cosa in vostro servigio che non avesse avuto desio di farne altro tanto.

DON FLAMINIO. Io ho voluto rammemorargli e ringra- 25 ziarti, acciò conoschi con che memoria gli serbo, e che voglia ho di remeritargli; fa' conto che se per te schivo questa ruina che mi sta sopra, da te ricevo la sposa, la vita, e l'onore insieme, ché perdendo lei perderò il tutto

ACT III

SCENE I

Don Flaminio, Panimbolo.

DON FLAMINIO. Battered by so cruel a tempest of contrary fortune which looses wave upon wave against me, my soul, stunned by fear, is tossed in a terrible storm and so travailed that I think there can be no man alive more besieged on all sides by conflicting cares. I fear many things and in such fear I cannot resolve to act. A hidden force, one alone, robs me of any ready counsel and decision: fear of my brother's spirit, which always dominates me. Although I am abandoned by fortune, Panimbolo, do not you abandon me too; arrange it so that if I cannot win, I may at least not be defeated by him. You are my rudder and my star; my eyes look only to you; do not let me be shipwrecked.

PANIMBOLO. This tempest that threatens shipwreck, this is the very thing that will guide you into port.

DON FLAMINIO. I cannot bear that my brother should have done better than I.

PANIMBOLO. If he has done, you will undo.

DON FLAMINIO. I have often accomplished my ends through your clever deceits, hatched by mature prudence, for which I am greatly obliged to you.

PANIMBOLO. Whatever I have done in your service, I have always wished could be twice as much.

DON FLAMINIO. I bring them to mind and thank you so that you may know how I remember and intend to match them with rewards. Consider that if by your means I avoid this ruin which is upon me, I receive from you my bride, my life and my honor together, for los-

miseramente: renderai me stesso a me stesso, e mi torrai 30
dalle mani della morte: se sei stato mio servidore, d'oggi
innanzi sarai mio fratello, e dal guiderdone che riceverai
da me, conoscerai che so conoscere e guiderdonare i servigi.

PANIMBOLO. Padron caro, allor sarò conosciuto e gui- 35
derdonato da voi quando conoscerete quanto i vostri
servigi mi sieno a caro.

DON FLAMINIO. Il fatto è passato molto innanzi, le
nozze son vicine, il tempo breve, i rimedi scarsi; temo
dell'impossibile. 40

PANIMBOLO. Non può l'uomo oprar bene, il quale si
avvilisce nell'impossibile. Quando non ci valerà ragione, bontà e giustizia, poneremo mano agl'inganni e fur-
fanterie, ché queste vincono e superano tutte le cose,
e poi che egli cerca con inganni torvi l'amata, sarà bene 45
che con i medesmi inganni gli respondiamo, e facciamo
cader inganno sopra l'ingannatore. E che val l'uomo che
non sa far bene e male? ben a' buoni, e mal a' cattivi? Or
mentre ho lingua ed ingegno state sicuro.

DON FLAMINIO. Comincio a respirare. 50

PANIMBOLO. Ma mentre parlo, rivocate voi stesso in
voi stesso.

DON FLAMINIO. O dolor, o rabbia che tu sei, fa' tanta
tregua con me fin che ordisca qualche garbuglio, e poi
tormentami ed uccidimi come a te piace. 55
Ma dimmi, hai pensato alcuna cosa?

PANIMBOLO. Cose belle a dire, e grate all'orecchie, ma
non riuscibili; e nelle riuscibili non vorrei valermi di
mezi così pericolosi.

DON FLAMINIO. Mai si vinse periglio senza periglio. 60
Ma perché corremo per perduti e per me è morta ogni
speranza, e non spero se non nella disperazione, prima
che muoia vo' tentar ogni cosa per difficile e perigliosa

ing her, I shall wretchedly lose all: you will return me to myself and wrest me from the hands of death. If till now you have been my servant, from today you shall be my brother, and the reward you receive from me will show you that I know how to recognize and reward services.

PANIMBOLO. Dear master, it will be enough recognition and reward for me that you realize how dear it is to me to serve you.

DON FLAMINIO. The matter has gone very far forward, the wedding is nigh at hand, the time short, the remedies hard to find: I fear the case is impossible.

PANIMBOLO. He who is dismayed by the impossible can accomplish nothing. If reason, goodness and justice are useless, we shall turn our hand to deceits and knavery, for these defeat and triumph over all things; since with tricks he aims to deprive you of your beloved, we may well answer him with the same tricks and turn the tricks against the tricker. What's a man worth if he cannot do both good and ill: good to the good and ill to the evil? While I yet have tongue and wit, count on me and have no fear.

DON FLAMINIO. I begin to breathe freely.

PANIMBOLO. But while I speak, call yourself back to yourself.

DON FLAMINIO. Oh pain, or rage, whichever passion you are, make a truce with me long enough to plot some intrigue, and then torment and kill me as you please!

But say, have you thought of anything?

PANIMBOLO. Things fine to speak of and welcome to hear, but not feasible; or things feasible requiring means more dangerous than I would wish to use.

DON FLAMINIO. Danger was never overcome without danger. But because we play a desperate game and all hope is dead for me and I have no hope but in my very hopelessness, before dying I want to try every means,

153

che sia, e morendo, io vo' che tutto il mondo perisca
meco. Ma tu imagina qualche cosa, fa' che veggia i fiori 65
della mia felicitade.

PANIMBOLO. Farò come il fico, che prima ti darà i
frutti, che ti mostri i fiori.

DON FLAMINIO. Presto: come la guadagnaremo?

PANIMBOLO. Ancora non avemo cominciato ad or- 70
dire, e volete la tela tessuta, né qui bisogna tanta fretta,
ché la fretta è ruina de' negozii, e le subbite resoluzioni
son madri de' lunghi pentimenti. Sappiate che non è più
facil cosa che guastar un matrimonio prima che sia contratto: uno solo sospetto scompiglia il tutto. Diremo 75
che molto tempo prima, voi ci avete fatto l'amore, e
godutala.

DON FLAMINIO. La sua fama ci è contraria, perché è
tenuta la più onesta ed onorata giovane che sia in Salerno.   80

PANIMBOLO. Un poco di vero mescolato con la bugia
fa creder tutta la bugia: aggiungeremo che la povertà sia
stata cagione della sua disonestà.

DON FLAMINIO. Non lo crederà mio fratello, ancorché
lo vedesse con gli occhi suoi.   85

PANIMBOLO. E bisognando, faremo che lo veggia: come fargli veder di notte che alcuno entri in casa sua,
mostrargli veste sue, gioie che portò quel giorno della
festa, o de' doni proprii mandati, e per mezzo della notte
agevolmente si può far veder una cosa per un'altra.   90

DON FLAMINIO. E ciò come farassi?

PANIMBOLO. Il parasito potrà aiutarvi, che è portinaio
della casa, in farvi entrar ed uscire, e prestarvi alcune
delle sue robbe.

DON FLAMINIO. Intendo ch'il padre, se ben per altro 95
riguardevole, è molto iracondo e tenace del suo onore e
buona riputazione; ci ponemo in pericolo d'un irrepara-
bil danno, e ne ponno accader molti disordini.

however difficult or dangerous; and dying, I want the whole world to die with me. But think of something: let me see the flowering of my felicity.

PANIMBOLO. I shall do as the fig tree, that gives you fruits before it shows you flowers.

DON FLAMINIO. Quickly: how are we to win her?

PANIMBOLO. We've not yet begun the design, and you want the cloth woven; nor is so much hurry needed here, for haste makes waste and what's quickly done is long repented. You know there's nothing easier than to spoil a match before the wedding: a single suspicion undoes all. We'll say that long ago you made love to her and enjoyed her favors.

DON FLAMINIO. Her reputation denies it, for she is held to be the chastest and most honorable young lady in Salerno.

PANIMBOLO. A little truth mixed with the lie makes the whole lie believed: we'll add that poverty was the reason for her wantonness.

DON FLAMINIO. My brother wouldn't believe it even if he saw it with his own eyes.

PANIMBOLO. Well, if necessary, we'll arrange for him to see it: make it appear as if someone entered her house at night, show him her clothes, jewels she wore the day of the festival or some of his own gifts to her, and by means of the night one thing can easily be made to seem another.

DON FLAMINIO. And how shall this be done?

PANIMBOLO. The parasite can help us, for he is doorkeeper of the house, in letting you in and out and lending you some of her garments.

DON FLAMINIO. I understand that her father, although estimable in other respects, is very irate and intransigent concerning his honor and good name; we risk doing irreparable damage, and great turmoil may result.

PANIMBOLO. A questi disordini rimediaremo con molti ordini; come vostro fratello rifiuterà la sposa, vi 100 appresentarete col prete e la sposarete.

DON FLAMINIO. Carizia or ama Don Ignazio, che l'ha legitimamente chiesta per isposa e complito con molti presenti; come s'accorgerà che per il nostri poco fedeli uffici riceverà questa macchia nel suo onore, non m'ac- 105 cetterà per isposo.

PANIMBOLO. Gli animi delle donne sono volubili: con nuovi benefici cancellaremo la vecchia ingiuria.

DON FLAMINIO. L'atto è pieno di speranza e di paura; non so a qual appigliarmi, perché essendomi forzato 110 mentre son vissuto di non macchiar la mia vita con al- cuna poco men che onesta azione, or facendo un così gran tradimento, con che faccia comparirò più mai fra cavalieri onorati? mio fratello arderà di sdegno contro di me, e ci uccideremo insieme. 115

PANIMBOLO. Noi lo battezaremo più tosto un genero- so inganno, che vituperoso tradimento. Ad un amante è lecito usar ogni atto indegno di cavaliero contro qual si voglia, pur che rivale, per acquistarsi la donna amata, e negli amori non si ha rispetto né ad amicizia né a stret- 120 tezza di sangue, ed ogni inganno e tradimento per vin- cere è riputato ingegno, e grande onore. Non si pren- dono molte città e castelli per tradimenti, e pur non «tradimenti» ma «stratagemmi militari» si chiamano, e quando si combatte per vincere, non si fa mostra per 125 ferir nell'occhio, e si percuote nel cuore? Voi per diverse vie aspirate alle nozze di Carizia: ella è posta nel mezo a chi per valore o per ingegno la sa guadagnare. Or di- temi, non ha egli usato a voi tradimento? mentre ocultá- mente trattava averla per isposa, vi facea trattar matri- 130 monio con la figlia del Conte; egli cerca ingannar voi; serà ben che inganniate lui. Poi fatto il sponsalizio, acciò che si vergogni, gli improverarete che, non trattando

PANIMBOLO. We'll remedy such turmoil with much concord. When your brother rejects his bride, you will appear with the priest in hand and marry her yourself.

DON FLAMINIO. Carizia now loves Don Ignazio, who has lawfully asked for her in marriage and sealed it with many gifts; when she realizes that through our treacherous offices her honor will receive this blemish, she won't accept me as her husband.

PANIMBOLO. Woman's resolution is mutable: with new benefactions we shall cancel out the old injury.

DON FLAMINIO. The act is charged with hope and fear; I do not know which to heed, for having all my days strictly avoided sullying my life with any less than honorable action, now perpetrating such a great treachery, how can I ever again show my face among men of honor? My brother will burn with anger against me and we shall end by killing each other.

PANIMBOLO. We'll christen it a generous deceit rather than a shameful betrayal. A lover is permitted to perform any unchivalrous act against anyone at all, provided that he is a rival, in order to win the woman he loves; and in love affairs neither friendship nor close kinship of blood is respected, and every deceit and betrayal used to win is deemed cleverness and great honor. Are not many cities and castles taken by treachery? And yet it is not called "treachery" but "military strategy." When one fights to win, doesn't one feint to the eye and strike to the heart instead? You two aspire by different ways to a wedding with Carizia. She is placed midway between you for the one who by valor or by wit knows how to win her. Now tell me, hasn't he used treachery toward you? While he secretly courted her for his bride, he caused you to arrange a marriage with the count's daughter. He seeks to deceive you; it's right that you should deceive him. Once the marriage is concluded, to make him ashamed, you can reprove him,

con voi alla libera, l'avete fatto conoscere che, facendo
professione di strasavio, e d'esser vostro maestro, non è 135
buono ad imparar da voi; e poi fatto l'errore, si tra-
pongono gli uomini da bene, e frati, e preti, anzi il
vostro zio, a por accordi fra voi: ed al fin bisogna che si
cheti: ché se ben v'uccidesse, non per questo otterebbe il
suo intento. 140

DON FLAMINIO. E non riuscendo quest'apparenza di
notte, non so come andarebbe la cosa.

PANIMBOLO. Perché addur tante teme o perigli contro
voi stesso? chi molto considera non vuol fare: lontani
da' pericoli, lontani dalle lodi della sperata vittoria: né 145
valoroso né degno uomo può esser quello che schiva i
pericoli che aprono la via all'onore: temendo i pericoli si
guastano i desegni.

DON FLAMINIO. Chi non teme con ragione, incorre
spesso in disordine, e la tema fa riuscire i consigli vani. 150

PANIMBOLO. Quei che col nome di «prudenza» cuo-
prono il natural timore, non fanno mai cosa buona.
Quando mai facessimo altro, poneremo il tutto in disordine e confusione, e chi scampa un punto, ne scampa
cento. 155

DON FLAMINIO. Se ben è ardito ma pericoloso il consiglio, e da spaventare ogni gran cuore, essendo disposto o di posseder Carizia o di morire, esseguiamolo: né
vo' per una ignobil paura mancar a me stesso.

PANIMBOLO. Sete risoluto? 160

DON FLAMINIO. Risolutissimo. O come con gli occhi
del pensiero la veggio riuscir bella e netta! E mentre sto
in questo pensiero, sento un secreto spirito nel cuore,
che mi conforta, e spinge ad esseguirlo. Resta solo si
parli al parasito se vuol aiutarci. 165

PANIMBOLO. Bisogna far presto, ché Don Ignazio è
d'ingegno destro e vigilante; se non si previene con pre-

saying that as he didn't treat openly with you, you have shown him that while claiming to be wiser than wise and your teacher, he's not fit to be your student; and once the misstep is taken, the intercession of virtuous men, friars and priests and, what's more, your uncle, will make peace between you. Finally he'll have to calm down: for even by killing you he wouldn't achieve his purpose.

DON FLAMINIO. And should this nocturnal imposture fail, I don't know how things would go.

PANIMBOLO. Why bring up so many fears and dangers to dismay yourself? He who hesitates is lost; nothing ventured, nothing gained; none but the brave deserves the fair; the road to honor is beset with dangers; when dangers are feared, plans are spoiled.

DON FLAMINIO. Reckless makes rueful; he who does not fear when there is reason, often falls into confusion; fear adds prudence and lends success to empty counsels.

PANIMBOLO. Those who cover their natural timidity with the name of prudence never achieve anything. If we accomplish nothing else, we shall at least throw all into disorder and confusion; he who averts one danger averts a hundred.

DON FLAMINIO. Though this is bold but dangerous counsel, and one to appall the greatest heart, as I am ready either to possess Carizia or to die, let us act on it: nor would I for an ignoble fear be untrue to myself.

PANIMBOLO. Are you determined?

DON FLAMINIO. Utterly determined. Ah, with my mind's eye I see the plan succeeding, beautifully and precisely! And while I am of this mind, I feel a secret motion in my heart which encourages and moves me to its execution. There remains nothing but to seek the parasite's aid.

PANIMBOLO. We must make haste, for Don Ignazio is quick and alert of wit; unless we quickly forestall him,

stezza, si torrà Carizia. Chi non fa conto del tempo, perde le fatiche, e le speranze dell'effetto.

DON FLAMINIO. Or mi par ogni indugio una gran lun- 170 ghezza di tempo: s'avesse le podagre, saria venuto.

PANIMBOLO. Se menasse così i piedi nel caminare come le mani ne i piatti, o le mascelle quando mangia, che l'alza in su e giù come un ballone, sarebbe venuto prima.   175

DON FLAMINIO. Eccolo, ma con una ciera annuncia- trice di cattive novelle.

SCENA II

LECCARDO, DON FLAMINIO, PANIMBOLO.

LECCARDO. [da sé] O Dio, che disgusto darò a Don Flaminio recandoli così cattive novelle!

DON FLAMINIO. Leccardo, ben venuto!

LECCARDO. Non son Leccardo, né mai fui Leccardo, ché non mai mi toccò leccar a mio modo.   5

DON FLAMINIO. Sempre sul mangiare!

LECCARDO. Sempre su gli amori!

DON FLAMINIO. Se ti scaldasse quel fuoco che scalda me, diresti altrimenti.

LECCARDO. Io credo che l'amor delle femine scaldi; 10 ma l'amor del vino scalda più forte assai.

DON FLAMINIO. Che novelle?

LECCARDO. Dispiacevolissime; Don Ignazio, avendo trattato col padre, ave ottenuto Carizia, ha mandato presenti sontuosissimi, or s'apparecchia un banchetto di 15 rari che s'han fatti al mondo. Le principali gentildonne addobbano Carizia, e se negletta parea così bella, or che fiammeggia fra quelli ori, e quelle gioie, par di bellezza indicibile.

160

he will win Carizia. Time waits for no man, and he who ignores it loses his labor and the hopes of success.

DON FLAMINIO. Now every delay seems interminable. Where is that parasite? Even if he had the gout he should have arrived by now.

PANIMBOLO. If he moved his feet to walk as he does his hands to snatch dishes or his jaws to eat, jerking them up and down like a balloon on a string, he would have arrived before this.

DON FLAMINIO. Here he is, but with a face announcing bad news.

SCENE II

LECCARDO, DON FLAMINIO, PANIMBOLO.

LECCARDO. [apart] Oh Lord, what displeasure I'll give Don Flaminio, bearing him such bad tidings!

DON FLAMINIO. Welcome, Leccardo!

LECCARDO. I'm not Leccardo, nor ever was Leccardo, for I've never been able to lick as I'd like.

DON FLAMINIO. Always harping on eating!

LECCARDO. Always harping on love!

DON FLAMINIO. If you were warmed by that fire which warms me, you'd speak otherwise.

LECCARDO. I believe that love for women is warming, but love for wine warms much better.

DON FLAMINIO. What news?

LECCARDO. The most unpleasant. Don Ignazio, having contracted with her father, has obtained Carizia. He has sent sumptuous gifts; now they are preparing one of the rarest banquets ever seen in the world. The foremost noblewomen are adorning Carizia, and if in her neglected state she seemed beautiful, now that she blazes amidst those gold ornaments and gems, she appears indescribably so.

161

DON FLAMINIO. Non mi recar più noia con le tue pa- 20
role che mi reca la presente materia.

LECCARDO. Mi dispiace che per mia cagione non sia
vostra sposa, ché la vostra tavola mi sarebbe stata sempre apparecchiata. Or temo il contrario: ché come
vostro fratello saprà che son stato dalla vostra parte, mi 25
arà adosso un odio mortale e sarò in capo della lista di
coloro che saranno sbanditi dalla sua casa.

DON FLAMINIO. Io non son così abandonato dalla fortuna che, aiutandomi, Carizia non possa divenir mia
moglie. E se darò ad intendere a Don Ignazio che abbi 30
goduto prima di Carizia, con manifesta speranza mi
guadagnarò le sue nozze. Onde vorrei che la notte che
viene mi aprissi la porta di sua casa, e mi facessi entrare,
e mi prestassi una di quelle vesti che portò il giorno della
festa, ed alcuni doni mandati da lui.   35

LECCARDO. Cacasangue, questa è una solenne ribalda-
ria, e discoprendosi, io sarei il primo a patire la penitenza, e non vorrei ch'avendomi io vivo mangiati molti uccelli cotti in mia vita, che or le cornacchie e corbi vivi se
avessero a mangiare me morto sovra una forca.   40

DON FLAMINIO. Tu sai che mio zio è Viceré di Salerno;
scoprendosi il fatto, saprà che il tutto arai oprato per mia
cagione; non offenderà te per non offender me.

LECCARDO. No, no, la forca è fatta per i disgraziati: la
giusticia è come i ragnateli, le moschette piccole, co- 45
m'io ci incappano, e ci restano morte; i signori come voi
sono gli uccelli grandi, che la stracciano, e portan via.

DON FLAMINIO. Io sarei il più ingrato uomo del mondo
se, tu incappando per amor mio, non spendessi quan-
t'ho per liberarti.   50

LECCARDO. De' poveretti prima si fa la giustizia, poi si
forma il processo, e si dà la sentenza.

DON FLAMINIO. Non temer quello che non sarà per
avvenir mai.

LECCARDO. Anzi sempre vien quello che manco si 55
teme.

DON FLAMINIO. Do not worry me with your words any more than the present matter demands.

LECCARDO. I regret that she can't be your bride by my means, for your table would always have been laid for me. Now I fear the contrary: for when your brother knows that I was on your side, he'll hate me mortally, and I'll head the list of those banished from his house.

DON FLAMINIO. I am not so much abandoned by fortune that, with your help, Carizia may not become my wife. If I make Don Ignazio think that I enjoyed Carizia first, I'll have a clear hope of marrying her. Wherefore I wish you to open the door of her house tonight, allow me to enter, and lend me one of the garments she wore the day of the festival and some of the gifts he sent her.

LECCARDO. Bloody shit! This is a piece of arrant knavery, and were it discovered, I'd be the first to suffer the penance; and I shouldn't like, I who alive have eaten many cooked birds, to be eaten dead on a gibbet by live crows and ravens.

DON FLAMINIO. You know that my uncle is viceroy of Salerno: if the deed is discovered, he'll know that you have done all at my bidding and to avoid harming me, he won't harm you.

LECCARDO. No, no, the gibbet is made for the unfortunate. Justice is like spiderwebs: small flies like me fall into them and die; lords like you are big birds who tear and carry them off.

DON FLAMINIO. I'd be the most ungrateful man in the world were you to fall into a web for my sake and I didn't spend all I have to free you.

LECCARDO. For poor folk the rule is execution first, trial and sentence later.

DON FLAMINIO. Don't fear something that will never happen.

LECCARDO. On the contrary, the thing that happens is always the thing too little feared.

DON FLAMINIO. Dài impedimento ad un gran disegno, ché non lo possiamo metter in atto, e nel felice corso della vittoria si rompe: mi distruggi in erba ed in spicca le già concette e mature speranze. 60

LECCARDO. Voi volete che i buoni bocconi, che ho mangiato in casa vostra, mi costino come il cascio a' topi quando incappano alla trappola.

DON FLAMINIO. Dunque non vòi aiutarmi?

LECCARDO. Crederò ben di no. 65

DON FLAMINIO. Dunque non vòi?

LECCARDO. Non voglio, e non posso; pigliatevi quale volete di queste due.

DON FLAMINIO. Troppo disamorevole risposta.

LECCARDO. Troppo sfacciata proposta. 70

DON FLAMINIO. Leccardo, sai che vorrei?

LECCARDO. Che fussi appiccato!

DON FLAMINIO. Che quel c'hai a fare, lo facessi tosto, ché il giorno va via, e la sera se ne viene, e'l beneficio consiste in questo momento di occasione. Usarò teco 75 poche parole, ché la brevità del tempo non me ne concede più; mi par soverchio ricordarti le cortesie che ti ho fatte; e'l volerti far pregar con tanta instanza diminuisce l'obligo che mi tieni: vorrei che mi facessi piacere pari alla cortesia; e questo servigio sarebbe il condimento di 80 tutti gli altri.

LECCARDO. L'impresa che mi proponi è di farmi essere appiccato.

DON FLAMINIO. Fai gran danno non aiutandomi.

LECCARDO. Maggior danno fo a me aiutandovi. 85

DON FLAMINIO. Leccardo, to', prendi questi danari.

LECCARDO. Ho steso la mano.

DON FLAMINIO. Togli questo argento.

LECCARDO. L'argento mi comanda.

DON FLAMINIO. You lay obstacles in the path of an excellent plan so that we cannot carry it out and it is shattered in its happy dash to victory; you blast the seedling and the ripe grain of my fully conceived and blooming hopes.

LECCARDO. You'd have the tidbits I've eaten in your house cost me what the cheese costs the mice when they fall into the trap.

DON FLAMINIO. Then you don't want to help me?

LECCARDO. I should say not.

DON FLAMINIO. You really don't want to?

LECCARDO. I don't want to and I can't: take whichever you like better.

DON FLAMINIO. A most unloving answer.

LECCARDO. A most shameless proposal.

DON FLAMINIO. Leccardo, do you know what I wish?

LECCARDO. That I hang!

DON FLAMINIO. That you would do quickly what you have to do, for day is ending and evening approaches, and our advantage lies in this moment's opportunity. I shall use few words with you, for time is short: it seems beyond the pale to remind you of the kindnesses I have done you, but by making me beg you so urgently you make light of your obligation to me. I wish you would return a favor equal to my kindness, and this service would give the crowning flavor to all the others you have performed.

LECCARDO. The undertaking you propose to me is to get myself hanged.

DON FLAMINIO. You do great harm by not helping me.

LECCARDO. I do worse harm to myself by helping you.

DON FLAMINIO. Leccardo, here, take this money.

LECCARDO. My hand is out.

DON FLAMINIO. Take this silver.

LECCARDO. Silver commands me.

165

DON FLAMINIO. Togli quest'oro.   90

LECCARDO. L'oro mi sforza; oh come son belli e lampanti: par che buttino fuoco, fanno bel suono e bel vedere!

DON FLAMINIO. Sai che ho de gli altri, che posso sodisfare alla tua ingordigia, e tu potrai taglieggiarmi a tuo   95
modo.

LECCARDO. Vorrei tornarteli, ma non posso distaccarmegli dalle mani.

DON FLAMINIO. Non sai quella pergola di presciutti, quei salciccioni alla lombarda, quei formaggi, e prova-   100
ture, non sai le compagnie de' polli, gli esserciti di galline, quei squadroni di galli d'India, le cantine piene d'eccellentissimi vini che ho in casa? ti chiuderò ivi dentro, e non ti farò uscir se non arai divorato e digesto il tutto, sederai sempre a tavola mia con maestà cesarea, e   105
ti saranno posti innanzi piatti di maccheroni di polpe di capponi, d'un pasto l'uno, sempre bocconi da svogliati.

LECCARDO. Panimbolo, che mi consigliaresti per non esser appiccato?

PANIMBOLO. Farti tagliar il collo prima.   110

LECCARDO. Il malan che Dio ti dia!

PANIMBOLO. A te ho detto quanto bisogna far per non esser appiccato.

LECCARDO. A tutti doi voi io lo posso insegnare.

DON FLAMINIO. Che dici eh, Leccardo mio?   115

LECCARDO. Che volete che dica? tanti presenti, tante carezze, tante promesse farebbono pormi ad altro pericolo di questo. Ma lassami retirar in consiglio secreto: [da sé] Leccardo, consiglia un poco te stesso, sei in un gran passo. Dall'una parte sta la fame, e dall'altra la   120
forca; e l'una e l'altra mi spaventano, e mi minacciano. La fame uccide subbito, la forca ci vol tempo a venire; la forca è una mala cosa, mi strangolarà che non mangiarò

DON FLAMINIO. Take this gold.

LECCARDO. Gold forces me. Oh how beautiful and bright they are, they seem to flash fire, they make a beautiful sound and a beautiful sight!

DON FLAMINIO. You know that I have others, that I can satisfy your greed, and you may tax me as you wish.

LECCARDO. I'd like to return them to you but they stick to my hands.

DON FLAMINIO. You know that arbor of hanging hams, those Lombard sausages, the cheeses of every kind, you know the companies of chickens, the armies of hens, those squadrons of turkeys, the cellars full of most excellent wines that I have at home? I'll shut you up inside and not let you out until you devour and digest it all; you shall sit always at my table with imperial majesty and there will be placed before you plates of macaroni stuffed with filet of capon, each one a meal in itself, nothing but tidbits to tempt a listless appetite.

LECCARDO. Panimbolo, what would you advise me to do to avoid being hanged?

PANIMBOLO. Get your head chopped off first.

LECCARDO. God's pox on you!

PANIMBOLO. I told you how to escape hanging.

LECCARDO. I can teach it to both of you.

DON FLAMINIO. What do you say, eh, Leccardo, my friend?

LECCARDO. What do you want me to say? So many gifts, so many blandishments, so many promises would make me put myself in worse danger than this. But let me retire in secret counsel. [*apart*] Leccardo, give yourself some advice: you've come to a momentous pass. On one side stands hunger, and on the other, hanging; both of them terrify and threaten me. Hunger is killing me now, hanging takes time to come; hanging is an evil thing, it will strangle me so that I'll never eat

più mai. Alla fame darò un perpetuo bando, e mi pro-
mette dovizia di tutte le cose. Ahi infingardo e senza 125
core: i soldati per tre ducati il mese vanno a rischio di
spade, di picche, di archibuggi, e di artegliarie, ed io per
sì gran prezzo non posso contrastar con la forca? Meglio è morir una volta che sempre mal vivere. Ho passati
tanti pericoli, così passerò quest'altro; cancaro, si man- 130
giano molte nespole mature, poi un'acerba t'ingozza, e
di errore antico penitenza nuova.

DON FLAMINIO. Risoluzione, ché l'indugio è pericoloso, e'l pericolo sovrasta.

LECCARDO. Son risoluto servirvi più volentieri che 135
non sapresti commandarmi, ed avvengane quello che si
voglia. Sete mio benefatore.

DON FLAMINIO. Averti, che avendomi a fidar di te, tu
sia di fede intiera.

LECCARDO. Interissima, non mai l'ho rotta, perché 140
non mai l'adoprai.

DON FLAMINIO. In che cosa mi serverai, ed in che
modo?

LECCARDO. Del modo non posso deliberare, se non
parlo prima con Chiaretta, ch'ella tien le chiavi delle sue 145
casse; è gran tempo ch'ella cerca far l'amor con me.

DON FLAMINIO. Bisogna far l'amor con lei, e dargli sodisfazione.

LECCARDO. Più tosto m'appiccherei; mai feci l'amor
se non con porchette e vitelle; ed è il peggio, ch'è una 150
simia, e pretende esser bellissima.

DON FLAMINIO. Bisogna tor la medicina per una volta.

LECCARDO. Quando la menerò a casa fingerò por la
mano alla chiave per aprir la porta; basta, l'ingannerò di
modo che mi aiuterà.   155

DON FLAMINIO. Lodo il consiglio; mandalo in essecu-
zione.

LECCARDO. Fra poco saperete la risposta.

again. But if I take the risk, I may exile hunger permanently and he promises me abundance of everything. Ah, fainthearted sluggard! For three ducats a month soldiers risk being killed by swords, pikes, harquebuses and artillery, and for such a great price can't I brave the gallows? It's better to die once than to live badly forever. I've survived many dangers, and I'll survive this one too. But, plague take it, after eating many ripe medlars, you can choke on a green one, and old sins make new repentance.

DON FLAMINIO. Come, decide, for delay is dangerous and danger threatens.

LECCARDO. I'm resolved to serve you more willingly than you can command, and let come of it what may. You are my benefactor.

DON FLAMINIO. Be warned that, as I must trust you, your fidelity must be absolute.

LECCARDO. Absolutely intact: I've never broken my faith because I've never used it.

DON FLAMINIO. In what will you serve me and how?

LECCARDO. Just how I can't determine until I talk with Chiaretta, for she holds the keys of Carizia's coffers. For a long time she has wanted to make love with me.

DON FLAMINIO. You must make love and satisfy her.

LECCARDO. I'd hang myself first. I never made love except with suckling pigs and veals; and the worst of it is, she's an ape and yet claims to be a beauty.

DON FLAMINIO. You must swallow the medicine for once.

LECCARDO. When I lead her home, I'll pretend to reach for the . . . ah . . . key to open the . . . ah . . . door. Enough: I'll deceive her so that she'll help me.

DON FLAMINIO. I approve the idea; put it into execution.

LECCARDO. Before long you'll have the answer.

169

DON FLAMINIO. Non vo' risposta, ché non ci è tempo; gli effetti rispondino per te.   160

LECCARDO. La notte viene, non mi trattenete, ché è vostro danno: io vo con buona fortuna.

DON FLAMINIO. A rivederci.

LECCARDO. A riparlarci.

SCENA III

MARTEBELLONIO, LECCARDO.

[MARTEBELLONIO.] Non ho lasciato fornai, salicciai, macellari, osterie e piscatori[1] che non abbia cerco per trovar Leccardo, e non ho avuto ventura di ritrovarlo.

LECCARDO. [*da sé*] Ecco il ballon da vento: oh come gionge a tempo: muterò parere, e farò disegni più a   5 proposito, ché, per esser ignorantissimo, gli potrò dar ad intendere ciò che voglio.

[MARTEBELLONIO.] Certo sarà imbriacato, e ficcatosi in qualche stalla: si sarà disfidato con la paglia a chi più dorme. M'è salito capriccio in testa di Callidora e vorrei   10 sborrar fantasia.

LECCARDO. [*da sé*] O come servirò ben l'amico.

Ben venghi il bellissimo ed innamoratissimo Capitano!

[MARTEBELLONIO.] Oh Leccardo, ti son ito cercando   15 tutt'oggi.

LECCARDO. Se foste venuto dov'era, m'areste ritrovato al sicuro.

[MARTEBELLONIO.] Perché m'hai detto «bellissimo»?

LECCARDO. Perché fate morir le principalissime gen-   20 tildonne della città, e fra tutte Callidora, la mia padrona, che quando le muovo ragionamenti di voi fa atti da spiritata.

DON FLAMINIO. I don't want an answer, there's not time; the results will answer for you.

LECCARDO. Night is falling; don't keep me, it would be against your interests. Good luck is going with me.

DON FLAMINIO. Until we next meet.

LECCARDO. Until we next talk.

SCENE III

MARTEBELLONIO, LECCARDO.

MARTEBELLONIO. There isn't a baker, sausage-vendor, butcher, tavern or fishmonger I've missed in searching for Leccardo, and yet I haven't had the luck to find him.

LECCARDO. [aside] Here comes the bag of wind! Oh how opportunely he arrives! I'll change my plan and lay others more appropriate, for he's so exceedingly ignorant, I can make him think whatever I like.

MARTEBELLONIO. Doubtless he's drunk and, having poked himself into some stall or other, has challenged the straw to a sleeping match. I've a fancy for Callidora and want to indulge it.

LECCARDO. [aside] Oh, how well I'll serve my friend! Welcome, most handsome captain and passionate lover.

MARTEBELLONIO. Oh Leccardo, I've been looking for you all day.

LECCARDO. If you'd looked where I was, you'd certainly have found me.

MARTEBELLONIO. Why did you call me "most handsome"?

LECCARDO. Because you drive mad with love the foremost noblewomen of the city, and among them my mistress, Callidora, who, when I speak to her of you, behaves like one possessed.

171

[MARTEBELLONIO.] Vorrei che la finissimo una volta, ché io non facessi penar lei né ella me; vorrei che le faces- 25 si un'ambasciata da mia parte.

LECCARDO. Farò quanto m'imponete.

[MARTEBELLONIO.] Dille che non è picciol favore che un mio pari s'inchini ad amar lei, ché son amato dalle più grandi donne del mondo. 30

LECCARDO. Andrò a dirglielo.

[MARTEBELLONIO.] Ma non con certe parole umili che cagionino disprezzo, ma con un certo modo altiero che cagioni verso me onore, e riverenza.

LECCARDO. Le dirò che se non vi ama, con un soffio la 35 farete volar per aria o, con un fulgore de gli occhi vostri mirandola, l'abrusciarete.

[MARTEBELLONIO.] Dille ciò che tu vuoi, ché le cortesi parole d'un mio pari minacciano tacitamente.

LECCARDO. Ella spasima per voi. 40

[MARTEBELLONIO.] Poi che è cosi, dimmi: quando? come? non m'intendi?

LECCARDO. V'intendo bene, ma non so che dite.

[MARTEBELLONIO.] Mi porrai con lei, da solo a solo?

LECCARDO. Questa notte. 45

[MARTEBELLONIO.] Or sì che puoi comandarmi; son assai amico delle preste risoluzioni, e per tal cagione nelle guerre ho conseguito grandissime vittorie. Ma venghiamo all'ora più comoda a lei.

LECCARDO. Quando dorme la vicinanza, alle due ore, 50 la farò venir in questa casa terrena,[2] e vi sollazzarete con lei tutta la notte. Ma che segni mi darete quando venite di notte ché vi conosca?

[MARTEBELLONIO.] Quando sentirai tremar la casa, e la terra, come se fusse un terremoto, son io che camino. 55

MARTEBELLONIO. I wish we could end this once and for all, so that I wouldn't make her suffer nor she me; I wish you'd undertake an embassy to her from me.

LECCARDO. I'll do whatever you command.

MARTEBELLONIO. Tell her that it is no small condescension for one of my standing to stoop to love her, for I am loved by the greatest ladies in the world.

LECCARDO. I'll go tell her.

MARTEBELLONIO. But not with the sort of humble words which invite contempt, but with a certain haughty manner arousing respect and reverence for me.

LECCARDO. I'll tell her that if she doesn't love you, with a puff of your breath you'll make her fly through the air or, looking at her with a flash of your eyes, you'll burn her up.

MARTEBELLONIO. Tell her what you will; from such a man as I am, courteous words are silently threatening.

LECCARDO. She's panting for you.

MARTEBELLONIO. In that case, tell me: when, how? Don't you understand me?

LECCARDO. I understand you, but I don't know what you're saying.

MARTEBELLONIO. Will you put me where I can be all alone with her?

LECCARDO. Tonight.

MARTEBELLONIO. Now indeed you may command me; I'm a friend to prompt resolutions, for which cause in the wars I have achieved the greatest victories. But let us come at the hour most convenient to her.

LECCARDO. When the neighborhood is asleep, at two o'clock, I'll bring her to this groundfloor chamber and you shall sport with her all night. But what signs will you give me when you come by night so that I may recognize you?

MARTEBELLONIO. When you feel the house and the earth tremble as if in an earthquake, it is I, walking.

LECCARDO. Andrò ad ordinar con lei l'ora, che possa venir senza saputa di suo padre. Venite sicuramente.

[MARTEBELLONIO.] Andrò a cenare, e sarò qui ad un tratto.

LECCARDO. Oh com'è stata la venuta di costui a pro- 60
posito; dalla cattiva via m'ha posto nella buona; quando la fortuna vuol aiutare, trova certe vie che non le trovarebbono cento consigli. Da Chiaretta non era possibile averne alcun piacere senza venir a' ferri, dove pensandovi sudava sudor di morte; l'accoppiarò con costui 65
di modo che l'uno non s'accorgerà dell'altro, e l'altro sarà contento ed ingannato. Veggio Chiaretta che toglie i ragnateli dalla porta della casa.

SCENA IV

CHIARETTA, fantesca, LECCARDO.

CHIARETTA. Ho tanta allegrezza che Carizia la mia padrona sia maritata che pare ch'ancora io sia a parte delle sue dolcezze.

LECCARDO. Maggior dolcezza aresti, se gustassi quello che gustarà ella quando staranno abbracciati insieme. 5

CHIARETTA. E se fusse a quei piaceri, ne gusterei ancor io com'ella; che pensi che non sia di carne e d'ossa come lei; o le membra mie non siano fatte come le sue?

LECCARDO. Ci è qua uomo che ti farà gustare le medesime dolcezze. 10

CHIARETTA. Sei tu forsi quello?

LECCARDO. Così Dio m'aiuti!

CHIARETTA. Tengo per fermo che non ti aiuteria: ché tu hai più a caro un bicchier di vino che quante donne son al mondo. 15

LECCARDO. I'll go arrange with her the hour when she may come, unknown to her father. Be here without fail.

MARTEBELLONIO. I'll go sup and return presently.

[*Martebellonio departs.*]

LECCARDO. Oh how opportune was the arrival of that fellow! From the wrong road he has put me on the right one. When fortune wants to help, she finds out ways which a hundred wise counsels would never turn up. It wasn't possible to obtain any favors from Chiaretta without bringing matters to a head in bed, the mere thought of which made me break out in a deathly sweat; I'll couple her with that one in such a way that neither will know the other and both will be satisfied and deceived. I see Chiaretta sweeping cobwebs from the door of the house.

SCENE IV

CHIARETTA, serving-maid, LECCARDO.

CHIARETTA. I'm so happy my mistress Carizia is to be married that I feel as if I were sharing her delight.

LECCARDO. You'd have sweeter delight if you could enjoy what she will enjoy when they're locked in each other's arms.

CHIARETTA. If I were at those pleasures, I'd enjoy them the way she will; do you think I'm not of flesh and bone too or that my body isn't shaped like hers?

LECCARDO. There's a man here who will make you taste the same delights.

CHIARETTA. Is it you, maybe?

LECCARDO. So help me God.

CHIARETTA. I'm sure He never would, for you care more for a glass of wine than for all the women in the world.

LECCARDO. Dici il vero, ma tu sei tanto graziosa che faresti innamorar i sassi.

CHIARETTA. S'io facessi innamorar i sassi, starei sicura che farei innamorar te, ché sei peggio d'un sasso.

LECCARDO. Son risoluto esser tuo innamorato. 20

CHIARETTA. Che ti ho ciera di vitella, o di porca, che ti vòi innamorar di me?

LECCARDO. T'apponesti. Hai certi labruzzi scarlatini come un prosciutto, una bocchina uscita in fuori com'un porchetto, gli occhi lucenti come una capra, le 25 poppe grassette come una vitella, le groppe grosse e ritonde come un cappone impastato. In somma non hai cosa che non mi muova l'appetito: ebbe torto la natura non farti una capra.

CHIARETTA. E tu che vòi esser mio marito, un becco.[1] 30

LECCARDO. E quando starò abbracciato con te, mi parrà di gustare il sapor di tutti quest'animali, o mia vacca, o mio porchetto, o mia agnella, o mia capra!

CHIARETTA. Starò dunque mal appresso te, che non mi mangi. Ma arei caro darti martello.[2] 35

LECCARDO. Sei più atta a riceverlo che a darlo. Oh come par bella Carizia or che pompeggia fra quelle vesti?

CHIARETTA. Altro che tovaglia bianca ci vuol a tavola, altro che vesti ci vuole a far bella una donna; gli in- 40 namorati non amano le vesti, ma quello che sta sotto le vesti. Bisogna aver buone carni, sode, grasse e lisce come abbiamo noi fantesche che sempre fatichiamo: le gentildonne che sempre stanno a spasso l'hanno così flaccide, e molli, che paiono vessiche sgonfiate. 45

LECCARDO. Mi piace quanto dici.

CHIARETTA. E le lor faccie son tanto imbellettate che paiono maschere, e portano tal volta sul volto una bot-

LECCARDO. You speak truth, but you're so charming you'd make a stone fall in love.

CHIARETTA. If I made stones fall in love, I'd be sure to do the same to you, for you're worse than a stone.

LECCARDO. I'm determined to be your lover.

CHIARETTA. Do I look to you like veal or pork, that you're in love with me?

LECCARDO. You've hit it. You have such fetching little lips, red as prosciutto, a little pouting mouth like a suckling pig's, eyes bright as a goat's, fat little tits like a she-veal's, a rump as plump and round as a pastied capon. In short, there is nothing about you that doesn't whet my appetite; nature was wrong not to make you a nanny goat.

CHIARETTA. And you who want to be my husband, a billy goat, horns and all.

LECCARDO. And when I am entwined in your embrace, I'll seem to taste the flavor of all that livestock, oh my moo cow, oh my suckling pig, oh my ewe-lamb, oh my nanny goat!

CHIARETTA. In your company I'll be in danger of being eaten. But I'd enjoy making you suffer, hammered by love for me.

LECCARDO. You are more fit to be hammered than to hammer. Oh, Carizia must look very beautiful, eh, now that she is arrayed in those splendid robes?

CHIARETTA. It takes more than a white cloth to lay the table and more than clothes to make a woman beautiful: lovers don't love clothes, but what's under them. One needs good flesh, firm, plump, smooth, such as we serving-maids have, being always hard at work: highborn ladies who are always idle have flesh as flaccid and soft as empty bladders.

LECCARDO. I like what you say.

CHIARETTA. And their faces are so painted that they're like masks, and sometimes they carry on their coun-

tega intiera di biacche, di solimati, di litargiri, di verzini,[3] ed altre porcherie. Oibò, se le vedessi la mattina   50
quando s'alzano da letto, diresti altrimente. Ma noi mi-
sere e poverelle abbiamo carestia d'acqua per lavarci la
faccia; triste noi, se non ci aiutasse la natura.

LECCARDO. Veramente come una donna si parte da un
buon naturale e l'piglia artificiale, non può parer bel-   55
la. Ma tu m'hai fatto risentir tutto; ti vorrei cercar un
piacere.

CHIARETTA. Che piacere?

LECCARDO. Che mi presti una cosa.

CHIARETTA. Che cosa?   60

LECCARDO. Per un'ora, anzi mezza, anzi per un quarto, e te la ritorno come me la prestasti.

CHIARETTA. Dimmi, che voresti?

LECCARDO. Vorrei . . .

CHIARETTA. Che vorresti?   65

LECCARDO. Dubito non me la presterai.

CHIARETTA. Ti presterò quanto ho per un'ora, per un
quarto, per quanto tu vuoi; a me più tosto manca l'occasione che la voluntà di far piacere, e se non basta in
presto, te la dono.   70

LECCARDO. So che sei d'una naturaccia larga e liberale,
chi ciò che ti è cercato in presto, tu doni.

CHIARETTA. Su, di' presto, che vuoi?

LECCARDO. Che mi presti la . . .

CHIARETTA. La che?   75

LECCARDO. La . . . , mi vergogno di dire.

CHIARETTA. Se ti vergogni dirmelo di giorno, ed in
piazza, dimmelo all'oscuro in casa.

LECCARDO. Vorrei che mi prestassi . . . , la gonna de
Carizia.   80

tenances a whole shopful of white leads, sublimates, litharges, brazilwood dyes and other abominations. Ho, if you saw them in the morning when they get out of bed, you'd talk differently. But we unlucky girls who are poor barely have water to wash our faces; woe to us if nature didn't help us!

LECCARDO. Truly, when a woman departs from her good natural gifts and puts on artificial aids, she can't look beautiful. But you remind me, I want to ask a favor of you.

CHIARETTA. What favor?

LECCARDO. That you lend me something?

CHIARETTA. What thing?

LECCARDO. For an hour, even a half hour, even only a quarter of an hour, and I'll return it to you just as you lent it to me.

CHIARETTA. Tell me, what would you like?

LECCARDO. I should like . . .

CHIARETTA. What would you like?

LECCARDO. I'm afraid that you won't lend it to me.

CHIARETTA. I'll lend you all I have for an hour, for a quarter of an hour, for as long as you like: when it comes to granting favors, I don't lack for will, only for opportunities, and if lending isn't enough, I'll give it to you.

LECCARDO. I know you're so big-hearted and generous that when you're asked to lend something, you give it away.

CHIARETTA. Come on, out with it, what do you want?

LECCARDO. That you lend me the . . .

CHIARETTA. The what?

LECCARDO. The . . . , I'm ashamed to say.

CHIARETTA. If you're ashamed to tell me by daylight in the piazza, tell me in the dark at home.

LECCARDO. I would like you to lend me Carizia's skirt.

CHIARETTA. Il malan che Dio ti dia, non vòi altro di questo?

LECCARDO. E che pensavi, qualche cosa trista?

CHIARETTA. Che vuoi farne?

LECCARDO. Vestirla a te, ed alcuna di quelle cose che 85
l'ha mandato Don Ignazio, o di quelle che portò quel
giorno della festa, ché s'ella si vuol sposar dimani, noi ci
sposaremo questa notte. Tu sarai Carizia, io Don Ignazio.

CHIARETTA. Tu mi burli. 90

LECCARDO. Se ti burlo, facci Dio che mai gusti vino
che mi piaccia!

CHIARETTA. A questo giuramento ti credo; a che ora?

LECCARDO. Alle due, in questa casetta terrena.

CHIARETTA. Perché non in casa nostra? 95

LECCARDO. Ché facendo romore non siamo sconci.
Ne parlaremo più a lungo in casa.

CHIARETTA. Bene.

LECCARDO. Non mancarmi della tua promessa.

CHIARETTA. Né tu della tua. 100

SCENA V

DON FLAMINIO, LECCARDO, PANIMBOLO.

DON FLAMINIO. Eco il veggiamo a punto: Leccardo,
hai appontato con la fantesca?

LECCARDO. No.

DON FLAMINIO. Perché?

LECCARDO. L'aco era spuntato, ed avea la testa rotta. 5

DON FLAMINIO. Hai scherzato a bastanza; non più
scherzi.

LECCARDO. Non abbiamo fatto cosa veruna.

CHIARETTA. God's pox on you, is that all you want?

LECCARDO. And what were you expecting, some wicked thing?

CHIARETTA. What do you want it for?

LECCARDO. To dress you in, and in some of those things Don Ignazio sent her, or those which she wore the day of the festival; for if she is to be married tomorrow, we shall be married tonight. You'll be Carizia, I, Don Ignazio.

CHIARETTA. You're joking with me.

LECCARDO. If I'm joking, may God never let me taste good wine!

CHIARETTA. By this oath I believe you; at what time?

LECCARDO. Two o'clock, in this little groundfloor storehouse.

CHIARETTA. Why not at home?

LECCARDO. So that if we make noise we won't be in trouble. We'll talk more about it inside.

CHIARETTA. Very well.

LECCARDO. Don't go back on your promise.

CHIARETTA. Nor you on yours.

SCENE V

DON FLAMINIO, LECCARDO, PANIMBOLO.

DON FLAMINIO. Here's the very man. Leccardo, have you made an appointment with the maid?

LECCARDO. No.

DON FLAMINIO. Why?

LECCARDO. My needle lost its point and had a broken head.

DON FLAMINIO. You've jested enough: no more.

LECCARDO. We've accomplished nothing at all.

DON FLAMINIO. Fortuna traditora, se tu volgi le spalle una volta, non volgi più la faccia! 10

LECCARDO. Anzi la fortuna s'è incontrata con te, senza saper chi fussi, e tu senza conoscerla sei incontrato con lei.

DON FLAMINIO. Che m'apporti?

LECCARDO. Le vesti, gioie, e l'istessa Carizia; più di 15 quel che m'hai chiesto e sapresti desiderare.

DON FLAMINIO. Perché dicivi di no?

LECCARDO. Per farvi saper la nuova più saporita, ché si t'avessi detto così il tutto alla prima, non ti sarebbe piaciuta: non solo aremo da Chiaretta quanto vogliamo, 20 ma m'è venuto fra' piedi quel capitano balordo, innamorato di Callidora, il qual ci servirà molto a proposito di modo che ci si trovarà gentilmente beffato, e vostro fratello tradito.

DON FLAMINIO. Da così buona fortuna fo argumento 25 che la cosa riuscirà assai netta; conosco il Capitano: ma come si sentirà beffato da te, ti farà una furia di bravate.

LECCARDO. Ed io una furia di bastonate.

DON FLAMINIO. Leccardo mio, come arò per tuo mezo conseguito il mio bene, arai sempre la gola piena, ed or- 30 nata di catene d'oro.

LECCARDO. Purché non rieschino in qualche capestro.

DON FLAMINIO. Che resta a far, Panimbolo?

PANIMBOLO. Come il fratello vi darà la nuova, mostrate non sapere nulla. Dilli che sia disonesta. Tu, Lec- 35 cardo, tieni in piedi la prattica della fantesca, ché noi ti avisaremo di passo in passo quanto è da farsi.

LECCARDO. Raccomando alla fortuna la vostra audacia.

PANIMBOLO. Abbi cura spiar se Don Ignazio prepara 40 alcuna cosa.

DON FLAMINIO. Treacherous fortune, if once you turn your back, you never again show your face!

LECCARDO. On the contrary, fortune has encountered you without knowing who you were, and without recognizing her, you have met her.

DON FLAMINIO. What do you bring me?

LECCARDO. The clothes, the jewels, and Carizia herself: more than you asked me or would know how to wish for.

DON FLAMINIO. Why did you say not?

LECCARDO. To make you savour the news more, for if I had simply told you everything at first, it wouldn't have pleased you. Not only shall we have whatever we want from Chiaretta, but I stumbled upon that dunce of a captain who is in love with Callidora and who will serve our purpose very well, in such wise that he will find himself nicely diddled and your brother betrayed.

DON FLAMINIO. From such good fortune I deduce that the business will succeed very neatly. I know the captain: when he finds himself tricked by you, he'll treat you to a fit of blusters.

LECCARDO. And I'll show him a fit of cudgeling.

DON FLAMINIO. Leccardo my friend, when by your means I achieve my aim, your gullet will always be full inside and decorated outside with chains of gold.

LECCARDO. As long as they don't turn out to be some kind of noose.

DON FLAMINIO. What remains to be done, Panimbolo?

PANIMBOLO. When your brother tells you the news, act completely surprised. Tell him that she is unchaste. You, Leccardo, keep up your affair with the maid, and we shall instruct you as need arises what has to be done.

LECCARDO. May fortune approve your boldness.

PANIMBOLO. Take care to spy out whether Don Ignazio is planning anything.

183

SCENA VI

Don Ignazio, Simbolo, ed Avanzino.

DON IGNAZIO. Tal che noi abbiamo gentilmente bur-
lato il fratello, il quale si pensava burlar me.

SIMBOLO. Se non era il mio consiglio, ti saresti trovato
in un gran garbuglio.

AVANZINO. Padrone, datemi la mancia, ché me l'ho   5
guadagnata da vero.

DON IGNAZIO. E di che cosa?

AVANZINO. Non la dico se prima non me la prometteti.

DON IGNAZIO. Ti prometto quanto saprai tu diman-   10
darmi.

AVANZINO. Quando voi mi mandaste a casa del Conte
se vi fusse, non so che mi fe' far la via della porta della
città che va a Tricarico.

DON IGNAZIO. E ben?   15

AVANZINO. Trovai il Conte, il quale perché se gli era
sferrato il cavallo di tre piedi, s'era fermato a farlo ferra-
re, e li feci l'ambasciata da vostra parte.

DON IGNAZIO. E che ambasciata?

AVANZINO. Come vostro fratello avea concluso il ma-   20
trimonio per questa sera, e che voi non potevate aspettar
fin alla sera, che volevate passar i capitoli allora allora e
venire a casa.

DON IGNAZIO. Il Conte che disse?

AVANZINO. Se ne rallegrò molto, e cavalcato se n'andò   25
alla via di palazzo a vostro zio, e credo che adesso adesso
serà spedito il negozio.

DON IGNAZIO. Chi t'ha ordinato che gli facessi quel-
l'ambasciata?

AVANZINO. S'io vedeva che voi vi attristavate per   30
quell'indugio, io per levarvi da quella tristezza, ho pre-

SCENE VI

DON IGNAZIO, SIMBOLO, and AVANZINO.

DON IGNAZIO. So we have sweetly tricked my brother, who thought to trick me.

SIMBOLO. If it hadn't been for my advice, you'd have found yourself in an awful mess.

AVANZINO. Master, give me a reward, for I've surely earned it.

DON IGNAZIO. What for?

AVANZINO. I won't say unless you promise it to me first.

DON IGNAZIO. I promise you anything you can think to ask.

AVANZINO. When you sent me to the count's house to see if he were there, something moved me to take the street to the city gate leading to Tricarico.

DON IGNAZIO. And so?

AVANZINO. I found the count, who had stopped to have his horse shod, because it had cast three shoes, and I delivered your message to him.

DON IGNAZIO. What message?

AVANZINO. That your brother had arranged the marriage for this evening, and that you couldn't wait till evening, and that you wanted to come to sign the articles immediately and to wait on him at his house.

DON IGNAZIO. What did the count say?

AVANZINO. He was delighted, and as soon as he was mounted he headed for the palace and your uncle, and I believe that at this very moment the matter is being settled.

DON IGNAZIO. Who told you to take him that message?

AVANZINO. As I saw that you were grieving over the delay, to spare you that sadness, on your behalf I be-

gato il Conte da vostra parte ch'avesse differito l'andare
a Tricarico per quel giorno.

DON IGNAZIO. Ah traditore, assassino!

AVANZINO. In che vi ho offeso io?   35

DON IGNAZIO. Non so perché non ti spezzi la testa in
mille parti, come m'hai rovinato dal fondo, e spezzato-
mi il cuore in mille parti!

AVANZINO. Queste sono le grazie che mi rendete del
piacer che vi ho fatto?   40

DON IGNAZIO. Un simile piacere sia fatto a te dal boia,
gaglioffo!

SIMBOLO. Padrone, non bisogna irarvi contro costui.

DON IGNAZIO. Egli m'ha rovinato della vita e scom-
pigliato il negozio.   45

SIMBOLO. Per questo non deve mai il padrone trattare i
suoi fatti dinanzi a' servi, i quali quando non vi nocciono per malignità, almeno vi nocciono per ignoranza.

DON IGNAZIO. Non so che farmi, son rovinato del
tutto; m'ha posto in un garbuglio, che non so come di-   50
staccarmene: andrà il Conte al mio zio, dirà che l'ha trattato Don Flaminio, e che io ne sia contentissimo, effet-
tuarà il negozio.

SIMBOLO. Il caso è da temerne, ma i consigli de' vecchi
son tardi, e non si muovono con tanta fretta, e poi egli   55
ha desio maritarvi in Ispagna.

DON IGNAZIO. Or conosco la mia sciocchezza a lasciar-
mi persuadere da te di accettar il partito di mio fratello;
con non men infelice che ignobil consiglio tu m'hai
posto in tanti travagli.   60

SIMBOLO. Chi arebbe potuto imaginar tanta ignoranza
d'uomo, a far di sua testa quel che non gli era stato ordinato?

seeched the count to put off for the day his journey to Tricarico.

DON IGNAZIO. Ah traitor, assassin!

AVANZINO. What have I done to offend you?

DON IGNAZIO. I don't know why I don't break your head in a thousand pieces just as you've destroyed me and shattered my heart!

AVANZINO. Are these the thanks you give for the favor I've done you?

DON IGNAZIO. May the hangman do a like favor to you, worthless wretch!

SIMBOLO. Master, there's no call to be angry with the fellow.

DON IGNAZIO. He has ruined my life and wrecked my plan.

SIMBOLO. This is why masters should never discuss their affairs before servants, who, if they don't harm you out of malice, at the least hinder you through ignorance.

DON IGNAZIO. I don't know what to do, I'm utterly ruined; he has got me into a mess that I don't know how to get myself out of: the count will go to my uncle, say that Don Flaminio has arranged it and that I am delighted, and conclude the business.

SIMBOLO. That is to be feared, but the consultations of old men are slow, they don't move with such haste and, besides, your uncle wants to arrange a marriage for you in Spain.

DON IGNAZIO. Now I realize my foolishness in letting you persuade me to accept the match my brother made; with advice no less unfortunate than ignoble you have thrust me into all these troubles.

SIMBOLO. Who would have imagined that any man could be so stupid as to do on his own what he hadn't been ordered to do?

DON IGNAZIO. Fa' che mai tu comparischi ove io mi sia; se non, che farò pentirtene. 65

AVANZINO. Questi sono i premi d'aver dieci anni fidelmente servito, esser cacciato di casa!

SIMBOLO. Taci e non parlar più in collera; ecco vostro fratello.

DON IGNAZIO. Don Flaminio, son andato gran pezzo 70 ricercandovi: voi siate il ben venuto!

SCENA VII

DON FLAMINIO, PANIMBOLO, DON IGNAZIO, e SIMBOLO.

DON FLAMINIO. E voi ben trovato; che buona nuova, poi che mostrate tant'allegrezza nel volto?

PANIMBOLO. [da sé] O quanto il cuore è differente dal volto!

DON FLAMINIO. Che cosa avete degna di tanta fretta e 5 di tanta fatica?

DON IGNAZIO. Per farvi partecipe d'una mia allegrezza, ché so che ve ne ralegrarete come me ne ralegro io, amandoci così reciprocamente come ci amiamo.

PANIMBOLO. [da sé] Mentite per la gola ambo doi! 10

DON FLAMINIO. Rallegratemi presto, di grazia.

DON IGNAZIO. Perché, partito che fui da voi, andai in casa del Conte, e mi dissero ch'era andato a Tricarico, e che trattava con altri dar la sua figlia, io mi ho tolto un'altra per moglie, secondo il mio contento. 15

DON FLAMINIO. Non credo sia maggior contento nella vita che aver moglie a suo gusto e suo intento. Quella signora d'Ispagna che trattava Don Rodorigo nostro zio?

DON IGNAZIO. Ho tolto una gentildonna, povera ben 20 sì ma nobilissima: ma la sua nobiltà è avanzata di gran

DON IGNAZIO. See to it that I never lay eyes on you again; otherwise I'll make you regret it.

AVANZINO. These are the rewards of ten years of faithful service, to be turned out of the house!

SIMBOLO. Hush, and speak no more in anger. Here is your brother.

DON IGNAZIO. Don Flaminio, I've been looking for you everywhere: welcome to you.

SCENE VII

Don Flaminio, Panimbolo, Don Ignazio, and
Simbolo.

DON FLAMINIO. Well met. What good news brings such happiness to your countenance?

PANIMBOLO. [aside] Oh, what a difference between heart and face!

DON FLAMINIO. What have you in hand worth such haste and effort?

DON IGNAZIO. To make you share a joy of mine, in which I know you will rejoice as I do myself, loving one another as reciprocally as we do.

PANIMBOLO. [aside] You both lie in your teeth.

DON FLAMINIO. Give me this joy quickly, I pray.

DON IGNAZIO. Since, after leaving you, I went to the count's house and was told that he had gone to Tricarico and was arranging a different match for his daughter, I have taken another bride, to my own satisfaction.

DON FLAMINIO. I believe that there is no greater satisfaction in life than to have a wife to one's taste and to one's own mind. Is it that Spanish lady for whom our uncle, Don Rodorigo, was negotiating?

DON IGNAZIO. I have taken a gentlewoman, poor but most noble, yet her nobility is far surpassed by her ex-

189

lunga della sua somma bellezza, e l'un' e l'altra dalla onestà e da gli onorati costumi.

DON FLAMINIO. Ditelami di grazia, acciochè mi rallegri anche io della vostra allegrezza, ché per aver ricusata una figlia de' grandi d'Ispagna, dev'esser oltre modo bella ed onorata.

DON IGNAZIO. È Carizia.

DON FLAMINIO. Chi Carizia? non l'ho intesa mai nominare.

PANIMBOLO. [da sé] Ah, lingua mendace, non la conosci?

DON IGNAZIO. Carizia, figlia di Eufranone.

DON FLAMINIO. Forsi volete dire una giovenetta che nella festa de' tori comparve fra quelle gentildonne con una sottana gialla?

DON IGNAZIO. Quella istessa.

DON FLAMINIO. E questa è quella tanto onesta ed onorata?

DON IGNAZIO. Quell'istessa.

DON FLAMINIO. Or veramente le cose non sono com'elle sono, ma come l'estima chi le possiede.

DON IGNAZIO. Che volete dir per questo?

DON FLAMINIO. Che non è tanta l'onestà e 'l suo merito quanto voi dite.

DON IGNAZIO. Dite cose da non credere.

DON FLAMINIO. Ma piene di verità. Ma dove nasce in voi tanta meraviglia?

DON IGNAZIO. Anzi io non posso tanto meravigliarmi che basti.

DON FLAMINIO. Avete fatto molto male.

DON IGNAZIO. Si ho fatto bene o male, non l'ho da riporre nel vostro giudizio.

DON FLAMINIO. Or non sapete voi ch'ella col far di sé copia ad altri dà da viver alla sua casa, la qual è più povera di quante ne sono in Salerno, e che senza la sua mercanzia non potrebbe sostenersi?

ceeding beauty, and both are surpassed in their turn by her chastity and her honorable manner of life.

DON FLAMINIO. Tell me who she is, please, so that I too may rejoice in your joy, for to be worth refusing a daughter of the grandees of Spain, she must be beautiful and honorable beyond measure.

DON IGNAZIO. It is Carizia.

DON FLAMINIO. Carizia who? I have never heard of her.

PANIMBOLO. [aside] Ah, lying tongue, you don't know her, eh?

DON IGNAZIO. Carizia, daughter of Eufranone.

DON FLAMINIO. Perhaps you mean a girl who appeared at the tourney of the bulls among those gentlewomen, wearing a yellow skirt?

DON IGNAZIO. The same.

DON FLAMINIO. And this is she who is so virtuous and esteemed?

DON IGNAZIO. The same.

DON FLAMINIO. Well, truly, things are not as they are but as they seem to their possessor.

DON IGNAZIO. What do you mean by that?

DON FLAMINIO. That her chastity and her merit are not so great as you say.

DON IGNAZIO. What you say is incredible.

DON FLAMINIO. But full of truth. Whence comes such amazement?

DON IGNAZIO. Indeed I cannot be amazed enough.

DON FLAMINIO. You have done very ill.

DON IGNAZIO. Whether I have done well or ill, I don't have to submit it to your judgment.

DON FLAMINIO. Are you aware that by giving herself to men she earns a living for her family, which is the poorest in all Salerno and could not maintain itself without her commerce?

PANIMBOLO. [*da sé*] Oh come i colori della morte escono ed entrano nel suo volto?

DON IGNAZIO. Si fusse altro che voi, ch'ardisse dirme questo, lo mentirei per la gola. 60

DON FLAMINIO. Perdonatemi si son forzato passar i termini della modestia con voi, ché quanto le dico tutto è per l'affezione che li porto.

PANIMBOLO. [*da sé*] Ah, lingua traditora! 65

DON FLAMINIO. Dico che fate malamente, ché per sodisfare ad un vostro momentaneo appetito, e di una finta bellezza di una donnicciola, non stimate una vergogna che sia per risultar al vostro parentado, ché ben sapete che una picciola macchia nella fama di una donna 70 apporta vituperio ed infamia a tutti.

PANIMBOLO. [*da sé*] L'ammonisce per carità fraterna, che Dio le benedica!

DON IGNAZIO. Io per diligente informazione, che per molti giorni n'ho presa da molte onoratissime persone, 75 ne ho inteso tutto il contrario.

DON FLAMINIO. Dovete credere più a me che a niuno.

DON IGNAZIO. Credo a voi, non al fatto.

DON FLAMINIO. Anzi vo' che crediate al fatto istesso non a me. 80

DON IGNAZIO. Ella è tanto onorata che la mia lingua s'onora del suo onore, ed avendola, ne resto io più onorato: e voi, per farla da cavaliero, d'una gentildonna dovresti dirne bene, ancor che fusse il falso; né dirne male, ancor che fusse il vero. 85

DON FLAMINIO. Io non ho detto ciò perché sia mala lingua, ma perché sappiate il vero: ma che non può la forza d'una gran verità? Perciò non vorrei che correste con tanta furia in cosa ove bisogna maturo consiglio: e poi fatta non può più guastarsi, e poi dal rimorso di voi 90 stesso, vi aveste a pentir d'una vana penitenza.

PANIMBOLO. [*aside*] Oh, how the colors of death come and go in his countenance!

DON IGNAZIO. If anyone but you dared say this to me, I'd tell him he lied in his throat.

DON FLAMINIO. Forgive me if I am impelled to exceed the bounds of decency with you, for whatever I say comes from the affection I bear you.

PANIMBOLO. [*aside*] Ah, treacherous tongue!

DON FLAMINIO. I say that you do ill if, in order to satisfy a momentary appetite, and for the false beauty of a woman of no account, you disregard the shame which would fall on your family, for well you know that a small blemish on the good name of a woman brings disgrace and infamy on all.

PANIMBOLO. [*aside*] His admonitions spring from brotherly love, God bless him!

DON IGNAZIO. In days of diligent inquiry among many highly esteemed people, I have heard exactly the contrary.

DON FLAMINIO. You ought to believe me more than anyone else.

DON IGNAZIO. I believe you, but not what you state as fact.

DON FLAMINIO. On the contrary, I wish you to believe the fact itself, not me.

DON IGNAZIO. She is so honorable that my very tongue is honored in speaking of it, and possessing her, I should enjoy an increase in my own honor. And you in all chivalry ought to speak well of a lady, though it were false, nor speak ill, though it were true.

DON FLAMINIO. What I have said was not to defame her but to let you know the truth. But what cannot the power of a great truth do? For this reason I don't want you to rush hastily into a thing which requires mature counsel and which, once done, cannot be undone, and then, full of remorse, to repent in vain.

DON IGNAZIO. A me sta il crederlo.

DON FLAMINIO. A voi il credere, a me dir la verità, la qual m'apre la bocca, e ministra le parole; ma io che tante volte v'ho fatto veder il falso leggiermente, or con   95
tante ragioni non posso farvi creder il vero?

DON IGNAZIO. E però non vi credo nulla, perché solete dirmi le bugie, e conosco i vostri artifici.

PANIMBOLO. [da sé] O come mal si conoscono i cuori!

DON FLAMINIO. Ma se vogliamo adeguar il fatto, bi-   100
sogna che ambo doi abbiamo pazienza, voi di ascoltare, io di parlare.

DON IGNAZIO. Dite suso.

DON FLAMINIO. Son più di quattro mesi che me la godo a bell'aggio, né io son stato il primo, o secondo; e   105
vi fo sapere che non è tanto bella quanto voi la fate, ché toltone quel poco di visuccio imbellettato e dipinto, sotto i panni è la più sgarbata e lorda creatura che si veda.

DON IGNAZIO. Non basto a crederlo.   110

DON FLAMINIO. Né la sorella è men disonesta di lei, ed un certo Capitano ciarlone, che suol pratticar in casa, se la tiene a' suoi commodi. Or questo, che è il peggior uomo che si trovi, sarà vostro cognato, e ci son altre cose da dire e da non dire.   115

DON IGNAZIO. Mi par impossibile.

DON FLAMINIO. Farò che ascoltiati da molti il medesimo.

DON IGNAZIO. Se non lo credo a voi, meno lo crederò a gli altri.   120

PANIMBOLO. [da sé] Li è restata la lingua nella gola e non ne può uscir parola.

DON FLAMINIO. E se non lo credete, farò che lo veggiati con gli occhi vostri.

DON IGNAZIO. I'd have to believe it first.

DON FLAMINIO. Yours to be convinced, mine to tell the truth, the truth which opens my mouth and dictates my words. But can't I, who so often have easily in jest made you believe what was false, now with such good reasons make you believe the truth?

DON IGNAZIO. And that is why I believe you not at all, because you usually tell me lies, and I know your tricks.

PANIMBOLO. [aside] Oh, how little can hearts be known!

DON FLAMINIO. But if we want to straighten out the matter, we must both have patience, you to listen, I to speak.

DON IGNAZIO. Speak on.

DON FLAMINIO. For more than four months I have enjoyed her whenever I liked, nor was I the first nor even the second; and I inform you that she is not as beautiful as you make her out to be, for take away that powdered and painted bit of face, under her clothes she is the most graceless and foul creature ever seen.

DON IGNAZIO. I can't believe it.

DON FLAMINIO. Nor is her sister less wanton than she, and a certain blabbermouth captain, who has access to the house, keeps her at his convenience. Now this fellow, the worst kind of man there is, will be your brother-in-law, and there is still more to say and to be left unsaid.

DON IGNAZIO. It seems impossible to me.

DON FLAMINIO. I can arrange for you to hear the same thing from many others.

DON IGNAZIO. If I don't believe it from you, I'll believe it even less from the others.

PANIMBOLO. [aside] His tongue is stilled in his throat and he can't get a word out.

DON FLAMINIO. Well, if you can't believe it, I can make you see it with your own eyes.

DON IGNAZIO. Che cosa? 125

DON FLAMINIO. Poi che volete sposarla dimani, vo' dormir seco la notte che viene; io sarò sposo notturno, voi diurno. State stupefatto?

DON IGNAZIO. Se mi fusse caduto un fulmine da presso, non starei così attonito. 130

DON FLAMINIO. Da un buon fratello, come vi son io, bisogna dirsi la verità, poi in cose d'importanza e dove ci va l'onore.

PANIMBOLO. [da sé] O mondo traditore, tutto fizioni!

DON IGNAZIO. Odo cose da voi non più intese da altri. 135

DON FLAMINIO. Se vi fusse più tempo, ve lo farei udir da mille lingue; ma perché viene la notte più tosto che arei voluto, venete meco alle due ore che andrò in casa sua, vi farò veder le sue vesti, e i doni che l'avete mandati, e ce ne ritornaremo a casa insieme. 140

DON IGNAZIO. Se me fate veder questo, farò quel conto di lei che si deve far d'una sua pari.

DON FLAMINIO. Andiamo a cenare, e verremo quando sarà più imbrunita la notte.

DON IGNAZIO. Andiamo. 145

DON FLAMINIO. Andate prima, ché verrò dopoi.

PANIMBOLO. Già è gito via.

DON FLAMINIO. Panimbolo, a me par che la cosa riesca bene.

PANIMBOLO. Avete finto assai naturale; mi son accorto 150 che la gelosia li attaccò la lingua che non possea esprimere parola.

DON FLAMINIO. Io non mi dispero della vittoria.

PANIMBOLO. Andiamo al fratello, acciò non prenda suspetto di noi, e gli ordini presi non si disordenino. 155

DON FLAMINIO. Andiamo.

DON IGNAZIO. What?

DON FLAMINIO. Since you want to marry her tomorrow, I intend to sleep with her tonight: I'll be the bridegroom by night, you by day. Are you astounded?

DON IGNAZIO. If a bolt of lightning had struck nearby, I couldn't be more stunned.

DON FLAMINIO. Like the good brother I am, I must tell the truth, especially in important matters which touch on honor.

PANIMBOLO. [aside] Oh treacherous world, all pretense!

DON IGNAZIO. I hear things from you never heard from others.

DON FLAMINIO. If there were more time, I'd have you hear it from a thousand tongues; but because the night comes on faster than I could wish, come with me at two o'clock, for I'll get into her house, show you her clothes and the gifts you have sent her, and we'll go home together.

DON IGNAZIO. If you show me this, I'll value her as such a one deserves.

DON FLAMINIO. Let's go to supper and come again when the night is darker.

DON IGNAZIO. Let's go.

[Don Ignazio and Simbolo depart.]

DON FLAMINIO. You go first and I'll come after.

PANIMBOLO. He is already gone.

DON FLAMINIO. Panimbolo, it seems to me that the thing is turning out well.

PANIMBOLO. You lied very credibly. I observed that jealousy gripped his tongue so that he couldn't press out a word.

DON FLAMINIO. I don't despair of victory.

PANIMBOLO. Let's join your brother lest he become suspicious of us and our plans be undone.

DON FLAMINIO. Let's go.

SCENA VIII

EUFRANONE solo.

EUFRANONE. Già ho dato la nuova a' parenti, a gli amici, ed a tutta la città, e ciascuno ne ha infinito piacere ed
allegrezza, veggendo che la nostra casa anticamente così
nobile e ricca per una disgrazia sia venuta in tanta miseria e povertade, ed ora per una così insperata occasione   5
risorga a quel primiero splendore e grandezza; e che la
bellezza ed onorati costumi di Carizia, che meritava
questa, e maggior cosa, abino sortito così felice ventura
per esser ne le sue parti tali da farsi amar insin dalle
pietre. O quanto sarà la mia allegreza dimani, quando   10
vedrò la mia figliola sposar da così degno cavaliero, con
tanta grandeza e concorso di nobili, e gionta a quell'eccelso grado che merita la sua bontade! Dubito che non
passarà mai questa notte ché veggia quell'alba, per lo
gran desiderio che ho di vederla. Ma perché trattengo   15
me stesso in tante facende? Andrò sù, cenerò subito, ed
andrò in letto, acciochè dimani mi levi per tempo. Sommo Dio, appresso cui son riposte tutte le nostre speranze, fa' riuscir queste nozze felici per tua solita bontade,
ché so ben che noi tanto non meritiamo!   20

SCENA IX

MARTEBELLONIO solo.

[MARTEBELLONIO.] Credo che non sia minor virtute e
grandezza ferir un corpo con la spada, che un'anima con
i sguardi; ben posso tenermi io fra tutti gli uomini glorioso, ché posso non men con l'una che con l'altra; ché
non può starmi uomo, per gagliardo che sia, con la   5
spada in mano innanzi, né men donna, per onesta e

SCENE VIII

EUFRANONE alone.

EUFRANONE. There, I have told the news to our relatives and friends, and to the whole city; and everyone is boundlessly pleased and overjoyed by it, seeing that our house, of old so noble and rich, through misfortune having fallen into such want and poverty, now by such an unhoped-for event is rising again to its original splendor and greatness, and that the beauty and the estimable behavior of Carizia, which deserve this and better, have made things turn out so happily, her qualities being such as to make the very stones love her. Oh, how great will be my joy tomorrow when I see my daughter married to so worthy a gentleman with such grandeur and noble company, and placed in that high rank which her goodness deserves! I fear this night will never pass that I may behold the dawn, so great is my desire to behold it. But why do I linger when there is so much to do? I'll up to supper immediately and then to bed, so that tomorrow I may rise early. God on high, repository of all our hopes, bring to pass these happy nuptials, through your wonted goodness, for well I know that of ourselves we do not deserve so much.

SCENE IX

MARTEBELLONIO alone.

MARTEBELLONIO. I believe it's no less a sign of power and greatness to wound a body with one's sword than a soul with one's glances: well may I deem myself glorious among men, for I'm as powerful in the one way as in the other; for no man, no matter how hardy, can stand up to me when I have my sword in hand, nor any

rigida, a i colpi de' sguardi miei: e se con la spada fo ferite, che giungono insin al cuore, con gli occhi fo piaghe
profondissime, che giungono insin all'anima: eco Callidora che appena mi guardò una volta, che non sostenne   10
il folgore del lampeggiante mio viso, onde ne restò
sconquassata per sempre. Ma io con un generoso ardire
non men uso mesericordia a quei che prostrati in terra
mi chiedeno la vita in dono, che a quelle meschinelle e
povere donne che si muoiono per amor mio. Or io mi   15
son mosso a darle soccorso, ché non la vegga miseramente morire: ed è gran pezza che mi deve star aspettando. Ma io non veggio per qui Leccardo, come re-
stammo d'appontamento.

SCENA X

DON FLAMINIO, DON IGNAZIO, CAPITANO
[MARTEBELLONIO], PANIMBOLO, SIMBOLO.

DON FLAMINIO. Io sento genti in strada, non so se potremo mandar ad effetto quanto desideriamo. Doveva-
mo cenar prima.

DON IGNAZIO. A me non parea mai che venisse l'ora di
veder un tanto imposibile, per poter dire liberamente   5
poi, che onore e castità non si trova in femina: poiché
costei, di cui si narrano tanti gran vanti della sua onestà,
si trovi sì disonesta.

DON FLAMINIO. Così va il mondo, fratello; quella donna è tenuta più casta che con più secretezza fa i suoi fatti. 10

[MARTEBELLONIO.] Sento stradaioli. Oh là, date la
strada, se non volete andar per fil di spada!

200

woman, no matter how chaste and unbending, can resist the onslaught of my glances; and if with the sword I
can pierce to the heart, with my eyes I make the deepest
wounds, which penetrate to the very soul. Take Callidora, who barely glimpsed me once and couldn't bear
the thunderbolt of my flashing countenance, whence
she remained shattered forever. But I, with generous
warmth, show mercy equally to those who, prostrate
on the ground, beg for their lives, and to those poor little miserable women who die for love of me. Now I am
moved to succour her, that I may not see her die
wretchedly; and by now she must have been waiting for
me a long while. But I don't see Leccardo here, as we
had agreed by appointment.

SCENE X

Don Flaminio, Don Ignazio, Martebellonio,
Panimbolo, Simbolo.

DON FLAMINIO. I hear people in the street; I don't
know if we can accomplish all we wish. We should have
supped first.

DON IGNAZIO. I couldn't wait; it seemed the hour
would never come for seeing such an impossibility, to
be able to declare afterward without fear of contra-
diction that honor and chastity are not to be found in
woman, since she whose purity is so greatly vaunted is
found to be impure.

DON FLAMINIO. That's the way of the world, brother:
the woman esteemed most chaste is the one who manages her affairs with greatest secrecy.

MARTEBELLONIO. I hear passersby. Ho there, make
way unless you want to be helped along by a sword.

PANIMBOLO. Se non taci, poltronaccio, andrai per fil di bastone!

[MARTEBELLONIO.] [*da sé*] Costui par che sia indo- 15
vino, ché son poltrone.

DON IGNAZIO. Chi è costui?

SIMBOLO. Quel Capitan vantatore.

[MARTEBELLONIO.] [*da sé*] Vo' farmi conoscere, ché
non m'uccidano in scambio.   20

O signori Don Flaminio e Don Ignazio, son il Capitan Martebellonio! E dove così di notte senza la mia
compagnia? ché è meglio aver me solo che una compagnia d'uomini d'arme.

DON FLAMINIO. E tu dove vai, a donne ah?   25

[MARTEBELLONIO.] L'hai indovinata, a fé di Marte!

DON FLAMINIO. A qualche puttana?

[MARTEBELLONIO.] Se non foste voi, a' quai porto
rispetto, li farei parlar altrimente. Io a puttane? che ho le
principali gentildonne della città, e tutto il mondo, che 30
spasima del fatto mio? vo ad una signora, che è ridotta a
pollo pesto per amor mio, ed or la vo a soccorrere.

DON FLAMINIO. Signora di casa, fantesca eh?

[MARTEBELLONIO.] E pur là! È Callidora, figlia d'Eufranone; conoscetela voi?   35

DON FLAMINIO. Che ti dissi, fratello? cominci a scoprir
paese. Noi la conosciamo molto bene; ma dove voi conoscete lei o sua sorella Carizia?

[MARTEBELLONIO.] Gran tempo fa che l'una e l'altra è
impazzita del fatto mio, ma a me piace Callidora per es- 40
ser di ciglio più rigido, e più severo. Mi ha chiesto in
grazia che vada a dormir seco per questa notte; or vo ad
attenderle la promessa; ma s'apre la porta e vegio il parasito che viene per ritrovarmi; perdonatemi.

PANIMBOLO. If you don't shut up, vile coward, you'll be helped along with a cudgel.

MARTEBELLONIO. [aside] That fellow seems to be a seer, for I *am* a coward.

DON IGNAZIO. Who is that?

SIMBOLO. That braggart captain.

MARTEBELLONIO. [aside] I'm going to make myself known, lest they kill me by mistake.

Oh my lords Don Flaminio and Don Ignazio, it is I, Captain Martebellonio! And where are you going thus at night without me? For it is better to have me along than a company of armed men.

DON FLAMINIO. And you, where are you going, to the women, eh?

MARTEBELLONIO. You've guessed it, by Mars.

DON FLAMINIO. To some whore?

MARTEBELLONIO. Were you not who you are and whom I respect, I'd make you talk differently. I go to whores? I who have the greatest noblewoman of the city and the whole world panting for me? I am on my way to a lady who is reduced to chopped chicken for love of me, and now I go to give her succor.

DON FLAMINIO. A lady of a noble house, that is to say a housemaid, eh?

MARTEBELLONIO. Still not convinced! It is Callidora, Eufranone's daughter: do you know her?

DON FLAMINIO. What do you say to that, brother? Now you begin to see how the land lies. We know her very well; but how do you know her or her sister Carizia?

MARTEBELLONIO. Quite a while ago both of them fell madly in love with me, but I prefer Callidora for her more forbidding and haughty aspect. She has asked me the favor of sleeping with her tonight, and now I go to keep my promise. But the door is opening and I see the parasite who comes to meet me. Excuse me.

SCENA XI

LECCARDO, CHIARETTA, [MARTEBELLONIO], DON
IGNAZIO, DON FLAMINIO, [SIMBOLO, PANIMBOLO].

LECCARDO. Entrate, signora, in questa camera qui
vicino.

CHIARETTA. T'obedisco.

LECCARDO. Serratevi dentro, ed aspettatemi un pochetto. Capitano, sete voi?   5

[MARTEBELLONIO.] Pezzo d'asino, non mi conosci?

LECCARDO. Non vi conoscea, perché mi diceste che
venendo la vostra persona, arei sentito il terremoto; son
stato gran peza atendendo se tremava la terra, però du-
bitavo se foste voi.   10

[MARTEBELLONIO.] Dite bene, e ti dirò la cagione.
Poco anzi mi è venuta una lettera dall'altro mondo; Plutone[1] mi si racomanda, e mi prega che non camini così
gagliardo, che vada pian piano, ché tante sono le pietre e
le montagne che cascono da gli altissimi volti della ter-   15
ra, che mancò poco che non abissasse il mondo, e sot-
terasse lui vivo con Proserpina la sua mogliere: gli l'ho
promesso e per ciò non camino al mio solito.

LECCARDO. Entrate, ché Callidora vi sta aspettando.

DON FLAMINIO. Che dici, fratello, è vero quanto vi ho   20
detto? Io farò il segno: fis, fis.

LECCARDO. Signor Don Flaminio, Carizia vi prega a
disagiarvi un poco, perché sta ragionando col padre.

DON FLAMINIO. Se ben è alquanto bellina, io non la
teneva in tanto conto quanto voi.   25

DON IGNAZIO. Non vi ho io dimandato più volte se in
quel giorno della festa vi fusse piaciuta alcuna di quelle
gentildonne, e mi dicesti di no?

SCENE XI

LECCARDO, CHIARETTA, MARTEBELLONIO, DON IGNAZIO,
DON FLAMINIO, [SIMBOLO, PANIMBOLO].

LECCARDO. Come, my lady, into this room nearby.

CHIARETTA. I obey you.

LECCARDO. Lock yourself in and wait for me a short while. Captain, is that you?

MARTEBELLONIO. Jackass, don't you know me?

LECCARDO. I didn't, because you told me that at the approach of your person I would hear an earthquake: for some time I've been waiting for the earth to tremble, and that's why I doubted that it was you.

MARTEBELLONIO. You're right, and I'll tell you the reason. Just a while ago I received a letter from the other world. Pluto greets me and begs me not to walk so powerfully, to go very softly, because so many rocks and mountains fall down from the earth's towering vaults, that the world has come close to collapsing into the underworld and burying him alive with his good wife, Proserpine: I gave him my promise, and that's why I don't walk in my usual way.

LECCARDO. Enter, for Callidora awaits you.

[*Martebellonio and Leccardo go within.*]

DON FLAMINIO. What do you say to that, brother? Have I told you the truth? I'll give the signal: psst, psst.

[*Leccardo reappears.*]

LECCARDO. My lord Don Flaminio, Carizia begs your indulgence for a short while, as she is in conversation with her father.

[*Leccardo returns within.*]

DON FLAMINIO. Although she is rather a pretty little thing, I never regarded her as highly as you did.

DON IGNAZIO. Didn't I ask you repeatedly if on that day of the festival any of those noble ladies had caught your eye, and you said not?

DON FLAMINIO. Era così veramente, ma essendomi offerta costei con mio poco discomodo, me ce inchinai. 30

LECCARDO. Signor Don Flaminio, Carizia v'aspetta a gli usati piaceri, e che le perdoniate se vi ha fatto aspettar un poco.

DON FLAMINIO. Don Ignazio, non vi partite: forse vi porterò alcuni de' suoi abbigliamenti e de' doni mandati. 35

DON IGNAZIO. Aspettarò sin a domani.

Che dici, Simbolo, aresti tu creduto ciò mai?

SIMBOLO. Veramente delle donne se ne deve far quel conto che dell'erbe fetide ed amare che serveno per le 40 medicine, che, cavatone quel succo giovevole, si butano nel letamare: come l'uomo si ha cavato quel poco di diletto che s'ha da loro, nasconderle ché più non appaiano.

DON IGNAZIO. Veramente la femina è un pessimo animale, e da non fidarsene punto. Ahi, fortuna, quando 45 pensava che fussero finite le pene, e cominciar la felicità, allor ne son più lontano che mai!

DON FLAMINIO. Don Ignazio, dove sete? Conoscete voi questa sottana gialla che portò quel giorno? non è questo l'anello che l'avete mandato a donare, le catene e 50 gli altri vezzi di donne?

DON IGNAZIO. Le conosco, e mi rincresce conoscerle.

DON FLAMINIO. Vi lascio le sue cose invece di lei, per questo breve tempo che mi è concesso goderla.

DON IGNAZIO. Eccole, tornatele a dietro. 55

DON FLAMINIO. Vi lascio la buona notte.

DON FLAMINIO. It was truly so, but when she offered herself to me, with so little trouble required on my part, I yielded.

[*Leccardo reappears.*]

LECCARDO. My lord Don Flaminio, Carizia awaits you for the wonted pleasures, and asks your pardon if she has made you wait a little.

DON FLAMINIO. Don Ignazio, don't go away; perhaps I shall bring you some of her apparel and some of the gifts you sent her.

DON IGNAZIO. I'll wait even till tomorrow.

[*Leccardo and Don Flaminio go within.*]

What do you say, Simbolo, would you ever have believed that?

SIMBOLO. Truly one must value women as one does the stinking and bitter herbs used for medicines, which, once the useful juice is extracted, are tossed onto the dung-heap: when men have extracted that small measure of delight to be had from them, they should be hidden away, to appear no more.

DON IGNAZIO. Truly the female is a vile animal, in no wise to be trusted. Ah, fortune, just when I thought suffering at an end and happiness about to begin, I am farther away from it than ever.

[*Don Flaminio emerges.*]

DON FLAMINIO. Don Ignazio, where are you? Do you recognize this yellow skirt, which she wore that day? Isn't this the ring that you sent her, these the necklaces and other feminine adornments?

DON IGNAZIO. I recognize them and it grieves me to do so.

DON FLAMINIO. I leave you her belongings in place of herself for this brief time given me to enjoy her.

DON IGNAZIO. Here they are, take them back.

DON FLAMINIO. I bid you good night.

[*Don Flaminio returns within.*]

DON IGNAZIO. Anzi notte per me la più acerba e d'infelice memoria che sia mai stata; o stelle nemiche d'ogni mio bene, ben posso io chiamarvi crudeli, poi che nel nascer mio v'armaste di così funesti e miserabili influssi! 60 Deh, fuggite dal cielo, spengete il vostro lume, e lasciate per me in oscure tenebre il mondo! O luna, oscura il tuo splendore, e cuopra il tuo volto ecclisse orribile e spaventoso; ed in tua vece veggansi orrende comete con le sanguigne chiome! O maledetto giorno ch'io nacqui e 65 che la viddi, e che tanto piacque a gli occhi miei! Ahi, dolenti ochi miei, a che infelice spetacolo sete stati serbati insin ad ora, veder ch'altri goda di quella donna che mi era assai più cara dell'anima istessa! Ahi, che sento straciarmi il cuore dentro da mille orsi, e da mille tigri, e 70 la gelosia m'impiaga l'anima di ferite inmedicabili ed immortali! Ahi, Carizia, così onori il tuo sposo? queste sono le parole che ho intese da te questa mattina? non avevi altri uomini con chi potevi ingannarmi, e lasciar mio fratello? e se mi dispiace l'atto, mi dispiace più assai 75 con chi l'hai tu adoperato.

SIMBOLO. Padrone, fate resistenza al male, ché non è maggior male che lasciarsi vincere dal male.

DON IGNAZIO. Ma io non sia quel che sono se non ne la farò pentire. 80

SIMBOLO. Dove andate?

DON IGNAZIO. A consigliarmi con la disperazione, con le furie infernali, ché non so qual in me maggior sia, l'ardore, il dolore, o la gelosia.

DON FLAMINIO. Panimbolo, son partiti? 85

PANIMBOLO. Sì, sono.

208

DON IGNAZIO. Nay, rather, night to me most bitter and of memory most unhappy that has ever been. Oh stars inimical to all my weal, rightly may I call you cruel, since at my birth you armed yourselves with such baneful and desolating influences! Ah, flee from the heavens, quench your light, and leave me the world shrouded in dark shadows! Oh moon, dim your brightness, let a horrid and fearful eclipse cover your visage, and in your stead let terrifying comets with bloody locks be seen! Oh cursed be the day I was born, and the day I saw her and she so pleased my eyes! Alas, my sorrowing eyes, for what an unhappy spectacle have you been preserved till now, to see another enjoy that woman who was much dearer to me than my very soul! Alas, I feel my heart within me rent by a thousand bears and a thousand tigers, and jealousy stabs my soul with incurable and eternal wounds! Alas, Carizia, thus do you honor your bridegroom? Are these the words I heard from you this morning? Could you not have deceived me with other men and dispensed with my brother? If I am displeased by the act, I am still more displeased that you committed it with him.

SIMBOLO. Master, steel your spirit against this ill hap, for there is no greater ill than to let oneself be defeated by ill.

DON IGNAZIO. But I am not I if I do not make her repent it.

SIMBOLO. Where are you going?

DON IGNAZIO. To take counsel with despair, with the infernal furies, for I know not which is stronger in me, desire, sorrow, or jealousy.

[*Don Ignazio and Simbolo depart; Don Flaminio, Panimbolo and Leccardo emerge.*]

DON FLAMINIO. Panimbolo, are they gone?

PANIMBOLO. Yes, they are.

LECCARDO. Don Flaminio, come sei stato servito da me?

DON FLAMINIO. Benissimo, meglio che s'io fussi stato nel tuo cuore, o tu nel mio. 90

LECCARDO. Che dici del Capitano, del suo non aspettato e fattoci beneficio?

DON FLAMINIO. La fortuna non ha ingannato punto il nostro desiderio.

LECCARDO. Mai mi son compiaciuto di me stesso 95 come ora, tanto mi par d'aver fatto bene.

DON FLAMINIO. Te ne ho grande obligo.

LECCARDO. Ne avete cagione.

DON FLAMINIO. Panimbolo, par che siamo fuori di periglio. 100

PANIMBOLO. Anzi or siamo nel periglio; e poi che si è cominciato, bisogna finire, ché non facci a noi egli quel che pensiamo di far a lui.

LECCARDO. La fortuna scherza con noi, ché scambivolmente abbassa l'uno, ed inalza l'altro. 105

DON FLAMINIO. Patisca or egli quelle pene che ha fatto patir a me: egli piange, ed io rido.

LECCARDO. Ben sarà se non s'appicca con le sue mani!

DON FLAMINIO. Questo bisogno sarebbe a punto per farmi felice! Andiamo. 110

LECCARDO. Ed io vo' entrar qui dentro, e prendermi spasso di Chiaretta col Capitano.

LECCARDO. Don Flaminio, how have you been served by me?

DON FLAMINIO. Well indeed, better than if I had been in your heart or you in mine.

LECCARDO. What do you say of the captain, of the unexpected good turn he has done us?

DON FLAMINIO. Fortune has not deluded our hopes in the least.

LECCARDO. I was never so pleased with myself as now, so well do I think I've done.

DON FLAMINIO. I am much obliged to you for it.

LECCARDO. You have reason to be.

DON FLAMINIO. Panimbolo, it seems we are out of danger.

PANIMBOLO. On the contrary, now we are in danger; and since we have begun, we must finish it, lest he do to us what we aim to do to him.

LECCARDO. Fortune plays with us, for in turn it sinks the one and exalts the other.

DON FLAMINIO. Now let him suffer the pains he made me suffer: he weeps and I laugh.

LECCARDO. It will be well if he doesn't hang himself with his own hands.

DON FLAMINIO. That's all I would need to make me happy. Let us go.

[*Don Flaminio and Panimbolo depart.*]

LECCARDO. And I want to go in here and have a laugh at the pairing of Chiaretta with the captain.

ATTO IV

SCENA I

SIMBOLO, DON IGNAZIO.

SIMBOLO. Padrone, vi è passata ancora quella rabbia?

DON IGNAZIO. Anzi me n'è sovragionta dell'altra.

SIMBOLO. Stimava che, la notte, come madre de' pensieri, avendovi meglio consigliato, foste mutato di parere.   5

DON IGNAZIO. Più mi ci son confirmato.

SIMBOLO. Frenate tanto sdegno che impedisce il dritto della raggione, ché le vostre parole potrebbono cagionar qualche gran scandolo.

DON IGNAZIO. Che vorresti dunque che facessi?   10

[SIMBOLO.] Ch'avendola a rifiutare, la rifiutaste con modi non tanto obbrobriosi.

DON IGNAZIO. Il fuoco d'amore è rivolto in fuoco di sdegno, e l'uno e l'altro m'hanno inperversato di sorte che mi parebbe poco se la sbranassi con le mie mani.   15

SIMBOLO. Fareste cosa che ve ne pentireste.

DON IGNAZIO. Vo' che sia a parte della pena, poiché è stata a parte del diletto.

SIMBOLO. Or non potrebbe esser che quella notte vostro fratello v'avesse ingannato?   20

DON IGNAZIO. Non sai che dici.

SIMBOLO. Dico cose possibili e dubbiose ancora. Considerate che nella sua famiglia si raccoglie tutta la nobiltà di Salerno, e facendo ingiuria ad uno, minacciate molti.

DON IGNAZIO. Non merita una sua pari le sia portato   25
tanto rispetto.

SIMBOLO. Ecco il padre, e i principali della città, che

ACT IV

SCENE I

SIMBOLO, DON IGNAZIO.

SIMBOLO. Master, has your rage passed yet?

DON IGNAZIO. No, rather it has increased.

SIMBOLO. I thought that when night, the mother of thought, had brought you better counsel, you'd have changed your mind.

DON IGNAZIO. I'm the more confirmed in it.

SIMBOLO. Rein in such anger, which impedes the right working of reason, for your words could cause some great scandal.

DON IGNAZIO. What, then, would you have me do?

SIMBOLO. Since you must reject her, do it in some less insulting manner.

DON IGNAZIO. The fire of love has turned to fire of wrath, and both have so deranged me that I could easily tear her to pieces with my own hands.

SIMBOLO. You might do something you'd repent.

DON IGNAZIO. I want her to share in the pain, since she's had her share of pleasure.

SIMBOLO. Think, isn't it possible that your brother may have deceived you last night?

DON IGNAZIO. You don't know what you're saying.

SIMBOLO. I say things that are both possible and probable. Consider that her family is related to all the nobility of Salerno and by defaming one, you endanger the honor of many.

DON IGNAZIO. Her kind doesn't deserve so much consideration.

SIMBOLO. Here is her father with the foremost men of

vengono incontro per ricevervi con molt'amorevolezza; ma troveranno in voi tutto il contrario.

SCENA II

EUFRANONE, DON IGNAZIO, SIMBOLO.

EUFRANONE. Caro signore, siate il ben venuto, per
mille volte molto desiato dalla sposa e da' principali di
Salerno!

DON IGNAZIO. Io vengo con voluntà assai diversa da
quel che pensi: stimi che venghi a sposar tua figlia, ed io   5
vengo a rifiutarla.

EUFRANONE. Non sperava sentir tal nuova da voi! Ma
in che ha peccato mia figlia che meriti tal rifiuto?

DON IGNAZIO. D'impudicizia e disonestà.

EUFRANONE. Onesta è stata sempre mia figlia, e così   10
stimata da tutti, e non so per qual cagione sia impudica
appresso voi solo.

DON IGNAZIO. Tal è come dico.

EUFRANONE. Or non vi pregai io, allor che tanto an-
siosamente m'era chiesta dalla vostra leggierezza, che ci   15
aveste pensato prima, ed al fin vinto dalla vostra ostinazione, ve la concessi? Ché il cuor mi presaggiva
quanto ora m'accade, che passati quei furori vi pentireste; e per mostrar giuste cagioni del rifiuto, offendete me, lei, e tutta la cittade. Bastava mandare a dire   20
ch'eravate pentito, ché io contentandomi d'ogni vostro
contento, mi sarei chetato, senza svergognarmi in tal
modo.

DON IGNAZIO. Io non spinto da giovenil leggierezza
ciò dico, ma da giustissime cagioni.   25

the city, all come to receive you with great affection; but they'll meet with quite the contrary from you.

SCENE II

EUFRANONE, [GENTLEMEN], DON IGNAZIO, SIMBOLO.

EUFRANONE. Welcome, my dear lord, whose coming has been a thousand times eagerly longed for by the bride and by the nobles of Salerno.

DON IGNAZIO. I come with intentions very different from what you expect: you think that I come to marry your daughter, and I come to refuse her.

EUFRANONE. Indeed I did not expect to hear such a statement from you! But of what is my daughter guilty, that she deserves such a refusal?

DON IGNAZIO. Of wantonness and unchastity.

EUFRANONE. My daughter has always been chaste and esteemed so by all, and I do not know by what reason your opinion alone may hold her wanton.

DON IGNAZIO. It is as I say.

EUFRANONE. Now did I not beg you then, when out of lightness you so anxiously asked for her, that you would first think carefully, and did I not give her to you at last because I was won by your persistence? For my heart foreboded what is now happening, that once those wild ardors were passed, you would repent; and in order to give some color of justification to your refusal, you insult me, her, and the whole city. It would have sufficed to send word that you had repented of your choice, for then I, making my wishes conform to yours, would have held my peace, without your shaming me in this way.

DON IGNAZIO. I say what I said not moved by youthful levity, but by most just reasons.

EUFRANONE. Dunque dite che mia figlia è infame?

DON IGNAZIO. Ce lo dicono l'opre.

EUFRANONE. Se non foste quel che sete, ed io men di tempo, vi risponderei come si converrebbe; ma che cose infami avete udite di lei?   30

DON IGNAZIO. Quelle che non arei mai credute.

EUFRANONE. Nelle cose degne ed onorate si trapone sempre mordace lingua.

DON IGNAZIO. Qui non mordace lingua ma gli occhi istessi furon testimonii del tutto.   35

EUFRANONE. Né in cosa così lontana dall'esser di mia figliuola dovrebbe un par vostro creder a gli occhi suoi, che ben spesso s'ingannano.

DON IGNAZIO. Che un uomo possi ingannar un altro è facil cosa, me se stesso è difficile; ché quel che vidi, mol- 40
to chiaramente il viddi, e per non averlo veduto arei vo-
luto esser nato senz'occhi.

EUFRANONE. Lo vedeste voi a lume chiaro?

DON IGNAZIO. Anzi a sì nimico spettacolo rimasi senza lume.   45

EUFRANONE. Gran cose ascolto!

DON IGNAZIO. Or ditele da mia parte che desiava lei per isposa, stimandola onesta ed onorata, ma avendone veduto tutto il contrario, si goda per sposo chi la passata notte goduto s'ave.   50

EUFRANONE. Farò la vostra ambasciata, e farò che le penetri ben nel cuore. Ahi, misero padre d'infame figlia, e quanto son dolenti d'averti generata!

SIMBOLO. Non v'ho detto, padrone, che il vostro parlare arebbe cagionato qualche ruina? ch'essendo egli 55
molto superbo, né punto avezzo a sopportar ingiurie,
con che rabbiosa pacienza ascoltava, e con gli occhi lam-

EUFRANONE. You assert, then, that my daughter has dishonored herself?

DON IGNAZIO. Her actions say so.

EUFRANONE. Were you not who you are and I less advanced in years, I would answer you as you deserve. What shameful things have you heard of her?

DON IGNAZIO. Those which I would never have believed.

EUFRANONE. Evil tongues always meddle in worthy and honorable matters.

DON IGNAZIO. In this case not evil tongues but my own eyes were the witnesses to it all.

EUFRANONE. In a thing so alien to my daughter's nature, one of your worth should not believe his eyes either, for very often they deceive themselves.

DON IGNAZIO. A man may easily deceive another, but to deceive oneself is difficult; for what I saw, I saw very clearly, though rather than see it, I would have wished to be born without eyes.

EUFRANONE. You saw it yourself in clear light?

DON IGNAZIO. Nay, more, that hateful sight struck me blind!

EUFRANONE. What enormities I hear!

DON IGNAZIO. Now tell her from me that I desired her for my wife, believing her chaste and honorable, but as I have seen quite the contrary, let her enjoy as husband him who enjoyed her last night.

EUFRANONE. I shall deliver your message, and see to it that it is fixed well in her heart. Alas, unhappy father of a wicked daughter,—and how I grieve to have sired you!

[*Eufranone goes within.*]

SIMBOLO. Didn't I tell you, master, that your speech would cause some disaster? Being very proud and quite unaccustomed to bear affronts, with what wrathful patience he listened, and with eyes flashing with sudden

217

peggianti di un subbito sdegno, ripieno di un feroce dolore, die' di mano al pugnale, e se n'è gito sù, dove farà qualche scompiglio. L'onda che batte ne' scogli si fa 60 spiuma,[1] sfoga, e finisce il furore, ma se non fa né rumor, né spiuma, s'ingorga in se stessa, si gonfia e fa crudelissima tempesta. Dal ferro delle vostre parole, come da una spada, ha rinschiuso[2] il dolor dentro; sentirete la tempesta. Sento tutta la casa piena di gridi, e di romore. 65 Andiamocene, se non volete ancor rallegrar gli occhi vostri del suo sangue, ché se foste constretto vederlo, dovreste serrar gli occhi per non mirarlo.

SCENA III

Capitano [Martebellonio], Chiaretta, Leccardo.

[MARTEBELLONIO.] Or mira che bizzari incontri vengon al mio fantastico cervello, ché pensando far correre un poco il mio cane dietro una bella fiera, s'è incontrato con una pessima fiera.

CHIARETTA. Buon can per certo, che, per aver avuto 5 tutta notte la caccia tra' piedi, è stato sì sonnacchioso che non ha voluto mai alzar la testa né indrizzarsi alla via per seguitarla.

[MARTEBELLONIO.] Il mio can ha più cervello che non ho io, che conosce all'odor la fiera, ché né per stuzzicar- 10 lo né sferzarlo si volse mai spinger innanzi.

CHIARETTA. Va' e fa' altre arti, ché di caccia di donne tu non te n'intendi.

[MARTEBELLONIO.] Troppo gran bocca avevi tu aperta, che aresti ingiottito il cane ed il padrone intiero in- 15 tiero.

CHIARETTA. Non bisognava altrimenti, avendo a combatter con can debole di schiena.

anger, full of fierce sorrow, he put his hand to his dagger and betook himself up there where he will wreak some havoc. If the wave beating on the rocks foams, it vents and spends its fury, but if it makes neither noise nor foam, it chokes on itself, swells, and unleashes a cruel storm. Lanced by the iron of your words, as by a sword, the sorrow within him has erupted: you shall feel the tempest. I hear all the house full of outcries and noise. Let's depart, if you don't want your eyes cheered by the sight of his blood; were you forced to see that, you would shut them fast rather than look upon it.

SCENE III

MARTEBELLONIO, CHIARETTA, LECCARDO.

MARTEBELLONIO. See now what strange encounters occur to my fanciful brain: thinking to make my hound run a bit after a lovely beast, it has met with a foul one.

CHIARETTA. A fine hound to be sure, that having had the chase afoot all night was too sluggish to lift his head or take the road to follow it.

MARTEBELLONIO. My hound has more sense than I, for he knows the beast by its smell, and neither for prodding nor whipping would he ever push on.

CHIARETTA. Go and ply another trade, for you know nothing about chasing women.

MARTEBELLONIO. You opened up too big a mouth, which would have swallowed up hound and master whole.

CHIARETTA. There was nothing else to do, pitted against a hound so weak-spined.

[MARTEBELLONIO.] Io non so punger così con la spada come tu pungi con la lingua; ma ti scampa ché sei ignobil feminella, che vorrei con una stoccata passarti da un canto all'altro. 20

CHIARETTA. Non temo le tue stoccate, ché la tua spada si piega in punta.

[MARTEBELLONIO.] O Dio, se non temessi che, cavando la spada fuori, la furia dell'aria conquassata movesse qualche tempesta, vorrei che la provassi! Ma me la pagherà quel furfante di Leccardo. 25

LECCARDO. Menti per la gola, ché son meglio uomo di te! 30

[MARTEBELLONIO.] Dove sei, o tu che parli e non ti lassi vedere?

LECCARDO. Non mi vedi perché non ti piace vedermi: eccomi qui!

[MARTEBELLONIO.] Mi farai sverginar oggi la mia spada nel sangue di poltroni. 35

LECCARDO. E tu mi farai sverginar un legno che non ha fatto peccato ancora.

[MARTEBELLONIO.] Sei salito sul tetto ché non ti possa giungere; come ti arò in mano te squarterò come una ricotta. 40

LECCARDO. E tu sei posto in piazza per aver molte strade da scampare, ché dubbiti che non voglia spolverizarti la schena.

[MARTEBELLONIO.] Se m'incappi nelle mani . . . 45

LECCARDO. Se mi scappi dalle mani . . .

[MARTEBELLONIO.] Ti sbodellerò!

LECCARDO. Tu non sai sbudellar se non borse.

[MARTEBELLONIO.] Ah, poltronaccio, ti farò conoscer chi son io! 50

LECCARDO. Ti conosco molto tempo fa, che fosti facchino, aiutante del boia, birro, sensale, ruffiano.

MARTEBELLONIO. I can't prick with my sword as you can with your tongue; but it's well for you that you are a worthless little female, or I'd run you clean through with one thrust.

CHIARETTA. I'm not afraid of your thrusts, for your sword bends at the point.

MARTEBELLONIO. Oh Lord, if I didn't fear that at the drawing of my sword the violence of the shattered air would arouse a tempest, I'd like to give you a taste of it. But that knave of a Leccardo will pay for this.

LECCARDO. [*from above*] You lie in your throat, for I'm a better man than you are.

MARTEBELLONIO. Where are you, you who speak but won't show yourself?

LECCARDO. You don't see me, because you don't want to see me: here I am.

MARTEBELLONIO. You'll make me sully my sword to-day for the first time with coward's blood.

LECCARDO. And you'll make me sully a hitherto sinless virgin cudgel.

MARTEBELLONIO. You've climbed up on the roof so that I can't reach you: when I lay hands on you, I'll quarter you like a curd.

LECCARDO. And you've set yourself in the piazza so as to have many avenues of escape, for you fear I may want to dust your backside for you.

MARTEBELLONIO. If you fall into my hands . . .

LECCARDO. If you slip out of my hands . . .

MARTEBELLONIO. I'll disembowel you.

LECCARDO. You don't know how to disembowel anything but purses.

MARTEBELLONIO. Ah, cringing slug, I'll show you who I am.

LECCARDO. I know you of old; you were a porter, hangman's helper, thug, fence, pimp.

[MARTEBELLONIO.] Ah, mondo traditore, ciel torchino,[1] stelle nemiche! fai del bravo perché non posso salir
sù, dove sei.   55

LECCARDO. E tu fai del bravo perché non posso calar
giù dove tu sei.

[MARTEBELLONIO.] Cala qua giù e pigliati cinquanta
scudi.

LECCARDO. Sali qua tu e pigliatene cento.   60

[MARTEBELLONIO.] Cala qua giù, traditore, e piagliati
mille scudi.

LECCARDO. Sali qua tu, forfante, e pigliatene dumila.

[MARTEBELLONIO.] O Dio, che tutto mi rodo per aver
in man quel traditore!   65

LECCARDO. O Dio, che tutto ardo per non poter cas-
tigar un matto!

[MARTEBELLONIO.] Con un salto verrò dove tu sei, se
ben la casa fusse più alta di Mongibello.[2]

LECCARDO. Con un salto calarò giù, se la casa fusse più   70
alta della torre di Babilonia.

[MARTEBELLONIO.] Tu sai che ti feci e che ti ho fatto, e
che ti soglio fare, né cesserò di far fin che non t'abbi fatto
e disfatto a mio modo.

LECCARDO. Non potendo far altro tirerò una pietra   75
dove sei: ti vo' acciaccare i pidocchi su la testa.

[MARTEBELLONIO.] O Dio, che montagna è questa!

LECCARDO. È la montagna di Mauritania, che è caduta
dal cielo, che ti manda Marte tuo padre, messer Caca-
merdonio.   80

[MARTEBELLONIO.] Questo incontro alle genti di Marte! [da sé] San Stefano,[3] scampami!

Mi partirò, t'incontrerò e ti gastigherò all'ordinario
come soglio.

LECCARDO. Ed io bastonate estraordinarie come so-   85
glio.

222

MARTEBELLONIO. Ah treacherous world, infidel blue heaven, inimical stars! You can swagger because I can't get up to you.

LECCARDO. And you swagger because I can't get down to you.

MARTEBELLONIO. Come down here and collect fifty crowns.

LECCARDO. You come up here and collect a hundred.

MARTEBELLONIO. Come on down, traitor, and get a thousand.

LECCARDO. You come on up, you knave, and get two thousand.

MARTEBELLONIO. Oh Lord, I'm gnawed by desire to have that traitor in my hands.

LECCARDO. Oh Lord, I'm all afire at not being able to punish the madman.

MARTEBELLONIO. With one jump I'll leap up to you, were the house higher than Etna.

LECCARDO. With one jump I'll leap down on you, were the house higher than the tower of Babel.

MARTEBELLONIO. You know what I did to you and what I have done to you and what I usually do to you, nor will I stop doing it, until I've done and undone you as I please.

LECCARDO. Since I can't do anything else, I'll throw a stone at you: I want to squash the lice on your head.

MARTEBELLONIO. Oh Lord, what mountain is this!

LECCARDO. It's the mountain of Mauritania fallen from heaven, sent you by your father Mars, Sir Farty-Craponio.

MARTEBELLONIO. This to the family of Mars? [*aside*] Saint Stephen, save me!

I'm leaving, I'll meet and chastize you in the ordinary way, as usual.

LECCARDO. And I—extraordinary cudgel blows, as usual.

[MARTEBELLONIO.] [*da sé*] In somma bisogna l'uomo serbar la sua dignità; che onor posso guadagnar con costui? Alla smenticata, ed alla muta, incontrandolo al buio, li darò la penitenza delle parole e della burla che 90 m'ha fatto.

LECCARDO. Io ho avuto a crepar della risa della battaglia fatta all'oscuro con Chiaretta; vo' andar a raccontarla a Don Flaminio; ma andrò prima a casa a veder che si faccia. 95

SCENA IV

DON FLAMINIO, PANIMBOLO.

DON FLAMINIO. Finalmente è pur stato vinto colui che era così malagevole a vincere, e preso chi pensava prender altri. Il volpone è caduto nella trappola e poco l'ha giovato la sua astuzia, ché ha trovato chi ha saputo più di lui. 5

PANIMBOLO. Or drizzisi un trofeo all'inganno, un mausoleo alla fraude, un arco trionfale alla bugia, un colosso alla falsità, poi che per lor mezo avete conseguito il sommo de' desideri.

DON FLAMINIO. Petto mio, se ben per l'addietro sei 10 stato bersaglio di tanti affanni, ricetto di tante pene, respira, e scaccia da te tanta amaritudine. Or andiamo a tor il possesso di Carizia, non temiamo più il fratello.

Gran meraviglia, ch'essendo gionto a quel segno ove solo aspirava il cor mio, non sento quell'allegrezza che 15 devrei, né ho passata notte più fastidiosa da che nacqui: avendo gli occhi rivolti alle prime passioni, non l'ho mai chiusi, né verso l'alba riposai molto; sogni, ombre, lar-

MARTEBELLONIO. [*aside*] After all, a man must maintain his dignity. What honor can I win fighting that fellow? Unexpectedly and stealthily, coming upon him in the dark, I'll give him his penance for the words and the trick he has dealt me.

[*Martebellonio departs.*]

LECCARDO. I nearly died laughing at the battle in the dark with Chiaretta. I want to go and tell Don Flaminio about it, but first I'll go home and see what's happening there.

SCENE IV

DON FLAMINIO, PANIMBOLO.

DON FLAMINIO. He who was so set on winning has finally been defeated, and he who thought to take in others has been taken in himself. The fox has fallen into the trap and his slyness availed him little, for he has met with a slier one still.

PANIMBOLO. Now let there be erected a monument to deceit, a mausoleum to fraud, a triumphal arch to mendacity, a colossus to falsehood, since by their means you have achieved the peak of your desires.

DON FLAMINIO. Oh my breast, although in the past you have been the target of so many afflictions, refuge of so many pains, breathe freely and expel such bitterness. Now we go to take possession of Carizia; we fear my brother no more.

It's a great wonder to me that having reached the sole aim of my heart's aspiration, I don't feel the joy that I should; nor have I ever in my life passed a worse night. My eyes, turned in remembrance to the beginnings of my passion, did not close once nor did I rest much near dawn: dreams, nightmarish shades and unrest disquiet-

ve, e turbolenze m'avean inquietato l'animo, e tutti i
sogni son stati travagli di Carizia: mi destava per non   20
conportargli, e pur dormendo sognava travagli. Veramente i travagli son ladri del sogno.

PANIMBOLO. Don Ignazio è di spiriti ardenti; non arà
indugiato fin adesso farli intendere che più non l'accetta
per isposa.   25

DON FLAMINIO. L'animo mio teme, e spera: spera nel
timore, e teme nella speranza; se ben desio Leccardo,
ché mi porti felice novella, pur temo qualche sinistro
successo. Vorrei venisse presto, ché ogni indugio mi
potrebbe apportar danno.   30

PANIMBOLO. Ecco s'apre la porta, e ne vien fuori.

SCENA V

LECCARDO, DON FLAMINIO, PANIMBOLO.

LECCARDO. [*da sé*] Se mi fussero stati posti innanzi
galli d'India cotti senza essere impillottati, caponi duri,
brodo macro e freddo, non arei potuto aver maggior
dispetto di quel che ho avuto quando viddi morta Carizia. O come intesi darmi colpi mortali allo stomaco ed   5
alla gola! Veggio Don Flaminio molto gioioso, ma di-
verrà subito doglioso come saprà quanto sia per dirgli.

DON FLAMINIO. Leccardo mio, i segni di mestizia che
porti scolpiti nel fronte mi dan segno d'infelice novella;
parla con la possibil brevità. Ohimè, tu taci, e par che   10
col tuo silenzio vogli significar qualche sinistro acci-
dente!

LECCARDO. [*da sé*] Desia saper quello che li dispiacerà
d'averlo saputo, ma vo' meno amareggiarlo al possibile.   15

DON FLAMINIO. Dhe, comincia presto!

ed my spirit, and all the dreams were of Carizia in distress; I woke myself to avoid them, but falling asleep yet again, I dreamed of troubles still. Indeed, troubles are thieves of sweet dreams.

PANIMBOLO. Don Ignazio is impetuous in spirit; he won't have waited this long to announce that he no longer accepts her as his bride.

DON FLAMINIO. My spirit fears and hopes: hopes in fear and fears in hope. Though I wish for Leccardo to bring me good news, yet I fear some evil occurrence; I wish he'd come quickly, for every delay could work my harm.

PANIMBOLO. Here, the door is opening and he's coming out.

SCENE V

LECCARDO, DON FLAMINIO, PANIMBOLO.

LECCARDO. [*apart*] If I had been served turkeys cooked unbasted, tough capons and thin, cold broth, I couldn't have been more distressed than I was to see Carizia lying dead. Oh, what mortal blows I felt to my stomach and my throat. I see Don Flaminio very joyful, but he will instantly become sorrowful when he knows what I have to tell him.

DON FLAMINIO. Leccardo my friend, the marks of sadness which you bear engraved on your brow signify unhappy news to me; speak with all possible brevity. Alas, you are silent, and it seems that with your silence you would communicate some dire event.

LECCARDO. [*aside*] He wants to know what it will displease him to know; I wish to pain him as little as possible.

DON FLAMINIO. Come, begin quickly.

227

LECCARDO. Di grazia, portami al monte di Somma,[1] dove nasce quella benedetta lacrima che bevendola ti fa lacrimare, acciò bevendone assai, possa lacrimar tanto che basti: ché or mi stanno gli occhi asciutti come un corno.   20

DON FLAMINIO. Col tardar più m'accresce il sospetto.

LECCARDO. Oimè, quella faccia più bianca d'una ricotta, quelle guancie vermiglie di vin cerasolo, quei labrucci più cremesin d'un presciutto, quelli . . . , ahi,   25 che mi scoppia il core!

DON FLAMINIO. Che cosa? sta male?

LECCARDO. Peggio!

DON FLAMINIO. Ecci pericolo della vita?

LECCARDO. Peggio!   30

DON FLAMINIO. È morta?

LECCARDO. Peggio!

DON FLAMINIO. Che cosa più peggio della morte?

LECCARDO. È morta, e morta disonorata!

DON FLAMINIO. O Dio, che nuova è questa che tu mi   35 dài?

LECCARDO. E mi dispiace darvela, e non vorrei sentiste da me quello che sete per intendere; ma avendolo a sapere, fate buon animo: Don Ignazio, non so che ingiuriose parole disse ad Eufranone, il quale, vinto in   40 quel punto dal furore ed inasprito dall'ira, con la schiuma in bocca com'un cignale, venne sù, e caricando la figlia di villanie, correa col pugnale in mano per infilzarla come un tordo al spedo. A questo la moglie se li fe' incontro e lo risospinse a dietro: instupedì la povera   45 figlia, ed aiutata dalla sua innocenza, diceva: «Padre mio, ascolta le mie ragioni; se conosci che ho fallato, ti porgerò il petto che mi ammazzi! » Egli, come un vitello che cerca di scappar di mano di coloro che lo conducono al macello, cercava scappar da man di quelli che   50 'l tenevano. Carizia cercava parlare, ma le chiome l'im-

LECCARDO. Oh carry me, pray, to the mount of Somma, whence springs that blessed tear the drinking of which makes you weep, so that drinking deeply of it I may weep enough, for my eyes are now dry as a bone.

DON FLAMINIO. With this delay he increases my doubt the more.

LECCARDO. Alas, that face whiter than a curd, those cheeks of cherry-red wine, those delicious lips more crimson than prosciutto: those . . . ,—ah, my heart bursts.

DON FLAMINIO. What is it? Is she ill?

LECCARDO. Worse.

DON FLAMINIO. Is her life in danger?

LECCARDO. Worse.

DON FLAMINIO. Is she dead?

LECCARDO. Worse.

DON FLAMINIO. What is worse than death?

LECCARDO. She is dead, and dead dishonored.

DON FLAMINIO. Oh God, what news is this you give me?

LECCARDO. And it distresses me to give it to you, and I wouldn't wish you to hear from me what you are about to learn; but as you have to know it, be brave. Don Ignazio said I don't know what injurious words to Eufranone, who, overcome in that instant by fury, and embittered by rage, foaming at the mouth like a wild boar, came up into the house and charging his daughter with vile deeds, rushed with his dagger in hand to run her through like a spitted thrush. At this his wife barred his way and pushed him back. The poor girl was stunned and, aided by her innocence, said: "My father, listen to my defense; if you know that I have sinned, I myself shall offer you my breast that you may kill me." He, like a calf seeking to escape the grasp of those who lead it to the slaughter, tried to evade the grasp of those who held him. Carizia attempted to speak, but her

pedivano; poi disse a fatica: « La conscienza mia pura mi
liberarà dall'obrobrio della calumnia, ché questa sola ha
lassato Iddio per consolazione degli innocenti! » Queste
ultime parole morir fra le labra, ché appena fur udite; e 55
morì prima della ferita: s'affoltavan i parenti per so-
venirla: ma « Lasciate, lasciate » gridava Eufranone,
« che l'uccida il dolore prima che l'abbi ad uccider il
ferro, e che prevenga la violenza la voluntaria morte; e
questo volerla far vivere è più tosto opra di crudeltà che 60
di pietà! » Così morì com'un agnello, e rimase con la
bocca un poco aperta com'un porchetto che s'arroste al
foco: ancor morta par bella e t'innamora, perché è morta senza offesa della sua bellezza.

DON FLAMINIO. Ahi, padre troppo austero, e troppo 65
nemico del suo sangue!

LECCARDO. Gli occhi miei, che mai piansero, piansero
allora. Eufranone la fe' subbito inchiudere in un'arca e
fecela sotterrar nella chiesa vicina per la porta di dietro
per non poner a romor la cittade. 70

DON FLAMINIO. Dunque è pur vero che l'anima mia sia
morta, e seco morto ogni mio bene, e sepolta ancora, e
con tanta bellezza sepolta ogni mia gioia, e me sepolto in
un infinito dolore? Gli occhi, che avanzavan il sol di
splendore, son chiusi in eterno sonno, e la bella bocca in 75
perpetuo silenzio. Ahi, non fia vero già ch'essendo tu
morta, io voglia restar in vita: è morta la sposa nel più
bello delle speranze, o com'in van s'affatica chi vuol
contrastar col Cielo, il qual'è più possente d'ogni uma-
no consiglio! Ho dato la morte da chi sperava la vita; ed 80
io, che di tanto mal son caggione, vivo ed ardisco spirar
quest'aria! Ho nociuto a me stesso, e patisco il mal che
ho fatto a me medesimo. Che m'ha giovato aver trava-
gliato tanti anni nella guerra,[2] esposto il petto a mille
perigli, imitar tanti esempi onorati per segnalarmi cava- 85
lier d'eterna lode, ed or per un sensual appetito son stato

loosened tresses prevented her; then she said with difficulty: "My pure conscience will free me from the disgrace of calumny, for this alone has God left to console the innocents." These last words died on her lips barely heard, and she died before the blow fell. Her relatives crowded about to help her: but "Let be, let be," cried Eufranone, "Let sorrow kill her, before the knife must do so, and let voluntary death forestall violence; this wish to revive her is an act of cruelty rather than of pity." Thus she died like a lamb, and remained with her mouth a little open, like a suckling pig roasting on the fire. Even dead she looks beautiful and makes you love her, for she died without damage to her beauty.

DON FLAMINIO. Alas, father too stern and too much an enemy to his own blood!

LECCARDO. My eyes, which never before wept, wept then. Eufranone had her immediately shut up in a casket and buried in the nearby church, carried through the back door, in order not to noise it abroad in the city.

DON FLAMINIO. Then is it really true, that my soul is dead, and with her all my good, and already buried too, and with such beauty buried all my joy and myself in infinite sorrow? The eyes that surpassed the sun in brightness are closed in eternal sleep, and the beautiful mouth in perpetual silence. Ah, never can I wish to live while you are dead. The bride is dead just as hope neared fruition. Oh, how vainly he labors who would combat heaven, which is more powerful than any human counsel! I have brought death to the one from whom I hoped for life; and I, the cause of so much evil, am alive, and dare to breathe this air! I have harmed myself, and I suffer a self-inflicted evil. What has it availed me to have toiled so many years in war, exposed my breast to a thousand dangers, imitated so many honored examples to distinguish myself as a knight of lasting fame, if now for a sensual appetite I have been the harm-

231

nocevol cagione della morte d'una innocente, tradito un fratello, infamato lei ed il padre, e disonorato il parentado? Ecco oscurata la gloria di tanti anni e di tante fatiche, e divenuto non cavalier d'onore, ma d'infamia, non di pietà, ma d'impietade. Dove mi nasconderò che non sia visto da uomo vivente? Dove andrò, dove mi nasconderò ché fugga e mi nasconda a me stesso, ché la conscienza afflige più di quanti tormenti può dar uomo vivente? Or sù, come cagione di tanto male, bisogna che pigli vendetta di me medesimo, che con un laccio mi toglia da tanto vituperio. Ahi, Panimbolo, tu fosti autor del malvaggio e da me mal preso consiglio, ed io più isconsigliato che lo presi, ché da si cattivo principio non poteva aspettar altro che l'infame e doloroso fine.

PANIMBOLO. Padrone, non è stato così mal il mio consiglio, come la mala Fortuna, ché l'una è sovraggionta all'altra, e noi per ischivarne una siamo incorsi in una peggiore; e da un error ne vengono mille, ed ogni cosa è riuscita in nostro danno: ed il mal sempre è andato crescendo di mal in peggio, né la fortuna istessa arebbe potuto rimediar a tanti infortunii: e quando la mala fortuna vuol rovinar alcuno, fa possibile l'impossibile.

DON FLAMINIO. Non è stato tanto la mala fortuna quanto il tuo cattivo consiglio, né in cose disconvenevoli dovevi tu prestarmi consiglio né agiuto.

PANIMBOLO. Voi che mi avete sforzato con tanti comandi m'accusate contro ragione. Ma chi può gir contro il Cielo? Ed essendo il mondo così sregolato ed insconsigliato, con che ragione o consiglio potete regolarvi con lui? non conoscete, come umana creatura, che tutte le cose son instabil ed incerte, e che il mondo inchina or ad una ed or ad un'altra parte? E l'uomo accorto nella necessità de' pericoli deve accomodar l'animo suo alla prudenza; ma la nobiltà del vostro sangue dovrebbe

ful cause of an innocent's death, betrayed a brother, defamed her and her father, and dishonored her house? Here now is tarnished the glory won by so many years and pains, and I have become the knight not of honor but of infamy, not of pity and devotion but of pitilessness and desecration. Where shall I hide myself from the sight of living man? Where shall I go, where shall I hide, to flee and hide from myself, for conscience afflicts me more than any torments living man can devise? Well then, as the cause of so much evil, I must take vengeance on myself and with a noose put myself beyond the reach of such great blame. Alas, Panimbolo, you were author of this ill and by me ill-taken advice, and I was the more ill-advised to take it, in that from so bad a beginning nothing could be expected but an infamous and woeful end.

PANIMBOLO. Master, it wasn't so much my bad advice as it was bad luck, for one misfortune followed another, and to avoid one we ran into a worse; and from one error came a thousand, and everything turned out wrong for us, and the evil went on growing from bad to worse, nor could fortune herself have remedied so many misfortunes; and when bad fortune wants to ruin someone, it makes possible the impossible.

DON FLAMINIO. It was not so much bad fortune as it was your wicked advice; nor should you have lent me advice or aid in improper things.

PANIMBOLO. Unreasonably you accuse me, you who forced me with so many commands. But who can go against the will of Heaven? And the world being so out of rule and ill-advised, by what reason or advice can you take your rule from it? Do you not know, as a human creature, that all things are unstable and uncertain and that the world inclines now to one side, and now to the other? And the wise man, when danger makes it necessary, must shape his spirit to prudence; but the nobility

destar in voi l'ardire, e caminar nel termine della modestia, soffrir, e conservar voi stesso a più liete speranze.

DON FLAMINIO. Io non temo più i colpi della Fortuna,
ché è morta ogni Fortuna per me. Non bisogna più ordir fraudi ed inganni; non ho più sospetto di niuno, 125
poiché è morta la cagion di tutte queste cose; ahi, che
pena converrebbe al mio fallo? mi conosco degno di
maggior pena che la morte: bisognaria che morisse d'u-
na morte che mai finisse; ma prima che morisse, deside-
rarei restituir l'onor che l'ho tolto, e scoprir l'inganno 130
che l'ho fatto.

PANIMBOLO. Ecco il vostro fratello che viene a voi.

SCENA VI
Don Ignazio, e Don Flaminio.

DON IGNAZIO. Veggio Don Flaminio assai doloroso.

DON FLAMINIO. Don Ignazio (ché al tradimento che
v'ho fatto, non son degno d'esservi né di chiamarvi fratello), vengo a voi ad accusar il mio fallo: io son quello
iniquo che avanzo d'iniquità tutti gli uomini.   5

DON IGNAZIO. Fratello, che aspetto pallido è il vostro?
che pianto, che parole son queste che intendo da voi?

DON FLAMINIO. Io son quello che attorto ho accusato
appo voi quella donna celeste, il cui corpo fu tanto bello
che non si vidde mai cosa tale.   10

DON IGNAZIO. Io non so ancora di che cosa parliate.

DON FLAMINIO. Io son quello che v'ho ingannato, e
tradito, e con quelle false illusioni di notte ho fatto veder
che Carizia fusse inonesta.

DON IGNAZIO. O estremo dolor, cessa alquanto fin 15
ch'intenda da costui come il fatto è seguito.

of your blood ought to arouse your hardihood; proceed within the limit of restraint, bear this and keep yourself for brighter hopes.

DON FLAMINIO. I fear no more the blows of fortune, for all fortune is dead to me. There is no more need to plan frauds and deceits; I beware no man now, since the reason for all these things is dead. Alas, what punishment would fit my crime? I know I deserve a greater pain than death: I should die a never-ending death. But before dying I wish to restore the honor of which I robbed her and to reveal the deceit which I perpetrated.

PANIMBOLO. Here, your brother approaches.

SCENE VI

DON IGNAZIO, and DON FLAMINIO, [PANIMBOLO].

DON IGNAZIO. I see Don Flaminio very sorrowful.

DON FLAMINIO. Don Ignazio (for by the treachery I have done you I am unworthy to be your brother or to call you mine), I come to you to denounce my crime: I am the evildoer whose iniquity surpasses all men's.

DON IGNAZIO. Brother, whence this pale countenance? What burst of grief, what words are these I hear from you?

DON FLAMINIO. I am he who falsely accused to you that heavenly woman whose earthly body was the loveliest thing ever seen.

DON IGNAZIO. I still don't know what you're talking of.

DON FLAMINIO. I am he who has deceived and betrayed you, and with those false illusions by night made Carizia appear to you unchaste.

DON IGNAZIO. Oh fiercest grief, hold off a little, until I learn from him how the deed was done.

235

DON FLAMINIO. Io, essendo innamorato di Carizia da quel infelice giorno che fu la festa de' tori, nascondei l'amor mio verso lei a voi quanto potei. Poi avendo inteso quanto voi più degnamente avevate oprato di me, 20 accecato da una nebbia di gelosia, vi feci veder quell'apparenza di notte, nella quale il parasito e la serva di casa sua mi fur ministri; e fu il mio intento che, voi ricusandola, io col prezzo del tradimento mi avesse comprato le sue nozze. Ma il mio pensiero ha sortito contrario fine, 25 perché è morta.

DON IGNAZIO. O Dio, quante mutazioni in un tempo sente l'anima mia: un intenso dolor della sua morte, pena della sua infamia ed innocenza, gelosia dell'inganno, rabbia dell'offesa che hai fatta al padre! Ed è pos- 30 sibil che si trovi un cuore, non dico di cavaliero, ma così barbaro ed inumano in cui abbia potuto cadere così mostruosa invenzione? In qual anima nata sotto le più maligne stelle del cielo, in qual spirito uscito dalle più cupe parti dell'inferno, vestito d'umana carne, ha potu- 35 to capire sceleraggine come questa?

DON FLAMINIO. Eccomi, buttato in terra, abbraccio le tue ginocchia, ti porgo il pugnale; la crudeltà che ho usata contra voi, usate voi contro me: qua si tratta del vostro onore; io son quello che t'ho tradito, infamato, e 40 tolta la sposa. Tu sei infame di doppia infamia se non te ne vendichi. Vorrei trovar le più pungenti parole che si ponno, per provocarti ad un giustissimo sdegno.

DON IGNAZIO. O tu, che non vo' dir mio fratello, fatti indietro, non mi toccare, allontana da me le tue mani 45 profane, ché non macchino il mio corpo! patirò che mi tocchino quelle mani che m'hann'uccisa la sposa? non contaminar le mie orecchie con le tue accuse; gli occhi miei rivolgono lo sguardo altrove, perché schivano di mirarti: sgombra questa terra, purga l'aria e 'l cielo in- 50 fetto dal tuo abominevole spirito: porta fuora del mondo anima così scelerata e traditrice, e come hai saputo

DON FLAMINIO. Being in love with Carizia ever since that unlucky day of the festival of the bulls, I hid my love from you as well as I could. Then having learned how much more worthily than I you had proceeded, blinded by a fog of jealousy, I caused you to see by night that nocturnal appearance, in which the parasite and the maidservant of her house were my ministers. And it was my intention, when you had refused her, to buy marriage with her at the price of treachery; but my design has turned out to the contrary, for she is dead.

DON IGNAZIO. Oh God, how many upheavals my soul feels in one moment: an intense grief for her death, pity for her innocence defamed, jealous anger at the deceit, rage at your affront to her father! And is it possible that anyone, not to say a gentleman, has a heart barbarous and inhuman enough to have hatched such a monstrous plan? What soul born under heaven's most evil star, which of darkest hell's spirits clothed in human flesh has harbored such wickedness?

DON FLAMINIO. Here I am, prostrate, I embrace your knees, I offer you my dagger: use me with the cruelty I have used toward you. Your honor is at stake: I am he who betrayed, defamed and robbed you of your bride. You are twice dishonored if you do not avenge yourself. I would find the sharpest of words, to goad you to a most just anger.

DON IGNAZIO. Oh you—I will not say my brother— stand back, do not touch me, take away your impious hands lest they defile me! Shall I suffer the touch of those hands which have killed my bride? Do not contaminate my ears with your self-accusations; my eyes turn away their gaze, loth to look at you. Free the earth, purge the air and the polluted sky of your abominable spirit, remove from the world a soul so wicked and treacherous,

machinar tante fraudi, così machina un modo da fuggir
dal mondo. Tu non morrai dalle mie mani; lascio che la
tua vita sia la tua vendetta: vo' che sopravivi al tuo   55
biasmevole ed infame atto, vo' che venghi in odio a te
stesso. Ma qual spirito dell'inferno ti spinse a tanta
sceleraggine?

DON FLAMINIO. Le fiamme de' suoi begli occhi, ch'accesero te dell'amore suo, accesero ancor me, e come la   60
desiavate voi, la desiava pur io; e quel tradimento che
v'ho fatto per possederla, m'imaginava che voi l'aveste
fatto a me; ma il caso, che maneggia tutte le cose, ha
fatto succedere il tutto contro il mio pensiero: ramentati
quella infinita bellezza, e secondo quella giudica l'error 65
mio. Qua ha peccato la sorte non la voluntà; e quando
l'effetto che succede è contrario alla voluntà, purga il
biasmo di chi il commette.

DON IGNAZIO. O falsa defension di ver' accusa! te accesero fiamme amorose de' suoi begli occhi? Tesifone   70
tenne l'esca, Aletto il focile, Megera percosse la pietra, [1]
e ne scagliò fuori faville tartaree accese nel più basso ba-
ratro dell'inferno. O notte, che fosti tanto cieca che non
scernesti l'inganno, t'ingrossasti di folte tenebre, ti co-
pristi di scuro manto per occultar fatto sì abominevole;   75
vergognandoti di te stessa ti nascondesti in te medesima! Te nascondesti nella tua notte, o luna, che con disu-
gual splendore facevi incerto lume, la nefandità ti fe'
nascondere la tua faccia, per che ti turbò e ti spense il
lume! O cielo, gira al contrario, e conturba le stagioni,   80
ed il sole non dia splendore a questo secolo infame, poi
che un fratello non è sicuro dall'insidie dell'altro fratello!
Non so che nome potrà aguagliar l'opre tue, sì inumano, barbaro, traditore senza vergogna e senza timor di
Dio. Il mondo non ha nome con che possa chiamarti.   85

DON FLAMINIO. Supplice e lacrimoso ti sta dinanzi a'
piedi la cagion del tuo affanno. Non chiede né perdono

and as you have cleverly contrived so many snares, now go and contrive your own escape from the world. You shall not die by my hand: I leave your life as my revenge on you. I want you to survive your blameworthy and infamous act, I want you to become hateful to yourself. But what devil of hell moved you to such wickedness?

DON FLAMINIO. The fires of her beautiful eyes which inflamed you to love, inflamed me too; and as you desired her, so did I; and the treachery I practiced on you to possess her, I imagined that you had practiced on me. But chance, which directs all, made everything go contrary to my intention. Remember that infinite beauty and judge my error accordingly. Chance, not will, has sinned here; and when the resulting effect is contrary to the will's intention, he who caused it is purged of blame.

DON IGNAZIO. Oh, false defense against a true charge! You were inflamed by amorous fires from her beautiful eyes, were you? Tisiphone held the tinder, Alecto the steel, Megaera struck the flint, and there leapt forth Tartarean sparks, ignited in the deepest pit of hell. Oh night, you who were so blind that you did not discern the fraud, you muffled yourself in thick shadows, you covered yourself with a dark mantle to hide so hateful a deed; ashamed, you hid yourself in yourself. You hid in your night, oh moon, who with wavering beams made doubtful light; the wickedness of it made you hide your face, for it shook you and doused your light. Oh heaven, reverse your motion and disorder the seasons, and let not the sun give brightness to this bad world, since here one brother is not safe from the snares of another. I know not what name can fit your actions, shameless traitor so inhuman, barbarous, without fear of God. The world has no name for you.

DON FLAMINIO. Suppliant and tearful, the cause of your affliction is at your feet. He asks neither forgive-

né vita, perché non la merita e non l'accetta, ché quando
l'uomo ha fatto quel che non deve, non deve più vivere,
per non vivere vita pessima ed infame; ma chiede ven- 90
detta; e se in te è rimasta qualche scintilla di fraterna
pietà, uccidimi, non invidearmi morte così desiata; anzi
per rimedio delle mie pene non chiedo morte ordinaria,
non assegno luoco alle ferite; ferite dove volete, trovate
voi nuove sorti di morti, com'io ho trovate nuove sorti 95
di tradimenti.

DON IGNAZIO. La vendetta facciala Eufranone suo
padre, a cui hai uccisa la figlia, e che figlia? quella ch'a-
mava più che l'anima sua, a cui se è pesata la morte, assai
più pesarà il modo della sua morte. 100

DON FLAMINIO. Andrò ratto a lui; forsi troverò in lui
quella pietà che non ho potuto trovar in voi, e li resti-
tuirò la fama come posso.

DON IGNAZIO. Ecco che giunge: fuggirò il suo aspetto,
ch'avendoli così a torto ingiuriato la figlia, non ho più 105
animo di comparirgli innanzi.

SCENA VII

EUFRANONE, DON FLAMINIO.

EUFRANONE. [da sé] Veggio il fratello di Don Ignazio
che vien verso me. Che voglion costoro? forsi uccider-
mi la rimasta figliuola?

DON FLAMINIO. Onoratissimo Eufranone, ve si appre-
senta innanzi il reo di tanti mali, acciò che con mol- 5
tiplicato suplicio lo castighiate. Io essendo ardentemen-
te innamorato della bellezza ma assai più dell'onestà di
Carizia, e veggendo che mio fratello m'avea prevenuto
a torsela per moglie, l'invidia, l'amor, la gelosia facen-
dono lor ultimo sforzo in me, l'infamai appresso lui, ac- 10

ness nor life, because he does not deserve the one or accept the other—for when a man does what he ought not to do, he should live no more, so as not to live a vile and wicked life—but he asks vengeance. If there remain in you some sparks of brotherly feeling, kill me. Do not begrudge me the death I so desire; nor to remedy my suffering do I ask an ordinary death, I do not point out where to wound me: strike where you will, invent new kinds of death, as I have invented new kinds of treachery.

DON IGNAZIO. Let vengeance be Eufranone's, the father whose daughter you have killed, and what a daughter! One he loved more than his own soul, he to whom however crushing her death, much more crushing will be its manner.

DON FLAMINIO. I'll go to him instantly; perhaps I shall find in him the pity I could not find in you, and I'll restore his honor to him as best I can.

DON IGNAZIO. Here he comes now. I shall flee his sight, for having so falsely defamed his daughter, I cannot bear to appear before him.

SCENE VII

EUFRANONE, DON FLAMINIO.

EUFRANONE. [apart] I see the brother of Don Ignazio coming toward me. What do they want? To kill my remaining daughter, perhaps?

DON FLAMINIO. Most honored Eufranone, the perpetrator of many wrongs comes before you, that with torture heaped on torture you may punish him. Being ardently in love with the beauty, but still more with the virtue, of Carizia and seeing that my brother had forestalled me in marrying her, moved by the utmost force of envy, love and jealousy, I defamed her to him, so that

cioché, egli rifiutandola per onorar la sua fama, me la togliesse io per moglie; e Leccardo, vostro servo di casa, m'aperse la porta di notte, . . .

EUFRANONE. O Dio, a che sorte d'uomini ho dato in guardia la casa mia! 15

DON FLAMINIO. . . . non pensandomi che la vostra iracondia avesse a terminar in atto sì sanguinoso. Tu, giusto monarca del Cielo, a cui solo è concesso di penetrar gli occulti seni del cuore, tu mi sia testimone come non fu mai mia intenzione offender voi, né d'infamar 20 lei, ma sol ch'ei la lasciasse, per tormela io per moglie; e tu mi sia ancor testimone come non fu mai donna di più candido onore, né mai macchiato di picciol neo di brutezza; prego la vostra bontà, ché sovra di me pigliate la vendetta della morte di vostra figliuola, e dell'offesa del- 25 l'onor vostro.

EUFRANONE. Ohimè, che le vostre parole m'hanno passato l'anima: voi avete ucciso lei, me e la madre in un colpo, ed uccisi nel corpo e nell'onore! Ohimè, che or ora m'uccidi la mia figliuola, ché allora pensando al 30 mancamento ch'avea fatto all'onor suo, mosso dalla disonestà del fatto, il desio della vendetta non mi facean sentir la doglia. O sfortunata fanciulla, o anima innocentissima, o figlia viva e morta unicamente amata da me, tu sola eri l'occhio, mente, mano e piedi del tuo 35 padre infelice; con teco compartiva gli affanni della mia povertà, e come un comun peso, la sopportavamo insieme; la tua compagnia non mi faceva sentir i difetti del tempo, e mi faceva cara la vita. O invano nata bella ed onorata: o nocente bellezza: o dannoso e mortale dono 40 di natura, misera ed infelice onestà! Dunque per esser tu nata bella ed onorata hai voluto perder l'onor e la tua vita? Dhe, qual prima piangerò delle tue morti, quella del corpo o quella dell'onore? Di quella del corpo non devo pianger molto, ch'essendo nata mortale e figlia 45

242

when he repudiated her for his honor's sake, I might take her as my wife. And Leccardo, your house servant, opened the door to me at night, . . .

EUFRANONE. Oh God, to what kind of men have I entrusted the safety of my house!

DON FLAMINIO. . . . I not thinking that your wrath might end in such a bloody deed. Just monarch of heaven, You to whom alone it is given to penetrate the hidden recesses of the heart, be my witness that I never intended to injure you, Eufranone, or to defame her, but only to make him leave her, so that I might have her for my wife; and God be witness also that there never was a lady of more spotless honor, not ever blemished with the least mole of ugliness. I beg your goodness to avenge on me the death of your daughter and the affront to your honor.

EUFRANONE. Alas, your words have pierced my soul: you have killed her, me, and her mother in one blow, left us dead in both body and honor. Alas, now at this moment truly you bereave me of my daughter, for then, thinking of her fault toward her honor, being stricken by the wantonness of the deed, desire for vengeance, all made me impervious to grief. Oh hapless maiden, oh most innocent soul, oh my daughter, living and dead singularly beloved, you alone were eye, mind, hand, and feet of your unhappy father; with you I shared the trials of my poverty and we bore it together, like a common burden: your company kept me from feeling the defects of age and made life dear to me. Oh in vain were you born beautiful and good: oh harmful beauty, oh injurious and deadly gift of nature, unhappy and ill-fated virtue! For being born beautiful and good, then, you had to lose your honor and your life? Ah, for which of your deaths shall I weep first, that of your body or that of your honor? For that of your body I need not weep much, for being born mortal and daughter of

243

d'uomo mortale, non ti potea mancare il morire; ma
piangerò la morte della tua fama, ch'essendo nata figlia
di padre onorato, col innocente tua morte hai infamato
te e 'l tuo parentado.

DON FLAMINIO. Il reo, pentito del suo errore, ti porge 50
il pugnale, ché vendichi con la tua mano il torto che ti ha
fatto.

EUFRANONE. A che mi giova il vostro pentimento, e la
vendetta, che cercate da me, mi restituirà forsi viva ed
onorata la mia figliuola? Infelice e sconsolato conforto! 55
Ahi, figlia, ahi, cara figlia, essendo io falsamente informato che tu avessi fatto torto all'onor tuo, fu tanto l'impeto dell'ira ch'estinse l'affetto paterno e ti corsi col
pugnale adosso. Tu pur volevi dir le tue ragioni, e la
furia non me le fece ascoltare. O che bei doni maritali 60
che ti portai: un pugnale! O che bel letto che ti aparec-
chiai: l'arca e la sepultura! Figlia d'infelice e sfortunato
padre, chi t'ha prodotto al mondo t'ave ucciso! Aresti
trovato più pietà in un barbaro che in tuo padre! O dolore insopportabile, o calamità mondane! E perché vivo, 65
per che non m'uccido con le mie mani? Ahi, che tu con
un leggerissimo sonno sei passata da questa vita, e sei
uscita di travagli, son finiti i tuoi dolori, ma a me, che
resto in vita, resteranno perpetuamente impressi nel
cuore i tuoi costumi, la tua bontà, la tua onestà, e la 70
riverenza che mi portavi. M'hai lasciato orbo, afflitto, e
pieno di pentimento: oh fossi morto in tua vece, vecchio canuto e stanco dal lungo vivere!

DON FLAMINIO. Eufranone, ascoltate di grazia.

EUFRANONE. Non voglio ascoltar più, ché quanto più 75
apro ed apparecchio l'orrecchie al vostro dire, più apro
ed apparecchio gli occhi al pianto. Ma perché i cavalieri
d'onore sogliono difendere e non opprimere gli onori
delle donne, vi priego, se le ragioni divine ed umane vi
muovono punto, fatte che quella bocca che l'ave accu- 80
sata, quella l'escusi: usate questa pietosa gratitudine, an-

mortal man, you could not have escaped death; but I shall weep for the death of your good name, for being born the daughter of a man of honor, by your innocent death you have dishonored yourself and your family.

DON FLAMINIO. The repentant criminal offers you his dagger, that with your own hand you may avenge the wrong he has done you.

EUFRANONE. What good to me is your repentance; can the revenge you look for from my hand give back my daughter alive and whole in her honor? Miserable and unconsoling comfort! Ah daughter, ah dear daughter, falsely informed that you had wronged your honor, I felt such force of wrath that it extinguished a father's love and I ran at you with dagger upraised. You wished to clear yourself, but rage would not let me listen. Oh what beautiful wedding gifts I took you: a dagger! Oh what a beautiful bed I decked for you: a tomb and burial! Daughter of an ill-starred, luckless father, he who brought you into the world has killed you! You would have found more fatherly feeling in a barbarian! Oh woe unendurable, oh calamities of earthly life! And why do I go on living? Why do I not kill myself with my own hands? Ah, with a gentle sleep you have passed out of this life and escaped its troubles! Your sufferings are ended, but I, who remain alive, will bear forever stamped on my heart your ways, your goodness, your purity and your reverence toward me. You have left me bereaved, afflicted, and full of repentance: oh, that I had died in your stead, a hoary old man weary of a long life!

DON FLAMINIO. Eufranone, listen, I beg you.

EUFRANONE. I will listen no more, for the more I open and dispose my ears to your speech, the more I open and dispose my eyes to tears. But as gentlemen of honor are wont to defend rather than oppress the honor of ladies, I pray you, if divine and human right can move you, let the mouth that accused her excuse her. Make this com-

date in palazzo dinanzi al Viceré vostro zio, raccontate la
verità, acciochè, divolgatosi il fatto per sì autorevoli
bocche, le restituiate l'onore, e si toglia tanto cicala-
mento dal volgo. 85

DON FLAMINIO. Poi che non posso giovarle col spender la robba, la vita, e l'onore, le giovarò con la lingua:
onorerò lei, infamerò me stesso; e son tenuto farlo per
obligo di cavaliero. Andiamo insieme innanzi al mio
zio, acciochè di quello che farò ne siate buon testimone. 90

SCENA VIII

LECCARDO, BIRRI.

LECCARDO. Aspettar che si mangi in casa è opra dis-
perata. Tutti stanno colerichi: intrighi di amori, di morti, di cavalieri, e cacasangui che venghino a quanti sono!
Al fuoco non son pignate né spedi su le brage: i cuochi e
guattari son scampati; la casa di Don Flaminio deve star 5
peggio; il budello maggior mi gorgoglia «cro, cro», la
bocca mi sta asciutta, la lingua mi si è attaccata al palato,
il collo è fatto stretto e lungo, e che peggio mi potrebbe
far un capestro? e si temo d'esser appiccato, così mi par
d'esser appicato due volte. 10

BIRRI. Ci incontra a tempo; costui è desso.

LECCARDO. [da sé] Veggio birri, e devono cercar me;
chi si arrischia a molti perigli, sempre ne trova alcuno
che lo fa pericolare. Ho scampato la furia di un legno,
non so come scamparò quella de' tre legni.[1] 15

BIRRI. [primo] Prendetelo, e cercatelo bene.

[secondo] Ha molti scudi.

[terzo] Questi son nostri.

passionate acknowledgment: go to the palace and in the presence of your uncle, the viceroy, recount the truth, so that when the fact is published by such authoritative voices, you may restore her honor and stop the gossiping of the crowd.

DON FLAMINIO. Since I cannot be of use to her by spending my substance, my life, and my honor, I shall serve her with my tongue: I shall honor her, I shall defame myself; and I am obliged to do this by my honor as a gentleman. Let us go together to my uncle's presence, that you may be a true witness of what I shall do.

SCENE VIII

LECCARDO, [THREE] CONSTABLES.

LECCARDO. To wait for dinnertime at home is hopeless. They're all in an uproar: tangled webs of loves, deaths, gentlemen's honor; and I say a bloody pox on the whole lot! There's not a pot on the fire nor a spit on the coals; the cooks and the scullions have run off. Don Flaminio's house must be worse still. My gut is gurgling "cro, cro," my mouth is dry, my tongue is stuck to my palate, my throat is tight and stretched; what greater harm could a noose do me? If I'm afraid of hanging, this is like being hanged twice.

CONSTABLE. Here he comes now: he's the one.

LECCARDO. [aside] I see constables, and they must be looking for me. He who risks danger always finds someone to brew it for him. I escaped the force of one cudgel, but I don't know how I'll escape that of three blockheads.

CONSTABLES. Take and search him well.
He has plenty of crowns.
Now they're ours.

LECCARDO. [*da sé*] O dinari rubati, ve ne tornate al vostro paese: oh quanto poco avete dimorato meco! 20

BIRRI. Camina camina!

LECCARDO. Dove mi strascinate?

BIRRI. Al boia!

LECCARDO. Nuova di beveraggio; che vuol il signor Boia da me? 25

BIRRI. Accomodarti un poco le lattucchiglie della camiscia intorno al collo con le scarpe,² che non stanno bene accomodate.

LECCARDO. Il ringrazio del buon' animo; mi contento che stiano come stanno, e volendole accomodare, me 30 l'accomodarò con le mani mie.

BIRRI. Presto presto!

LECCARDO. Ché tanta fretta?

BIRRI. Ti vol appicar caldo caldo.

LECCARDO. Che l'importa che sia freddo freddo? 35

BIRRI. Le cose fatte calde calde son buone.

LECCARDO. Che son' io piatto di maccheroni, che bisogna che sia caldo caldo? Ma io vo' morir appiccato per non morir sempre di fame; ma se volete appicarmi, fatemi mangiar prima che non muoia di doppia morte, e 40 della fune, e della fame.

BIRRI. Camina!

LECCARDO. Son debole, e non posso caminare.

BIRRI. Le buon'opre tue ti fan meritevole d'una forca.

LECCARDO. Per vostra grazia, non per mio merito: ed 45 io ne fo un dono alle Signorie Vostre come più meritevoli di me.

BIRRI. Là tua gola ti ha fatto incappare.

LECCARDO. I topi golosi incappano al laccio.

BIRRI. Sei stato cagione che sia morta la più degna 50 gentil donna di questa città per la tua golaccia.

LECCARDO. Oh stolen money, you're returning whence you came! Oh how short a time you dwelt with me!

CONSTABLE. Step lively, move!

LECCARDO. Where are you dragging me?

CONSTABLE. To the hangman.

LECCARDO. Give me a tip: what does Sir Hangman want with me?

CONSTABLE. To adjust the shirt ruffles around your neck for you with his shoes, because they're not neat.

LECCARDO. I thank him for the kind intention: I like them the way they are, and if I wanted them rearranged, I'd do it for myself, with my hands.

CONSTABLE. Faster, faster!

LECCARDO. What's the hurry?

CONSTABLE. He wants to hang you piping hot.

LECCARDO. What difference would it make to him if I were stone cold?

CONSTABLE. Piping hot things are good.

LECCARDO. Am I a dish of macaroni, that I must be piping hot? Still—I'll die on the gallows so as not to be always dying of hunger; but if you're going to hang me, feed me first, so that I don't die a double death, by hemp and by hunger.

CONSTABLE. Move!

LECCARDO. I'm weak and can't walk.

CONSTABLE. By your good works you deserve a gibbet.

LECCARDO. By your grace, not by my desert, and I'll make a gift of it to Your Worships, as more deserving than I.

CONSTABLE. Your greed has been your downfall.

LECCARDO. Greedy mice fall into the snare.

CONSTABLE. You have caused the death of the worthiest gentlewoman of this city, by and for your gluttonous maw.

249

LECCARDO. E se non lo faceva per la mia gola, per chi l'aveva io a fare?

BIRRI. Ma tu troppo ti tratteni.

LECCARDO. Avendo a morir strangolato, ponetemi di 55
grazia un fegatello in gola, ché quando il capestro mi stringerà il collo di fuori, la gola mi stringerà il fegadello di dentro, ed il succo, che calerà giù, mi confortarà lo stomaco e lo polmone; e quello che ascenderà sù mi confortarà la bocca e 'l cervello; così morendo non mi parrà 60
morire.

BIRRI. Se non camini presto, ti darrò delle pugna.

LECCARDO. Al manco dite a i confrati, che m'hanno a ricordar l'anima, che portino seco scatole di confezioni, e vernaccia fina, ché mi confortino di passo in passo. 65

BIRRI. Non dubbitar, ché andrai su un asino, con una mitra in testa,[3] con trombe, e gran compagnia, ed il boia ti sollicitarà con un buon staffile.

LECCARDO. O, pergole di salciccioni alla lombarda, o provature, morrò io senza gustarvi! o caneva, non as- 70
saggiarò più i tuoi vini! Prego Iddio che coloro, che t'hanno a godere, sieno uomini di giudizio, e non sciagurati che ti assassinino; a Dio, galli d'India, caponi, galline, e polli, non vi goderò più mai!

BIRRI. Presto, finimola. 75

LECCARDO. Fratelli, di grazia, dopo che sarò morto, sepellitemi in un magazin di vino, ché a quell'odore risusciterò ogni momento.

BIRRI. Camina, forfante Leccardo!

LECCARDO. Forfante no, Leccardo sì. 80

LECCARDO. For whom should I have done it, if not for my maw?

CONSTABLE. You're dawdling.

LECCARDO. Since I must die throttled, for pity's sake put a chicken liver in my mouth, so that when the noose squeezes my neck on the outside, my throat will squeeze the liver on the inside, and the juice that trickles down will comfort my stomach and my lungs, and what spurts up will comfort my mouth and my brain: to die thus will not seem to me like dying.

CONSTABLE. If you don't walk faster, I'll help you along with my fists.

LECCARDO. At least tell the friars who will accompany me to the gallows for my soul's sake to bring with them boxes of sweets and some of the best *vernaccia* to solace me at each step.

CONSTABLE. Have no fear, you'll ride on an ass with a mitre on your head, to the sound of trumpets, surrounded by a great company, and the hangman will urge you on with a fine whip.

LECCARDO. Oh garlands of Lombard sausages, oh fresh cheeses, I shall die without tasting you: oh buttery, I'll not sample your wines again! I pray God that they to whom it is given to enjoy you may be men of judgment, and not wretches who will ruin you. Farewell, turkeys, capons, hens and chickens; I shall enjoy you nevermore!

CONSTABLE. Make haste, let's be finished.

LECCARDO. Brothers, when I am dead, please bury me in a wine cellar, for at that smell, I shall ever rise up again.

CONSTABLE. Move, you rascally lickchops.

LECCARDO. Rascal, no; lickchops, yes.

ATTO V

SCENA I

DON RODORIGO, Viceré della provincia, EUFRANONE,
DON FLAMINIO.

DON RODORIGO. Dunque mi sarà forza, per non mancar ad una giustissima causa, incrudelir nel mio sangue,
che la prima giustizia ch'abbia a far in Salerno sia contro
il mio nipote, qual amo come proprio mio figliuolo?

EUFRANONE. Signor Viceré, chi non sa reggere e co- 5
mandare a' suoi affetti, lasci di reggere e comandar agli
altri, né si deve prepor la natura alle leggi; però non
dovete far torto a me perché costoro sieno a voi con-
gionti di sangue e di amore.

DON RODORIGO. In me non può tanto la passione che 10
mi torca dal dritto della giustizia, né mi muove rispetto
d'altri, né proprio affetto; ché quanto mi sento vincer
dall'amore, tanto mi fo raffrenar dalla raggione.

DON FLAMINIO. Giudice, non zio, io vengo ad accusar
me stesso: ho infamata ed uccisa l'amante mia! Non 15
chiedo pietà, né perdono; usate meco le vostre raggioni,
datemi tanti supplicii quanti ne può soffrir un reo: vuo'
con presta e vergognosa morte purgar gli errori che per
me son avvenuti, ché i fatti dell'onore ricercano testimonio d'un chiaro sole. Toglietemi questo avanzo di 20
vita, toglietemi da tanta miseria; qua non lenti consigli
di vecchi, ma un espedito decreto ché muoia, e voi sete
reo giudice ed inumano, se non volete che con la morte
finisca la mia miseria, e perdonatemi se non uso con voi

ACT V

SCENE I

DON RODORIGO, viceroy of the province; EUFRANONE, DON FLAMINIO, [GENTLEMEN and ATTENDANTS].

DON RODORIGO. So, shall I be forced, in order to render justice to a most righteous suit, to turn cruel toward my own blood; must the first judgment I hand down in Salerno be against my nephew, whom I love as my own son?

EUFRANONE. My lord viceroy, he who cannot rule and command his affections should leave off ruling and commanding others, and ties of nature should not take precedence of the law; therefore, you must not wrong me because the evildoers are related to you by blood and by love.

DON RODORIGO. Passion has not such sway in me as to turn me from the straight way of justice, nor does respect of persons move me, nor my own affection; for as much as I feel myself overcome by love, equally do I restrain myself by reason.

DON FLAMINIO. Judge, not uncle, I come to accuse myself: I have maligned and killed my beloved. I ask no pity nor pardon; pass sentence on me as you see fit, condemn me to as many tortures as ever criminal can suffer. By prompt and shameful death I wish to expiate the wrongs occasioned through my fault, for matters of honor require the testimony of the bright light of day. Take from me this remnant of life, take me from such wretchedness; let us have here not the slow deliberations of old men, but a speedy decree that I die; and you are a wicked and inhuman judge if you do not will that I finish my wretchedness by death. And forgive me if I

253

quelle parole rispettevoli che a voi si devon per ogni 25
ragione.

DON RODORIGO. Non si deve condennar a morte chi
sommamente desia di morire, e che la morte gli sarebbe
premio, non castigo; egli, desiando la vostra figliuola
per isposa, fece l'errore, e l'error fu più tosto dell'età che 30
suo, ché non gionge ancora a diciotto anni.[1]

EUFRANONE. E voi con la giustizia vincete gli animi;
né un error fatto per poca età deve privar un padre di sua
figlia. E voi sete giudice, e non avvocato che debbiate
escusarlo. 35

DON RODORIGO. Perché gli innamorati han l'animo in-
fermo d'amore, e la ragione annebbiata da furori, i loro
errori son più degni di scusa che di pena, e la giustizia ha
gran riguardo ne' casi d'amore.

EUFRANONE. Se l'amor bastasse ad escusar un delitto, 40
tutti gli errori si direbbono esser fatti da innamorati, e
l'amor si comprarebbe a denari contanti.

DON RODORIGO. Perché le sete padre, la soverchia passion non vi fa conoscer il giusto, ed un cor turbato ed
agitato da l'ira non ascolta ragione. 45

EUFRANONE. Fui padre d'una e, se mi è lecito dir,
onestissima figlia, e i vostri nepoti per particular inte-
ressi me l'hann'uccisa, infamata.

DON RODORIGO. Quando il reo è di gran merito si pro-
cede alla sentenza con più riguardo. 50

EUFRANONE. La morte ed innocenza di mia figlia gridano dinanzi al tribunal di Dio giustizia contro i vostri
nepoti, ché non restino invendicate.

do not use the respectful language which is owed to you by all rights.

DON RODORIGO. He who of all things desires to die ought not be condemned to death, for death would be a reward to him, not a punishment. By desiring your daughter for his wife, he committed the fault, and it proceeded from his age more than from himself, for he is not yet eighteen years old.

EUFRANONE. By doing justice you win your subjects' trust; moreover, an error committed by reason of youth should not be allowed to deprive a father of his daughter. You are a judge, not the advocate who must defend him.

DON RODORIGO. Because lovers' souls are sick with love and their reason clouded by fits of madness, their faults deserve excuse rather than punishment, and justice gives special consideration to cases of love.

EUFRANONE. If love sufficed to excuse a crime, all transgressions would be blamed on being in love and love would be bought for cash.

DON RODORIGO. Because you are her father, overwhelming passion prevents your recognizing what is just; a heart disturbed and agitated by wrath does not hear reason.

EUFRANONE. I was the father of a daughter, if I may say so, most chaste; and your nephews, for their own selfish ends, have killed her, with her good name destroyed.

DON RODORIGO. When the malefactor is someone of great regard, we move toward the sentence with more care.

EUFRANONE. The death and the innocence of my daughter, that they may not go unavenged, cry out before the tribunal of God for justice against your nephews.

DON RODORIGO. Dio sa quanto desio uscir da questo
intrigo con onor mio, e mi contenterei volentieri spen-   55
der una parte del mio proprio corpo, e mi parrebbe
come nulla mi levassi, anzi mi parrebbe esser intiero e
perfetto. Eufranone mio, poniam caso che Don Flaminio morisse publicamente, resuscitarà per questo la tua
figliuola?   60

EUFRANONE. No, ma da un publico supplicio vien a
verificarsi la sua innocenza.

DON RODORIGO. Anzi questo garbuglio ha nobilitato
la fama della sua pudicizia, perché Leccardo è già preso
e, menato dinanzi al giudice, ha confessato che il tutto   65
sia successo con non men scelerato che infelice suo aiuto; e come caggion del tutto è stato condennato a morire, se il capestro non gli fa grazia della vita. Ma ditemi,
fratello, non ci è altro modo di restituir l'onore alle donne che far morir il reo publicamente?   70

EUFRANONE. Ditelo voi che reggete.

DON RODORIGO. Ne dirò uno, e credo che ne restarete
sodisfatto, se sete così galante uomo come sete predi-
cato da tutti. Voi avete un'altra figliuola chiamata Callidora, non men bella ed onorata che Carizia: facciamo   75
che Don Flaminio sposi costei, a ciò che le genti, che
hanno inteso il caso della sorella, non sospettino più
cosa contraria all'onor suo. Voi con la sua ricchezza vi
ristorerete in parte del danno avvenuto, e se la vostra
famiglia Della Porta è famosa per antica gloria d'uomini 80
illustri, or si rischiara con i titoli di questo nuovo parentado, per esser la casa di Mendozza delle più chiare
d'Ispagna; ed a lui poi per penitenza del suo fallo gli resti
un perpetuo obligo di servitù e di amore verso la vostra
dilettissima figlia. Il Viceré non vuol mancar alla giusti- 85
zia; ma Don Rodorigo vi priega che questo Viceré non
sia constretto a farla; e voi, se sete prudente e savio,

DON RODORIGO. God knows how I desire to emerge from this perplexity with my honor unharmed, and I would give a limb of my body as gladly as if it were nothing; nay, I would think myself whole and intact. Eufranone, my friend, let us suppose that Don Flaminio were to die publicly, would this restore your daughter to life?

EUFRANONE. No, but a public execution will declare her innocence.

DON RODORIGO. No need—this tumult has in fact increased the fame of her modesty, for Leccardo has been apprehended and, led before the judge, has confessed that everything happened by means of his no less wicked than unlucky assistance; and as the cause of it all, he has been condemned to die, if the noose does not refuse to hang him. But tell me, brother, is there no way to restore ladies' honor other than public execution of the malefactor?

EUFRANONE. Say what it is, you who rule.

DON RODORIGO. I'll tell you a way, one that I believe will satisfy you, if you are as true a gentleman as you are reputed to be. You have another daughter, named Callidora, no less beautiful and honorable than Carizia; let us marry Don Flaminio to her, so that people who have heard of her sister's case will no longer suspect anything contrary to her honor. By his wealth you will restore in part your damaged fortunes, and if your Della Porta family is already famous for the ancient glory of its illustrious men, let it now be brightened with the titles of this new connection, the house of Mendoza being among the noblest in Spain; and let the penance for his fault be a perpetual obligation of service and of love to your cherished daughter. The viceroy does not wish to fail in his duty to justice, but Don Rodorigo begs that this viceroy may not be forced to uphold its rigor; you yourself, if you are prudent and wise, should forestall

dovreste prevenirmi con i prieghi di quello che or priego voi.

EUFRANONE. Signor Viceré, se ho parlato così senza 90
rispetto, ne è cagion il dolor acerbo della morte della
mia figliuola, non il desio della morte di vostro nipote;
purché venghi reintegrato nell'onor pristino, facciasi
quanto ordinate.

DON FLAMINIO. O zio, non di minor osservanza e di 95
amor di colui che mi ha generato, che più onorata giustizia, più santa vendetta non arei saputo desiderare; io
ben conosceva che la mia morte non toglieva la macchia
impressa nell'onestà di donna, né per morte fineva l'amor mio; desiava servir e riverir Callidora sotto l'i- 100
magine della morta sorella; accettarla per moglie indignissimo mi conosco; l'accetto per mia signora col
tributo impostomi d'averla a servir sempre, e mentre
duri la vita, duri l'obligo. A voi, mio suocero Eufranone, m'inchino, con ogni umiltà che devo, a ricevermi 105
per servo: la vostra dote saranno i suoi meriti, le mie
facultà communi a tutto il parentado.

EUFRANONE. Ed io per genero vi accetto e per figliuolo.

DON FLAMINIO. Concedetemi che vi baci la mano se ne 110
son degno; se non, i piedi.

EUFRANONE. Alzatevi, signor Don Flaminio, ché la
vostra soverchia creanza non facci me mal creato: ardisco abbracciarvi perché me lo comandate.

me with prayers for the very thing I now pray you to accept.

EUFRANONE. My lord viceroy, if I have spoken thus without respect, the reason is bitter sorrow for my daughter's death, not desire for the death of your nephew. Provided that her name be restored to its pristine honor, let whatever you order be done.

DON FLAMINIO. Oh uncle, no less worthy of obedience and of love than he who sired me, I could not have wished for a more honorable justice or a more holy revenge. I was well aware that my death could not cancel the stain on womanly honor, nor was my love to be ended by death. I longed to serve and to revere Callidora as the image of her dead sister. I know myself most unworthy to receive her as my wife: I accept her as my lady with the tribute levied on me to serve her forever, and while life endures, so also may this obligation. To you, my father-in-law Eufranone, I bow with all due humility, in supplication that you receive me as a servant: her virtues will be the dowry you bestow, my fortune will belong equally to the whole family.

EUFRANONE. And I accept you as son-in-law and as son.

DON FLAMINIO. Permit me, if I am worthy of it, to kiss your hand; if not, your feet.

[*Don Flaminio kneels.*]

EUFRANONE. Arise, my lord Don Flaminio, that your exceeding courtesy may not put me to shame: I make bold to embrace you, because you command it.

SCENE II

Don Ignazio, Don Rodorigo, Don Flaminio, ed
Eufranone.

DON IGNAZIO. Intendo, signor Don Rodorigo, che per
accomodar il fallo di Don Flaminio, l'avete ammogliato
con l'altra sorella.

DON RODORIGO. Io per non partirmi dalle leggi del
giusto, e per non veder la disperazion di tuo fratello, mi   5
è paruto accomodarlo in tal modo.

DON IGNAZIO. Ma non vuol la legge del giusto che per
accomodar uno si scomodi un altro.

DON RODORIGO. A chi ho fatto pregiudizio io?

DON IGNAZIO. A me, a cui la rimasta sorella si con-   10
venia per più legittime cagioni.

DON RODORIGO. Per che ragioni?

DON IGNAZIO. Prima, avendo io ingiuriato Eufranone, a me tocca la sodisfazione, togliendo io la rimasta
sorella, ed egli allor sarà reintegrato nel suo onore: ap-   15
presso, restando io offeso da' suoi inganni e vituperevoli
frodi, a me tocca disacerbarmi il dolore con le nozze
dell'altra sorella, ché niuna bastarebbe a farmi partir dal
cuore la bellezza, onestà, maniere, e tante maravigliose
parti di Carizia che sua sorella: egli, che con tanta scele-   20
ratezza ha turbato il tutto, sarà rimunerato, ed io verrò
offeso, che ho operato bene. Né convien ad un occisor
della sorella che divenghi marito dell'altra; ed avendomi
tolto la prima moglie, non è convenevole che mi toglia
la seconda; e tante e tante altre raggioni, che se volessi   25
dirle tutte non si verrebbe mai a capo.

DON RODORIGO. Caro figliuolo, non sapeva l'animo
vostro: ho avuto pietà della sua vita come una imagine

SCENE II

Don Ignazio, Don Rodorigo, Don Flaminio and
Eufranone, [Gentlemen and Attendants].

DON IGNAZIO. I understand, my lord Don Rodorigo,
that to repair the fault of Don Flaminio, you have married him to the other sister.

DON RODORIGO. In order to uphold just laws and
to rescue your brother from hopeless straits, it has
seemed well to me to repair the damage in this way.

DON IGNAZIO. But a just law does not intend to right
one by wronging another.

DON RODORIGO. To whom have I done wrong?

DON IGNAZIO. To me, whose rights to the surviving
sister are better founded.

DON RODORIGO. What are these rights?

DON IGNAZIO. First, as I am the one who injured Eufranone, it is incumbent upon me to make reparation by
taking to myself the remaining sister, and his honor will
then be healed; besides, as I have been wronged by Don
Flaminio's deceits and execrable frauds, it is due to me
to assuage my sorrow by marriage to the other sister,
for no one but her sister could suffice to erase from
my heart the beauty, the chastity, the manners and the
many wondrous charms of Carizia; he who so wickedly
made all the trouble will be rewarded, while I who have
acted well shall be injured. Nor is it fitting that the murderer of one sister should become the husband of the
other; that having robbed me of my first wife, he should
rob me of my second; and there are so many, many
other rights and reasons that if I had to name them all, I
would never end.

DON RODORIGO. Dear son, I did not know your mind:
I had compassion for his life as an image of yours; and I

della vostra, e stimava che a questo vostro fratello, ancor che fusse vostra moglie, per compiacergli glie l'avessi concessa. 30

DON IGNAZIO. Il voler tor a sé, e dar ad altri, mi par cosa fuor de' termini dell'onesto.

DON FLAMINIO. Ella è mia moglie, e non comporterò mi sia tolto quello con violenza che mi ho procacciato 35 per l'affezion del mio zio, ed acquistato con ragioni dal padre, e con la fede: fatto il contratto, volete voi rompere le leggi del matrimonio?

DON IGNAZIO. Io non rompo le leggi del matrimonio, ma difendo le mie ragioni con un'altra legge: ed io non 40 patirò che un frettoloso decreto sia fatto con infame pregiudizio dell'onor mio, e ti consiglio che lasci tal impresa, perché verremo a cattivo termine insieme.

DON FLAMINIO. Pazzo è colui che accetta consigli dal suo nemico; e meco venghisi a qual si voglia termine, 45 ché con l'armi son per difendere quel che la mia sorte m'ha donato, e te lo giuro da quel che sono.

DON IGNAZIO. D'ingannatore, e di traditore!

DON FLAMINIO. Don Ignazio, se, mentre siamo vissuti insieme, t'ho fatto altro inganno, e tradimento, fuor di 50 questo, veramente son un ingannatore, e traditore: se questo, che ho fatto per amore si ha da chiamar «tradimento», diffiniamolo con l'armi.

DON RODORIGO. Don Flaminio, tu parli troppo liberamente e fuor de' termini. 55

DON IGNAZIO. Zio, voi ne sete cagione, ché la vergogna de gli errori commessi, quando vi si trapone autorità d'uomo degno, diventa audacia: si è fatto superbo per la mia viltà, ché se per l'offesa fattami l'avesse dato il dovuto castigo, non saria tale. Ma ella sarà mia, o che tu 60 voglia, o non voglia; e diffiniamolo con l'armi, e ti ricordo che alla vecchia, tu aggiungi nuova offesa.

thought that you would have given anything, even your wife, to make your brother happy.

DON IGNAZIO. To despoil oneself in order to give to another seems to me to exceed what is right.

DON FLAMINIO. She is my wife, and I will not be deprived by violence of what I have obtained through my uncle's affection and acquired with her father's approval, our promise sealed. The contract being made, can you wish to break the laws of marriage?

DON IGNAZIO. I break no laws of marriage, but defend my rights with another law; I shall not suffer a hasty decree to be passed with slanderous harm to my honor; and I advise you to abandon such an enterprise, for otherwise you and I must come to evil terms.

DON FLAMINIO. Only a madman would take advice from his enemy; let anyone come to whatever terms he will with me, for I am ready to defend by arms what my destiny has bestowed on me; and that I swear to you by all I am.

DON IGNAZIO. A deceiver and a traitor!

DON FLAMINIO. Don Ignazio, if in all the time we have lived together, I have perpetrated any deceit or treachery but this one alone, then truly I am a deceiver and a traitor; whether this that I did for love is to be called treachery, let us resolve with our swords.

DON RODORIGO. Don Flaminio, you speak too freely and transgress the limits of order.

DON IGNAZIO. Uncle, it is your doing that shame for faults committed, taking sanction from the intercession of worthy authority, turns into effrontery: he has become arrogant through my unmanly mildness, for if I had punished his offence to me as it deserved, he would not be as he is. But she shall be mine, whether you will or not; let us decide it by arms. And I remind you that to the old offence you add a new one.

DON FLAMINIO. Chi m'ha da tor Callidora me la torrà per la punta della spada!

DON IGNAZIO. Grida come fusse ingiuriato, e non avesse ingiuriato altri. Ma se m'hai vinto con le forfantarie, non mi vincerai con l'armi, e vedremo se saprai così menar le mani come ordir tradimenti. 65

DON RODORIGO. Cercando accomodar uno, ne ho sconcio doi. Fermatevi, fermatevi! questo è il rispetto che mi portate? Questo cambio rendete a chi ve ha allevati, e nodriti, come padre? Non vi son'io padre in età, e maggiormente in amore? Così abusate la mia amorevolezza? 70

DON IGNAZIO. Zio, chi può soffrir le stoccate delle sue parole, che pungeno più della punta della sua spada? Ma io sarò giusto punitore dell'ingiuste sue azioni. 75

DON RODORIGO. Ferma, Don Ignazio! ferma, Don Flaminio! o che confusione di sdegno e di furore, o che misero spettacolo d'un abbattimento di doi fratelli! 80

SCENA III

POLISENA, DON IGNAZIO, DON FLAMINIO, e DON RODORIGO, ed EUFRANONE.

POLISENA. Fermate, cavalieri! fermate, fratelli, e non fatte che lo sdegno passi insin al sangue!

DON IGNAZIO. Di grazia, madre, toglietevi di mezzo, acciochè, mentre cerchiamo offenderci l'un'all'altro, non offendessimo voi e facessimo error peggior del primo. 5

POLISENA. Se le figliole mie sono cagione delle vostre risse, offendendo la madre loro, offendete il ventre che

DON FLAMINIO. Who takes Callidora from me does so by the point of his sword.

DON IGNAZIO. He raves as if he were the injured instead of the injurer of others. But though you defeated me with your scoundrel's tricks, you will not defeat me with arms; we shall see if you are as dextrous in combat as in planning your treacheries.

DON RODORIGO. Seeking to settle one, I have marred two.

[*The brothers fight.*]

Cease! Cease! Is this the respect you owe me? Is this the return you make to him who reared and nourished you like a father? Am I not father to you in years and still more in love? Do you thus abuse my loving kindness?

DON IGNAZIO. Uncle, who can bear the thrusts of his words, which pierce more than the point of his sword? But I'll be the just punisher of his unjust actions.

DON RODORIGO. Stop, Don Ignazio! Stop, Don Flaminio! Oh what turmoil of wrath and unreason! Oh what a grievous spectacle, this clash of two brothers!

SCENE III

POLISENA, DON IGNAZIO, DON FLAMINIO, DON RODORIGO and EUFRANONE [GENTLEMEN and ATTENDANTS].

POLISENA. Hold, noble sirs, hold, brothers, and do not let anger proceed to bloodshed!

DON IGNAZIO. Please, mother, do not interfere, lest, seeking to wound each other, we wound you and commit an error worse than the first.

POLISENA. If my daughters are the cause of your quarrels, by wounding their mother, you strike the womb

l'ha prodotte: questo ventre sia bersaglio de' vostri
colpi! 10

DON IGNAZIO. Di grazia appartatevi, madre, ché per
tema d'offender voi non posso offender 'l mio nemico.

POLISENA. O figlie nate sotto che fiero tenor d'iniqua
stella, poi che in cambio di doti, apportate a i vostri
sposi scandalo, e sangue? Ed a che sposi, a che fratelli 15
poi: a i più chiari e valorosi che vivono a i nostri secoli!
Non son le mie figlie di tanto merito che le lor nozze
siano comprate col prezzo del sangue di sì onorati cavalieri. Cari miei figliuoli, se amate le mie figliuole, è debito di ragione che amiate ancora la lor madre, la qual vi 20
priega che lasciate il furor e l'armi, ed ascoltiate quello
che son per dirvi.

DON IGNAZIO. Io non lasciarò la mia spada s'egli prima
non lascia la sua.

DON FLAMINIO. E s'egli prima non lascia la sua, io non 25
lasciarò la mia.

POLISENA. Io sto in mezzo ad ambi doi, e l'uno non
può ferir l'altro se non ferisce prima me, e la spada pas-
sando per lo mio corpo facci strada all'altrui sangue; ma
a chi prima di voi mi volgerò, carissimi miei generi, ca- 30
rissimi miei figliuoli? Mi volgerò a voi primo, Don Ignazio: voi prima mi chiedesti amorevolmente la mia
figliuola per isposa. Se non è in tutto in voi spenta la memoria dell'amor suo, s'ella vi fu mai cara, mostratelo in
questo, che siate il primo a lasciar l'armi. Com'io posso 35
stringervi la destra, se sta nella spada? Come posso abbracciarvi, se spirate per tutto odio, e veleno?

DON IGNAZIO. Non mi comandar questo, cara madre,
ché costui, solito a far tradimenti, veggendomi disar-
mato, che non mi tradisca di nuovo. 40

DON FLAMINIO. Tien mano alla lingua, se vòi ch'io
tenghi le mani all'armi.

POLISENA. Ed è possibile che possa tanto la rabbia in

which produced them: let this womb be the target of your thrusts.

DON IGNAZIO. Please retire, mother, for fearing to injure you, I cannot injure my enemy.

POLISENA. Oh daughters, born under what fierce influence of an evil star, that instead of dowries you bring your bridegrooms scandal and blood? And what bridegrooms, what brothers, indeed: the brightest and bravest of our times! My daughters are not of such great desert that their marriages should be bought with the blood of such honored noblemen. My dear sons, if you love my daughters, it follows accordingly that you also love their mother, who begs you to lay aside your fury and your weapons and to listen to what I shall tell you.

DON IGNAZIO. I will not lay down my sword unless he first lays down his.

DON FLAMINIO. And if he does not first lay down his, I won't lay down mine.

POLISENA. I stand between the two, and one may not strike the other unless he strikes me and the sword, passing through my body, opens the way to the other's blood. But to which of you shall I turn first, my dearest sons-in-law, my dearest children? I'll turn to you, Don Ignazio: you first asked me lovingly for my daughter's hand. If the memory of her love is not quite extinguished in you, if she was ever dear to you, show it in this: be the first to lay down your arms. How can I clasp your hand if it grasps a sword? How can I embrace you if you breathe only hatred and poison?

DON IGNAZIO. Do not command this, dear mother, for he, practiced in treachery, seeing me disarmed, will betray me once again.

DON FLAMINIO. Hold your tongue if you want me to hold my hand.

POLISENA. Is it possible that rage can be so strong be-

voi, che pur sete stati in un'istesso ventre, rabbia più
convenevole a barbari che a' vostri pari?   45

DON IGNAZIO. Noi non siamo più fratelli, ma cru-
delissimi nemici: sono rotte le leggi fra noi della natura,
e del convenevole: un fratello che offende non è differente dal nemico.

POLISENA. Non fate vostre le colpe che son della for-   50
tuna: questa sola ha peccato nell'opere vostre, questa
sola ha conspirato ne i vostri danni! L'un fratello vuol
uccider l'altro fratello: cercati una vittoria nella quale è
meglio restar vinto che vincere: per acquistar una moglie perdernosi duo mariti? Volete che le vostre spose   55
siano prima vedove che spose? volete che coloro,
ch'eran venuti per onorar le vostre nozze, onorino le
vostre esequie?

DON IGNAZIO. Dite presto, madre, che sete per dire.

POLISENA. Che voce potrà formar la mia lingua tutta   60
piena d'orrore, e di spavento, veggendovi con l'armi in
mano, e che state di ponto in ponto per ferirvi? Almeno
ponete le punte in terra, e colui che sarà primo ad'inclinar la spada, darà primo testimonio dell'amor che mi
porta.   65

DON IGNAZIO. Ecco ch'io v'obedisco.

DON FLAMINIO. Ed io pur voglio obedirvi.

POLISENA. Don Ignazio, di che cosa vi dolete del fratello?

DON IGNAZIO. Egli, senza averlo giamai offeso, tra-   70
dendomi, mi ha tolto il mio core, che era la Carizia, la
qual essendo morta, son certo che mai morirà nel mio
core quella imagine che prima Amor vi scolpì di sua
mano, né spero vederla più in questo mondo se non ve-
stita di bella luce innanzi a Dio. Per non morirmi di pas-   75
sione avea pensato tormi la sorella per isposa, la qual
sempre che avesse veduta, avrei veduto in lei l'imagine
sua, e gustato l'odor del sangue e del suo spirito. Or ei,
cagion di tanto male, mi vuol tor la seconda: io che ho

tween you who issued from one womb, rage more proper to barbarians than to such as you?

DON IGNAZIO. We are no longer brothers, but cruelest enemies. The laws of nature and of propriety between us are broken: a brother who wounds is not different from an enemy.

POLISENA. Do not lay to your own charge the blows which came from fortune: it alone has sinned through your works, it alone has conspired to harm you! One brother wants to kill the other! You seek a victory in which it is better to be vanquished than victor. To win one wife, must two husbands be lost? Would you have your brides widows before they are wives? Would you have your wedding-guests perform your obsequies?

DON IGNAZIO. Say quickly, mother, what you have to say.

POLISENA. What word can my tongue form when it is full of horror and dismay, seeing you with weapons in hand and on the verge of wounding one another? At least point them downward, and he who first lowers his sword will give first proof of his love for me.

DON IGNAZIO. There, I obey you.

DON FLAMINIO. And I too wish to obey you.

POLISENA. Don Ignazio, what is your complaint against your brother?

DON IGNAZIO. Without my having ever harmed him, by treachery he robbed me of my heart, of Carizia; she being dead, I am sure that her image will never die in my heart, first engraved there by the hand of Love, nor do I hope to see her again in this world but only in God's presence, clothed in beautiful light. So as not to die of grief, I had thought of taking her sister as my wife, looking on whom I would ever have seen Carizia's image and tasted the fragrance of her kinship and her spirit. Now he, the cause of so much evil, wants to take the

oprato bene ricevo male, ed egli che ha oprato male sarà 80 guiderdonatto.

DON FLAMINIO. Egli cerca tor a me Callidora concessami dal padre, e dal mio zio, della qual son' acceso talmente che sarò più tosto per lasciar la vita che lei: l'amor mio non è de gli ordinarii, ma insopportabile, in- 85 medicabile, non vuol ragione.

POLISENA. Se amavate Carizia, com'or amate Callidora?

DON FLAMINIO. Non potendo amar quella che è morta, l'anima mia si è nuovamente invaghita di costei. 90

POLISENA. Or poi che l'amate tanto, vostra sia, e farò che Don Ignazio ve la conceda.

DON FLAMINIO. Con una medicina mi sanarete due infirmità, di amore e di gelosia, e vi arò sempre obligo delle due vite che mi donate. 95

DON IGNAZIO. O madre, non vi promettete tanto di me, ché ancor ch'io volessi non potrei.

POLISENA. Ben potrete, sì.

DON IGNAZIO. E s'avesse il potere non avrei il volere.

POLISENA. Vi darò rimedio, che avrete Carizia. 100

DON IGNAZIO. La morte sola saria il rimedio, ché cavandomi dal mondo, il spirito mio s'unisse col suo.

POLISENA. Vo' che senza morir godiate la vostra Carizia; sperate bene.

DON IGNAZIO. Come può sperar bene un afflitto dalla 105 fortuna?

POLISENA. Carizia ancor vive per voi.

DON IGNAZIO. So che lo dite a ciò che fra noi cessino l'ire e li sdegni, ma con queste speranze più m'inacerbite le piaghe. 110

POLISENA. Dico che è viva.

second sister from me: I, who have acted rightly, receive evil, and he, who has done evil, is to be rewarded.

DON FLAMINIO. He seeks to rob me of Callidora, bestowed on me by her father and my uncle, the one I love so ardently that I will sooner relinquish my life than her. My love is no ordinary kind, but one unbearable, incurable, not subject to reason.

POLISENA. If you loved Carizia, how is it that now you love Callidora?

DON FLAMINIO. Being unable to love her who is dead, my soul is newly charmed by the other.

POLISENA. Then since you love her so much, let her be yours: and I shall cause Don Ignazio to yield her up to you.

DON FLAMINIO. With one medicine you will heal me of two diseases, love and jealousy, and I shall forever be indebted to you for the two lives you bestow.

DON IGNAZIO. Oh mother, do not promise so much on my part, for even if I wished to, I would be unable to do it.

POLISENA. You will be quite able.

DON IGNAZIO. And were I able, I would not wish to.

POLISENA. I'll give you a remedy: you shall have Carizia.

DON IGNAZIO. Only death could be the remedy, releasing me from this world that my spirit might unite itself with hers.

POLISENA. I wish you to enjoy your Carizia without dying: be of good hope.

DON IGNAZIO. How can there be hope for one afflicted by fortune?

POLISENA. Carizia still lives for you.

DON IGNAZIO. I know that you say this so that anger and resentment may cease between us, but with these hopes you exacerbate my wounds.

POLISENA. I say she is alive.

271

DON IGNAZIO. O Dio, sognando ascolto, o sogno ascoltando?

POLISENA. Dico che vegilando ascoltate il vero.

DON IGNAZIO. Il mio cuore non è capace di tanta alle- 115 grezza, e s'io non muoio per allegrezza, è segno che nol crede: non sapete che l'innamorati appena credeno a gli occhi loro? Ma se è vero, fa' che veggia colei da cui dipende la vita mia.

POLISENA. Va' tu e fa' venir qui Carizia. 120

Quando voi li mandaste quella cruda ambasciata, il dolor la fe' cader morta. Il mio marito per l'offesa dell'onor, che s'imaginava aver ricevuto da lei, la fece conficcare in un'arca, volea farla sepellire. Io, non potendo soffrir che la mia cara figlia fosse posta sotterra senza 125 darle le lacrime e gli ultimi baci, feci schiodar l'arca; e mentre la baciava tutta, intesi che sotto le mammelle li palpitava il core. Oprai tanti remedi che rivenne: rivenuta, fu veramente spectacolo miserabile, stracciandosi i capelli, si dolea della sorte che l'avesse di nuovo 130 ritornata in vita assai peggior che la morte, pensando al torto che l'era fatto. Io reimpiendo l'arca di un altro peso, la mandai a sepellire: ella volea entrarsene in un monastero e servir a Dio, per non aver a cadere mai più in podestà di uomo. 135

DON IGNAZIO. O madre, cavami fuor delle porte della morte, dimmelo certamente se è viva, per che ella sarà mia, ancor che voglia o non voglia tutto il mondo!

POLISENA. Ed ella più tosto vol esser vostra che sua; e per non esser d'altri, volea esser più tosto della morte. 140

DON IGNAZIO. Donque gli occhi miei vedranno un'altra volta Carizia, ed aran pur lieto fine le mie disperate speranze?

EUFRANONE. O moglie cara, tu arrechi in un tempo nuove dolcezze a molti, tu pacifichi i fratelli, allegri il 145

DON IGNAZIO. Oh God, do I hear in a dream, or dream that I hear?

POLISENA. I say that, awake, you hear the truth.

DON IGNAZIO. My heart cannot hold so much joy, and if I do not die of joy it is a sign that my heart does not believe it. Do you not know that lovers find it hard even to believe their eyes? But if it is true, let me see her on whom my life depends.

POLISENA. [to a servant.] Go and fetch Carizia. [to Ignazio.] When you sent her that brutal message, grief made her fall lifeless. My husband, because of the imagined wound to his honor, ordered her thrust into a coffin and intended to have her buried. Unable to bear that my dear daughter be put in the earth without my bestowing tears and last kisses upon her, I ordered the coffin unnailed; and as I was kissing her all over, I realized that beneath her breasts her heart still beat. I applied such remedies that she revived. Once conscious, she was a piteous spectacle: tearing her hair, she lamented the destiny that had returned her to a life much worse than death, thinking of the wrong that had been done her. Refilling the coffin with a substitute weight, I sent it to be buried. She wanted to enter a convent and to serve God in order to avoid ever falling again into the power of man.

DON IGNAZIO. Oh mother, bring me back from death's doors, tell me with certainty if she is alive, for she shall be mine in despite of the whole world!

POLISENA. And she would rather be yours than her own, and rather than belong to anyone else, she would belong to death.

DON IGNAZIO. Then my eyes will see Carizia once more, and my desperate hopes will have a happy end?

EUFRANONE. Oh dear wife, in one moment you bring new delight to many: you make peace between the brothers, you rejoice the uncle, you give sweet joy, not

273

zio, dài dolcezza, non al padre amorevole di colei, ma a chi le fu rigido ed inumano, e consoli tutta questa città.

DON FLAMINIO. Ma io come uscirò di tant'obligo? che grazie vi potrò rendere, essendo stato cagione di tante rovine? 150

POLISENA. Rendete le grazie a Dio, non a me indegna serva. Egli solo ha ordinato nel Cielo che i fatti così difficili ed impossibili ad accommodarsi siano ridotti a così lieto fine.

DON IGNAZIO. Ecco che l'aria comincia a dischiararsi 155 da' raggi di suoi begli occhi; o come il mio core si ralegra della sua dolce e desiata vista!

SCENA IV

CARIZIA, DON IGNAZIO, DON FLAMINIO, POLISENA, DON RODORIGO, ed EUFRANONE.

CARIZIA. Madre, che comandate?

POLISENA. Conoscetela ora? v'ho detto la bugia?

DON IGNAZIO. O Dio, è questa l'ombra sua, o qualche spirito ha presa la sua stanza?

POLISENA. Toccala, e vedi si è ombra, o spirito. 5

DON IGNAZIO. O Don Ignazio, sei vivo o morto? e se sei vivo, sogni, o vaneggi? e se vaneggi, per lo soverchio desiderio ti par di vederla? Io vivo, e veggio, ed odo, ma l'infinito contento che ho nell'alma mi accieca gli occhi, mi offusca i sensi, e mi conturba l'intelletto, 10 ché veggiundo dormo, vivendo moro, ed essendo sordo e cieco, ed odo e veggio. Ma se eri sepolta e morta, come or sei qui viva? o quello o questo è sogno: e se sei

to the loving father of Carizia, but to one who was hard and inhuman to her, and you console this whole city.

DON FLAMINIO. But how shall I ever repay you? What thanks can I return, having been the cause of so much destruction?

POLISENA. Give thanks to God, not to me his unworthy servant. He alone has decreed in Heaven that events so difficult and impossible to resolve be brought to so happy an end.

DON IGNAZIO. Lo, how the air begins to brighten again from the rays of her lovely eyes. Oh how my heart rejoices at the sweet and yearned-for sight of her!

SCENE IV

CARIZIA, DON IGNAZIO, DON FLAMINIO, POLISENA, DON RODORIGO and EUFRANONE, [CALLIDORA, GENTLEMEN and ATTENDANTS].

CARIZIA. Mother, what do you command?

POLISENA. Do you know her now? Have I lied to you?

DON IGNAZIO. Oh God, is this her shade, or has some spirit inhabited her earthly dwelling?

POLISENA. Touch her and see if she is a shade or a spirit.

DON IGNAZIO. Oh Don Ignazio, are you alive or dead? And if you are alive, are you dreaming or imagining? And if you are imagining, does excess of longing make you think you see her? I live, and see, and hear, but the infinite happiness in my soul blinds my eyes, clouds my senses, and confuses my mind, so that wide awake I sleep, living I die, and deaf and blind I hear and see. But if you were buried and dead, how are you here alive? Either that or this is a dream. And if you are alive, how

275

viva, come posso soffrir tant'allegrezza e non morire? O
tanto desiato oggetto de gli ochi miei, hai sofferte tante   15
ingiurie insin'alla morte, insin'alla sepoltura, ed or volevi finir la vita in un monastero!

CARIZIA. Veramente avea così deliberato per non aver
a trattar più con uomo, poi che era stata ingiuriata e rifiutata dal primo a cui avea dato le premizie de' mia   20
amori, ed i primi fiori d'ogni mio amoroso pensiero.

DON IGNAZIO. Dhe, signora della mia vita, poiché sei
mia, fammi degno che ti tocchi, e non potendoti ponere
dentro il cuore, almeno che vi ponga in queste braccia.
Io pur ti tocco e stringo; donque io son vivo; ma ohimè,   25
che per lo smisurato contento par che sia per isvenirmi, i
spiriti del core sciolti dal corpo per i meati troppo aperti[1] per lo caldo dell'allegrezza, par che se ne volino via, e
l'anima abbandonata non può soffrir il corpo, ed il corpo afflitto non può sostener l'anima: mi sento presso al   30
morire. Ma come posso morire, se tengo abbracciata la
vita? O cara vita mia, quanto sei stata pianta da me, dal
tuo padre, fratello, e zio mio, e da tutto Salerno!

CARIZIA. Donque mi spiace che viva sia, essendo onorate le mie essequie da persone di tanto conto.   35

DON IGNAZIO. Ecco, o vita mia, hai reso il cor al corpo, lo spirito all'anima, la luce a gli occhi, e'l vigore alle
membra.

DON FLAMINIO. Ecco, o signora, l'infelicissimo vostro
innamorato, gettato innanzi a' vostri piedi, quale, spin-   40
to da un ardentissimo amore e gelosia, con falsa illu-
sione per ingannar il fratello, ha offesa ancor voi; ed arei
offeso e tradito anco mio padre, e zio, e tutto il parentado insiememente per possedervi, tanto è la vostra
bellezza, e pregio delle dignissime vostre qualitadi, deg-   45
ne d'essere invidiate da tutte le donne: ma il disegno

276

can I bear such happiness and not die? Oh, you whom my eyes so yearned to behold, how much you have suffered, even to death, even to burial; and just now you wished to end your life in a convent!

CARIZIA. Truly I had determined to do so, in order to have no more to do with men, since I had been defamed and rejected by the man to whom I had given the first fruits of my love and the first flowers of even my thoughts of love.

DON IGNAZIO. Ah, lady of my life, since you are mine, let me be worthy to touch you; and if I cannot lock you within my heart, at least let me hold you in my arms. I touch you indeed, and I press you close; it is true, then, I am alive. But, ah me, I feel as if I were going to faint for boundless joy! My heart's spirits, released from my body through conduits distended by the heat of happiness, seem to fly away, my deserted soul cannot endure my body and my afflicted body cannot support my soul: I feel nigh to death. But how can I die if I hold life in my embrace? Oh, my dear life, how your loss has been wept by me, by your father, by my brother and my uncle, and by all Salerno!

CARIZIA. Then I am sorry to be alive, my obsequies having been honored by persons of such importance.

DON IGNAZIO. Here, oh my life, you have restored the heart to my body, the spark to my soul, the light to my eyes, and the strength to my limbs.

DON FLAMINIO. Here, oh lady, your most unhappy lover is cast at your feet, he who impelled by burning love and jealousy with false illusion to deceive his brother, has injured you as well; and I would have injured and betrayed my father, my uncle and my whole clan together, in order to possess you, so great is your beauty and the value of your supreme qualities, worthy to be envied by all women; but the design turned out

277

sortì contrario fine; ma chi può contrastar con gli inev-
itabili accidenti della fortuna? Vi prego a perdonarmi
con quella generosità d'animo, eguale all'alte sue virtù,
offerendomi in ricompensa, mentre serò vivo, servir   50
voi, e 'l vostro meritevolissimo sposo.

CARIZIA. Signor Don Flaminio, a me i travagli non mi
son stati punto discari, perché da quelli è stato cimentato
l'onore e la mia vita: questo sì m'ha dispiaciuto, che la
mia infelice bellezza, che che ella si sia, abbi data occa-   55
sione di turbar un'amorevolissima fratellanza di duo valorosi cavalieri.

DON FLAMINIO. Generosissimo mio fratello, le mie
pazzie vi hanno aperto un largo campo di esercitar la
vostra virtute: io non ardirei cercarvi perdono, se amore   60
e la disgrazia non me ne facessero degno, la quale, quando viene, viene talmente che l'uomo non può ripararla.
Essendo tolta la cagione, si devono spengere gli odii ancora, e poi che sete gionto a quel segno dove aspiravano
tutte le vostre speranze, e possedete già il caro e glorioso   65
pregio[2] delle vostre fatiche, pregovi a perdonar le mie
inperfezioni e smenticarle, e ricevermi in quel grado di
servitù ed amore nel quale prima mi avevate, restando
io con perpetuo obligo di pregar Iddio che con la vostra
desiata sposa in lunga e felicissima vita vi conservi.   70

DON IGNAZIO. Caro mio Don Flaminio, se è disdice-
vole a tutti tener memoria dell'ingiurie, quanto si denno
in minor stima aver quelle che accaggiono tra fratelli? e
poi per liti amorose? E questo ch'avete voi fatto a me,
l'avrei io fatto a voi parimente. Mi sete or così caro ed   75
amorevole più che mai foste, ed in fede del vero io vengo ad abbracciarvi.

DON FLAMINIO. Abbattuto dalla propria conscienza, e
confuso da tanta cortesia, io non so che respondervi, né
basto ad esprimere il mio obligo: arò particolar memo-   80
ria della grazia ch'or mi fate.

contrarily. Well, who can combat the inevitable accidents of fortune? I beg you to forgive me with that generosity of spirit which is equal to your lofty virtues, and in recompense I offer, while I live, to serve you and your most deserving husband.

CARIZIA. My lord Don Flaminio, the ordeals have not been at all unwelcome to me, for by them my honor and my life have been tested. Only this has displeased me: that my unlucky beauty, whatever it may be worth, has been the occasion of disturbing the loving brotherliness of two valiant gentlemen.

DON FLAMINIO. Most generous brother, my mad actions have opened to you a wide field in which to exercise your virtue. I would not dare to seek your pardon, were I not made fit for it by love and by misfortune, which, when it comes, comes so that it cannot be withstood. The cause being removed, hate must be extinguished too; and as you have reached that goal to which all your hopes aspired and you now possess the rich and glorious crown of your endeavors, I beg you to forgive my imperfections, to forget them and to receive me in that degree of service and of love in which you held me formerly, I forever bound to pray God to preserve you with your beloved bride in a long and most happy life.

DON IGNAZIO. My dear Don Flaminio, if it is unfitting for anyone to harbor the memory of injuries, how much less regarded should be those which occur between brothers—and for rivalries in love, at that? What you have done to me, I would have done to you likewise. You are now more than ever dear and lovable to me, in pledge of which I embrace you.

DON FLAMINIO. Cast down by my own conscience and overwhelmed by so much courtesy, I am unable to answer or to express my obligation; I shall never forget your mercy to me.

EUFRANONE. Ed io, soprapreso da diversi effetti, non so qual io mi sia: allegro dell'amorevol fratellanza, ripieno d'ineffabil meraviglia della prudenza di mia moglie, allegro della figlia risuscitata, confuso e pieno di 85 vergogna, veggendomi dinanzi a quella che ho ingiuriato a torto con la lingua, ed uccisa con le mie mani; però, figlia, perdona a tuo padre, il quale falsamente informato ha cercato d'offenderti; e ti giuro che io ho sentito la penitenza del mio peccato senza che voi me l'avesti 90 data. Vieni ed abbraccia il tuo non occisore, ma carissimo padre.

CARIZIA. Ancor che m'aveste uccisa, o padre, non mi areste fatto ingiuria; la vita che voi m'avete data la potevate repetere quando vi piacea; mi è sì ben or di somma 95 sodisfazione che siate chiaro che non ho peccato; questo sì mi è di contento: che la mia morte v'ha fatto fede dell'innocenza mia.

EUFRANONE. La tua bontà, o figlia, ha commosso Iddio ad aiutarti: egli ne' secreti del tuo fato aveva or- 100 dinato che per te ogni cosa si fusse pacificato, e perciò di tutto si ringrazii Iddio, che ha fatto che le disaventure diventino venture, e le pene allegrezze.

DON RODORIGO. Veramente mi son assai meravigliato, essendo spettatore d'un crudel abbattimento di dui 105 per altro valorosi e degni cavalieri: ma or che veggio tanta bellezza in Carizia, e così ancor stimo la sorella, gli escuso e non gl'incolpo; e giudico che l'immenso Iddio governi queste cose con secreta e certa legge de' fati, e che molto prima abbi ordinato che succedano questi 110 gravi disordini, acciochè così degna coppia di sorelle si accoppionò con sì degno paro di fratelli, che par l'abbi fatti nascere per congiungerli insieme; e come il mio sangue onorerà voi, così dal vostro il mio prenderà splendore ed onore, e già veggio scolpite nelle lor fronti 115 una lunga descendenza di figliuoli e nepoti che mi nasceranno dalla mia indarno sperata successione, per non

EUFRANONE. And I, surprised by warring emotions, do not know what I feel most: happy at this loving brotherliness, full of inexpressible wonder at the prudence of my wife, happy for my daughter restored to life, confused and ashamed before her whom I have wrongly injured with my tongue and killed with my hands; therefore, daughter, forgive your father, who, falsely informed, tried to harm you; I swear to you that I have suffered penance for my sin without your imposing it. Come and embrace, not your murderer, but your dearest father.

CARIZIA. Even if you had killed me, oh father, you would not have wronged me: the life you gave me you might require of me when it pleased you. But truly it gives me the greatest contentment that you know I have not sinned; this indeed is happiness to me, that my death has proved to you my innocence.

EUFRANONE. Your goodness, oh daughter, moved God to aid you: he had ordered in the secrets of your fate that all be made serene for you; therefore, thanks for all be to God, who has so wrought that misfortunes become good fortune and sorrows become joys.

DON RODORIGO. In truth, as spectator, I greatly wondered at the cruel battle between two otherwise valorous and worthy noblemen; but now that I see so much beauty in Carizia—and likewise in her sister—I excuse and do not blame them, and I judge that God in his vastness governs these matters with secret and sure laws of the fates, and that long ago He had ordained these grave disorders that so worthy a pair of sisters might be matched with so worthy a pair of brothers, for it seems that by His will they were born to be joined together. As my blood will honor you, likewise from yours mine will gain luster and honor. I see already decreed in their aspects a long posterity of children and grandchildren born from my succession, till now a vain hope, as there

esservi altro germe nel nostro sangue. E perché queste gentildonne mancano di doti, io li faccio un donativo degno dell'amore e generosità loro, di ventimila ducati 120 per una, dopo la mia morte a succedere non solo alla eredità ma nell'amore: e se a gli altri si danno per usanza, vo' donarli a voi per premio, e per segno d'amore, vuo' abbracciarvi: il sangue mi sforza a far l'offizio suo.

CARIZIA. E noi saremo perpetue serve e conservatrici 125 della vostra salute.

EUFRANONE. E noi quando di tanta largità vi renderemo grazie condegne?

DON IGNAZIO. Carissimo padre e nostro zio, vi abbiamo tal obligo che la lingua non sa trovar parole per rin- 130 graziarvi.

DON RODORIGO. Or, poi che tutti i travagli han sortito sì lieto fine, ordinisi un banchetto reale per le nozze, e corte bandita per dieci giorni per tutti gentiluomini e gentildonne di questa città, acciò un publico dolore si 135 converti in una publica allegrezza. E perché non vi sia cosa melancolica in Salerno, si scarcerino tutti i prigioni per debito, e si paghino del mio, e si facci grazia a tutti quei che han remissioni dalle parti. E per voi, Eufranone caro, scriverò e supplicherò Sua Maestà³ che vi si re- 140 stituisca quello che ingiustissimamente vi è stato tolto.

DON FLAMINIO. Poi che a tutti si fa grazia, sarà anco giusto che l'abbi Leccardo il parasito.

DON RODORIGO. O là, ordinate che Leccardo sia libero. Ma mi par oggimai tempo che questi felici sposi ed 145 amanti, dopo tanti travagli, colgano il desiato frutto degli disperati loro amori. Entriamo.

DON FLAMINIO. Ma ecco Panimbolo.

is no other offshoot of our blood. And because these ladies lack dowries, I make them a gift, worthy of their love and generosity, of twenty thousand ducats each, and declare them heirs not only to my fortune but also of my love. While to other brides dowries are given by custom, I give you yours as a reward. And as a mark of love, I wish to embrace you: the blood of my ancestors compels me to this office.

CARIZIA. And we shall be perpetual servants and preservers of your health.

EUFRANONE. How are we ever to give adequate thanks for such liberality?

DON IGNAZIO. Dearest father and uncle, we are so much obliged to you that our tongues cannot find words to thank you.

DON RODORIGO. Now since all these troubles have come to so happy a conclusion, let a regal banquet be ordered for the wedding, and court proclaimed for ten days for all gentlemen and ladies of this city, so that a public sorrow may be converted into a public joy. And that there may be nothing of melancholy left in Salerno, let all imprisoned debtors be freed, and their debts paid at my expense, and let pardon be granted to all those whose accusers are willing. And for you, dear Eufranone, I shall write to supplicate His Majesty that what was unjustly taken from you be restored.

DON FLAMINIO. Since pardon is being granted to all, it is only just that Leccardo the parasite should have it too.

DON RODORIGO. [to the guards.] Ho there, order Leccardo to be freed. And now, it seems to me time that these happy bridegrooms and lovers, after so many troubles, gather the desired fruit of their desperate loves. Let us go in.

[All go within but Don Flaminio.]

DON FLAMINIO. Here comes Panimbolo.

SCENA V

PANIMBOLO, DON FLAMINIO, e LECCARDO.

PANIMBOLO. Padrone, che allegrezza è la vostra?

DON FLAMINIO. È tanta che non basto dirla. Panimbolo, la fortuna secondo il suo costume tutt'oggi ha scherzato con noi, valendosi della varietà de' casi, ed all'ultimo Iddio ha essauditi i nostri desiri. Ralegrati, 5 ché la poco dinanzi infelice miseria mia or sia ridotta in tanta felicità.

PANIMBOLO. Stimo che di questo giorno vi ricorderete ogni giorno che viverete.

DON FLAMINIO. O dolcezza infinita degli innamorati, 10 quando, dopo i casi di tanti infortunii, fortunatamente li è concesso di giunger a quel desiato segno che bersagliò da principio! O come ottimamente dissero i savi, che Amor alberga sovra un gran monte, dove solo per miserabili fatiche e discoscese balze si perviene, volendo 15 inferir che negli amori gran pene ed amaritudini si soffriscono, ma quelle pene son condimento delle lor dolcezze!

Ma ecco Leccardo.

LECCARDO. [da sé] Io ho avuto tanta paura d'esser ap- 20 piccato che la gola si è chiusa da se stessa senza capestro, e mi ha data la stretta più de mille volte, e senza morir mi ha fatto patir mille morti, ed ancora che io abbi avuto grazia della vita, per ciò non sento allargar il cappio: e sono appicato senza esser stato appiccato. 25

A Dio, cavaliero! O come presto m'era riuscito il pronostico che mi feci questa mattina! Ma per prender un poco di fiato, bisogna al meno bermi un barril di greco, e quattro piatti di maccheroni; se non, che or mi mangerò voi vivo e crudo. 30

DON FLAMINIO. Or non si parli più di scontentezza, poi che la fortuna dal colmo delle miserie mi ha posto

SCENE V

PANIMBOLO, DON FLAMINIO, and LECCARDO.

PANIMBOLO. Master, what joy has befallen you?

DON FLAMINIO. So much that it is beyond my power to say. Panimbolo, according to her wont, fortune has toyed with us all day, taking advantage of the various coincidences, and at last God has fulfilled our desires. Rejoice that my recent unlucky wretchedness is now resolved into such happiness.

PANIMBOLO. I think you will remember this day for all the days of your life.

DON FLAMINIO. Oh what infinite sweetness lovers enjoy, when after the vicissitudes of so many misfortunes, fortunately it is granted them to reach the mark they aimed at longingly from the start. Oh how truly said the sages, that Love dwells atop a great mountain, to be reached only by wretched struggles and steep cliffs, meaning that in love great pains and bitterness are suffered, but those pains are the seasoning of love's sweetness.

But here is Leccardo.

LECCARDO. [apart] I was so afraid of hanging that my throat closed up by itself without a noose, has strangled me a thousand times over and made me suffer a thousand deaths without dying, and though my life has been pardoned, I don't feel the noose loosened thereby, and I'm hanged without being hanged.

Greetings, noble sir. Oh how soon my morning's prophecy has come true! To breathe a little more easily, I must suck up at least a barrel of Greek wine and four plates of macaroni; otherwise I'm going to eat you, alive and raw.

DON FLAMINIO. Now let us speak no more of discontent, since fortune has taken me from the utmost mis-

285

nel colmo di tutte le sue felicità. Starai meco tutto il
tempo della tua vita, e comune sarà la tavola, le robbe, le
facultadi e le fortune. Licenzia costoro che son stati a di-   35
saggio, ascoltando le nostre istorie, e vien a prender
possesso della mia tavola.

[LECCARDO.] Spettatori, ho la gola tanto stretta che
non posso parlare. Andate in pace, e fate segno d'allegrezza.   40

eries to the utmost of her joys. You shall stay with me all your life long and share my table, goods, riches and fortunes. Bid depart those present who have been put to some discomfort listening to our histories, and come take possession of my table.

LECCARDO. Spectators, my throat is so tight that I cannot speak. Go in peace and signify your merry approval.

FINIS

Notes to the Text

Dedica

1. *Alessandro Gambalonga:* Gambalonga, or Gambalunga (d. 1619), member of a Riminese family enriched by his father's and grandfather's success in the building and iron trades, was given a gentleman's education in civil and canon law at Bologna. He held the office of Podestà in Rimini in 1591 and for many years patronized learning and the arts. Gambalonga played Maecenas to Cesare Ranucci and to Malatesta Porta as well as to Ciotti. By bequeathing his palace and his books to the public, he founded the Biblioteca Gambalunghiana of Rimini.

2. *cotesta città:* Rimini

3. *Gio. Batt. Ciotti:* Sienese printer, bookseller and editor, active from 1583 to at least 1622 in Venice, "al segno della Minerva e dell'Aurora," and in 1594 official printer to the Accademia Veneta.

Persone

1. *luogo:* The set should be envisaged as the fixed street scene recommended for comedies pretending to unity of place, affording views of urban architecture, approaches from at least three directions and practicable entrances to the Della Porta house and to the *casa terrena*, a balcony, and a corner around which an eavesdropper can hide.

2. *Persone:* Della Porta was as eclectic in naming his characters as in piecing together his plots. He mixes historically real or plausible names for the "serious" male figures with charactonyms and mythologizing fantasies from the *commedia dell'arte* or the *commedia regolare* for several of the comic types, and with romantically Hellenistic names for the Della Porta mother and daughters. Both *Ignazio* and

Flaminio were names in ordinary use in the late cinquecento, but the former has Spanish and Counter-
Reformation overtones appropriate to the "good"
brother, while the latter is relatively pagan and even
a shade stagey. The rhymed pair of fanciful names,
Simbolo and *Panimbolo*, also imply a constrast between the coherent and morally consistent advice
given by Ignazio's clever servant and the wide-
open, often self-contradictory, pragmatic counsels
of Flaminio's. *Leccardo*, from *leccare* (to lick), is typical of the descriptively unrealistic names attached
to the stock characters of the glutton in scores of
Renaissance comedies. *Martebellonio*, a name in
which the god and goddess of war are joined, belongs to the tradition of character-labelling which
also includes Plautus's Pyrgopolinices and Francesco Andreini's Capitan Spavento. The name *Eufranone* (Della Porta) is echoed in history by one
"Eufranon de Porta," listed as "Vicarius Generalis
Regni" in Salerno by Mazza, while that of *Don
Rodorigo* (di Mendozza), the viceroy, has been in-
conclusively associated with the "Roderico di Mendozza" named among regents and pro-regents in
the Regno di Napoli in 1541. See Introduction, pp.
11–12.

Prologo

1. *O là, che rumore*: From among the styles of induc-
   tion sanctioned by contemporary practice, Della
   Porta chooses the "critical" prologue, continuing
   the genre in which Terence defended his principles
   of dramaturgy.
2. *boccaccevole . . . regole di Aristotle*: Despite Aristotle's approval of verse for comedy, as despite several illustrious Italian examples of comedy in un-
   rhymed hendecasyllables, a general preference for
   prose became evident early in the sixteenth century. The language of Boccaccio's *Decameron*, recommended by Bembo as a model for prose com-

position and adopted for comedy by Bibbiena, among others, was in Della Porta's time still widely regarded as the touchstone of vernacular prose in comedy. The wave of commentary on the *Poetics* in the second half of the cinquecento gave to Aristotle in other respects, however, a powerful authority, which encouraged the development of "rules" for dramatic structure.

3. *legista . . . poeta*: The university degree in law and the practice of poetry are features by which Della Porta characterizes the small fry of the intellectual milieu in which questions of literary and dramatic theory were debated, often with Tuscan affectations. The frequenters of academies, universities and courts addressed here as carping critics are further represented in the prologue to *Carbonaria* as inept rival playwrights. See Appendix, p. 315.

4. *stampate . . . tradotte . . . ristampate*: By 1601, six of Della Porta's comedies had been printed in Italy; three had gone into more than one edition. It is not known which translations he refers to here. In 1585 *L'Olimpia* had been published in Paris in Fabrizio Fornaris's adaptation, *Angelica*, itself translated into French in 1599, probably by Pierre Larivey. Walter Hawkesworth's Latin version of *La Cinzia*, under the title *Labyrinthus*, may also have been ready before 1601, but the other authenticated translations and foreign printings of Della Porta's comedies occurred after this date.

5. *sorelle . . . in publico ed in privato*: The earliest documented performance in Italy of a comedy by Della Porta was that of *L'Olimpia* between 1586 and 1589 for the Count of Miranda, viceroy of Naples. There were undoubtedly earlier and less elaborate productions in private homes, as well as professional performances of the adaptation *Angelica* (see preceding note), which was certainly staged in Paris in 1584 and probably still earlier in Italy, to judge by the fact that Cornelio Lanci plagiarized its

prologue for his *Mestola*, printed in 1583. The second printing, in 1597, of a trio of Della Porta's comedies, *L'Olimpia, La trappolaria* and *La fantesca*, also was very likely the result of successful performances.

6. *Dottor della necessità*: a representative specimen of the *legisti senza legge* referred to above, a university graduate with a degree in law but lacking both knowledge and clients. Neediness was also the characteristic condition of the *commedia erudita* stock figure of the pedant, viz. Campanella's phrase, "pedanti superstiziosi nel parlare, bisognosi sempre" (*Poetica*, Cap. XXII). In the *commedia dell'arte* too, the masks of Dottore Graziano, the Bolognese lawyer, and even that of the usually rich Pantalone were often surnamed "dei Bisognosi."

7. *sei tratti di corda*: In this technique of interrogation, the victim was lifted by a rope attached to his wrists, then dropped and jerked to a halt, short of the ground. In England *strappado* could refer to the kind, the instrument or the single episode of torture; cf. Florio's dedication to his Italian dictionary of 1598 in a passage echoing a phrase of Aretino's prologue to *La cortigiana*: "One saies of Petrarche for all: A thousand strappadas coulde not compell him to confesse, what some interpreters will make him saie he ment."

8. *favola* . . . : The statement of structural principle that follows is a fairly typical late Renaissance adaptive paraphrase of Aristotle, with traces of tribute to Horace and Donatus.

9. *Menandro . . . Epicarmo . . . Plauto*: As representatives of the classical tradition of comedy, Della Porta chooses Epicharmus (ca. 528–ca. 438 B.C.), held to be the Sicilian Doric precursor of Attic Old Comedy; Menander (343–292 B.C.), prime exponent of Attic New Comedy; and Plautus (ca. 254–ca. 184 B.C.), the playwright of Roman New Com-

edy whose complete works Della Porta is said to have translated.

10. *se avesse saputo di filosofia*: The slap at Aristotle is more in raillery than in rebellion, as the Aristotelian characters of Della Porta's emphasis on plot and peripety suggests. The absence of the mocking from the otherwise similar prologue to *Carbonaria*, however, suggests that the joke could sometimes be judged unseasonable, by the author or by the Paduan censors.

11. *scherzi . . . fanciullezza*: In the prologue to *Carbonaria*, the corresponding phrase is "scherzi de' suoi studi più gravi." Although such deprecation, in either version, is a conventional display of *sprezzatura*, Della Porta undoubtedly considered his scientific works to be his major bid for fame; nevertheless, he showed concern for the printing of his plays. See Appendix, p. 315.

I.i

1. *Tricarico*: a town near Matera in the Basilicata region east of Salerno, long held by that line of the Sanseverino family from which the princes of Bisignano descended. A Salernitan branch of Della Porta's own family reputedly was connected by marriage with Giacomo Sanseverino, Count of Tricarico.

2. *pregio*: prezzo, premio. In the late cinquecento the word denoted concrete winnings or a prize, not merely prestige. The custom of turning the victory into a compliment to a lady was part of the protocol of the bullfight, in the Kingdom of Naples as in Spain.

3. *Ferrante di Corduba*: Consalvo di Cordova, or Gonzalo Fernández de Córdoba (1453–1515), known as "el Gran Capitán," was the general by whose victory over the French at the River Garigliano in 1503 the power of Ferdinand the

Catholic of Spain became absolute in the Kingdom
of Naples. Gonzalo Fernández was Ferdinand's
viceroy in the Regno until 1507.

4. *Rodorigo di Mendozza . . . Viceré*: Spampanato's
identification of the viceroy as the "Roderico di
Mendozza" listed among regents and pro-regents
for the Kingdom of Naples in 1541 is undermined
by Ignazio's statement that his uncle received office
from Ferrante di Corduba. It is likely that Don
Rodorigo and his nephews are fictional characters
in a historical setting, specifically in the period immediately after the "Gran Capitán's" conquest of
1503 but before the Spanish Crown had restored the
rule of Salerno to the Prince of Sanseverino. If the
fiction is intended to bear comparison with the realities of Spanish administration, the appointment to
rule both the province of Salerno and the city must
be counted as an extraordinary double honor. See
Introduction, pp. 10–16.

5. *giochi di canne, e di tori*: The game of hollow poles,
referred to also by Ariosto (*Orlando Furioso,* XIII,
xxxvii) and by Castiglione (*Il libro del cortegiano*, I,
xxi; II, viii), was a Moorish contest introduced into
Italy by the Spaniards. Divided into teams, the
players hurled poles at each other from opposite
sides of the field, and defended themselves with
shields. Bullfighting was likewise recommended
by Castiglione as a proper sport for the courtier,
and in his day already flourished as a festive spectacle at various Italian courts. A description of the
game of "cane" and of bullfighting at the papal
court of Leo X in 1519 is found in Alfonso Paolucci's
letter to Duke Alfonso I d'Este, reprinted by Borlenghi, vol. I.

6. *Della Porta . . . le parti del Principe di Salerno*: The
Prince of Salerno, referred to again when Eufranone Della Porta is said to have followed "le
parti Sanseverinesche" (II,vi), is not further identified in the play. Spampanato's conjecture that Eu-

franone was ruined by the rebellion of Ferrante Sanseverino, who left the Regno in 1551 and fled to France in 1552, is not borne out by the chronology of the plot. Eufranone's family has been impoverished for some time when the Mendoza brothers and their uncle come to Salerno as a consequence of the "Gran Capitán's" victory in 1503. It is more reasonable to conclude that the rebellion was the "Congiura dei Baroni," an uprising led by Antonello Sanseverino against Ferrante I of Aragon in 1485–86. It ended in Antonello's flight, the execution of some of the conspirators, and the confiscation of property, much of which was restored after 1503 by Ferdinand the Catholic. See Introduction, pp. 13–14.

7. *riversivi*: The medical vocabulary rings curiously in Ignazio's speech, and the resulting metaphor of the anticoagulant likewise sounds forced in reference to a conventional comic trick borrowed from Terence; both the scientific terms and the yoking of disparate subjects and sources, however, are typical of Della Porta's dramaturgy.

I.ii

1. *40.000 docati*: The terms *ducati* and *scudi* are used interchangeably here and later (II.iv), but the gold *scudo* coined in the Kingdom of Naples during the reign of Philip II (1554–98), the period in which the play was composed, was worth a little more than the gold *ducato*. According to Dell'Erba, the *scudo* was valued in 1573 at twelve-and-a-half *carlini*, the *ducato* at ten. Between 1582 and 1597 the *scudo* was worth thirteen *carlini*. Despite references in this scene in the 1601 and 1606 editions to 4,000 and 3,000 *ducati* and *scudi*, later references (II.i; II.iv) establish the sums at 40,000 and 30,000 *ducati* or *scudi*. Leccardo mentions that soldiers earn three ducats a month (III.ii). In *La tabernaria* Della Porta values a rich Neapolitan character's fortune at "più di 40.000

ducati." Della Porta's own inheritance from his well-to-do father was 20,000 ducats, not counting real estate, and his earnings from his scientific works came to 12,000. The dowry requested from the Count of Tricarico and Don Rodorigo's gifts of 20,000 ducats apiece to the two brides (V.iv), therefore, are very considerable amounts of money.

2. *pallido*: The colorlessness evoked is nearer in hue to sickly yellowish green or blue than to white.

3. *galli d'India*: tacchini. The turkey was first named for its origin in the New World, i.e., the West Indies.

I.iii

1. *lacrima . . . vin greco*: *Lacrima*, or *lachryma Christi*, is a sweet wine produced on the slopes of Vesuvius in both golden and red varieties. It is one of the "Greek" wines, so called because they come from a species of grapes imported in antiquity from Greece and continuously cultivated in Italy ever since.

2. *vernaccia di Paula*: The strong white wine named for Vernazza in Liguria is also produced in southern regions, including the ancient town of Paola, situated on the Tyrrhenian coast near Cosenza and known for its fruit and wine.

3. *vin d'amarene*: Like maraschino, this mildly bitter liquor is produced from the *visciolo* cherry.

4. *caso marzollino*: March is the traditional season for the round cheese made from *bufala* cows' or from ewes' milk. It is a specialty of the Florentine countryside but is also produced elsewhere in Tuscany, as well as in other regions, especially Romagna and Lazio.

I.iv

1. *Di Tunisi*: Leccardo probably intends to turn the insult into a compliment by making a feeble and

rather outdated pun on the name of Muley Hassan (Muleassen, re di Tunisi), restored to the hereditary throne of Tunis in 1535 by the campaign of the Emperor Charles V and well-known in Naples, where he took refuge in 1543.

2. *quinto cielo*: Della Porta had read Copernicus, but Martebellonio subscribes to the Ptolemaic cosmic system, in which the planet Mars dominated the fifth of nine spheres encircling the earth.

3. *sfera stellata*: In Ptolemy's universe the sphere of fixed stars is the eighth circle, placed between the sphere of Saturn and the *primum mobile*.

4. *canchero (cancaro)*: cancro. Often used as a solitary expletive, the word expresses a cinquecento formula of abuse, literally, "canker eat you."

5. *battaglia . . . con la Morte*: The fantastic contests described in this scene by Martebellonio and Leccardo, joining traits of the braggart and the parasite of Roman comedy with those of late medieval *contrasti* between personifications of ideas, were also characteristic set-pieces in the repertories of the *comici dell'arte*. Similar boasts of Capitano Spavento's duel with La Morte and of a glutton's challenging Hercules to an eating contest were published six years after *Fratelli rivali* in Francesco Andreini's *Le bravure del Capitano* (Ragionamenti 36 and 53).

6. *Atlante . . . toglio il mondo da sopra le spalle*: The Atlas mountains of North Africa, their height appearing to support the firmament, were identified by legend with the Titan Atlas, who bore the weight of the world on his back. Like many boasts in the braggart captain's repertory, this one of Martebellonio is an imitation of Hercules, the ur-*miles gloriosus*. In one version of the account of his eleventh labor, Hercules holds the world long enough to allow Atlas to gather the apples of the Hesperides.

7. *Mona*: Madonna.

8. *Dorindana*: Orlando's sword, called Durindana in Boiardo's *Orlando Innamorato* and Ariosto's *Orlando Furioso*, Durlindana in Pulci's *Morgante* and Durendal in the *Chanson de Roland*.

9. *occidente . . . ucciso*: By opposing *occidente* to *uccidente*, Della Porta plays on Latin *occidere* (*ob+caedo* = to kill or fell in battle), from which derives Italian *uccidere*, and Latin *occidere* (*ob+cado* = to fall, as the sun falls in the west), whence Italian *occidente, occaso*.

10. *fede*: From the handshake signifying a pledge of good faith, *fede* by metonymy means *hand*, here and again in II.iii, line 43 and II.vi, line 49.

II.ii

1. *fuggono le tenebre*: According to the time scheme of the play, it is still full daylight, but the minor inconsistency does not deter Della Porta from using the generic scene in which the window is likened to the east and the lady to the sun, an amalgam of long-established lyrical image and stage action, developed as a movable unit of dramatic construction decades before appearing here and in *Romeo and Juliet*. See Introduction, pp. 35–38.

II.iii

1. *fedi*: See I.iv, *n*10. In modern Italian the wedding-ring is called *la fede*, and the *Vocabolario dell'Accademia della Crusca* notes that wedding-rings used to be engraved with clasped hands instead of set with a gem; Ignazio's *anello*, however, is an engagement ring, bearing both a gem and an engraving of the joined hands called *fedi*.

2. *mensa di Tantalo*: Zeus's son Tantalus, king of Lydia in some versions of the legend, of Phrygia in others, because of divulging secret divine counsels was condemned to be eternally tormented by thirst and

hunger, in sight of inaccessible drink and food. Homer represents him in a lake, where the waters recede from his lips and the winds blow the branches of fruit trees out of his reach (*Odyssey*, XI, 582–92). Della Porta alters the common version of the myth by making Tantalus drink, to suit Ignazio's claim that Carizia makes thirsty where most she satisfies.

3. *mi sieda ne gli occhi . . . il peso della sua persona*: Ignazio's raptures, attributing real weight to the memory of Carizia's image, and in supposition lodging her in a rarefied atmosphere suggesting that of "il Padre eterno/ch'è ne la parte più del ciel sincera" (Tasso, *Gerusalemme Liberata* I.vii.3–4), parody the excesses of neoplatonic theories of love, and of the Petrarchan lyric tradition. The rhetorical question put to Simbolo (line 116) comically domesticates Petrarch's famous opening, "In qual parte del ciel, in qual idea" (*Rime*, CLIX).

II.iv

1. *Aldonzina*: Commentators on *Don Quijote*, I.1, often point out that Aldonza, the real name of the peasant girl whom Don Quijote idealizes as Dulcinea, was considered vulgar and rustic, in keeping with the proverb "a falta de moza, buena es Aldonza." In the contemporary Spanish-ruled Naples of Della Porta, the same connotations probably obtained, but the joke seems gratuitous.

II.vi

1. *Copritevi*: Eufranone has doffed his hat as a sign of respect to his social superior.
2. *fede*: See I.iv, *n*10.
3. *le parti Sanseverinesche*: See I.i, *n*6.

II.vii

1. *Dottor*: university graduate. See *Prologo*, *n*6.
2. *sale*: a Hispanism (*salir* = to go out) found in both

seicento editions and changed by the two later editors in order to avoid confusion with Italian *salire* (to ascend).

II.ix

1. *Ca . . . Cari . . .* : It is a stock device of cinquecento comedy to play off a subordinate's linguistic blundering against his superior's impatience and to use breathlessness or stuttering for bawdy or, as in this instance, coprocomic effect.

III.iii

1. *piscatori*: The standard distinction between a fisherman (*pescatore*) and a fishmonger (*pescivendolo*, *pesciaiolo*) would not have been observed in the port of Salerno, where fishermen sold their own catch.
2. *casa terrena*: rooms or detached apartments on the ground floor, essential to much of the intricate traffic on and off stage in Italian comedy, were relatively safe for assignations because they were separated from the family habitation proper, which used the *piano nobile* upstairs and extended to the higher storeys.

III.iv

1. *becco*: The male goat is a traditional metaphor for a cuckold; cf. Spenser's Malbecco (*The Faerie Queene*, book 3, cantos 9–10).
2. *dar martello*: an idiomatic phrase that denotes persistent tribulation and inevitably invites *double entendre*.
3. *biacche . . . verzini*: Chiaretta's knowledge of technical terms is still more surprising than Ignazio's (see I.i, *n*7) and similarly illustrates Della Porta's practice of varying the conventions of comedy, here the generic discourse on cosmetics, with details from his scientific studies. See Introduction, pp. 17–18.

III.xi

1. *Plutone . . . Proserpina*: When the gods divided the universe after the fall of the Titans, the underworld fell to Pluto, as the sea and the heavens did to his brothers Neptune and Jupiter respectively. Pluto's queen is the nymph Proserpine, whom he kidnapped from her mother, the goddess Ceres.

IV.ii

1. *spiuma*: The distortion of *schiuma*, crossing it with *spuma*, is apparently intentional, as it occurs twice in this scene in both seicento editions. *Schiuma* also occurs in both, in IV.v.

2. *rinschiuso*: The insertion of an *s* in *rinchiudere*, found in both seicento editions and in Muzio's of 1726, should change the meaning of the verb from *to close within* to *to unclose within*. The translation depends on treating *rinschiudere* as an imaginative neologism rather than as a solecism or a typographical error.

IV.iii

1. *torchino*: turchino. The reasoning behind the wordplay is this: because the stars are inauspicious to Martebellonio and the universe has betrayed him, the sky deserves to be called unfaithful or infidel, especially since it wears the Turkish color, turquoise or deep blue.

2. *Mongibello*: the popular name for the Sicilian Mount Etna, from a fusion of the Italian and Arabic words for *mountain*: *monte* and *giabal*.

3. *San Stefano*: Saint Stephen, deacon and martyr, was stoned to death in Jerusalem, ca. A.D. 35–36, by a crowd which received his Christian proselytizing as blasphemy against the Sanhedrin. His death is recorded in the *Acts of the Apostles*, chapters 6–8, and he is traditionally represented in art with stones on his head.

301

IV.v

1. *monte di Somma*: the jagged remains of the ancient crater from which Vesuvius erupted. The vines cultivated on the surrounding slopes produce the wine called *lacrima* (See I.iii, *n*1).

2. *tanti anni nella guerra*: Although the discrepancy between Flaminio's extreme youth (See V.i, line 31) and his Othello-like claim to many years of military experience accords with his mendacious and self-dramatizing character, it remains one of those collisions of theatrical effects which Della Porta's methods constantly risked. The topos of the warrior's self-recrimination, contrasting past honor with present woe, is not satisfactorily integrated with the topos of youth's susceptibility to passion, encountered later in the viceroy's plea for indulgence toward his nephew's deceits.

IV.vi

1. *Tesifone . . . Megera:* the sister Furies, or Eumenides, generated by the blood of the castrated Titan Uranus. Tisiphone is called "the Avenger," Megaera "the Jealous One," and Alecto "the Unresting." They especially pursue offenders against blood relations.

IV.viii

1. *tre legni:* The number of *birri* may be deduced from the number of cudgels and of sentences in the following speech.

2. *accomodarti . . . con le scarpe:* Spampanato accepts the passage without emendation as it stands in the 1601 edition, apparently thinking that the shoes belong to Leccardo. The 1606 editor and Muzio in 1726 assign them instead to the hangman, the former by making plural a singular noun and the latter by making singular a plural adjective (see Variants).

That they are correct in regarding the shoes as the means of adjusting Leccardo's neckwear is confirmed by testimony from another of Della Porta's comedies, *La turca*. To a modern reader, *scarpe*, taken in the technical sense of *rope-supports*, *skids* or *drags*, might suggest mechanical parts of a gallows. Scenes from *Turca*, however, make it clear that at least some hangmen (including, perhaps, Della Porta's celebrated acquaintance, the Neapolitan *boia*, Antonello Cocozza) actually kicked their victims off the ladder and into eternity. The character called simply "Boia," pleased at the prospect of acquiring a well-dressed victim's clothes, promises:

Io ti accomoderò una cordicina sotto il Capestro, che per esser sottile, fa il groppo stretto, e ti strangolerà senza, che lo senti, ti parrà un pulice che ti morda il collo, *ti salto sopra le spalle* con tanta destrezza, come un daino. . . . (*Turca*, IV.vi. Italics mine.)

Taking his characteristically sardonic way with literal details, Della Porta makes Boia continue:

. . . à me è licito abbassar le più superbe teste del mondo, e *calcar il collo* de' maggiori. . . . (IV.vi)

Later, when the victim, Dergut, has bestowed his rich garb on the poor and appears wearing rags, Boia angrily refuses to hang him:

Guai ti dia Dio, e la Madonna, ho comprato la fune con li miei danari: mi costa un'occhio; nè meno vò *logorar le scarpe*, per amor tuo. . . . (V.i)

Then he changes his mind ferociously and threatens in the following exchange:

BOIA. Hor ti vò appiccare in nome del Diavolo.
DERGUT. Mai ho havuto simil adversità sù le mie spalle.
BOIA. Maggior l'harai quando *ti calcherò sopra*. Vò appiccarti solo, per farti dispiacere, tu non potevi esser se non un rustico villano, & il tuo collo me lo

pagherà ben sì, le carezze, che soglio fare à gli altri,
non le vò fare à te, questo nodo grosso te lo porrò
sotto la gola, ti farò stralunar gli occhi, torcer la
bocca, e ti farò uscir la lingua fuori un palmo, à tuo
dispetto, ti stringerò tanto, che ti farò uscir l'anima
per l'oculo. Bagnerò la fune, che non scorra, accio-
che più tardi facci l'effetto, & facci morir con maggior tormento. *Ti farò una pavana sù le spalle* senza
suoni, che non ti piacerà molto, poiche mi vai do-
nando le cose mie, il mio stento, il mio sudo-
re. (V.i)

Marabeo's line in Annibal Caro's *Gli Straccioni*,
II.ii, "il boia mi pesti in su le spalle" (in Borsellino,
vol. 2) suggests that Roman hangmen may have
used the same technique.

3.　　*su un asino con una mitra in testa*: Condemned prisoners were often led through the streets in mock-
ery, seated backwards on donkeys and wearing
high caps of rolled paper inscribed with vitupera-
tions. These grim preliminaries to public execution
were travesties of the ceremonial marks of respect
paid to dignitaries; by succinct reference to the literal facts, the *birro* can pretend to promise high
honors to Leccardo.

V.i

1.　　*non gionge ancora a diciotto anni*: See IV.v, *n*2.

V.iv

1.　　*meati troppo aperti*: From Plato's concept of the tri-
partite soul, Renaissance neoplatonic love theory
explained the diffusion of the intermediate vital
spirits heated by the heart. Castiglione uses the
same terms in describing the opposite effect caused
by the absence of the beloved lady, " . . . essendo
la bellezza lontana, quell' influsso amoroso non
riscalda il core come faceva in presenza, onde i
meati restano aridi e secchi" (*Il libro del cortegiano*
IV, lxvi). The idea of the vital spirits situated in the

heart also belonged to the Galenic system of human physiology still generally accepted in the sixteenth century.

2. *pregio*: See I.i, *n*2.

3. *Sua Maestà*: the king of Spain and of the Kingdom of Naples. If the action of the play is supposed to occur in 1504 (see Introduction, pp. 10–16, and I.i, *nn*3, 4, 6), the king is Ferdinand the Catholic (1452–1516), who restored to the Sanseverino party much of the property confiscated by Ferrante I of Aragon after the Congiura dei Baroni in the 1480s.

APPENDIX:

Editing the Text

THERE ARE FOUR EDITIONS of the complete text of *Gli duoi fratelli rivali*:

A. GLI DVOI / FRATELLI / RIVALI / Comedia / NVOVAMENTE / data in luce, / DAL SI-GNOR / GIO. BAT. DELLA PORTA / Gentil-huomo Napolitano. / CON PRIVILEGIO. / IN VENETIA, / Appresso Gio. Batt. Ciotti Sanese, 1601. [Stiefel incorrectly names Francesco Ciotti as the printer of this first edition.]

B. GLI DVOI / FRATELLI / RIVALI / Comedia / NVOVAMENTE / data in luce, / DAL SI-GNOR / GIO. BAT. DELLA PORTA / Gentil-huomo Napolitano. / CON PRIVILEGIO. / IN VENETIA, M.D.CVI. / Appesso [sic] Francesco Ciotti.

C. *Delle commedie di Giovanbattista de la Porta*, v.II. Napoli: Gennaro Muzio, 1726.

D. *Giambattista Della Porta. Le commedie*, a cura di Vincenzo Spampanato, v.[II]. Bari: G. Laterza, [1911].

In 1943 an acting version was published, following Anton Giulio Bragaglia's production at the Teatro delle Arti di Roma on 27 January:

"*I due fratelli rivali*, commedia di Gian Battista Della Porta, riduzione in tre atti di Gerardo Guerrieri," in *Il Dramma*, Anno XIX, numero 408–409, 15 agosto–1 settembre, 1943.

Because Della Porta was under surveillance by the Inquisition, the licensing of his scientific works called for an unusual amount of correspondence, and from 1592 he was forbidden to publish anything at all without obtaining permission directly from the Roman censor; the approval of local inquisitors no longer sufficed. Taken

together, Pompeo Barbarito's prefaces to Della Porta's first two printed plays, *L'Olimpia* in 1589 and *La Penelope* in 1591, show that behind a conventional show of reluctance to publish light works, the author was more than cooperative with his editor. Whether or not he was in Venice in 1601 when three of his comedies were printed there, moreover, it is clear from his having issued three comedies and a tragicomedy to presses between 1589 and 1596 that he actively forwarded such undertakings. Among his plays in manuscript listed by Barbarito and by Bartolommeo Zannetti in 1610 there is no mention of *Fratelli rivali*, however, and as no manuscripts of any of the fourteen comedies have come to light, we do not know in what form or condition most of them were delivered to the printers. Another of Della Porta's editors, Lucrezio Nucci, records in the dedication to *La sorella* in 1604 that copies of *La furiosa*, *La turca* and *L'astrologo* were circulating "scattered, incorrect and ill-treated." The discontinuity in the action and the often imperfect fitting of formulaic *battute* to situations in *Fratelli rivali* could be interpreted as evidence that Ciotti's typesetters worked from a copy modified or reconstructed by a troupe of *comici*. This hypothesis, however, would not explain why the 1606 edition, obviously set from the 1601 edition, contains two variants pointing to the collaboration of actors: "tal cosa pacienza" for "rabbiosa pacienza" in IV.ii, line 57, suggesting faulty aural memory; and the addition of "posto" to expand the wordplay on "pesta . . . pasta . . . pasto" in I.iv, lines 160–161, an improvement which, admittedly, might as well have come from a would-be-witty printer as from an improvising player. In any case, it is certain that Della Porta's comedies were in favor with the professional actors and it seems that he was liberal with his manuscripts. His earliest published comedy, *L'Olimpia*, in fact, first appeared in print in 1585 as the work of the *capo-comico* Fabrizio de Fornaris, who, on receiving it in Venice "a few years ago from an exceedingly accomplished Neapolitan gentleman," had re-

named it *Angelica*, made a few changes and taken it to Paris, where it was performed in 1584 and published the following year. In this connection it may be useful to compare the *Prologo* of *Fratelli rivali* with the version of it attached to *La carbonaria*, another of Della Porta's comedies, published likewise in Venice in 1601 but by a different printer. The version in *Fratelli rivali* is more pungently phrased, that in *Carbonaria* is better printed; both contain inconsistencies in grammar. In the *Carbonaria* prologue the jibe at Aristotle has been deleted, perhaps by "Domino Fabio Paulini lettor publico," or by one of the other members of the University of Padua who were deputized by the Council of Ten to examine *La Cintia* and *La carbonaria* and passed them on 26 October 1600, for licensing on 16 November. The absence of a notice of licensing attached to *Fratelli rivali* suggests more perfunctory scrutiny by the censors. The texts of the two prologues could represent separate reconstructions by actors, but they might also be two versions by Della Porta himself. His manner of composing was hospitable to influence from the *commedia dell'arte*, and as his style (including inconsistencies, formulae, oscillations in orthography and irregularity of syntax) is much the same in the first editions of the fourteen comedies issued over a span of twenty-seven years, in six cities, and from eleven printers, it may be supposed that Ciotti's text was a manuscript acknowledged, if not directly transmitted, by the author.

Like the greater number of cinquecento and seicento printed plays, the 1601 edition of G. B. Ciotti (called *A* in the variants to the text of my edition) and the 1606 edition by Francesco Ciotti based on it (*B*) are full of typographical anomalies, many of them garbles or easily corrigible misprints, some of them gaps or puzzles, and some of them possibly variations or oscillations of spelling, grammar or syntax. Muzio's 1726 edition in four volumes (*C*), the only complete collection of Della Porta's comedies, is carefully executed; but because he adhered to the standards of the eighteenth century by

modernizing and normalizing the grammar and spelling, and by not infrequently replacing Della Porta's words with seemlier ones of his own, Muzio will be consulted but not imitated by modern editors. Spampanato's edition of eight comedies in two volumes in 1910 and 1911 (D) attempted to return to first editions; had the attempt succeeded, I might have reprinted the D text of *Fratelli rivali* with my translation. Despite its undeniable utility in the absence of other modern editions, however, Spampanato's not only is noteless but also contains incorrect transcriptions and numerous errors of which the two Ciotti and the Muzio editions are innocent.

Until there exists a critical edition of Della Porta's complete comedies, the surest approach to the text of any of them will be to take Spampanato's way, but with greater care. This has been my aim in returning to the first edition (A), collating it with the other three (B, C, D), correcting egregious errors but preserving the ambiguities, ellipses, inconsistencies and oscillations of the original, modernizing the spelling and punctuation only as much as is necessary to avoid pedantry or more than momentary confusion.

Accordingly, I have not reproduced the typographical interchanges of *u* and *v*, *i* and *j*, nor the etymological *h* (*hoggi*, *abhominevole*, *humile*). The Latinate *tti* and *ti* (*perfettione*, *gratia*) have been replaced with *zi*, and *ij* with *ii* in plural endings (*negozij*). I have expanded all of the many abbreviations, substituting *e* and *ed* for ampersands before consonants and vowels respectively, as also for the Latinate *et*. I have sparingly changed the punctuation, sometimes following Spampanato's modernizations in D, especially when the plethora of commas or the length of periods in A invites confusion, but at other points I have added commas, apostrophes and exclamation points; whenever possible, however, I have preserved the punctuation of A. Neither A nor B admit acute accents; following D and departing from

modern usage, I add acute accents to the isolated adverbial conjunctive *ché* when it is used in lieu of compound conjunctions, such as *purché*, *perché*, etc. I likewise accent these compound conjunctions and a few other *e*'s, where stress (*Viceré*) or distinction from homonyms (*né*) is needed, and in rare cases I have added grave accents (*dà* as verb, *sì*) or removed them (*ho*, *a*). Capitalization in *A* and *B* is generous and erratic; I have reduced and standardized it somewhat, but very much less than Spampanato does in *D*. One arbitrary change in my edition is the standardized spelling of given names: oscillations in *A* and *B* between Callidora-Calidora, Flaminio-Flamminio, Polisena-Polissena, Rodorigo-Roderico-Rodorico, and so on, figure among the variants but not in the text, where the form most common in *A* is invariably used. The paragraphing follows that of *A*, except when I have begun new paragraphs to point up a dramatically significant change of tone or to indicate a shift from delivery aside to directed speech. Brackets are used to indicate extraneous material, usually stage directions.

Other oscillations in spelling of *A* have been preserved with as much care as have the invariable archaisms, even though this practice results in juxtapositions disconcerting to modern readers not familiar with the unfixed orthography of Renaissance texts: for example, *struger* and *strugger*, *allegreza* and *allegrezza*, *ragione* and *raggione*, *accetar* and *accettar*, *ochi* and *occhi*, even the misleading *eco* and *ecco* may appear side by side. Without knowledge of the manuscript behind Ciotti's printed text (*A*), we cannot yet determine how close the *editio princeps* brings us to the author. It is noteworthy, however, that Sirri's recent study of the language of Della Porta's tragedies shows that in the autograph manuscript of *Il Georgio* he twice used the abnormal diphthongization *nuovol-o*, *i* (subsequently changed by the printer to *nuvolo* and *nuvoli*) that I have transcribed from the *A* and *B* texts of *Fratelli rivali* II.ix (*nuovola*).

Except in one case, where they would be seriously misleading, inconsistencies in person (unexplained shifts from second person plural to second person singular or to third person singular) are preserved, as are the obsoletely lax verb-endings (*io avesse*) corrected scrupulously in *C* and haphazardly in *D*. One of the functions of the translation is to clarify ambiguities of this sort that stand in the original.

The textual variants given for the body of the play include all points required by the above principles, with a small number of readings in *A* that accordingly have been excluded from my text, with all variants in *B*, with some variants in *D* selected to illustrate its distance from *A*, and with only those variants in *C* which are needed to clarify the relationship of the other texts. The *C* edition is sometimes cited to explain or to suggest alternatives to the solutions that my text offers, but the regular variants in *C*, so consistent and extensive as to alter the linguistic character of the original, are not included. A few of the changes in the *D* edition are consistent: *e'l* always becomes *e il*, *Dhe* becomes *Deh*, final *ii* or *ij* becomes *i*. Many others are sporadic, however: some of these are unprecedented and inexplicable, such as *O* and *Oime* become *Oh* and *Ohime*, but, again, *Oh* and *Ohime* become *O* and *Oime*; others are unconscious carry-overs from *C*, such as the occasional addition of *e* to a truncated infinitive, or the intermittent modernizations of spelling and changes of *vuol* to *vuole*, *ciel* to *cielo*, *da la* to *dalla*, *constretto* to *costretto*, *stessi* to *istessi*, etc. Except where there is a clear reason, the variants to the present edition make no account of such errors in transcription and departures from the *A* text by the editor of *D*.

Because Ciotti's letter is omitted in *C* and *D*, variants to the text of the dedication are limited to *A* and *B*. Variants to the prologue are the most inclusive: in this section only, in order to suggest the range of variation in the four texts from 1601 to 1911, I give in full all the

differences among the four editions and reprint the version of the prologue that appeared with *La carbonaria* in 1601. The meanings of the words, whatever the form, are glossed by the translation, which has been kept literal for that purpose and as an invitation into the Italian text. Although I have not annotated archaisms per se, leaving it to the reader and his Italian dictionary to distinguish between the quaint and the current, I have included in the notes some necessary observations on definitions and untranslatable aspects of lapsed usages.

Variants

Dedication
(omitted in *C* and *D*)

3 *B* picciola   4 *B* obligo   7 *B* peregrinaggio   10 *B* accettare   16 *A B* novenirsi   30 *A B* non lettare

Persone

1 *B* inamorato   3 *B* Flamminio   6 *A B* Martibellonio (elsewhere in the *A* text most frequently Martebellonio)   10 *A B C D* Polissena (elsewhere in the *A* text most frequently Polisena)   14 *A B D* Roderigo, *C* Roderico (elsewhere in the *A* text most frequently Rodorigo)

Prologo

1 *C* strepito è quello?   3 *B* vilisima   5 *C* di Commedie, or ghigna di qua   9 *B* versimile   12 *C* la Commedia non dia soddisfazione agl' intendenti   17 *B* parer un'opera di mano, ch'ella si sia come il mondo, *C* parere un'opera men, che ella sia, come se il mondo, *D* parere un'opera di manco ch'ella sia, come il mondo   18 *A* gradirasse, *B* gradisse, *C* bilanciasse, *D* graduasse, (*Carbonaria* giudicasse)   19 *C* che siete, che l'opere;   20 *C universale*   21 *A B* stampare . . . tradotte, *C D* stampate . . . tradotte, (*Carbonaria* stampare . . . tradurre)   22 *B* spa-

gnuolo   23   *A* piaccino e son, *C* piacciono e sono
25   *C* pubblico   27   *B* cõffessaresti, *C* confesseresti
28   *C* scienzie; *B* soterra   29   *C* Commedia;   30   *B*
parlare giamai, *C* parlarne giammai   31   *C* maravi-
gliosa   32   *C* questo è l'anima della Commedia
34   *D* moto, che se   35   *C* farla cadere   36   *A* stirocc-
chiamenti   39   *C* degli occhi dello 'ntelletto, *D* degli
occhi dell'intelletto   41   *C* vagare   41   *B* comedia sia
giunta, *C* Commedia sia gionta   44   *C* quale   45   *D*
o di altro; *C* Commedia, forse non averebbe   48   *A*
B fuor de limitar, *C* fuori del limitare   51   *C* Commedie furono   52   *B C* di morti;   53   *C*
provocherete   54   *C* conoscere   55   *C* siete; *C*
quest'ignorantoni   56   *C* uficio
Title–page and prologue to *La carbonaria*, as in first
edition:

La/ Carbonaria/ Comedia/ Dell'Illustre/ Sig. Gio.
Battista/ Della Porta/ Napolitano./ Nuovamente
data in luce./ con Privilegio,/ & licenza de' Superi-
ori./
In Venetia,/ Presso Giacomo Antonio Somasco./
M.DCI.
O là, che rumore, ò là che strepito è questo? egli è
possibil pure, che fra persone tanto illustri e di persone, e di sangue v'habbia à venir sempre mischiata
questa vilissima generatione, la qual per mostrare à
quel popolaccio, che gli stà intorno che s'intende di
comedie (come se la comedia fusse qualche poema
da suoi pari) hor ghigna di quà, hor torce il muso di
là, par che li puzzi ogni cosa. Questa parola s'haria
potuto dir meglio altrimente, quell'altra non è vsata
dal Boccaccio. Questo è fuor delle regole di Aristotele, l'altro non mi par verisimile, e pascendosi di
quella vil aura popolare, ne intende egli, ne lascia
intendere à gli altri. Altri pieni d'invidia e di veleno,
per mostrar che la comedia non dia sodisfattione à
gli intendenti, empiono di strepito, e di gridi tutto il
teatro. Ma che gente son queste poi? qualche Leg-

gista senza legge, ò qualche Poeta senza versi. Credete ignorantoni, che voi con le vostre insipide chiacchiere bastar à far parer vn'opra, che sia di men grado, di quella che sia? come il mondo dal vostro bestial giuditio giudicasse il valor dell'opere? O goffi, che sete, che l'opre son bilanciate dall'vniversal giuditio dei dotti, e di tutte le nationi: perche quando son commendate da tutti, si veggono stampare per tutte le stampe del mondo, e tradurre in varie lingue; e quanto più s'odono, e si veggono più si considerano, e più piacciono, e più son ristampate, come è accaduto all'altre sue sorelle, che in publico, & in privato cōparse sono. Vien qua dottor della necessità, che non sapendo della tua, presumi saper tutte le scienze; e tu che ogn'hor più gonfi co'l dir mal d'altri; se sapeste che cosa sia comedia, vi porreste sotterra per nō parlarne giamai. Ignorantissimi considerate la favola se sia nuova, piacevole, e meravigliosa, con l'altre parti sue convenevoli, che questa è l'anima della comedia: cōsiderate la peripctia, che è 'l spirito dell'anima, che le da moto, e l'avviva, e considerate gli antichi comici, che ordiscono venti Scene per far cader la peripetia in vna sola, & in queste cade da se stessa in tutto vn atto, anzi quando stimi, che sia finita, vedrai nasccr peripetia da peripetia, & agnitione da agnitione. E se non foste cosi ciechi de gl'occhi dell'intelletto, vedreste l'ombre di Menãdro, di Epicarmo, e di Plauto vagar su questa scena, e rallegrarsi, che la comedia di tēpo in tēpo hor sia salita à quel colmo, dove con tutto il sforzo si sforzò giongere la comica antichità. Ma voi non conoscere l'arte: à gli savi, & à gli ignoranti tutte le cose son chiare. Hor gracchiate tanto che scoppiate, che le vostre maledicenze non passano il limitare delle vostre camere, & i vostri scritti muoiono innanzi la vostra morte. Non sapete che le comedie son scherzi de suoi studi più gravi, e che non hà bisogno delle lodi delle comedie? Ma se pur troppo provocaretela sua modestia, farà co-

noscere le vostre non comedie, ma cadaveri, e
mostri di comedie rubbate: le inventioni, e le scene,
e le parole dall'altre vecchie mal attaccate, & mal
vnite insieme. Ma questi ignorantacci per la rabbia
m'han fatto smenticar del mio vfficio, ch'era venuto qui per farvi il prologo: Ma perche costoro che
vengono fuori vi narreranno l'argomento, mi par-
to. à Dio.

I.i

2 *B* presto: m'habbi   21 *B* Flamminio; *B* Conte che
ve   34 *B* che lo   36 *B* di me di   37 *B* non vi potete
fidar di parole   43 *B* fede di un   61 *B* cani, e di tori
62 *D* Palazzo;   63 *A B* vene (tilde missing)   63 *B*
cani;   63 *A B* vener (tilde missing)   78 *B* suprema
81 *B* pur si sentiva   83 *B* una nõ mai piu   88 *D*
fusse maggiore   90 *B* medicina   93 *B* crudilissima-
mente   104 *C D* ammazzaremmo senz'alcuna
105 *B* Segui, e   107 *A B* dimostrar   126 *B* havera
(haveva?) compassione   130 *B* vincitor   142 *B* di
tutta   144 *B* Flamminio   145 *B* reducemmo   150 *B*
mattina   152 *B* essernele   156 *B* di Tricarico   169 *B*
pensateci   170 *B* che'l   173 *B* vi vuol; *B* grandi di
175 *B* priverà   176 *B* nel matrimonio   180 *B* per
l'amor   181 *B* la robba   187 *B* m'havessi   189 *B*
subito   190 *B* Eco Don Flamminio

I.ii

Persone *B* Flamminio   7 *A B C* redirmele; *B* non
vuoi   11 *B* di buona voglia, che ragionava   13 *B* so-
pragiunse   21 *B* come sono io   25 *B* de' suoi   26 *B*
di quelle   32 *B* comprarsi   35 *B* che vuoi   39 *B*
patienza; *B* d'animo di vili   41 *B* presente nè   58 *B*
affetto   62 *B* il colsi   69 *A D* faldi; *B* quando imposi   71 *A* pensinò, *B* pensino, *C* pensano, *D* pensi
75 *D* delle ventiquattro   75 *D* più di trenta   81 *A*
4000 docati, *B* 4000 ducati, *C* 40000 ducati, *D*
quarantamila docati; *C* la sposerà, *D* sposaralla
82 *A B* 3000, *C* 30000, *D* trentamila   85 *A B* 10000,

C 100000, D centomila   86 A B 1000, C 10000, D
diecimila   93 B farebbono   100 B cruccia   110 A
volte, e m'è   116 A i 4000, B i 40000, C li 40000, D
li quarantamila   126 B affetto

I.iii

8 B di bietole   13 B gli spiriti   16 B maraviglia
17 A cosi 'l leggiero   30 B gli Scherzi   44 C D non
vuoi dir   50 D fu festa   62 B mi haria   68 B da'
colpi   92 B boglir   93 B di pan   95 B vengano
96 D e sarà un   102 B più di una   105 A B Pani.
Con certe animelle de Vitelluccie ti riporrò l'anima in
Corpo se fussi morto e sepellito resuscitarci per farmi
medicar da voi. I follow the division of speeches in C
and D.   108 B haverste (avreste) qualche   111 B addosso   115 A medicessi   128 C D apparecchi
132 B serò a voi   135 A afatto mile arti   140 C D
Valorosissimo

I.iv

1 A B Martebellonio indicated only as "Cap."
throughout scene   7 B francese   12 A venne; B
tamburo   34 B Gli attacco   38 B se non   44 B
nube   45 B se desse   59 B per l'historie   64 B di
sopra   70 B tre dita;   72 B sosteneavate   82 B
Bene, bene   93 B eleggeste   95 C D malaugurio
97 C D allessa   101 B Seguite   109 B se vuoi
114 B dita   120 B vi sete   122 D basta a ingiottire
127 A cãpagnia, B conpagnia   135 D più la Fame
136 A B Ma prima che queste due fami andiamo a
mangiare, C Or presto andiamo a mangiare, D Ma
prima andiamo a mangiare   144 A B Calidora
155 B stringonno, D stringe   160 B Prima sarò sotterra posto che sia pesta la pasta per questo pasto
177 D mi fa far certe   182 C D gli fo

II.i

5 B servigio   8 B cagion   14 C dare 40 mila, D
dare quarantamilla   17 C D spingi   18 B mi hai

22 *B* havesse certo   36 *D* dice   37 *B* stimai   46 *B* se dice; *C D* sera, voi

II.ii

3 *B* cessi (cossi?) stanca come si   5 *D* Vo innanzi 13 *B* honesta sia   15 *C D* qualità; ne l'importanza del negozio, né   22 *B* non so se debba; *A B* chiamarle 28 *B* ragionamento   72 *B* pur trapporrò, *C* pure frapporò, *D* pure traporrò   73 *B* di voi   85 *B* di sì 96 *A B* la tenebre

II.iii

13 *D* cara bellezza   18 *B* riccheza   23 *C D* ric- chezza   26 *B* sontuosa   29 *B* pellegrine virtù   29 *B* risiedeno   39 *B* meriti, per   46 *A B* nondimeno/ Ma ben sapete (line missing?), *C* nondimeno ben sapete, *D* nondimeno . . . , ma   51 *B* accettatelo 59 *B* Accetto l'anello   62 *B* diseguale alla sua gran- dezza, accettarlo come   66 *B* occhi miei   69 *B* pa- tiscono   70 *B* eccomi   90 *B* ardeva   99 *B* con- vitto   104 *A* celesti bellezza, *C D* celesti bellezze 108 *C* quanto l'amerò, *D* quanto l'amarò   112 *D* ac- cettar   114 *C D* lasciarsi   119 *B* l'Aria più tranquilla, e

II.iv

Persone *A B* omit Simbolo   17 *D* complimenti 26 *C* i 40 mila, *D* i quarantamilla   34 *C* 40 mila, *D* quarantamilla   41 *A B* assign this speech to "Panim."   42 *B* inganato   58 *B* struggere   66 *A B* assign this speech to "Panim."   67 *D* abbiam   71 *D* mandiamo a   74 *B* di Tricarico   87 *B* movetevi 91 *B* lacciuoli   93 *A* donna vedersi

II.v

5 *B* deto che 'l matrimonio del conte era chiuso, *C* detto che'l matrimonio del Conte era conchiuso, *D* detto che il matrimonio con la figlia del Conte era

conchiuso   10 *D* come son vivo   11 *B* vivace,
pronto

II.vi

5 *B* leggiermente   16 *B* Servitevi   25 *B* sarei   28 *B*
farmivi   35 *B* figliuola   36 *B* forse   37 *B* di mia
53 *B* Caprici   63 *A* altri S ricchi, *B* altri Si ricchi
64 *B* de poveri Gentilhuomini, non havendo mo
84 *B* intepedisce   89 *D* contento vostro   92 *D* af-
fettuaremo   95 *B* della festa, fin hora sia potuto
105 *C D* ma né meno   107 *B* siete   119 *C D* vita e
l'onore   127 *A* fasci, *B* faccia   128 *B* facciasi
130 *A B* drappi, d'oro   141 *B* tratener   145 *B* Polissena

II.vii

3 *A* compagna mia, *B* compagnia mia   12 *B* mi-
glior   30 *B* raffredato   36 *B* vide   41 *C D* appena
va fuor   45 *C D* conducessi   46 *B* abbigliamenti
47 *D* pari, se disse   72 *C* me la lasciano, *D* me lo
lasciano

II.viii

Persone *B* Polissena   3 *C D* e di vostra   6 *C D*
maniglie d'oro   7 *B* abbigliamenti   10 *B* supplendo
de

II.ix

10 *B* beuto soverchio   41 *B* Dimmi la nuova   60 *D*
e venti e trenta   62 *B* Carizia maritata   74 *C D* pur
certo   75 *B* soffirirlo   78 *B* spedisca   82 *B* addoc-
chiai   100 *D* vostro fatto; *B* ragiona, che à voi
106 *D* anzi sia abbondantissimo   123 *B C* indovinate
da voi   128 *B* finiscela   135 *C D* non sentii   140 *C*
D Dunque taccio   151 *B* c'havea   158 *B* pensavassi
165 *B* Hor questo, Innomine   169 *B* Spediscemi
178 *B* Spetate, *C D* Spedazio   179 *C* spiedo, *D*
spede   180 *B* Forse Don Ignazio?   183 *B* son spiedi

196 *C D* nuvola; *A* ma circondato   202 *B* venga
203 *B* addatti   218 *B* fino a la   222 *B* di qua

III.i

2 *C D* addosso   3 *B* da la paura   5 *B* da si varij
13 *B* faccia   17 *B* habbia   27 *B* rimeritargli   31 *B*
da le mani de la morte   33 *B* guiderdonar   39 *A B*
noze   46 *B* rispondiamo   47 *B D* cader l'inganno
71 *B* freta, ché la freta   72 *B* risolutioni   74 *B*
guasta'   96 *B* e di buona   102 *B* Caritia c'hor ama,
C Carizia, or ama, *D* Carizia che or ama   108 *B*
cancelaremo   110 *B* sforzato   120 *B* nè strettezza
129 *B D* occultamente   132 *B* lo Spõsalitio   133 *B*
improverate   139 *B* chetti;   148 *B* dissegni   153 *B*
mai non facessimo   154 *B* confussione   158 *B* ese-
quiamolo   164 *B* esequirlo   173 *B* como le mani

III.ii

15 *B* de' rari che s'hà fatti   26 *B* addosso   27 *B*
sbandditi   28 *B* abbandonato   30 *B* habbia goduto
39 *B* si havessero   42 *D* operato per mia cagione e
non   45 *B* Giustitia; *B* ragnatelli   51 *D* si fa
giustizia   57 *B* Dal impedimento   58 *B* meter
59 *C* ed in spiga leggiera le concepite, *D* e in spica le
già concette   64 *B* non vuoi   65 *D* credo io ben
66 *B* non vuoi?   72 *B* appicato   83 *B* appicato
100 *C D* salsiccioni   101 *D* di polli   115 *B* dici, che
Liccardo mio?   122 *C D* ci vuol tempo   124 *D*
prometto   127 *B* Artiglierie   131 *B* accerba   136 *B*
sapreste comandarmi   137 *B* benefattore   142 *B* ser-
virai   149 *B* m'appicherei

III.iii

1 *A B* Martebellonio indicated only as "Cap."
throughout scene   6 *A* porrò   10 *A B* Calidora
13 *B* venga   37 *B* l'abracciarete (D11 verso, tag on
D11 recto is "abbra-")   60 *B* la ventura di costui
68 *B* ragnatelli; *D* dalla casa

III.iv

Persone *A* Chiaretta, Francesca, Leccardo, *B*
Chiaretta, Leccardo, *C D* Chiaretta fantesca, Leccardo 6 *B* gustarei 13 *B* aiuterei 22 *B* vuoi
30 *B* vuoi 32 *B* questi animali 47 *D* facce 55 *B*
e piglia l'artificiale, *D* e il piglia 56 *B* ti vorrei ricer-
car, *D* vorrei cercare 63 *C D* vorresti 72 *B* ti
è ricercato 77 *A* ti vergogno 79 *B* di Caritia
81 *B* altro che questo 86 *B* le hà 91 *B* faccia
96 *B* Perche facendo

III.v

1 *C D* Ecco 12 *D* Conoscerla ti sei *B* le gioie
19 *B* se t'havessi 22 *A B* Calidora 35 *A B* Dille
40 *B* cura di spiar

III.vi

8 *B* promettete 12 *C D* per veder se vi 12 *B* non
so chi 27 *B* sarà spedito 47 *B* nuoccono 48 *B*
nuoccono 55 *D* tardi che non 56 *B* desio di maritarvi 70 *D* transfers Don Ignazio's speech to the beginning of the next scene

III.vii

8 *B* rallegrarete; 10 *B* ambi doi 14 *B* altri di dar
18 *A B* Rodrigo 46 *A B* Cosa da non 53 *B*
giudicio 60 *B* dirmi 62 *B* Perdonate, se 63 *C* vi
dico, *D* ve dico 64 *C D* vi porto 67 *A* e da una,
C e ad una, *D* e d'una 95 *B* leggermente 101 *B*
ambi doi 108 *B* è più 112 *B* practicar 117 *B*
ascoltiate 123 *B* veggiate 138 *B* venite 151 *B* gli
attaccò; *B* potea 155 *B* disordinino

III.viii

8 *D* abbino 10 *D* Oh quanta 10 *C D* allegrezza
12 *C D* grandezza 15 *B* tratengo 18 *A* risposte

III.ix

1 *A B* Martebellonio indicated as "Cap." 3 *B* gli
sguardi 9 *B* ecco; *A B* calidora 13 *B* misericordia
18 *B* però qui

III.x

Persone *A B* Don Flaminio: Don Ignatio: Capitano:
Panimbolo: Simbolo 1 *C D* in istrada; *B* non se
potremo 5 *B* impossibile 6 *B* poiche in costei
7 *A B* la sua honestà la sua honestà si trovi si disho-
nesta 11 *A B* Martebellonio indicated only as
"Cap." throughout scene 20 *C D* in iscambio
20 *B* il farei, *C D* vi farei 30 *B* prencipali 37 *D*
conosceste 40 *A B* calidora 43 *D* veggio 44 *B*
perdonatimi

III.xi

Persone *A B* Leccardo, Chiaretta, D. Ignatio, Don
Flaminio 4 *B* Serrativi 6 *A B* Martebellonio indicated only as "Cap." throughout scene 9 *B* pezza;
attendendo 15 *B* cascano 16 *B* poco nõ 16 *B* sot-
terrasse; 17 *C D* Proserpina sua 19 *A B* Calidora
30 *B* discommodo, mi ci 35 *B* abbigliamenti, de'
41 *B* servono 42 *B* letamaro 42 *A B* ha cauto
quel 46 *B* le felicità 52 *A* conoscerli 54 *A B* che
vi e concesso, *C D* mi è 58 *A* stele 64 *A B*
co-/le 65 *B* ch'io nacqui l'e che 67 *C D* occhi; *B*
spettacolo 67 *B* sorbai ĩsin ad hora, e veder c'altri
70 *B* stracciarmi 79 *A B* nella farò 85 *D* assigns
line to Don Ignazio 99 *B* per che siamo 102 *B*
faccia 104 *B* scambievolmente

IV.i

11 *A B* attribute speech to "Pan."; *B* Che havendola
15 *B* parrebbe 23 *A B C D* place Ignazio's next
speech after Simbolo's sentence ending "dubbiose ancora," thereby concluding the scene with an uninter-

rupted speech by Simbolo, "Considerate . . . il
contrario." 24 *C D* macchiate molti 29 *B* tro-
varanno

IV.ii

2 *B* prencipali 5 *B* vēghe a sposar 15 *D* leggierezza 28 *D* sète e men di tempo, io vi risponderei 30 *A B* infame 30 *B* udito 35 *C D* stessi
39 *B* possa 56 *B* soportar ingiurie, con che tal cosa
pacienza 60 *B* batte scogli 61 *C* spuma, *D*
schiuma 62 *C* spuma, *D* schiuma 64 *D*
rinchiuso 67 *B* constreto

IV.iii

Persone *A* Capitano, Chiaretta, Leccardo, *B* Capitano, Chiareta, Leccardo 1 *A B* Martebellonio indicated as "Cap." throughout scene 10 *A* struzzicarlo;
D né per sfcrzarlo 47 *B* sbudellerò 53 *B*
turchino 63 *B* pigliaten 73 *B* cessarò 83 *A*
incon-/rerò, *B* in-/corerò 85 *C D* io con bastonate
93 *B* Chiareta

IV.iv

11 *B* affani 14 *B* giūto 17 *B* nō gli hò mai chiusi
22 *D* del sonno 24 *B* adesso a farle 28 *A B* felice
novelle, *C* felice novella, *D* felici novelle

IV.v

4 *B* vidi 9 *B* dan signo 25 *D* presciutto,
quella . . . 41 *A B* inasprite 43 *B* infelzarla come
un tordo allo spiedo 44 *C* se gli, *D* se le; 45 *B*
instupidì 50 *B* scappar di mano 51 *D* le lacrime
l'impedivano 65 *B* austere 68 *B* subito 76 *B* non
sia 80 *B* morte a q̄lla da chi sperava 81 *B* cagione
83 *A B* tragliato 94 *B* affligge 109 *C D* è stata
111 *B* aiuto 113 *B* mà che può 117 *B* instabili
121 *C D* e farvi caminar

IV.vi

8 *B* che a torto   10 *A* cose tale   28 *C D* mia! intenso   35 *B* del Inferno   50 *D* Sgombra da questa   58 *B* sceleragine   60 *B* dell'amor   67 *B* sucede e contrario alla volontà   69 *B* ti accesero   82 *B* dell'insidie dall'altro   92 *B* invidiarmi   95 *B* voi nuove sorti di tradimenti (line omitted)   101 *B* forse

IV.vii

2 *B* forse   4 *B* vi si   6 *B C D* supplicio   9 *B* facendo   22 *B* non fosse mai donna   23 *B* bruttezza   24 *B* pigli vendetta   32 *C D* mi facea   34 *B* è figlia   35 *D* piede   46 *B* poteva mancare   47 *B* de la tua fama   48 *B* con l'inocẽte   61 *B* apparecchiai   72 *B* oh fosse   80 *C D* fate   82 *B* a palazzo   84 *B* restituate   86 *B* cõ lo spender

IV.viii

1 *B* magni   2 *A B* di amori, di morità, di cavalieri   6 *B* gorgolia   9 *B* temo d'esser appicato due volte (line omitted)   15 *B* scamperò   16–18 *A B C* have each sentence on a separate line, *D* all in one continuous paragraph   26 *A D* la lattuchiglia . . . accomodate, *B* le lattuchiglie . . . accomodate, *C* la lattuchiglia . . . accomodata   30 *A B D* stiano . . . stanno volendole, *C* stia . . . sta . . . volendola   34 *B* ti vuol   44 *B* buone opre   46 *A* alla S vv. come piu meritevoli, *B* alla S.v. come più meritevole, *C* alle S.V. come più meritevoli, *D* alle Signorie Vostre come più meritevoli   54 *C D* trattieni   68 *B* solicitarà   69 *B* salcicioni   72 *B* giudicio   74 *B* galine

V.i

13 *B* reffrenar dalla ragione   16 *B* ragioni   25 *B* rispetievoli   28 *C* morire, a cui, *D* morire che   31 *B* dicioto   37 *B* annebiata   42 *B* denarii   47 *C* particolari, *D* particulari   48 *B* l'hã uccisa, ĩfamata   53 *B* nipoti   53 *B* invendicati   55 *A* e mi volentieri

contenterei, *C D* e volentieri mi contenterei   57 *B*
intiero perfetto   74 *B* Calidora   86 *B* Roderigo
90 *B* parlato cosa   93 *B* venga   95 *B* osservanza che
di amor   99 *B* finiva   101 *C D* sorella; d'accettarla
105 *A B* m'inchino, con ogni humilità, che devo à
ricevermi

V.ii

Persone *A B* Rodorico   1 *A B* Rodorico   11 *C D*
legittime ragioni   22 *B* uccisor;   23 *B* divenga
27 *D* sapevo   30 *A B* compiacergli, e gli l'havessi,
C l'avereste   33 *A B* de termine   42 *B* pregiudicio
65 *D* come se fusse   67 *B* vederemo   71 *B* chi vi
hà   80 *B* dui

V.iii

Persone *A B* Rodorico   2 *C D* fate   4 *C D* l'un
l'altro   6 *B* figliuole   13 *C D* sotto fiero   16 *B* vi-
vano   27 *B* duoi   29 *B* faccia   33 *A* figlila, *B*
figliuola, *D* figliola   42 *B* tenga   45 *A* convenevoli   53 *B* cercate   55 *A D* perdernosi, *B* per-
denosi, *C* perdendosi   63 *D* a inclinar   81 *B*
guiderdonato   82 *A* torrà me; *A B* Calidora   83 *B*
de la qual son   84 *A* por lasciar   87 *A* Calidora
90 *B* si nuovamente   91 *B* sia, le farò   93 *D* infer-
mità   98 *D* potreste   105 *B* un'afflito   114 *B* vigi-
lando   117 *B* gli innamorati   129 *B* spettacolo
139 *B* assigns Polisena's speech to Ignazio by fusing
it with his preceding one; *B* vuol esser vostra che
suia: et non esser   140 *B* de la morte./ tra volta Carizia (line omitted)   156 *B* rallegra; *C D* de' suoi
157 *D* desiata vita

V.iv

Persone *A* Rodovico, *B* Roderico, *D* Rodorico   4 *A*
prese, *B* presa, *C D* preso   11 *B* veggiando   12 *C D*
cieco odo   13 *B* è segno: se sei viva, come posso
sofrir   15 *C D* occhi   17 *A* Manastero, *B* Mone-
stero   20 *B* primitie de' miei   23 *B* tochi;   24 *D* e

no potendoti; *C D* ti ponga   28 *B* alegrezza   30 *B*
afflito   34 *B* Dunque   39 *A B* assign this speech to
"D. Ign."   43 *C D* tradito anche mio   44 *B* insieme
per;   49 *B* all'altre sue virtù   58 *A B* fratelo   84 *A*
B moglie. allegra   86 *C D* ho ingiuriata   90 *A B*
voi me l'avessi, *C* voi me l'aveste, *D* voi me l'avesti
95 *C D* ben ora di   96 *A* chiaro che/contento, che la
mia morte v'hà/ non hò peccato; questo si mi è di/
fatto fede (lines transposed, correctly reversed in *B*)
99 *B* commesso   100 *A B* secreti del tuo fatto
107 *B* belleza   112 *C* accoppiano, *D* accoppino
116 *B* de figliuoli   120 *B* vintimilla   124 *B* l'officio
136 *B* converta   139 *A B* premissioni dalle, *C* remissioni dalle, *D* remissioni delle

V.v

5 *B* Rallegrati;   6 *B* dianzi   22 *B* più di   27 *B* che
mi feci ma per prender questa/ mattina un poco di
fiato: bisogna al meno (half line transposed)   29 *B*
quatro   37 *A* prender postello   38 *A B* separate last
speech from the preceding one without assigning it to
any character.

Bibliography

In addition to the studies cited in the notes to the introduction and the editions of Della Porta's comedies referred to in the Appendix, the following have contributed to my work.

ANDREINI, FRANCESCO. *Le bravure del Capitano Spavento, divise in molti ragionamenti in forma di dialogo*. Venetia, 1607.

ARISTOTLE. *Aristotle's Poetics: The Argument*. Edited by Gerald F. Else. Cambridge, Mass., 1967.

BADALONI, NICOLA. "Fermenti di vita intellettuale a Napoli dal 1500 alla metà del '600." In *Storia di Napoli*. A cura di Ernesto Pontieri et al. Vol. 5, no. 1, pp. 643–89. Napoli, 1972.

BARGAGLI, GIROLAMO. *La pellegrina, commedia*. A cura di Florindo Cerreta. Firenze, 1971.

BATTAGIA, MICHELE. *Delle accademie veneziane*. Venezia, 1826.

BATTAGLIA, SALVATORE. *Grande dizionario della lingua italiana*. 9 vols. (A-MED completed). Torino, 1961–.

BATTISTI, CARLO, and G. ALESSIO. *Dizionario etimologico italiano*. 5 vols. Firenze, 1950–57.

BORLENGHI, ALDO, ed. *Commedie del Cinquecento*. 2 vols. Milano, 1959.

BORSELLINO, NINO, ed. *Commedie del Cinquecento*. 2 vols. Milano, 1962–67.

CAMPANELLA, TOMMASO. *Tutte le opere*. A cura di Luigi Firpo. Vol. 1 (subsequent volumes have yet to appear). Milano, 1954.

CARELLA, LUIGI. *Salerno: Storia e leggenda*. 2a ed. riv. Salerno, 1973.

CASTIGLIONE, BALDESAR. *Il libro del cortegiano*. A cura di Vittorio Cian. 4a ed. riv. e cor. Firenze, 1947.

CLUBB, L. G. *Giambattista Della Porta, Dramatist*. Princeton, N.J., 1965.

———. *Italian Plays (1500–1700) in the Folger Library*. Firenze, 1968.

———. "Italian Renaissance Comedy." *Genre* 9, no. 4 (Winter 1976–77): 469–88.

CONIGLIO, GIUSEPPE. *I vicerè spagnoli di Napoli*. Napoli, 1967.

CORTESE, NINO. "Feudi e feudatori napoletani della prima metà del cinquecento." *Archivio Storico per le Province Napoletane*, Nuova Serie, Anno XV, 1–4 (1929): 5–150.

CROCE, BENEDETTO. *La Spagna nella vita italiana durante la Rinascenza*. 4a ed. riv. ed acc. Bari, 1949.

D'AGOSTINO, GUIDO. "Il mezzogiorno aragonese (Napoli dal 1458 al 1503)." In *Storia di Napoli*. A cura di Ernesto Pontieri et al. Vol. 4, pp. 231–314. Napoli, 1974.

———. "Il governo spagnolo nell'Italia meridionale (Napoli dal 1503 al 1580)." In *Storia di Napoli*. A cura di Ernesto Pontieri et al. Vol. 5, no. 1, pp. 1–71. Napoli, 1972.

DELLA PORTA, G. B. *La fantesca, comedia*. Venezia, 1592.

———. *La Penelope, tragicomedia*. Napoli, 1591.

———. *La sorella, comedia*. Napoli, 1604.

———. *La tabernaria, comedia*. Ronciglione, 1616.

———. *La turca, comedia*. Venetia, 1606.

DELL'ERBA, LUIGI. "La riforma monetaria angioina e il suo sviluppo storico nel reame di Napoli." *Archivio Storico per le Province Napoletane*, Nuova Serie, Anno XIX, 1–4 (1933): 5–66.

DE VOTO, GIACOMO, and G. C. OLI. *Vocabolario illustrato della lingua italiana*. 2 vols. Firenze, 1967.

FLORIO, JOHN. *A Worlde of Wordes, Or Most Copious, and Exact Dictionarie in Italian and English*. London, 1598.

FORNARIS, FABRITIO DE. *Angelica, comedia*. Parigi, 1585.

GRENDLER, PAUL F. *The Roman Inquisition and the Venetian Press, 1540–1605*. Princeton, N.J., 1977.

MILANO, FRANCESCO. "Le commedie di Giovanbattista della Porta." *Studi di letteratura italiana* 2, no. 2 (Napoli, 1900): 311–411.

ODDI, SFORZA. *Prigione d'amore, commedia*. Venetia, 1591.

PASTORELLO, ESTER. *Tipografi, editori, librai a Venezia nel secolo XVI*. Firenze, 1924.

PECK, HARRY THURSTON. *Harper's Dictionary of Classical Literature and Antiquities*. New York, 1826, rpt. 1923.

PEDIO, TOMMASO. *Napoli e Spagna nella prima metà del cinquecento*. Bari, 1971.

PETROCCHI, GIORGIO. "La letteratura del pieno e del tardo

Rinascimento." In *Storia di Napoli*. A cura di Ernesto Pontieri et al. Vol. 5, no. 1, pp. 278–336. Napoli, 1972.

PONTIERI, ERNESTO. "La 'guerra dei baroni' napoletani e di Papa Innocenzo VIII contro Ferrante d'Aragona in dispacci della diplomazia fiorentina." *Archivio Storico per le Province Napoletane*, Terza Serie, 9 (1971): 197–347, and 10 (1972): 117–77.

―――. *et alii*. *Storia di Napoli*. 10 vols. Napoli, 1967–74.

SIRRI, RAFFAELE. "L'artificio linguistico di G. B. Della Porta: I—Le Tragedie." *Annali dell'Istituto Universitario Orientale, Sezione Romanza* 20, no. 2 (Napoli, 1978), 307–57, and 21, no. 1 (1979), 59–112.

STIEFEL, A. L. "Unbekannte italienische Quellen Jean de Rotrou's." *Zeitschrift für französische Sprache und Litteratur*, Supplementheft 5, pp. 1–159. Offeln and Leipzig, 1891.

TOMMASEO, NICCOLÒ, and B. BELLINI. *Dizionario della lingua italiana*. 8 vols. Torino, 1929.

TONINI, LUIGI. *Del riminese Alessandro Gambalunga della Gambalunghiana e de' suoi bibliotecari Brevi memorie*. Bologna, 1869.

Vocabolario degli Accademici della Crusca compendiato da un Accademico Animoso secundo l'ultima impressione di Firenze del MDCXCI. 4a ed. riv. 2 vols. Venezia, 1729.

Designer:	Wolfgang Lederer
Compositor:	G & S Typesetters, Inc.
Printer:	Thomson-Shore, Inc.
Binder:	Thomson-Shore, Inc.
Text:	VIP Bembo
Display:	VIP Bembo
Cloth:	Joanna Arrestox B 34000
Paper:	50 lb P&S offset B–32